BIONICLE®

ENCYCLOPEDIA
— UPDATED! —

BIONICLE®

FIND THE POWER, LIVE THE LEGEND

The legend comes alive in these exciting BIONICLE® books:

BIONICLE
ENCYCLOPEDIA
by Greg Farshtey

UPDATED!

SCHOLASTIC INC.

New York   Toronto   London   Auckland   Sydney

Mexico City   New Delhi   Hong Kong   Buenos Aires

*Dedicated with respect and gratitude
to Crystal Matrix, Peter Dolan, and
BIONICLE fans everywhere*

ISBN-13: 978-0-439-91640-0
ISBN-10: 0-439-91640-2

12 11 10 9 8 7 6 5 4 3   8 9 10/0

Cover Design by Henry Ng
Interior Design by Henry Ng and Bethany Dixon
Printed in the U.S.A.
First printing, October 2007

A

ACID SHIELD:

Tool carried by the LEHVAK. This shield secreted a special acid that could eat through any substance on MATA NUI (2) in a matter of seconds.

AHKMOU (OCK-moo):

AHKMOU

MATORAN carver originally from PO-METRU. His rivalry with ONEWA led him into a deal with the DARK HUNTER NIDHIKI to obtain the six GREAT DISKS. Frustrated in this and captured by Onewa, he reluctantly joined the TOA METRU in their efforts to find the disks and defeat the MORBUZAKH plant. He was briefly a part of the merged being MATORAN NUI, but split off to pursue his own destiny.

Ahkmou was one of six Matoran initially rescued from the COLISEUM by the Toa Metru. During the voyage to MATA NUI (2), Ahkmou's sphere was lost. It lay on the bottom of an underground river until found by MAKUTA. By that time, evidence had been discovered by the Toa Metru that Ahkmou may have been destined to become a Toa of Stone. That evidence later proved to be false. Ahkmou would later reappear on Mata Nui as a trader, selling KOLHII BALLS infected with Makuta's darkness.

AIR KATANA:

LEWA NUVA's tools, which allowed him to glide on air currents. One of these was later broken in combat with REIDAK, but eventually fixed by the MATORAN inventor VELIKA.

AIRSHIP:

Matoran flying vehicles used to transport cargo in METRU NUI. Airships were operated using a complicated system of KANOKA DISKS with the *levitation* and *increase weight* powers. When pulleys caused the *levitation* disks to strike the framework, the craft rose. When another set of pulleys brought the *increase weight* disks into contact with the frame, the craft would lose altitude. Forward thrust was provided by a portion of CHUTE capped at both ends, with only a small amount of liquid PROTODERMIS under high pressure allowed to jet from the back. Airships were built, maintained, and piloted by LE-MATORAN.

The VISORAK destroyed all of the airships in the MOTO-HUB when they invaded the city. Later, the TOA HORDIKA constructed six vessels to carry the sleeping MATORAN to the island of MATA NUI (2). Upon arrival, the ships were broken up and the parts were used to help build the island's six villages.

AIRWATCHER:

Winged DARK HUNTER who patrols the mountainous northern regions of ODINA. More powerful than he is intelligent, he has been known to attack rocks, trees, and even other Dark Hunters. His chest-mounted launcher projects energy webs and his staff fires acid.

AIRWEED:

Plant that grows in the undersea FIELDS OF AIR near MAHRI NUI. These plants produce pure air, which can be harvested from inside them by HYDRUKA or released due to significant impact tremors. The air produced by these plants made it possible for the MATORAN to survive underwater.

AKAKU (ah-KAH-koo):

The Mask of X-Ray Vision, which allowed the wearer to see through solid objects. Many Akaku were fitted with special lenses that allowed for telescopic vision as well.

AKAKU NUVA (ah-KAH-koo NOO-vah):

The more powerful Mask of X-Ray Vision worn by KOPAKA NUVA. He used this mask to spot the damage done to KO-KORO by the RAHKSHI. Like all KANOHI NUVA masks, its power could be shared by the user with those in close proximity. See KANOHI NUVA.

AKAMAI (OCK-kah-MY):

A TOA KAITA, the result of the merging of Toa TAHU, Toa POHATU, and Toa ONUA. Akamai fought the MANAS, MAKUTA's monstrous crablike guardians. Akamai wore the KANOHI AKI.

AKAMAI NUVA (OCK-kah-MY NOO-vah):

A TOA KAITA NUVA that could have been formed by TAHU NUVA, ONUA NUVA, and POHATU NUVA. There is no record that this being was ever brought into existence.

AKI (OCK-kee):

The Gold Mask of Valor, possessed of the powers of Shielding, Speed, and Strength.

AKILINI (AH-kih-LEE-nee):

The major sport of METRU NUI. Akilini was said to have been created by a MATORAN named KODAN, with the original version featuring a ball (see KODAN BALL). Later, it evolved into a popular sport in which players launched KANOKA DISKS through hoops. Akilini was played on small fields throughout Metru Nui and in the COLISEUM. The disks used by the winning team in a tournament would be sent to TA-METRU to be turned into KANOHI masks.

RULES OF AKILINI

1. Akilini matches are played between more than one, but not more than four, teams.
2. An akilini team consists of at least two, but not more than six, players.
3. At least one player on each team must serve as a defender. A defender is forbidden to take shots and may only launch disks to deflect the shots of opponents. A maximum of two players may serve as defenders.
4. At least one player on each team must be a launcher. If the team has more than two players, a maximum of four players may serve as launchers.
5. One point is scored for every disk that passes cleanly through an opposing team's hoop. Disks that strike the hoop are not considered goals.
6. Akilini tournament play ends when one team reaches 21 goals.
7. Disks in play may be retrieved by any launcher or defender from the launching team but may not be recovered by opposing players.
8. Disks that leave the playing field are considered to be open to all and may be retrieved by players from any team.
9. Players must keep at least one foot on their transport disk at all times. Transport disks may not be launched. Launching disks may not be used for transport.
10. Players who go more than one bio outside of the field of play on any side will be considered out of bounds. However, players may go as far above or below the field of play as they wish and still be considered in bounds.
11. Players may not make physical contact with a defender at any time.
12. Players may make physical contact with launchers, but only after their disk has been launched. Striking, tackling, or otherwise making physical contact with a launcher in the process of making a shot is considered "roughing the launcher" and will cost the offending team one launching disk.

At its most basic, akilini was played on a round field surrounded by posts upon which hoops were mounted. The field was not free of obstacles — in fact, the prevailing wisdom was: the more, the better. Matoran would surf on Kanoka disks up and down structures, through chutes, and even through tunnels in the ARCHIVES, popping up only long enough to make a shot. "Street akilini" became so popular, and such a menace to pedestrians, that the VAHKI eventually had to crack down on it.

AMAJA CIRCLE [ah-MAH-yah]:
A circular sandpit at KINI-NUI used by the TURAGA to tell stories using stones.

AMANA VOLO SPHERE [ah-MAH-nah VOH-loh]:
A powerful globe of dark energy discharged from certain RAHI upon the removal of an infected mask. These free-floating balls of energy could be absorbed by other beings and could restore health.

AMPHIBAX

AMPHIBAX [AM-fi-BACKS]:
Amphibious DARK HUNTER whose primary occupation is raiding BROTHERHOOD OF MAKUTA vessels and the coastlines of MATORAN-held islands. His weapons are sharp claws on one hand and a spiny whip in place of the other hand. He is a skilled swimmer, runner, and tree-climber. He was, at one time, a member of EHLEK's army, and is rumored to have lost his hand in a futile attempt to search for, and rescue, his leader after the failed rebellion against MATA NUI (1).

ANCIENT:
Veteran warrior who, along with the SHADOWED ONE, formed the DARK HUNTERS. He now serves as one of the Shadowed One's most trusted operatives. Ancient was responsible for recruiting both VEZOK and HAKANN into the Dark Hunter organization. In addition to his great strength and formidable armor, he possesses boots fitted with levitation disks that enable him to rise into the air. His modified RHOTUKA SPINNER robs targets of all physical coordination.

ANCIENT

ANTIDERMIS:
Name given by the PIRAKA to the green-black virus they used to enslave the MATORAN of VOYA NUI. In fact, the "virus" was actually the life essence of the MAKUTA of METRU NUI. The vat containing the antidermis was shattered by AXONN, forcing Makuta to search for another vessel to house his energy or risk being permanently dispersed into the atmosphere.

AQUA AXES:
GALI NUVA's tools. In addition to their cutting edge, they doubled as fins for swimming at great speed.

ARCHIVES:
The living museum of ONU-METRU, which extended far below the surface and below many other metru as well. Here could be found virtually every tool, artifact, and creature of METRU NUI's past. Staffed by a large number of ONU-MATORAN, it was once the workplace of WHENUA before his transformation into a TOA METRU.

RAHI kept in the Archives were held in stasis for safety purposes. Each Rahi was placed inside an inner stasis tube which was surrounded by a clear casing. While in the stasis tube, their life processes were slowed to an extreme degree. They were alive, but not aware, and could remain in that state for thousands of years. Damage to the outer case would not affect the Rahi, but damage to the inner case would cause it to awaken.

The Archives were known to contain levels, sublevels, and maintenance tunnels. Some sublevels featured creatures considered too dangerous to exhibit publicly. The museum could be accessed through a number of entrances, all of which were guarded. The locking mechanism was a series of hidden switches that had to be hit in a certain order.

Creatures known to have been in the Archives included RAHKSHI, the TWO-HEADED TARAKAVA, the USSAL hybrid, a NUI-RAMA, a MUAKA, and the ARCHIVES BEAST. KRAHKA and other creatures lived in the maintenance tunnels beneath the Archives.

The RAHAGA used the Archives as a base for years prior to the coming of the VISORAK and hid the AVOHKII there. A massive earthquake later shattered the Archives, releasing all of its exhibits into the city.

ARCHIVES MOLE

ARCHIVES BEAST:

A strange creature housed in the ONU-METRU ARCHIVES and believed to have some connection to the *reconstitutes at random* KANOKA DISK power. When encountered by TOA NUJU and Toa WHENUA, it had taken on the appearance of an empty room. Its attempts to trap the Toa were frustrated by a blizzard created by Nuju.

ARCHIVES MOLES:

Small, harmless creatures who migrated from PO-METRU to the ARCHIVES. They fed on insects and microscopic protodites and were known for their ability to cooperate with each other. These RAHI later made their way to LE-WAHI on MATA NUI (2).

ARTAKHA [arr-TOCK-ah]:

A place of peace and contentment for all MATORAN. Its location has never been discovered, and many Matoran now believe it to be a myth. The first mention of Artakha is in an ancient legend which speaks of a trouble-free site to which skilled Matoran workers were allowed to migrate.

ARTAKHA BULL [arr-TOCK-ah]:

A swift, strong, plant-eating RAHI who relied on its sharp horns for defense. The Artakha bull was considered to be one of the earliest RAHI known to MATORAN and was rumored to be extremely intelligent. The species lived in LE-METRU on METRU NUI, but none were ever seen on MATA NUI (2).

ARTHRON [ARE-thronn]:

KANOHI Mask of Sonar worn by TOA MAHRI JALLER. This mask allows the wearer to locate beings or objects through echolocation.

ARTAKHA BULL

ASH BEAR:

A large ursine creature known for its powerful teeth and claws. The TOA METRU encountered a wounded member of this species in the ARCHIVES and combined their powers to heal the she-creature. Hundreds of years later, this same ash bear would briefly menace JALLER and TAKUA in LE-WAHI, before being subdued and calmed by LEWA NUVA.

ASSEMBLER'S VILLAGE:

Small settlements scattered throughout PO-METRU on METRU NUI, home to the crafters who assemble Matoran goods. Parts were shipped to these villages via CHUTE, boat, AIRSHIP, and USSAL cart, and these were then painstakingly assembled by skilled PO-MATORAN. Due to the relative isolation of these villages, they were extremely vulnerable to RAHI attack. In the past, assembler's villages had been menaced by STONE RATS, KINLOKA, ROCK RAPTORS, and scores of other beasts. The TOA METRU fought NIDHIKI and KREKKA here, in a village later destroyed by a KIKANALO stampede.

AV:

A Matoran prefix meaning "light."

AV-MATORAN:

Name given to a MATORAN of Light. The dwelling place of these Matoran remains a mystery, as does the number in existence. TAKUA, unknown to himself and all those around him, was an Av-Matoran disguised as a TA-MATORAN. The Av-Matoran tribe includes both males and females. Their affinity with the element of light allows them to subtly alter its frequency so that they can change their color. Av-Matoran were "seeded" on various islands in disguise by the ORDER OF MATA NUI during the TIME SLIP to protect them from possible future actions by the BROTHERHOOD OF MAKUTA.

AVAK [ay-VACK]:

AVAK

One of the six PIRAKA who attempted to steal the KANOHI IGNIKA. Avak was originally employed as a jailer on ZAKAZ, where he used his powers to imprison DARK HUNTERS, among others. He was recruited into the Dark Hunter organization shortly after that. Avak possesses the elemental power of stone, X-ray and telescopic vision, and the ability to create the perfect prison for any target out of thin air using only his mind. He carries a ZAMOR SPHERE LAUNCHER and a seismic pickaxe/jackhammer. Avak is a skilled inventor who designed the Zamor Sphere Launchers for his fellow Piraka. He was ambushed and defeated by DALU and later joined with the other Piraka to battle the TOA NUVA and TOA INIKA. When last seen, he was with the Piraka on Voya Nui still scheming to get the Kanohi Ignika, unaware that his body was being affected by an earlier exposure to mutagenic seawater.

AVOHKII [ah-VOH-kee]:

KANOHI Mask of Light worn by TOA TAKANUVA.
The Mask of Light was originally forged on the island of ARTAKHA and intended for use by a prophesied Toa of Light. Many thousands of years later, the brotherhood of Makuta stole the mask from its creators and hid it in one of their fortresses in an effort to prevent this Toa from ever coming to be. Later, after discovering the Brotherhood's treachery, the TOA HAGAH raided the fortress and stole the mask themselves. Even after being turned into RAHAGA, they were able to successfully spirit the mask away.
The Rahaga hid the mask in the ARCHIVES in METRU NUI. The compartment in which it was concealed could only be opened using six MAKOKI STONES, which the Rahaga hid around the city to keep them from the VISORAK. The TOA HORDIKA retrieved all six stones and found the Avohkii, which gave off a bright glow. Fearing that the glow would attract the attention of the Visorak, Toa Hordika ONEWA used his RHOTUKA SPINNER to conceal the mask in a block of stone.

The TOA METRU later transported that stone to the island of MATA NUI (2) and hid it in a lava cave. Legend stated that the HERALD of the Toa of Light would have to find the mask, it could not be given to him, and so the location of it was kept secret. A MATORAN named TAKUA would eventually stumble upon the Mask of Light while exploring the cavern.

Takua and JALLER were charged by the TURAGA with the duty of finding the Toa of Light. Their adventure took them to many places on the island and exposed them to danger from RAHI and RAHKSHI. Takua later donned the mask and transformed into Takanuva, the Toa of Light. (How the mask was able to trigger such a transformation when normal Great Masks do not has not yet been revealed. It is rumored that the mask may have been infused with Toa power during its creation, and so acted like a TOA STONE.)

The Avohkii can project powerful beams of light energy and banish the darkness. It also brings understanding, turning anger into peace and enemies into allies.

AXE:

TOA tool carried by LEWA, used to focus his air power.

AXONN (AXE-on):

Member of the ORDER OF MATA NUI and former member of the HAND OF ARTAKHA. After the Hand was disbanded, Axonn wandered for some time, using his powers for petty conquests.

He was eventually recruited by the Order, who offered to put his talents to good use. Axonn was assigned to VOYA NUI, to guard the KANOHI IGNIKA, and was there when the landmass split off from its continent and rocketed to the surface of the ocean. Axonn and his partner, BRUTAKA, defeated a number of enemies who attempted to claim the Mask of Life, until the PIRAKA arrived. Brutaka betrayed Axonn and allied himself with the Piraka, forcing a confrontation between the two. In the battle, Axonn defeated Brutaka and destroyed the vat containing the ANTIDERMIS. Later, Axonn opened the way to the CORD so the TOA INIKA could travel to MAHRI NUI.

Axonn wears the Kanohi RODE, the GREAT MASK of Truth, which can pierce any disguise and spot any deception. His axe can fire energy blasts and cleave virtually any substance. In addition, Axonn has massive strength and a number of special powers, among them the ability to heal insanity with a touch of his hand.

B

BAHRAG (BAH-rag):

CAHDOK and GAHDOK, the twin queens of the BOHROK swarms. The Bahrag directed the rampages of the Bohrok, unaware that there were MATORAN living on the surface of MATA NUI (2). They possessed the elemental powers of the six Bohrok, plus the ability to create lifelike illusions. They created and were in contact with the KRANA that inhabited each Bohrok. The Bahrag were defeated by the TOA NUVA and imprisoned in a cage of solid PROTODERMIS. The Bahrag were later the subject of a failed rescue attempt by the BOHROK-KAL. The Toa Nuva recently released the Bahrag as part of their preparations for awakening the GREAT SPIRIT MATA NUI (1).

BALTA (BALL-tah):

TA-MATORAN member of the RESISTANCE on VOYA NUI. Balta was a skilled tinkerer, able to make a weapon out of whatever materials were at hand. When crossed, his twin repeller tools could block any enemy attack and strike back with equal force. Balta helped steal one of the ZAMOR SPHERE LAUNCHERS belonging to the PIRAKA, was saved from a cave trap by AXONN, and later organized the rescue of GARAN from the PIRAKA.

BARRAKI (BUH-rock-KEE):

Six powerful rulers who attempted to overthrow MATA NUI (1) and were condemned to the PIT for their crimes. The Barraki (Matoran for "warlord") were originally allied in the LEAGUE OF SIX KINGDOMS and ruled a significant portion of the known universe. Desiring more, they attempted a revolution 80,000 years ago, but were defeated by an army led by the MAKUTA of METRU NUI. Before they could be executed, they were spirited away to the Pit by BOTAR. There they remained until the Pit was shattered by the GREAT CATACLYSM. The Barraki escaped but found that they were at the bottom of a strange ocean. Since only one of the six breathed water naturally, it appeared they were doomed.

But the mutagenic seawater of the region affected all the Barraki, severely mutating them and making it possible for all to survive at great depths. No longer able to breathe air, they carved out what empires they could beneath the waves and dreamed of revenge against Mata Nui (1) and the BROTHERHOOD OF MAKUTA. After the appearance of MAHRI NUI in their midst, they periodically hunted MATORAN for the fun of it.

All of that changed when the KANOHI IGNIKA drifted down into the Pit. The Barraki knew its power could transform them back to the perfect physical specimens they once were and make it possible for them to reclaim their kingdoms on the surface. They seized the mask, but then lost it after entrusting it to NOCTURN. The Barraki were then tricked by the TOA MAHRI into warring among themselves, while the Toa took advantage of the opportunity to search for the mask themselves.

The Barraki have since realized their error and have banded together once again to battle the Toa Mahri for possession of the Ignika. The six Barraki are PRIDAK, EHLEK, KALMAH, TAKADOX, CARAPAR, and MANTAX.

BIO (BY-oh):

A unit of Matoran measurement. A bio is equal to roughly 4.5 feet or 1.37 meters in Earth measurement. A TOA averages 1.6 bio in height (7.2 feet/2.19 meters). There are 1,000 bio in a KIO.

BLADE BURROWER:

A creature of the ONU-METRU ARCHIVES. It used its powerful claws to carve tunnels that looked MATORAN-made, and then used the tunnels to lure archivists to their doom. Blade burrowers hunted mainly by smell, having poor eyesight, and rarely ventured to the higher levels of the Archives.

BLADE BURROWER

BLAZER CLAWS:

Tools carried by TOA HORDIKA VAKAMA. These could be used to charge his RHOTUKA SPINNER or produce small flames.

BOGGARAK (BOE-ger-rack):

One of the six breeds of VISORAK who invaded METRU NUI. Although not strong swimmers, Boggarak were capable of "skating" atop the water, speedily darting to and fro toward their prey. Their RHOTUKA SPINNERS had two powers. When used underwater, they caused the target to swell up and float helplessly to the surface. When used on land, they completely dehydrated the target, reducing it to a pile of dust. Boggarak were also capable of emitting a sonic hum that could transmute solid matter. ROODAKA's personal guard was made up of Boggarak. These Visorak also decimated a squad of VAHKI.

BOG SNAKE:

Nasty, venomous serpents that lived in the muddy shallows off ONU-METRU and fed on small amphibians. ONU-MATORAN walking along the shoreline learned to be extremely careful so that they did not disturb a bog snake nest.

BOHROK

BOHROK (BOH-rock):

Insectlike mechanoids who menaced the island of MATA NUI (2) shortly after the TOA arrived there. Each Bohrok contained a KRANA that provided additional power as well as direction to the machine. The krana, in turn, were in mental contact with the BAHRAG, who were the ultimate authority over the Bohrok swarms. Bohrok nests extended from below the surface of Mata Nui to below the city of METRU NUI. Each nest was home to hundreds of Bohrok and BOHROK-VA. There were six known breeds of Bohrok: GAHLOK, KOHRAK, LEHVAK, NUHVOK, PAHRAK, and TAHNOK (see individual entries).

HISTORY

The first recorded encounter between MATORAN and Bohrok occurred in Metru Nui, when ONU-MATORAN miners stumbled upon a nest filled with sleeping Bohrok. Not certain what the creatures were or why they could not be awakened, the miners turned the Bohrok over to the ARCHIVES. They were put on display and at the same time studied by Matoran researchers. (The name "Bohrok" came from a word carved in the wall of the nest.)
Their first discovery was that the Bohrok themselves were completely inorganic and not "alive" in the sense that Matoran understand life. They also learned that the dormant krana inside them were completely organic and living creatures, although the connection between krana and Bohrok was not yet known. Interestingly, an examination of the Bohrok revealed no traces of any assembly. An Onu-Matoran archivist, MAVRAH, theorized that perhaps the Bohrok were not built but were in fact originally biomechanical creatures that had somehow evolved to the point where all organic matter was lost. It would have meant their transformation from possibly a living, thinking state to a form of artificial life incapable of independent thought. Archivists were split on his theory, and since there was no way to prove it one way or the other, it was forgotten over time.
No active Bohrok presence ever existed on Metru Nui. In fact, the Bohrok and krana remained asleep for another 1,000 years after the fall of the city. The only other thing to be learned about them during this time was the result of VAKAMA's visions of the Bohrok attacking and destroying the island of Mata Nui.
Following his defeat by the Toa of Mata Nui, MAKUTA sent a signal that awakened the swarms. They immediately made for the surface of Mata Nui and went on a rampage, destroying mountains, forests, waterways, and every other obstacle that got in their way. It seemed as if their sole purpose was to eradicate everything on the surface of the island. The Toa and Matoran mobilized to stop them, fighting battles across the entire island.

Interestingly, the Bohrok showed no interest in harming Toa, TURAGA, or Matoran unless those beings prevented the swarm from carrying out its task.

The most devastating blow dealt by the Bohrok was the capture of almost the entire population of LE-KORO, including Turaga MATAU and Toa LEWA. These prisoners were fitted with krana in place of their masks and thus became slaves of the swarm. They were eventually freed, thanks to the efforts of Toa ONUA and four Matoran: KONGU, TAKUA, TAMARU, and NUPARU.

The Toa eventually tracked down the Bahrag and brought the fight to them. The defeat and imprisonment of the Bohrok queens caused the swarms to become disorganized and no longer any threat. The Matoran removed the krana from most of the Bohrok and put the machines to work rebuilding the villages.

Later, the Bohrok were summoned back to their nests by the BOHROK-KAL to await the call to invade Mata Nui again. The intervention of the TOA NUVA prevented the Bohrok-Kal from freeing the Bahrag, and so the signal was never sent. They remained in a dormant state until the Toa Nuva freed the Bahrag and sent the signal to awaken the swarms. At this writing, they are back on Mata Nui (2), working to return the island to its original barren state.

POWERS

The six breeds of Bohrok had elemental powers similar to the Toa for the most part, controlling fire, water, earth, stone, and ice. The Lehvak, however, were not connected to the air element but instead were identified with swamp terrain. The Bohrok were also capable of snapping their heads forward, delivering a powerful blow, as well as launching the krana they carried at a foe. If a krana affixed to the face of a target, that being would become mentally enthralled by the swarm.

PERSONALITY

Although different breeds of Bohrok had preferred tactics in battle, they could not be said to have actual personalities.

EQUIPMENT

Each breed of Bohrok carried two shields through which elemental power could be focused. These were the ACID SHIELD, EARTH SHIELD, FIRE SHIELD, ICE SHIELD, STONE SHIELD, and WATER SHIELD.

BOHROK-KAL (BOH-rock KAHL):

Six mutated BOHROK who challenged the TOA NUVA in an effort to free the BAHRAG, and so unleash the swarms against the island of MATA NUI (2) a second time. Each Bohrok-Kal contained a KRANA-KAL, which provided additional power and controlled the mechanoid. There were six Bohrok-Kal: GAHLOK-KAL, KOHRAK-KAL, LEHVAK-KAL, NUHVOK-KAL, PAHRAK-KAL, and TAHNOK-KAL (see individual entries). They were defeated by the Toa Nuva.

BOHROK-KAL

HISTORY

The six Bohrok-Kal appeared on Mata Nui following the defeat of the Bahrag. Their stated mission was to free the Bohrok queens so that the swarms could be active again. It later became clear that the Kal had been created by the Bahrag for just this purpose.

How the Bohrok-Kal were created has never been determined, though it is believed by some that the Bahrag discovered a means of distilling energy from a mutagenic substance, possibly Visorak venom or some variation of that. The energy was then used to bathe both the Bohrok and their KRANA, resulting in a number of mutations.

The Bohrok-Kal rapidly proved to be quite different from the Bohrok. They had different powers. Their krana-kal were capable of communication with other species and were not mentally linked to the Bahrag as the Bohrok krana were.

Knowing the Toa Nuva would attempt to prevent their rescue of the Bahrag, the Bohrok-Kal infiltrated the Matoran villages and stole the NUVA SYMBOLS. By doing so, they robbed the Toa Nuva of their elemental powers, severely weakening them. The Kal then began searching the island for the location of the Bahrag.

The Toa Nuva tried desperately to stop the Kal, doing everything from gathering KANOHI NUVA to forming WAIRUHA NUVA. Meanwhile, the Bohrok-Kal had discovered where the Bahrag were imprisoned. The prison was guarded by EXO-TOA running on automatic, but these were easily defeated by the Bohrok-Kal.

Faced with no choice, TAHU NUVA called upon the most powerful mask in his possession, the VAHI, or Mask of Time. He used its power to slow down time around the Kal and prevent them from freeing the Bahrag.

The Nuva symbols proved to be the Kal's undoing. Through force of will, the Toa Nuva were able to trigger the power stored in the symbols and cause it to flow into the Kal. This resulted in an overload as the Kal absorbed more power than they could control. They were defeated and have not been a threat since that time.

POWERS

The Bohrok-Kal's powers included control of magnetism, gravity, plasma, electricity, sound, and vacuum.

EQUIPMENT

Each breed of Bohrok-Kal carried two shields through which its power could be focused. These were the ELECTRIC SHIELD, GRAVITY SHIELD, MAGNETIC SHIELD, PLASMA SHIELD, SONIC SHIELD, and VACUUM SHIELD.

PERSONALITY

The Bohrok-Kal tended to be arrogant and cruel. Whereas the Bohrok did not go out of their way to harm living beings, the Bohrok-Kal were not only willing to attack Toa and Matoran but even members of the swarms.

BOHROK-KAL KAITA JA [BOH-rock KAHL KIGH-ee-TAH JAH]:
A merged being formed by the combination of KOHRAK-KAL, LEHVAK-KAL, and GAHLOK-KAL. It was dominated by the KRANA JA-KAL and controlled the powers of magnetism, vacuum, and sound. It defeated WAIRUHA NUVA in battle.

BOHROK-KAL KAITA ZA (BOH-rock KAHL KIGH-ee-TAH ZAH):

A merged being formed by the combination of TAHNOK-KAL, PAHRAK-KAL, and NUHVOK-KAL. It was dominated by the KRANA ZA-KAL, and controlled the powers of gravity, plasma, and electricity. It was never sighted on MATA NUI (2).

BOHROK VA (BOH-rock VAH):

Miniature mechanized assistants and couriers for the BOHROK swarms. The Bohrok Va traveled back and forth from the BAHRAG nest to the Bohrok in the field, carrying KRANA to those Bohrok who had lost theirs. The Va were also capable of hurling krana at opponents — if the krana affixed to the target's face, that being would become a servant of the swarm. Bohrok Va were present throughout MATA NUI (2) during the Bohrok invasion and frequently clashed with MATORAN, but rarely with the TOA.
When the Toa defeated the Bahrag, and thus the Bohrok swarms, the Matoran believed the Bohrok Va had been rendered harmless. They allowed both the Bohrok and Bohrok Va into the villages to repair some of the damage done by the swarms. But the Matoran had made a potentially fatal mistake. Since the Bohrok Va were not guided by krana like the Bohrok, the defeat of the Bahrag did not lessen their threat. They immediately began rendering aid to the BOHROK-KAL, assisting them in infiltrating the villages to steal the NUVA SYMBOLS.
There were six breeds of Bohrok Va: GAHLOK VA, KOHRAK VA, LEHVAK VA, NUHVOK VA, PAHRAK VA, and TAHNOK VA.

BOMONGA (bo-MAHN-gah):

Former TOA HAGAH of Earth, later mutated by ROODAKA into a RAHAGA. Bomonga had been part of an elite TOA team charged with being MAKUTA's personal guard. When the Toa discovered Makuta was oppressing and enslaving MATORAN, they turned on him and attacked a fortress of the BROTHERHOOD OF MAKUTA. Bomonga was struck by one of Roodaka's RHOTUKA SPINNERS and mutated into a shrunken creature with the head of a RAHKSHI. He was later rescued by Toa IRUINI and Toa NORIK, who also ended up being mutated.
What masks and tools Bomonga carried as a Toa has not yet been revealed.
As a Rahaga, Bomonga specialized in capturing RAHI hiders, such as FIREFLYERS and BLADE BURROWERS. He carried a Rhotuka Spinner that could fly in absolute silence and then adhere to and paralyze a target. Bomonga was known for his patience and his ability to remain motionless for long periods of time while waiting for a target to pass nearby.

BORDAKH (bore-DOCK):

VAHKI model assigned to GA-METRU on METRU NUI. These mechanoids were cunning and enjoyed to chase for the sake of chasing. Their staffs of loyalty made a target so enthused about maintaining order, he would turn in his friends to the Vahki if necessary. NOKAMA and MATAU clashed with Bordakh while trying to recover the Ga-Metru GREAT DISK.

BOTAR (BOH-tarr):

Member of the ORDER OF MATA NUI tasked with teleporting the condemned to the PIT. Botar brought the six BARRAKI, among many others, to that prison.

BOXOR (BOX-oar):

A defense vehicle designed by NUPARU, an ONU-MATORAN inventor. It was used by the MATORAN on MATU NUI (2) to defend themselves against the BOHROK swarms. A Matoran could ride inside the vehicle and manipulate its two arms to fight the invaders. Boxors were later disassembled for transport to METRU NUI. See NUPARU.

BRAKAS [BRAH-kahs]:
Mishievous monkeylike creatures who once roamed freely throughout LE-METRU and GA-METRU. They were such pests that the MATORAN petitioned Turaga DUME to have them banned. VAHKI later rounded up all specimens and put them in the ARCHIVES, from which they escaped. They later appeared on MATA NUI (2), where they continued to be an annoyance, often stealing fruit from KORO storehouses. Brakas are known for their distinctive "kau kau" cry.

BROTHERHOOD OF MAKUTA:
A secretive, powerful and dangerous group of renegades who have turned against the GREAT SPIRIT MATA NUI (1). According to legend, they were originally the beings closest to the heart of the Great Spirit, charged with creating whatever was needed to do the will of Mata Nui and safeguarding the MATORAN. They were a largely benevolent organization, even protecting the universe as a whole by crushing the rebellion of the LEAGUE OF SIX KINGDOMS.
Shortly after that, for reasons of greed, ambition, or a darker emotion, the MAKUTA of METRU NUI began oppressing and enslaving Matoran. The Brotherhood did nothing to stop him, even aiding him as he turned the knowledge and power he had against those he had sworn to protect.
Roughly 2,500 years ago, the Brotherhood staged an unprecedented raid on the island of ARTAKHA and stole the KANOHI AVOHKII, the Mask of Light. Their stated reason was that Artakha was not secure enough to protect such an important artifact, but the ORDER OF MATA NUI realized this was a prelude to further acts of aggression by the Brotherhood. As a result of this invasion, all those who knew the location of Artakha were hunted down and eliminated so that such an act could not take place again.
Over the centuries, the Brotherhood continued to grow in power while remaining relatively small in number. They were allied with the DARK HUNTERS and turned benevolent technology like the EXO-TOA into tools of conflict. Led by the Makuta of Metru Nui, the Brotherhood experimented with mutating RAHI as well as creating specialized beings like VOPORAK. They employed the TOA HAGAH as bodyguards with the Toa being unaware of the true nature of the organization.
Some 1,300 years ago, six Toa Hagah discovered that the Brotherhood had stolen the Avohkii and proceeded to steal it back. Although they were mutated into RAHAGA, they succeeded in making off with and hiding the artifact. Now realizing his corruption would be exposed, the Makuta of Metru Nui struck at Mata Nui (1), poisoning that powerful being. Armies of VISORAK went on the march, seizing the southernmost islands and working their way north. Although the attack on Mata Nui (1) eventually sent him into an unending slumber, the attempt by the Brotherhood to seize control of Metru Nui was thwarted by the TOA METRU, the Rahaga, and KEETONGU. A later effort to secure the Kanohi VAHI, the Mask of Time, was also stopped by Toa VAKAMA. During this period, a clash between the SHADOWED ONE and the Makuta of Metru Nui resulted in the start of the ongoing DARK HUNTER-BROTHERHOOD OF MAKUTA WAR.
The Brotherhood has remained active over the last 1,000 years, preparing for their eventual takeover of the universe. Despite some setbacks (like the apparent "death" of the Makuta of Metru Nui and his subsequent failed effort to secure the Kanohi IGNIKA), their plans continue on track. According to documents hidden in a Brotherhood base, the group actually intends for Mata Nui (1) to be awakened. Why and how they see that as being to their advantage remains unknown.

All Brotherhood members share certain powers, including shape-shifting, control of shadow energy, and the ability to make KRAATA. All have evolved past the point of needing a physical body, and now consist of energy inhabiting armor. They can also inhabit a living, but spirit-less, body, or a completely mechanical construct (see MAXILOS). The organization has shrunk a bit in recent years, owing to a purge by the Makuta of Metru Nui of those he did not consider sufficiently loyal and Dark Hunter attacks. At least one Brotherhood member has split from the group after a spectacular failure with regard to the island of ZAKAZ (see SKAKDI), and remains in hiding.

The Order of Mata Nui has recently received an unconfirmed report from the homeland of the AV-MATORAN that the Brotherhood has launched an assault and is attempting to seize control of the core of the universe. Should that succeed, they would have control over whether and when the Great Spirit Mata Nui's life could be saved, regardless of whether they possess the Ignika or not. The Order is relying on the TOA NUVA to defeat this invasion, but is also prepared to fully support them with Order members, other Toa, and any other force they can muster.

BRUTAKA (broo-TOCK-ah):

Former member of the ORDER OF MATA NUI who turned against that group and was banished to the PIT. Brutaka began his life as a lieutenant in the army of MAKUTA, but rapidly grew dissatisfied with the regimented existence he led. He was recruited by the Order and turned into a roving troubleshooter, achieving many great things but also causing his share of trouble (such as using his mask power to transport a TAHTORAK from its home island to METRU NUI). The Order finally decided to partner him up with AXONN and assigned them both to VOYA NUI. They spent most of the next 100,000 years there.

At some point, Brutaka suffered a crisis of faith. Convinced that MATA NUI (1) had either deserted the universe or died, he began to question why he should spend his time guarding a mask intended for the Great Spirit's benefit. When the PIRAKA invaded the island, Brutaka allied with them and used his power to defeat the TOA NUVA. He intended to let them steal the KANOHI IGNIKA and then take it from them. He survived an attempt by HAKANN and THOK to steal his power, but was eventually defeated in combat by AXONN. He was banished to the PIT by BOTAR and there offered to ally with the BARRAKI in an effort to claim the Ignika. The Barraki rejected him and he was last seen being dragged off by a giant squid. His fate remains unknown.

Brutaka carries a twin-bladed sword and wears the Kanohi OLMAK. Exposure to ANTIDERMIS had the strange effect of strengthening him rather than enslaving him. The extent of his powers has never been revealed, but he has enormous strength, the ability to shoot energy from his sword, and was formidable enough to have defeated Axonn in past combat.

BULA (BOO-lah):

A berry that grew on MATA NUI (2) and was famous for its ability to restore energy. MATORAN could absorb energy from direct physical contact with the berries, something that was particularly helpful when on long journeys.

BURNAK:

Four-legged RAHI found on VOYA NUI, believed to be a mixture of the canine, the feline, and some as-yet-unidentified creature. At least six breeds are known to exist. Some MATORAN keep burnak as pets.

CABLE CRAWLER:

A LE-METRU RAHI who made a home in the cables that overhung the district. Nocturnal hunters, cable crawlers fed on small birds and were extremely difficult to capture. They had the added ability of being able to unleash an energy blast that disrupted a foe's sense of balance.

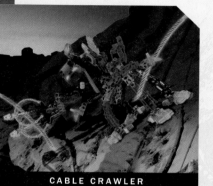

CABLE CRAWLER

CAHDOK (KAH-dahk):

This monstrous blue creature was one of the two BAHRAG twins.

CALIX (KAY-liks):

KANOHI Mask of Fate worn by TOA INIKA JALLER. The Matoran version of this mask was given to him during his time in the realm of KARZAHNI (1). The Calix allows the wearer to perform at the absolute peak of his natural abilities, making it possible for him to run, leap, dodge, etc. better than virtually any other unenhanced member of his species.

CANYON OF UNENDING WHISPERS:

Geographic feature in PO-METRU on METRU NUI, located near the PRISON OF THE DARK HUNTERS. The canyon got its name because of the abundance of echoes. VAKAMA, NOKAMA, MATAU, and the KIKANALO battled VAHKI here while attempting to save the other TOA METRU.

CARAPAR (Kah-RUH-parr):

One of the six BARRAKI who menace MAHRI NUI. Carapar was originally a member of the LEAGUE OF SIX KINGDOMS and ruled the southernmost empire in that alliance. He was known more for his brawn than his brains, and his army was the least disciplined of the League's six legions. But no one could deny his record of success, which included conquering entire civilizations through a combination of sheer might and the occasional bit of trickery.

Carapar joined in the League's efforts to rebel against MATA NUI (1), and he and his army were defeated by the BROTHERHOOD OF MAKUTA. He was condemned to the PIT by BOTAR and spent most of the next 80,000 years there. Then, some 1,000 years ago, a massive earthquake shattered the walls of his prison. He escaped, only to find himself in a strange ocean. Carapar would have drowned had it not been for the mutagenic effects of the seawater, which transformed him into a water-breathing, crablike being. He was now able to survive, but could not escape from this new Pit since he could no longer live on land.

CARAPAR

Assembling a new army of KERAS crabs and PIT WAR TORTOISES, Carapar staked a claim to a portion of this underwater world. Although he controlled an area rich in resources, his power was sufficient to keep any other Barraki from trying to take land away from him. When the KANOHI IGNIKA appeared underwater, Carapar and his army occupied the FIELDS OF AIR in an attempt to force the MATORAN to hand it over.

He later joined with KALMAH in an uneasy alliance with TOA MAHRI JALLER to get the Mask of Life, which he believed could reverse his mutation and make him an air-breather again. Carapar possesses monstrous claws (though one has now been detached in order for him to hold a SQUID LAUNCHER) and a thick armored shell.

CARAVAN CRAWLER:
RAHI of VOYA NUI repurposed by the PIRAKA into a war machine. Its hard shell was partially cut away to make room for a battle platform with multi-ZAMOR SPHERE LAUNCHER.

CATAPULT SCORPION:
A dangerous PO-METRU RAHI. The catapult scorpion had the ability to materialize a ball of molten magma at the end of its tail, which rapidly cooled to solid rock. The scorpion could then hurl it at enemies. Catapult scorpions fed on raw PROTODERMIS and were considered to be extremely hostile. None were ever reported on MATA NUI (2).

CATAPULT SCORPION

CAVE FISH:
A GA-METRU creature that defended itself by absorbing liquid PROTODERMIS through its skin. It used the fluid to "inflate" itself and give the appearance of being a larger creature. GA-MATORAN later used dead cave fish to absorb leaks in the protodermis purification vats. Cave fish were often seen in the waters around MATA NUI (2).

CHAMBER OF LIFE:
Cavern created by the GREAT BEINGS to house the KANOHI IGNIKA. It sits at the bottom of a 777-step staircase and has multiple guardians. The PIRAKA and TOA INIKA fought VEZON, FENRAKK, and KARDAS here.

CHAMBER OF TRUTH:
Interrogation cell used by the PIRAKA on VOYA NUI. GARAN was taken here following his capture and interrogated about the appearance of SPIRIT STARS over the island. The chamber was badly damaged when the other members of the MATORAN RESISTANCE came to Garan's rescue.

CHARGER:
A mutated KANE-RA bull who serves as a DARK HUNTER. Charger is known for his instinctive dislike of other animals. He carries two sharp blades and an axe capable of absorbing elemental energy and hurling it back at a foe.

CHARRED JUNGLE:
A forest of burnt trees in TA-WAHI on MATA NUI (2). TAKUA trailed TAHU through the jungle and discovered TA-KORO.

CHIEF ARCHIVIST:
Administrator in charge of the ARCHIVES in METRU NUI. Only the Chief Archivist had keys to certain sublevels of the structure. TURAGA DUME instructed the Chief Archivist to put an end to MAVRAH's researches.

CHARGER

CHRONICLER:

A MATORAN designated to record important events on the WALL OF HISTORY. The best-known Chronicler in METRU NUI was a PO-MATORAN named KODAN. His first experience was recording the defeat of the KANOHI DRAGON by TOA LHIKAN and 10 other Toa. He later traveled with some of Lhikan's fellow Toa on one of their missions, but neither he nor they ever returned. TURAGA DUME chose not to appoint a new Chronicler. No one knew at the time that the true Dume had been replaced by MAKUTA in disguise.

After the Matoran traveled to MATA NUI (2), the six TURAGA appointed TAKUA to serve as Chronicler. His position would lead to his being present at many of the most important events in Mata Nui history.

When Takua became TAKANUVA, Toa of Light, a GA-MATORAN named HAHLI stowed away on the USSANUI on its journey to Makuta's lair. Once there, she volunteered to serve as Chronicler in Takua's stead. She served in that role until shortly after the Matoran returned to Metru Nui, at which time she left the city with five others in search of the Toa Nuva. KOPEKE was later appointed to the position.

CHRONICLER'S STAFF:

The tool carried by the MATORAN charged with the task of recording events on the WALL OF HISTORY. In addition to being decorative, the staff can be used to scratch letters into the wall. The original Chronicler's staff was lost when KODAN disappeared. TURAGA NOKAMA carved another one for TAKUA to carry during his time of service. It has now been passed on to HAHLI.

CHUTE LURKER:

A dangerous RAHI known for its habit of hiding in chutes and ambushing travelers. The Rahi were both omnivorous and amphibious, though they seemed to prefer avoiding breathing air as much as possible.

CHUTE SPEAK:

Name given to the slang used by residents of LE-METRU in METRU NUI.

CHUTE STATION 445:

The busiest transport hub in PO-METRU. TOA ONEWA caught up to AHKMOU here.

CHUTE LURKER

CHUTES:

Primary transport system for the city of METRU NUI. Chutes were long cylindrical tubes made of liquid PROTODERMIS held in place by a sheath of magnetic energy. The protodermis flowed through the chutes at a high rate of speed, carrying cargo and MATORAN from place to place. Passengers were required to hold their breath while riding in a chute.

Most chutes ran aboveground, often supported by solid protodermis braces. Some chutes ran underground or underwater, but most of these were in poor repair and largely abandoned by the Matoran. These chutes were used by both RAHI and VISORAK to reach the city.

Chutes ran in a preset direction. Attempting to change that direction could cause severe damage to the system. KONGU was forced by NIDHIKI and KREKKA to reverse the flow of a chute in an effort to capture the TOA METRU.

Chutes could be boarded at a chute station or by "chute jumping," leaping onto a chute during the brief moments when the magnetic energy wavered and the outer layer could be penetrated. This was both dangerous and illegal.

Chutes faced a number of potential problems. A weakened magnetic energy sheath would cause liquid protodermis to leak out. Poorly constructed braces could break and cause the chute to collapse. It was also possible for a portion of the magnetic energy to break off and form a FORCE SPHERE.

CITY OF LEGENDS:

Nickname given to the city of METRU NUI. The name was actually coined as a dark joke by the SHADOWED ONE during the conflict between the TOA and the DARK HUNTERS. He claimed that Metru Nui would be "well and truly a city of legends since, as is well known, most legends are about the dead."

CLAW CLUBS:

Tools carried by TOA HORDIKA ONEWA, which could be used to hurl stones or charge up his RHOTUKA SPINNER.

CLIFF SCREECHER:

RAHI native to the island of ODINA. The cliff screecher is a batlike creature that legend says is effectively immortal because its spirit is housed somewhere other than its body. It emits a loud screech when it attacks, and seems to delight in knocking potential prey down a mountain, then scooping it up, bringing it back to the cliff face, and knocking it down again. Cliff screecher victims eventually die of fear and shock.

CLIMBING CLAWS:

POHATU NUVA's Toa tools. These claws could be hurled at opponents or combined to form a sphere called a KODAN BALL.

COLISEUM:

The sporting arena, power station, and seat of government for METRU NUI. The largest building in the city, it sat at the meeting point of the six metru boundaries. It was home to TURAGA DUME.

The central arena of the Coliseum was used for citywide AKILINI tournaments as well as VAHKI training exercises. Below that were storage areas. Farther down, there was a power station that relied on the flow of liquid PROTODERMIS to generate energy for the city.

The TOA METRU made their first major public appearance at the Coliseum, where they were challenged by MAKUTA (posing as Turaga Dume) to prove themselves to be TOA. The Coliseum floor was activated, causing the surface to move like ocean waves and huge pillars of protodermis to rise up in an irregular pattern. When the Toa failed to keep their footing, they were branded as impostors and their capture was ordered. NUJU, ONEWA, and WHENUA were captured in a whirlpool and VAKAMA, MATAU, and NOKAMA were forced to flee.

The Toa Metru later returned here to confront Makuta and attempt to save the MATORAN. The city's population had been placed in spheres and rendered comatose, and those spheres were then loaded into the storage area. The Toa managed to recover six of the spheres even as Makuta drained the energy from the city's power plant. They were forced to leave the remainder of the spheres behind as they made their escape from the city.

COLISEUM

Later, the Toa Metru returned to Metru Nui in an effort to save the rest of the Matoran. They discovered that the Coliseum had been taken over by the VISORAK horde and its leaders, SIDORAK and ROODAKA. Following their transformation into TOA HORDIKA, the heroes were able to defeat the Visorak in the Coliseum in a ferocious battle. During the fight, Sidorak was slain by KEETONGU in the building's main arena.

COLONY DRONE:
Harmless creatures whose RHOTUKA SPINNER energies were a food source for the VISORAK. The hordes brought large groups of colony drones with them whenever they went to a new land, keeping them penned up and under guard.

COMET:
A popular type of KOLHII BALL. AHKMOU sold comet balls infected with MAKUTA's darkness to unsuspecting MATORAN. His scheme was uncovered by TAKUA, and the tainted spheres were destroyed by Takua and POHATU.

CONJURER:
Former warrior-king of a southern island who joined the DARK HUNTERS. He relies on sophisticated technology to make it appear that he has "magical" powers. Conjurer has powerful telekinetic abilities, a staff of disintegration, and RHOTUKA SPINNERS that can temporarily steal the power of an opponent and channel it into himself. He is currently in a coma after trying to absorb the power of a BROTHERHOOD OF MAKUTA member.

CONJURER

COPPER MASK OF VICTORY:
Ceremonial masks awarded to the winners of Matoran village games. These were originally forged on METRU NUI and worn by the champions of AKILINI tournaments.

CORDAK BLASTER:
Name of the weapons found by the TOA MAHRI in the undersea armory of the BARRAKI. The blasters had a revolving launcher that fired mini-charges capable of blasting apart huge sections of rock. The blasters were originally designed on XIA and sold to the DARK HUNTERS, then stolen from that organization by agents of the ORDER OF MATA NUI. They were stored on VOYA NUI and disappeared into the sea when a section of that island broke off. The weapons were recovered from the sea floor by the Barraki. Cordak is the Matoran word for "desolation."

CRYSTAL CLIMBER

CRYSTAL CLIMBER:
RAHI originally from KO-METRU, these creatures lived among the KNOWLEDGE TOWERS, feeding on ICE BATS. They were considered pests due to their habit of infesting tower chambers and refusing to leave. They later migrated to the frosty wastes of MOUNT IHU on MATA NUI (2).

CRYSTAL SERPENTS:
Four huge Rahi who dwell in the four corners of the realm of ARTAKHA. The serpents attack and defend themselves by maneuvering so that light strikes their

crystalline form, then they convert that light into a devastating heat ray. They are dormant most of the time, awakening only to feed every century or two.

CRYSTAL SPIKES:
Climbing tools carried by TOA METRU NUJU.

CYCLONE SPEAR:
Tool carried by TOA IRUINI. The cyclone spear could create massive windstorms strong enough to sweep away hundreds of foes at a time. Use of the spear weakened Iruini, making it necessary for him to be careful how often he used it.

DAGGER SPIDER:
RAHI insects of VOYA NUI who attack by stabbing their victims with their front legs, injecting a paralyzing venom.

DAIKAU (DIGH-cow):
A carnivorous plant that grew wild in the jungles of LE-WAHI on MATA NUI (2). It fed primarily on insects and small birds but was not above snatching a passing MATORAN if one wandered too close. Its apparent ability to think led the Matoran to classify it as a RAHI.

DALU (dah-LOO):
GA-MATORAN member of the RESISTANCE on VOYA NUI. A warrior by nature, Dalu was determined to fight for the freedom of her people and the safety of her home. She is best known for her single-handed defeat of AVAK. Her twin chargers enable her to temporarily increase one attribute of a target (i.e., strength, speed, etc.).

DARK HUNTERS:
A shadowy band of mercenaries and bounty hunters whose existence has been rumored for centuries. They are said to be as powerful as TOA but far less moral, willing to take on any job if the reward is great enough. In the past, Dark Hunters have been paid with everything from skillfully crafted tools to secrets to political power.
No one outside of the organization knows exactly how many Dark Hunters there are. They are allegedly led by a charismatic and powerful individual known only as the SHADOWED ONE, a being said to be respected even by MAKUTA. When a request for Dark Hunter assistance comes in, the Shadowed One decides how many Dark Hunters he will dispatch and who they will be. Often, he pairs up agents who on the surface seem like poor teams, such as NIDHIKI and KREKKA. In the end, they are inevitably successful, for all Dark Hunters know the price of failure.
The Dark Hunters have a history of conflict with Toa and METRU NUI. Early in the reign of DUME, the Shadowed One wished to establish a base in the city, but Dume refused. This resulted in a huge struggle between the Toa, led by LHIKAN, and the Dark Hunters. During this conflict, Toa Nidhiki attempted to betray the city and eventually defected to the enemy. The Toa eventually won the fight, leaving the Shadowed One embittered and determined to grind Metru Nui to dust beneath his heel.

As an organization, the Dark Hunters were at one time allied with the BROTHERHOOD OF MAKUTA. In addition, both ROODAKA and SIDORAK were frequent employers of Dark Hunters, using them to spy on each other. Later, Makuta himself, in the guise of Turaga Dume, would call for Dark Hunters to be sent to Metru Nui to capture Toa Lhikan. He also used Dark Hunters to capture or eliminate some of Lhikan's fellow Toa. The Dark Hunters later clashed with the Brotherhood when Makuta caused the deaths of Nidhiki and Krekka. That conflict continues to this day.

The Dark Hunters jealously hide their secrets and enforce their own rules. Summoning a Dark Hunter for no reason or refusing to pay them can result in truly hideous consequences. The worst offense of all is causing the death of a Dark Hunter, either directly or indirectly, a crime that risks attracting the direct attention of the Shadowed One.

Known current and former Dark Hunters include the Shadowed One, Nidhiki, Krekka, LARISKA, SENTRAKH, PHANTOM, SILENCE, DEVASTATOR, TRIGLAX, HAKANN, THOK, VEZOK, ZAKTAN, AVAK, REIDAK, AIRWATCHER, AMPHIBAX, ANCIENT, CHARGER, CONJURER, DARKNESS, DWELLER, ELIMINATOR, FIREDRACAX, GATHERER, GLADIATOR, GUARDIAN, HORDIKA DRAGONS, KRAATA-KAL, LURKER, MIMIC, MINION, POISON, PRIMAL, PROTOTYPE, RAVAGER, SAVAGE, SEEKER, SHADOW STEALER, SPINNER, SUBTERRANEAN, TRACKER, TYRANT, and VANISHER. See individual entries.

DARK HUNTER-BROTHERHOOD OF MAKUTA WAR:

Conflict sparked over 1,000 years ago by the discovery that MAKUTA had killed two DARK HUNTERS in his service, NIDHIKI and KREKKA. The war continues to rage across many lands, with the Dark Hunters employing guerrilla tactics against the more powerful Brotherhood. It was during this conflict that ZAKTAN discovered the true plans of the Brotherhood. At present, the war remains a stalemate, largely because the Brotherhood has been unwilling to devote its full attention to the struggle.

DARKNESS:

One of the most powerful of the DARK HUNTERS, Darkness's job is to keep watch over the organization's leader, the SHADOWED ONE, and kill him should he ever show any sign of weakness.

DAXIA (DACKS-ee-ah):

Island home of the ORDER OF MATA NUI and site of that organization's first and largest base. Mountainous and blazingly hot, it is a place that first seems intimidating but can offer great treasures to those who take the time to get to know the land. The fortress on the island is defended with cutting-edge weaponry. All Order of Mata Nui members have orders to fall back to Daxia in the event of a major attack.

DEFILAK (Deh-FILL-lack):

LE-MATORAN leader of the Matoran Council on MAHRI NUI. Defilak led an expedition into the PIT and was among those captured by PRIDAK. He later escaped and helped defend his city against a massive venom eel and the armies of the BARRAKI. It was he who gave the TOA INIKA their new name, TOA MAHRI, in honor of their service to Mahri Nui.

DEFILAK

DEKAR [day-KAR]:

PO-MATORAN resident of MAHRI NUI. An aquahunter, Dekar was the second MATORAN to come into possession of the KANOHI IGNIKA. As a result of his touching the mask, he was "cursed" in such a way that he could not cause a fatal injury to anything he fought. Convinced the mask was evil, he attempted to destroy it, but it was stolen from him by the BARRAKI before he could do so. Later, the power of the Ignika transformed him into HYDRAXON, erasing his memories of his previous life in the process.

DEKAR

DERMIS TURTLE:

Amphibious creatures who lived in GA-METRU and later migrated to GA-KORO. They were credited by MATORAN with being able to predict the weather — they retreated into their shells when storms were coming.

DERMIS TURTLE

DESTRAL [des-TRAHL]:

Site of the first and largest BROTHERHOOD OF MAKUTA fortress, and their headquarters in the war against the DARK HUNTERS. The island's location changes all the time — it's believed the Brotherhood is using some version of a KANOHI OLMAK to move it through dimensional gates. It is heavily defended by concealed weaponry and traps and the legions of VISORAK, RAHKSHI, and EXO-TOA. Beyond the fortress, Destral is a largely barren island and has no native inhabitants. The six TOA HAGAH stole the KANOHI AVOHKII, the Mask of Light, from the fortress on Destral.

DEZALK [day-ZAHLK]:

TA-MATORAN who was the first to be enslaved by ZAKTAN using ANTIDERMIS. Dezalk was ordered to lure the other MATORAN of VOYA NUI into a trap so they too could be enslaved, which he did. Dezalk was later freed from Piraka control by the actions of the TOA INIKA.

DIGGER:

A unique tool used by ONU-MATORAN miners on MATA NUI (2), the digger consisted of a short wooden staff with a pointed metal spiral at the end. It could be planted and twisted to loosen rock, much like a drill.

DIKAPI [DIGH-kah-PEY]:

A flightless desert bird known for its ability to run great distances without tiring. Although present on MATA NUI (2), these creatures were never seen on METRU NUI. It's believed they may have arrived on the island from some other underground region.

DISK OF TIME:

A KANOKA DISK made by combining all six of the GREAT DISKS. This disk had the power to speed up or slow down time around a target. VAKAMA later carved the disk into the VAHI, the Mask of Time.

DISKS:

See KANOKA DISKS.

DOOM VIPER:

Multi-headed serpent whose toxic breath was capable of killing any living thing it touched. Doom vipers came to GA-METRU via a trading boat from another land and proved extremely hard to capture. None seem to have made it to MATA NUI (2).

DOOM VIPER

DRAGON LIZARD:

See HIKAKI.

DRIFTS:

The icy snowfields of MOUNT IHU. POHATU NUVA followed KOPAKA NUVA through this treacherous area during the search for the KANOHI NUVA masks. TAKUA and JALLER later traveled this way as well on their quest for the Seventh TOA, encountering vicious RAHKSHI during the journey.

DRILL STAFF:

TURAGA WHENUA's tool and badge of office, also known as the drill of ONUA. The drill staff is an altered version of the EARTHSHOCK DRILLS that Whenua carried as a TOA; it transformed when Whenua became a TURAGA.

DUME (doo-MAH):

Former Toa of Fire and Turaga of METRU NUI. Dume's history as a Toa has not yet been revealed, although it is believed that he had some hand in LHIKAN's becoming a Toa. After becoming a Turaga, Dume led Metru Nui for thousands of years, helping it to become a thriving metropolis.

Under Dume's rule, the MATORAN constructed the KRALHI and the VAHKI. Dume also authorized MAVRAH's researches into ancient sea RAHI, then later ordered the experiments stopped when they threatened the city. It was also Dume who first summoned Lhikan and 10 other Toa to battle the KANOHI DRAGON that menaced Metru Nui.

Perhaps Dume's bravest act was opposing the DARK HUNTERS when they wished to establish a base in Metru Nui. Despite threats from the SHADOWED ONE, Dume refused to allow the mercenaries anywhere within the boundaries of the city. This set off a major conflict between the Dark Hunters and a small band of Toa in the city, led by Lhikan. The Toa were eventually victorious, despite the defection of Toa NIDHIKI and his attempts to betray the city into Dark Hunter hands.

Centuries later, Dume was captured by MAKUTA and placed inside a sphere which rendered him comatose. Makuta then impersonated Dume as part of his plan to capture all of the Matoran in the city. Although the TOA METRU uncovered the ruse, they were unable to rescue Dume prior to their initial escape from the city. After their return and transformation into TOA HORDIKA, they discovered that Dume's canister had malfunctioned and he was free. He refused to leave the city with them following the defeat of the VISORAK, preferring to watch over Metru Nui in their absence.

Dume was still there when the TOA NUVA returned with the Matoran, and it was he who dispatched the Nuva to VOYA NUI to retrieve the KANOHI IGNIKA. He continues to rule Metru Nui today.

DUST DARTERS:

Tiny insects who dwell in the realm of KARZAHNI and feed on metallic protodermis. Although relatively harmless individually, over time a swarm can do severe damage to anything metallic or mechanical. They are considered pests.

DWELLER:

DARK HUNTER assigned to monitor events on METRU NUI. His powers include the ability to read minds, screen his own mind from telepathy, and drive a target mad with nightmares.

DWELLER IN THE DEEP:

A massive underwater beast that lived in the sea beneath the GREAT TEMPLE. TOA NOKAMA encountered it during her search for the GA-METRU GREAT DISK, which turned out to be wedged between two of the creature's sharp teeth. The dweller's preferred prey was GREAT TEMPLE SQUID.

EARTH SHIELD:

Tool carried by NUHVOK. These shields could weaken a structure from below, causing it to tumble down. The Nuhvok used their earth shields in their successful invasion of LE-KORO.

EHLEK (AY-leck):

One of the six BARRAKI who menace MAHRI NUI. Ehlek was originally a member of the LEAGUE OF SIX KINGDOMS and dominated a number of western island chains that included the island of ZAKAZ. He was one of the harsher and more brutal dictators, which may have been because he was not a native land-dweller. Ehlek's native domain was beneath the waters surrounding Zakaz and he had to wear a complicated apparatus to breathe. This left him feeling vulnerable and led him to be extremely strict with any potential rebellion against his rule.

Ehlek joined in the League's efforts to rebel against MATA NUI (1), and he and his army were defeated by the BROTHERHOOD OF MAKUTA (that army included AMPHIBAX). He was condemned to the PIT by BOTAR and spent most of the next 80,000 years there. Then, some 1,000 years ago, a massive earthquake shattered the walls of his prison. He escaped, only to find himself in a strange ocean. Of all six Barraki, he was the least affected by the mutagenic seawater, being already a water-breather. His form did change radically, however, resulting in his growing a series of electrified spines. With his air-breathing equipment destroyed, he was unable to return to the lands he had once ruled.

EHLEK

Assembling a new army of venom eels, Ehlek took control of the northern reaches of this new world and built a massive fortress. That fortress was destroyed when the city of MAHRI NUI sank beneath the waves and crushed it. Since that time, Ehlek has nursed a deep hatred of MATORAN. When the KANOHI IGNIKA appeared underwater, Ehlek led his army against Mahri Nui, only to be stopped by order of PRIDAK. He was later suspected by Pridak of being responsible for the subsequent disappearance of the Mask of Life. Ehlek was then tricked by TOA MAHRI HEWKII into believing Pridak had betrayed him and led his army into battle against his former leader.

An interesting side note is that Ehlek's native species was tampered with by the ORDER OF MATA NUI in an effort to create a race that could successfully battle the BROTHERHOOD OF MAKUTA.

Ehlek carries a SQUID LAUNCHER and his sharp spines can give off an electric charge.

EHRYE [AIR-yay]:

A KO-MATORAN. Ehrye worked as a messenger in KO-METRU but dreamed of obtaining employment in a KNOWLEDGE TOWER. He blamed NUJU for preventing him from getting a better job and resolved to use his knowledge of the location of the Ko-Metru GREAT DISK to get what he wanted. NIDHIKI and KREKKA trapped Ehrye on a rooftop in their efforts to get the Great Disks, and he had to be saved by Toa Nuju. Later, Ehrye merged with VHISOLA, ORKAHM, NUHRII, TEHUTTI, and AHKMOU to form the MATORAN NUI and help the TOA METRU defeat the MORBUZAKH. Shortly after that, Ehrye was captured by the VAHKI and put into a sphere that rendered him comatose. Evidence was later discovered that Ehrye may have been destined to become a Toa of Ice. This evidence proved to be false.

Ehrye was eventually rescued by the Toa Metru and brought to MATA NUI (2).

EHRYE

ELDA [ELL-dah]:

KANOHI Mask of Detection worn by TOA INIKA HAHLI. She was given the MATORAN version of the mask while in the realm of KARZAHNI (1). The Kanohi Elda allowed Hahli to detect the presence of the Kanohi IGNIKA, as well as to see the spirit of MATORO when it was free of his body. The Elda was stolen from Hahli by MAKUTA while that being was in possession of Toa Matoro's body.

ELECTRIC SHIELD:

Tool carried by TAHNOK-KAL capable of releasing hundreds of thousands of volts at once.

ELIMINATOR:

DARK HUNTER charged with killing any members of that organization who fail in their missions, then carrying out the missions himself. Along with NIDHIKI and KREKKA, he was dispatched to METRU NUI to help MAKUTA in his efforts to seize control of the city. Eliminator's task was to track down and destroy the Toa guardians of Metru Nui, which he did very successfully. Eliminator is nearly invisible in low-light conditions and can harness and combine the powers of up to four KANOKA DISKS and then fire the energies from his claws.

ELIMINATOR

ENERGIZED PROTODERMIS:

The rarest form of PROTODERMIS, capable of inducing permanent mutations or causing instant destruction. Energized protodermis was silver in color and appeared to be charged with an unknown form of energy, but the origin of the substance was not known by the MATORAN. ONU-MATORAN miners occasionally stumbled across small samples of it beneath METRU NUI and GA-MATORAN scholars attempted to analyze it, but to no avail. In some strange way, energized protodermis appeared to be linked to the destiny of those beings exposed to it. A being destined to be transformed by energized protodermis would be; a being who was not so destined would be dissolved by the liquid. Energized protodermis apparently worked on inanimate objects as well, having been seen to transform KANOHI masks and give a semblance of life to solid stone. It is believed the rock creature called VATUKA may have been created using this substance as well.

Makuta worked with the ENERGIZED PROTODERMIS ENTITY to use the substance to mutate RAHI, for reasons still unknown. Later, the TOA METRU discovered an energized protodermis pool in one of Makuta's lairs outside of the city, guarded by the energized protodermis entity.

During the ensuing battle, the entity used its substance to mutate Rahi to fight the Toa. Later, the KARZAHNI (2) was destroyed after exposing itself to this fluid in an effort to gain greater power.

There has been speculation that VISORAK venom was a dilute form of energized protodermis, but no proof of that was ever found and the RAHAGA voiced doubts that it was true. VAKAMA later discovered that the GA-MATORAN of Metru Nui were attempting to create an artificial form of the substance.

Centuries after the Matoran left Metru Nui for MATA NUI (2), TAHU and his team of Toa were immersed in tubes of energized protodermis following a battle with the BAHRAG. Rather than being destroyed by it, the Toa were transformed into TOA NUVA. The chamber in which this occurred was later buried under tons of rubble.

The TOA INIKA used ZAMOR SPHERES filled with energized protodermis to destroy the ANTIDERMIS virus that was controlling the Matoran of VOYA NUI.

What future role, if any, energized protodermis will play in the lives of the Toa and Matoran remains to be seen.

ENERGIZED PROTODERMIS ENTITY:

A sapient being that consisted exclusively of ENERGIZED PROTODERMIS in a humanoid form. It was encountered by the TOA METRU in one of MAKUTA's lairs. It revealed that it had been allied with Makuta in experiments to mutate RAHI, as well as being a vital part of the creation of KARZAHNI (2) and the MORBUZAKH. The Toa Metru asked for a small portion of its substance to trade for a cure for NOKAMA's wounds, but the entity refused and engaged them in battle. The entity fought primarily through surrogates, Rahi creatures mutated by its substance. In the end, the Toa Metru defeated the Rahi and threatened to bring the chamber down on the protodermis pool if the entity did not comply. The entity allowed them to take a vial full of its substance but then attempted to slay the Toa Metru as they departed. Toa ONEWA brought down the last pillar supporting the ceiling and buried the entity under tons of rock.

It is highly unlikely the energized protodermis entity was killed in this incident. Since it was capable of appearing wherever any of its substance might be, it probably disappeared before the impact and reappeared at another pool somewhere else. It is no doubt planning revenge for its defeat.

ENERGY CROSSBOW:

Weapon carried by TOA INIKA KONGU. It fired bolts of pure laser energy to devastating effect.

ENSIGN:

A badge worn by members of the TA-KORO GUARD, bearing the volcanic emblem of that force.

EXO-TOA [EX-oh TOE-ah]:

Armored suits capable of enhancing the powers of the beings that wore them. The Exo-Toa were constructed under the orders of the BROTHERHOOD OF MAKUTA, both as a fail-safe against a possible rampage by the BOHROK and as automated guardians of the Brotherhood's many fortresses. Exo-Toa made up part of the Brotherhood army that defeated the BARRAKI. Later, a number of Exo-Toa were destroyed by the TOA HAGAH during their attack on a Brotherhood base.

Centuries later, the Exo-Toa were stumbled upon by TAHU and his team of Toa while attempting to stop the BAHRAG. They donned the armor and used its advanced equipment, including electro-rockets, to challenge the Bohrok queens. However, the armor inhibited the Toa's elemental powers, making them as much of a hindrance as a help.

Later, the six Exo-Toa suits, again running on automatic, challenged the BOHROK-KAL as they tried to free the Bahrag. The Kal destroyed the Exo-Toa. Unknown to anyone, NUPARU salvaged some of the armor and was hoping to study it, but events forced him to leave METRU NUI before doing so.

FADER BULL:
Plant-eating PO-METRU RAHI capable of limited teleportation to escape enemies.

FANG BLADES:
Tools carried by TOA HORDIKA MATAU, which can cut through webs and other substances and charge up his RHOTUKA SPINNER.

FAU SWAMP (FOW):
The marshy ground of LE-WAHI. Too soft and muddy to build homes upon, the presence of the Fau Swamp forced the LE-MATORAN to make their homes in trees. MATAU became lost in the swamp on his first visit to MATA NUI (2) and often complained about the terrain afterward. The swamp was later home to a large number of RAHI.

FADER BULL

FAXON (FACKS-on):
KANOHI Mask of Kindred worn by TOA MAHRI HAHLI. This mask allows the wearer to simulate the powers of creatures who share the same environment. In this case, Hahli was able to use it to duplicate the powers of certain sea beasts.

FENRAKK (FEN-rack):
Monstrous mutant spider found in the Chamber of Life on VOYA NUI. Fenrakk was mutated by the KANOHI IGNIKA to a larger size and fused to VEZON to provide an additional guardian for the mask. Already possessed of great strength and acidic saliva, Fenrakk also shared Vezon's ability to absorb kinetic energy. Defeated by the TOA INIKA, Fenrakk transformed into KARDAS.

FENRAKK SPAWN:
Native RAHI spider species on the island of VOYA NUI. A Fenrakk spawn was mutated by the KANOHI IGNIKA into the monstrous FENRAKK who guarded the Mask of Life. Like the larger Fenrakk, these creatures possessed great strength and acidic saliva.

FIELDS OF CONSTRUCTION:
A large, open area in PO-METRU where assorted pieces were assembled to make goods for use throughout METRU NUI.

FIKOU (fee-KOO):
Tree spiders that nested in LE-METRU cables, ONU-METRU tunnels, and, later, LE-WAHI vines. The Fikou were known for spinning incredibly intricate webs and for jumping out suddenly at passing prey.

"FIKOU WEB" [fee-KOO]:
Nickname given by ONU-MATORAN to a complex series of maintenance tunnels beneath the ONU-METRU ARCHIVES. The TOA METRU encountered RAHKSHI and KRAHKA here while attempting to repair a leak that threatened the Archives.

FIN BARBS:
Tools carried by TOA HORDIKA NOKAMA, which could dig through most substances and charge up her RHOTUKA SPINNER.

FIRE ENTITY:
A creature made completely of flame encountered and defeated by TOA VAKAMA during the TOA METRU's journey back to METRU NUI. Its exact nature was never discovered, but Vakama saw it as a reflection of himself if he were ever to let his power run out of control. He defeated the fire entity by using his Toa power to draw every last bit of heat from the chamber, causing the entity to freeze. It evidently survived, for it was gone when the other Toa arrived to find Vakama, unconscious from his effort.

FIRE GREATSWORDS:
Twin Toa tools carried by LHIKAN, through which he could focus his flame power. They could also be fitted together to form a shield and a flying board.

FIRE PITS:
Flame geysers in the center of TA-METRU, believed by the MATORAN to have been the source of all fire in the district. They were surrounded by a fence and guarded by VAHKI patrols. Due to the danger of the pits, Matoran had to receive special permission from TURAGA DUME to access them. TOA VAKAMA and NUHRII broke into the fire pit area to retrieve the Ta-Metru GREAT DISK, and fought a MORBUZAKH vine inside one of the pits.

FIRE SHIELD:
Tool carried by the TAHNOK. It was capable of melting any substance on the island of MATA NUI (2). Tahnok used fire shields in attacks on TA-KORO, PO-KORO, and elsewhere.

FIREDRACAX [FIRE-dray-KAX]:
A MATORAN transformed by ENERGIZED PROTODERMIS into an armored warrior with a hatred for VISORAK, Firedracax joined the DARK HUNTERS for a chance to kill the spider creatures. His shield is unbreakable and his RHOTUKA SPINNER absorbs thermal energy from the air and redirects it at a target in a burst of heat and flame.

FIREDRACAX

FIREFLYERS:
Flying insects with a fiery sting. Swarms of fireflyers were known to nest in furnaces and maintenance tunnels beneath TA-METRU.

FIRESTAFF:
TURAGA VAKAMA's tool and badge of office. His firestaff is in fact his mask-making tool that he used while living on METRU NUI as a MATORAN. This same tool was used by Vakama to create the KANOHI VAHI, the Mask of Time.

FORCE SPHERE:

A particularly dangerous phenomenon observed in CHUTES in the city of METRU NUI. When part of a chute was damaged, a portion of the magnetic force holding the liquid PROTODERMIS in place could fold in on itself and break off. It could then travel through the chute, absorbing everything that it passed and growing larger. At a certain size, it would wreck the chute and then implode, destroying everything contained within it. The LE-METRU GREAT DISK was freed from a force sphere by TOA MATAU.

FOUNTAINS OF WISDOM:

Decorative structures in GA-METRU from which jets of liquid PROTODERMIS emerged.

FROST BEETLES:

Insectoid KO-METRU RAHI rumored to have Matoran-level intelligence as a result of having consumed MEMORY CRYSTALS. These creatures were never spotted on MATA NUI (2).

FROST BEETLE

FROSTELUS (frost-TELL-lus):

A savage species somewhere between a RAHI and a TOA, Frostelus dwell inside floating "homes" that resemble icebergs. Highly territorial, a tribe of these beings once wiped out a Toa tower, killing all but one of the Toa inside. They were most recently spotted near Metru Nui and TAKANUVA has clashed with Frostelus scouts on more than one occasion.

FURNACE SALAMANDER:

Lizardlike RAHI that lived inside the foundries and furnaces of TA-METRU. Excellent climbers and jumpers, they were also capable of gliding short distances.

FUSA (FOO-sah):

A kangaroo-like RAHI and a natural enemy of the MUAKA. Fusa defended themselves using their powerful hind legs and could be extremely dangerous when cornered or in captivity.

FURNACE SALAMANDER

GA (GAH):

A Matoran prefix meaning "water."

GADUNKA (guh-DUNK-ah):

Vicious RAHI mutated by the KANOHI IGNIKA. Gadunka are, by nature, tiny sea creatures, not much longer than the length of a finger. One such specimen hid beneath the Ignika for refuge and was affected by its power, which was leaking out of the damaged mask. As a result, it grew to millions of times its size, large enough to pose a serious threat to the TOA MAHRI. Gadunka possess sharp claws and large metallic teeth. They are impervious to most physical attacks and do not have big enough brains to be badly affected by mental attacks.

GAFNA (GAFF-nah):
Small rodents native to Voya Nui. There are at least six known breeds of gafna, who were among the few Rahi to survive the traumatic events of the GREAT CATACLYSM.

GA-KINI (GAH-kin-NEE):
A temple dedicated to GALI located in GA-WAHI on MATA NUI (2).

GA-KORO (GAH-koar-OH):
Village on MATA NUI (2) and home to the GA-MATORAN. Ga-Koro was led by TURAGA NOKAMA and protected by TOA GALI. The village floated atop the waters off the northeastern coast of the island. Whirlpools and strong currents combined to make the village a dangerous place for outsiders to visit. TAKUA aided the village when it was invaded by RAHI, shortly after the arrival of Gali. Ga-Koro was menaced by PAHRAK during the BOHROK invasion.

GA-MATORAN (GAH-mat-OR-an):
A resident of GA-KORO or GA-METRU. Ga-Matoran had blue armor and often wore blue masks. All Ga-Matoran were female. On METRU NUI, most Ga-Matoran were students or teachers. On MATA NUI (2), their labors tended to involve boating, fishing, and other aquatic pursuits.

GA-METRU (GAH-MET-troo):
Spiritual and educational center of METRU NUI and home to the GREAT TEMPLE and the FOUNTAINS OF WISDOM. Ga-Metru was the site of numerous PROTODERMIS canals, as well as temples and schools. According to legend, Ga-Metru was the second region of the city built and was the one most favored by MATA NUI (1). Protodermis was pumped from the sea into Ga-Metru, and the purification process took place here. This metru was protected by TOA NOKAMA, who discovered a GREAT DISK in the waters beneath the Great Temple.

GA-METRU

GA-SUVA (GAH-soo-VAH):
A shrine to GALI NUVA in GA-KORO. KANOHI masks and Gali Nuva's symbol were kept here.

GA-WAHI (GAH-wah-HEE):
Region in northeastern MATA NUI (2), site of GA-KORO. Ga-Wahi was dominated by the waters of NAHO BAY and was home to numerous aquatic RAHI, including RUKI, MAKUTA FISH, TARAKAVA, and TAKEA. Seaweed and lily pads in the bay provided a foundation for the village to float upon.

GAAKI (gah-KEE):
Former TOA HAGAH of Water later mutated by ROODAKA into a RAHAGA. Gaaki had been part of an elite Toa team assigned to be MAKUTA's personal guard. When they discovered Makuta was oppressing and enslaving MATORAN, they turned on him and attacked a fortress of the BROTHERHOOD OF MAKUTA. Gaaki was struck by one of Roodaka's RHOTUKA SPINNERS and mutated into a shrunken creature with the head of a RAHKSHI. She was later rescued by Toa IRUINI and Toa NORIK, who also ended up being mutated. What masks and tools Gaaki carried as a Toa has not yet been revealed.

As a Rahaga, Gaaki specialized in capturing RAHI swimmers, such as TAKEA and MAKUTA FISH. She carried a Rhotuka Spinner with the *floater* power, which attached to its target and carried the Rahi to the surface of the water. She also carried a staff that she used to bait Rahi by striking the water with it.

GAHDOK (GAH-dahk):
This red creature was one of the two BAHRAG twins. See BAHRAG.

GAHLOK (GAH-lahk):
One of the six breeds of BOHROK, insectlike mechanoids controlled by KRANA who menaced the island of MATA NUI (2). The Gahlok were tied to the element of water, and their WATER SHIELDS could draw moisture from any source and redirect it at an opponent. The Gahlok were known for being sly and tricky, rarely reacting the same way twice to a given situation. Although most often seen in GA-WAHI, their most successful strike was the flooding of ONU-KORO. The Gahlok returned to their nests after the coming of the BOHROK-KAL but have since re-emerged.

GAHLOK-KAL

GAHLOK-KAL (GAH-lahk-KAHL):
One of the six mutant BOHROK who made up the BOHROK-KAL. Its tool was a MAGNETIC SHIELD, which could be used for defense or offense. After being fed TOA power via the TOA NUVA SYMBOLS (see BOHROK-KAL), Gahlok-Kal's power went wild and drew every metallic object in the room toward it. Its robotic body was crushed in the ensuing collision.

GAHLOK VA (GAH-lahk VAH):
One of the six BOHROK VA, Gahlok Va was connected to the water element. Their primary tools were twin hooks which could be used to climb slippery surfaces or defend themselves in combat. Although not fleet swimmers, they had incredible endurance, enabling them to travel long distances without stopping.

GALI/GALI NUVA (GAH-lee/GAH-lee NOO-vah):
Toa of Water and protector of GA-KORO.

GAHLOK VA

HISTORY

All that is known about Gali and her past prior to her first appearance on MATA NUI (2) comes from MATORAN legend. She was one of six Toa who had been floating in the ocean around the island for 1,000 years. They were inside unique canisters and each was partially disassembled. A signal unwittingly sent by TAKUA called the canisters to shore. Gali emerged on the shores of GA-WAHI and almost immediately had to act to save Ga-Koro from the rampage of a TARAKAVA.

Gali soon made contact with the other five Toa — ONUA, POHATU, TAHU, LEWA, and KOPAKA. Together and separately, they searched for KANOHI masks and battled the Rahi servants of MAKUTA. From the start, she had to spend a lot of time keeping Kopaka and Tahu from arguing. During a fight with the Rahi, Gali hit her head and had a vision in which the two TOA KAITA appeared and told her that it would be the destiny of the Toa to form those two

GALI

powerful beings. Later, she would indeed briefly merge with Lewa and Kopaka to form TOA KAITA WAIRUHA and fight the MANAS.

During the BOHROK invasion, Gali teamed with Pohatu, Onua, and Kopaka to trap a swarm of TAHNOK in TIRO CANYON.

Following the defeat of the twin Bohrok queens, the BAHRAG, the six Toa were transformed by energized protodermis into TOA NUVA. When Kopaka and Tahu decided to break up the team, Gali objected strongly. But no one, not even Onua, supported her. It would be some time before she forgave her friends. Later, after the BOHROK-KAL had stolen the Toa Nuva's powers, Gali teamed with Turaga NOKAMA to search for KANOHI NUVA masks and was almost killed by a GREAT TEMPLE SQUID.

Gali was the first to see the coming of the RAHKSHI, and she sped to TA-KORO to warn the village. But despite the best efforts of herself and Tahu, they were unable to prevent the village of fire from being destroyed or the Toa of Fire from being poisoned. Later, she led the other Toa in a healing ritual to save Tahu's life.

Gali was there to witness TAKANUVA's victory over Makuta and the rediscovery of METRU NUI. Back on Mata Nui, Gali Nuva helped with the construction of boats for a journey back to the city of legends. She also joined with the others in listening to Turaga VAKAMA's tales of life in Metru Nui centuries before.

Gali Nuva returned to Metru Nui with the other Toa Nuva, the Turaga, and the Matoran. Once there, she and her teammates were dispatched to VOYA NUI to retrieve the KANOHI IGNIKA. There they battled the PIRAKA and BRUTAKA, and were defeated in a treacherous attack from behind. They were imprisoned but later freed by the MATORAN RESISTANCE. They have since returned to Metru Nui, beginning the preparations for the awakening of Mata Nui (1), including the freeing of the Bahrag and the unleashing of the Bohrok.

POWERS

Gali controls the power of water. She can start or stop tidal waves and floods, draw moisture from the air and hurl it in a devastating water blast, or lash an opponent with fierce rainstorms. She is a strong swimmer and can survive prolonged periods of time at great depths.

PERSONALITY

On a Toa team filled with strong personalities, it normally falls to Gali to be the peacemaker. More than once, she has had to get between Tahu and Kopaka to keep them focused rather than fighting. Of all the Toa, she and Pohatu are probably closest to their respective Matoran, taking time to help them and guide them in between adventures.

EQUIPMENT

Gali carried HOOKS that allowed her to scale slippery surfaces. As Gali Nuva, she carries twin AQUA AXES that could be attached to

GALI NUVA

her feet to serve as scuba fins. Gali most often wore the Kanohi KAUKAU or KAUKAU NUVA, the Great Mask of Water Breathing.

GARAI (gah-RI):
KANOHI Mask of Gravity worn by TOA MAHRI HEWKII. This mask allows the wearer to increase or decrease the effect of gravity on a target.

GARAN (gah-RAN):
ONU-MATORAN leader of the RESISTANCE on VOYA NUI. His twin pulse bolt generators fire a ball of energy that grows more powerful the farther it travels. Garan led the mission to rescue the TOA NUVA from the PIRAKA STRONGHOLD.

GATE GUARDIAN

GATE GUARDIAN:
A deceptive creature that created a false image of itself to fool enemies. The Gate Guardian seen by others was small, perhaps 1.5 feet high. In reality, the creature was much bigger, but virtually impossible to see. An attacker targeting the small image would find itself beaten back by the larger, invisible Gate Guardian. The image mimicked the movements of the true creature. The only way to defeat a Gate Guardian was to first find some way to reveal its true form. NOKAMA was able to use her water power to do this on METRU NUI. It is believed that Gate Guardians were allied with the VISORAK.

GATHERER:
A MATORAN transformed by the SHADOWED ONE to be an armored colossus in service to the DARK HUNTERS. Gatherer has no need for food or sleep and carries a wide array of weapons. He also has a psychic connection to RAHI who dwell underground and can command them to do his bidding.

GHEKULA (GECK-you-LAH):
Amphibious creatures most often found in swampy waters. It was considered bad luck to harm one. Prior to selling infected KOLHII BALLS in PO-KORO, AHKMOU attempted to make a living selling "lucky Ghekula" to superstitious MATORAN, until TURAGA ONEWA put a stop to it.

GLADIATOR:
A native of SIDORAK and KREKKA's home island, Gladiator was a warrior in the arena before being freed from prison by a DARK HUNTER. He was recruited into that organization and put his brute strength, sharp claws, and incredible resistance to damage to work for them.

GNOMON:
The centerpiece of a sundial. Gnomon were in use on both the sundial on MATA NUI (2) and the massive sundial kept by MAKUTA in the COLISEUM.

GRAVITY SHIELD:
Tool carried by NUHVOK-KAL. This shield could completely eliminate gravity in a large area or increase it by up to 1,000 times. Nuhvok-Kal used this shield to erase gravity around a swarm of TAHNOK and send them flying into space.

GLADIATOR

GREAT BEINGS:

Immensely powerful entities who, according to MATORAN legend, dispatched the GREAT SPIRIT MATA NUI (1) from paradise to care for all living things. It is believed that the Great Beings came into existence long before Mata Nui — and dwarf even him in sheer power. How many Great Beings there are and where they reside is unknown. Among the things known to have been brought into existence by the Great Beings are the Matoran, KRANA, ARTAKHA, KARZAHNI, ZYGLAK, the KANOHI IGNIKA, the CHAMBER OF LIFE, and the GREAT SPIRIT himself.

GREAT CATACLYSM:

Name given to the universe-wide earthquake that resulted from MATA NUI (1) succumbing to unending slumber. Along with massive destruction in METRU NUI, the Cataclysm is known to have caused VOYA NUI to split off from its continent and the shattering of the PIT.

GREAT DISKS:

Six KANOKA DISKS of great power. According to legend, one was hidden in each of the six districts of METRU NUI. Their powers were *reconstitutes at random, freeze, weaken, enlarge, regenerate,* and *teleport*. Each Great Disk had a power level of 9.

Shortly after becoming a TOA METRU, VAKAMA had a vision that hinted the Great Disks were needed to save the city. He and the other Toa Metru went on a dangerous quest and succeeded in finding all six disks, despite efforts by NIDHIKI, KREKKA, and AHKMOU to stop them. They later used the disks to defeat the MORBUZAKH.

The heroes believed the recovery of the disks would prove them worthy to be TOA in the eyes of the MATORAN, but such did not prove to be the case. However, Vakama was successful in merging the disks into a DISK OF TIME and later carving the VAHI from it.

GREAT DISRUPTION:

Name given to the roughly 400-year period of the Matoran civil war in Metru Nui. MATA NUI (1) was so weakened during this time that Toa JOVAN and his team were dispatched to retrieve and use the KANOHI IGNIKA.

GREAT FURNACE:

Once the second highest structure in METRU NUI (after the COLISEUM), the Great Furnace was a massive foundry in TA-METRU used for the creation of VAHKI parts and other essential items. The heat from the furnace was so intense that even MATORAN could stand it for only a few minutes at a time before they had to retreat to a slightly cooler outer ring in the structure. The Great Furnace operated day and night, producing the largest amount of material of any forge or factory in the metru.

Shortly before the coming of the TOA METRU, mysterious vines began attacking workers in the Great Furnace. The workers eventually fled the structure, leaving it abandoned but still functioning. The Great Furnace became the home of the king root of the MORBUZAKH plant, from which it launched its attacks on the rest of the city. It was also the site of the final battle between the Toa Metru and the Morbuzakh, which resulted in the destruction of both the plant creature and the building. The Great Furnace was never rebuilt.

GREAT MASKS:

See KANOHI.

GREAT SPIRIT:

Designation given to MATA NUI (1) by the MATORAN. A Great Spirit is considered to be extremely powerful, though not at the level of a GREAT BEING. The GREAT TEMPLE in GA-METRU and KINI-NUI were both dedicated to the Great Spirit Mata Nui.

GREAT TEMPLE:

Arguably the most important building in METRU NUI, the Great Temple was the spiritual center of the city. It was built on a spit of land apart from the rest of GA-METRU and revered by

GREAT TEMPLE

MATORAN from all districts. It was heavily patrolled by VAHKI BORDAKH to protect it from RAHI attack.

The Great Temple was the home of the TOA SUVA, a round stone structure said to be the source of TOA power. The suva boasted six slots into which TOA STONES could be placed. Toa LHIKAN stole six Toa stones from this site and gave them to six Matoran — MATAU, NOKAMA, NUJU, ONEWA, VAKAMA, and WHENUA. These six were later transformed from Matoran into TOA METRU. KANOHI Masks of Power were also stored in the Great Temple.

Amazingly, the structure survived, relatively intact, the earthquake that struck Metru Nui. TOA HORDIKA Nokama and RAHAGA GAAKI encountered a GATE GUARDIAN here while searching for GREAT MASKS. The RAHAGA and Toa Hordika also journeyed here in search of clues to the location of KEETONGU.

The Great Temple was later largely destroyed due to the actions of Toa Hordika Vakama. It has since been restored by the Ga-Matoran.

GREAT TEMPLE SQUID:

Multi-tentacled beasts that lurked in the waters beneath the GREAT TEMPLE in GA-METRU. Long a menace to divers, the Great Temple squid feared only their natural enemy, the DWELLER IN THE DEEP. Each squid had twelve tentacles, each ending in a snapping beak, as well as a larger beak that acted as a mouth. Their sheer strength rivaled that of a TOA.

GALI NUVA was once trapped in the tentacles of a Great Temple squid that had made its way into an underwater tunnel between METRU NUI and MATA NUI (2).

GREAT USSAL RACE [uss-SUL]:

The major sporting event of ONU-KORO on MATA NUI (2). This competition pitted riders on USSAL crabs against each other in a test of speed and skill. ONEPU won the race five times.

GUARDIAN:

DARK HUNTER whose job it is to eliminate any others who might be captured before they can talk. His RHOTUKA SPINNERS contain powers tied to stone and earth.

GUARDIAN

GUKKO [GUCK-koh]:

These large, four-winged birds originally made their nests in the cables above LE-METRU. After the MATORAN fled METRU NUI to MATA NUI (2), the Gukko followed and found a home in the jungles of LE-WAHI. The LE-

MATORAN eventually learned to tame the Gukko birds. Gukko riders became the main defense force of LE-KORO. RAHAGA KUALUS insisted that Gukko was not the correct name for the species and that the term might have even been an insult in the language of these RAHI. Kualus and TOA HORDIKA NUJU are believed to have been the first to ride Gukko birds.

GUKKO BIRD FORCE:

A defense squad made up of LE-MATORAN mounted on GUKKO. Their most memorable feats were coming to the aid of the CHRONICLER's Company and their attack on a NUI-RAMA nest. The Gukko Bird Force was led by KONGU.

GUURAHK (GER-rahk):

One of the six RAHKSHI sent by MAKUTA to stop the HERALD and recover the KANOHI AVOHKII. Guurahk's staff emitted a powerful cone of energy capable of disintegrating anything it struck. This Rahkshi's special talent was the ability to divine the weakest point in any object or foe and target it. Along with LERAHK and PANRAHK, Guurahk destroyed the village of TA-KORO. These three Rahkshi were later trapped in a prison of glass, thanks to the combined powers of LEWA NUVA and TAHU NUVA.

HAFU (HAH-foo):

Extremely skilled PO-MATORAN carver. Hafu was widely considered the best of all the artisans in PO-KORO, as well as a great storyteller. Unfortunately, Hafu had a very high opinion of himself and tended to talk mostly about himself and his achievements. Hafu was part of the CHRONICLER's Company assembled by TAKUA to defend KINI-NUI against RAHI attack. Hafu's greatest moment occurred when he sacrificed some of his most beautiful statues to block the entryway to Po-Koro against the invading TAHNOK. Hafu later served on the Po-Koro KOLHII team with HEWKII, narrowly losing to the GA-KORO team.

HAHLI (HAH-lee):

Former GA-MATORAN CHRONICLER of the TOA NUVA's adventures, later TOA INIKA and TOA MAHRI.

HISTORY

Prior to the coming of the TOA, Hahli spent most of her time fishing and mending nets, too shy to voice her ideas or opinions. But she was thrust into danger during the BOHROK invasion and worked with MACKU to prevent the PAHRAK from entering GA-KORO. Following the defeat of the BOHROK-KAL, Hahli was unexpectedly tapped by Turaga NOKAMA to play on the Ga-Koro KOLHII team. Hahli led her team to victory against PO-KORO and TA-KORO squads. She had formed a close friendship with JALLER, captain of the TA-KORO GUARD, at this time, though the relationship had not progressed beyond that.
After TAKUA became TAKANUVA, Hahli stowed away on board his USSANUI vehicle to MAKUTA's lair. There she revealed herself to him and offered to be his Chronicler. He sent her back to the surface to gather the other Toa, the TURAGA, and the MATORAN and bring them down with her. This she did, returning in time to see Takanuva and Makuta merge into TAKUTANUVA.

Hahli was one of the Matoran who passed through the gateway leading to the shores of the silver sea around Metru Nui. She carried the late Jaller's mask with her. Takutanuva stopped her and used part of his life force to bring Jaller back to life.

After that time, Hahli has served as Chronicler, present for almost all of Turaga VAKAMA's tales of METRU NUI.

Following the return to Metru Nui, Hahli was one of five Matoran who accompanied Jaller in search of the missing Toa Nuva. After a number of harrowing adventures, the canisters in which they traveled landed on the shores of VOYA NUI. The canisters were struck by lightning from the RED STAR, which transformed all six into the Toa Inika. As Toa, they battled the PIRAKA, BRUTAKA, and others in an effort to claim the KANOHI IGNIKA.

TOA INIKA HAHLI

When the Kanohi was found, and then lost, it was Hahli who dove into the sea to try to retrieve it. The great pressure almost killed her, but she was saved by a Matoran from MAHRI NUI. She later accompanied the Toa Inika through the CORD, battling the ZYGLAK and Makuta, before arriving at Mahri Nui. As the Toa entered the water, a burst of energy from the Ignika transformed them into the aquatic Toa Mahri. They went on to battle the BARRAKI for possession of the Mask of Life.

When last seen, Hahli appeared to have struck up an alliance with MANTAX and was leading his army of rays toward Mahri Nui.

POWERS

Like GALI NUVA, Hahli controls the power of water. Although not as skilled as Gali, she is a quick learner.

PERSONALITY

Although Hahli understands the importance of what the Toa are doing, some part of her still fears the sheer amount of power they wield. A life of constant combat was never what she wished for, and she has a nagging intuition that tragedy will be the end result of their efforts.

EQUIPMENT

As a Toa Inika, Hahli wore the KANOHI ELDA, the Mask of Detection, and carried a LASER HARPOON and a ZAMOR SPHERE LAUNCHER. As a Toa Mahri, she wears the Kanohi FAXON, the Mask of Kindred, and carries a CORDAK BLASTER and PROTOSTEEL TALONS.

HAKANN (hah-CAN):

One of the six PIRAKA who attempted to steal the KANOHI IGNIKA. Hakann was recruited into the DARK HUNTER organization after being captured by ANCIENT while attempting to rob a TOA fortress. Treacherous and dishonest, Hakann betrayed the Dark Hunters during the TOA-DARK HUNTER war to save himself. When he and the others broke away from the group and traveled to MANGAIA to loot MAKUTA's lair, it was Hakann's error with the SPEAR OF FUSION that resulted in the creation of VEZON.

HAKANN

Later, on the island of VOYA NUI, Hakann made an unsuccessful bid to rebel against ZAKTAN and joined with THOK to steal the power of BRUTAKA. Defeated by the TOA INIKA, he rejoined the other Piraka in a failed attempt to steal the Mask of Life. When last seen, he was with the rest of his band of thieves on Voya Nui, still scheming how to get the Kanohi Ignika, and unaware that his body was being affected by an earlier exposure to mutagenic seawater. He possesses the elemental powers of fire, heat vision, and the ability to perform mental attacks. He carries a ZAMOR SPHERE LAUNCHER and a lava launcher.

HAND OF ARTAKHA:

Organization dedicated to the will of MATA NUI (2) and the pursuit of justice, which predated the formation of organized Toa teams. The Hand operated for more than 200 years, challenging threats to the new universe created by the GREAT BEINGS as well as stopping a number of natural disasters. Former members of the Hand include AXONN, HYDRAXON, and SHADOW STEALER. After a time, the group's leaders realized that its members were too undisciplined and their battles caused more damage than they prevented. It was decided to disband the Hand in favor of the more efficient Toa teams that had started to come into existence. The Hand reorganized itself as the ORDER OF MATA NUI, with many former members returning, and it continues under that name today.

HAPAKA (hah-PAH-kah):

Large hounds briefly employed by GA-MATORAN to drive away KAVINIKA, with mixed success. Although the Hapaka were certainly fierce enough for the job, they were also easily distracted by the chance to chase other RAHI.

HAU (HOW):

HAU

The Mask of Shielding. This mask created a force field around the user, protecting him from physical attack. Its sole limitation was that it could only protect against attacks that are expected, and so was ineffective against ambushes. Toa TAHU was wearing a Hau when he first appeared on MATA NUI (2), and it was Toa LHIKAN's mask of choice as well on METRU NUI. After his transformation into a TURAGA and subsequent death, Lhikan's Noble Hau was given to JALLER. It was later taken from him by KARZAHNI (1) and subsequently recovered by Tahu Nuva. In addition, the Hau is the symbol of the GREAT SPIRIT MATA NUI (1).

HAU NUVA (HOW noo-vah):

The more powerful version of the HAU worn by TAHU NUVA. This mask was able to project a stronger force field than the Hau, and the effect could be maintained for a longer duration. Like all Nuva masks, its power could be shared by the user with those in close proximity.

HEATSTONE:

A small, yellowish rock which gave off natural heat. It could be used to warm a chamber when open flame was not advisable. Heatstones are believed to be related to LIGHTSTONES, but most likely derive their power from a different source.

HERALD:

According to MATORAN legend, the Herald was the being charged with bringing the KANOHI AVOHKII, the Mask of Light, to the TOA of Light. This would bring about the dawn of a new age in which darkness would be defeated and peace would reign. TAKUA was the chosen Herald, but he attemped to pass the responsibility on to JALLER. After Jaller's death, it was discovered that Takua was not only the Herald but was, in fact, destined to become TAKANUVA, the Toa of Light.

HEWKII (HOO-kee):

Former PO-MATORAN carver and diskmaker, later TOA INIKA and TOA MAHRI.

HISTORY

During the time that he lived on METRU NUI, Hewkii was famous throughout the city for the quality of his KANOKA DISKS. So excellent was his workmanship that Turaga DUME was forced to make a rule that players from other metru could not use PO-METRU disks in AKILINI tournament play.

HEWKII

On MATA NUI (2), Hewkii was a KOLHII champion and a trusted aide to Turaga ONEWA. He was one of the only Po-Matoran strong enough to crush rocks with his both feet and his head. Athletic and powerful, he led the Po-Koro team to numerous kolhii championships and won the COPPER MASK OF VICTORY multiple times. Hewkii was credited with inventing the most popular current form of kolhii when he used his staff to save MACKU from a flying rock during the BOHROK invasion.

Following the return to Metru Nui, Hewkii was one of five Matoran who accompanied Jaller in search of the missing Toa Nuva. After a number of harrowing adventures, the canisters in which they traveled landed on the shores of VOYA NUI. The canisters were struck by lightning from the RED STAR, which transformed all six into the Toa Inika. Hewkii was somewhat disturbed that none of the others commented on the fact that the transformation had changed his armor color from brown to yellow and gray. As Toa, they battled the PIRAKA, BRUTAKA, and others in an effort to claim the KANOHI IGNIKA. Hewkii accompanied the Toa Inika through the CORD. It was Hewkii who first realized that MATORO's body had been possessed by MAKUTA. Arriving at Mahri Nui, a burst of energy from the Ignika transformed them into the aquatic Toa Mahri. They went on to battle the BARRAKI for possession of the Mask of Life. Hewkii used his mask power to trick EHLEK into thinking PRIDAK had betrayed him, sparking a war between the two.

POWERS

Like POHATU NUVA, Hewkii controls the power of stone. He is particularly adept at boulder slinging, given his past history as a kolhii champion.

PERSONALITY

Hewkii never asked to be a Toa, but he understands there is a job that needs to be done. His attitude is that the faster they do it, the faster the team can return to Metru Nui and see their friends again. He is a strong believer in being a team player, but doesn't have a lot of patience for sitting around and making complicated plans.

EQUIPMENT

As a Toa Inika, Hewkii wore the Kanohi SANOK, the Mask of Accuracy, and carried a LASER AXE and climbing chain. As a Toa Mahri, Hewkii wears the Kanohi GARAI and carries an AQUA WARBLADE.

HIATUS:
Term used by LESOVIKK to describe his tens of thousands of years wandering the universe. During this period, Lesovikk visited and explored the unknown lands far to the south, battled the RAHI NUI, and successfully defended an entire island from the VISORAK.

HIKAKI [hih-KAH-kee]:
A small lizardlike creature that thrived on molten PROTODERMIS and often shared territory with the FURNACE SALAMANDER. It was found most often in the vicinity of the MANGAI volcano on MATA NUI (2). Also known as the DRAGON LIZARD.

HIVE:
Bases for the VAHKI order enforcers in METRU NUI. Each hive contained an energy cradle through which Vahki could be recharged. When the METRU NUI power plant was destroyed, the resulting energy surge wrecked the hives as well.

HOOKS:
Tools carried by TOA GALI that allowed her to climb on slippery surfaces.

TOA INIKA HEWKII

HORDIKA

HORDIKA [hoar-DEE-kah]:
A Matoran word meaning "half beast." It was applied to the venom of the VISORAK, which could transform TOA into half-hero, half-RAHI forms.

HORDIKA DRAGONS:
Eight DARK HUNTERS transformed by VISORAK venom into lizardlike beasts. In addition to their natural strength and agility, they have an electric charge that flows through their claws. The SHADOWED ONE uses them primarily as debt collectors.

HORDIKA TEETH:
Tools carried by TOA HORDIKA NUJU, which could be used to summon flying RAHI or charge his RHOTUKA SPINNER.

HOTO [HOH-toh]:
Fire bugs known for tunneling through solid stone using the searing heat given off by their bodies to melt the way. On both METRU NUI and MATA NUI (2), they were considered a pest, often causing buildings and tunnels to collapse.

HUAI SNOWBALL SLING (HOOH-eye):
A popular sport in KO-KORO. Winners of the competition would receive a COPPER MASK OF VICTORY.

HUFA-MAFA RIVER (HOOH-fah MAH-fah):
A river that ran southwest from NAHO BAY on MATA NUI (2). MACKU thoroughly explored this waterway in the early years of her time on the island. She was almost killed here by a TAKEA shark that had wandered into the river and become lost.

HUNA

HUNA (HOO-nah):
KANOHI Mask of Concealment. TOA VAKAMA wore the Great Mask of Concealment, which could make him invisible, although he would still cast a shadow. As a TURAGA, Vakama wore the Noble version of this mask, which had the same effects but a shorter duration.

HUSI (HOO-see):
Ostrichlike birds that once roamed free on the rocky crags of PO-METRU before being hunted almost to extinction by MUAKA and other predators. They were later placed in the ARCHIVES for their own protection. Some Husi escaped after the quake shattered the facility and later made their way to MATA NUI (2).

HYDRAXON (high-DRACKS-on):
This name has been used by two identical but slightly different entities. The original Hydraxon was a member of the ORDER OF MATA NUI and the jailer of the PIT. He was a former member of the HAND OF ARTAKHA and was the one who later recruited AXONN into the Order. Badly wounded in the GREAT CATACLYSM that shattered the walls of that prison, Hydraxon was killed by the BARRAKI named TAKADOX.
Later, the KANOHI IGNIKA used its power to transform a PO-MATORAN named DEKAR into a new version of Hydraxon. Stripped of his memories, this new Hydraxon believed he was the original and set out to recapture all the escapees of the Pit. Using a variety of weapons, including razor-edged and explosive boomerangs, wrist knives, and a Cordak blaster, he proved a formidable opponent for beings such as TOA MAHRI MATORO and NOCTURN. When last seen, Hydraxon had defeated Nocturn and taken the Ignika with the intention of destroying it.

HYDRUKA (high-DROO-kah):
Sea creatures used by the MATORAN of MAHRI NUI to harvest air bubbles from the FIELDS OF AIR. The hydruka are able to sense which stalks of AIRWEED contain the most air. The creatures are notoriously stubborn and ill-tempered, and defend themselves by launching solid air spheres at enemies.

ICE BAT:
Winged creatures of KO-METRU, known for their destructive flights through KNOWLEDGE TOWERS. Their presence accounted for the reluctance of AIRSHIP pilots to fly over Ko-Metru.

ICE BLADE:

KOPAKA NUVA's twin Toa tools, through which he focused his ice power. The ice blade could be split in two and be used as power ice skates for rapid travel.

ICE PICK OF NUJU (noo-joo):

TURAGA NUJU's tool and badge of office.

ICE SHIELD:

(1) Tool carried by the KOHRAK. These shields were capable of freezing anything, including molten rock or open flames. Kohrak used their ice shields in an early attack on TA-KORO.
(2) Defensive tool carried by KOPAKA.

ICE SWORD:

Toa tool carried by KOPAKA through which he channeled his elemental power.

ICE VERMIN:

Small RAHI who became serious threats to METRU NUI after the earthquake. In some strange way, their RHOTUKA SPINNERS absorbed the seismic energy of the quake. They were then able to use them to cause earth tremors or make enemies actually shake apart.

ICE VERMIN

IDEN (EYE-den):

KANOHI Mask of Spirit worn by TOA INIKA MATORO. He was given the MATORAN version of the mask while in the realm of KARZAHNI (1). The Iden allows its users to unleash his spirit from his physical body for a limited amount of time. While free, the spirit can move at high speed, pass through physical objects, and observe events in the physical world. The spirit is invisible to anyone not wearing a Kanohi ELDA or Kanohi RODE. In spirit form, the user can only communicate with those wearing one of those two masks, and cannot interact with any other physical object.

IGNALU (igg-NAH-loo):

Lava surfing competition popular in TA-KORO. Participants used LAVABOARDS to travel rapidly across the flows. Winners of this competition received a COPPER MASK OF VICTORY.

IGNIKA (ig-NEE-kah):

KANOHI Mask of Life.
The Ignika was created by the GREAT BEINGS over 100,000 years ago. Its purpose was to replenish the failing energies of MATA NUI (1) should that ever become necessary. From the beginning, it proved a dangerous artifact, cursing anyone who touched it if they were not destined to do so. After driving a Great Being mad by giving him the ability to bring life to everything around him, the mask was taken and placed in the heart of VOYA NUI on a large continent. It was guarded by UMBRA, AXONN, BRUTAKA, and other guardians it created for itself. The mask was removed only once from its resting place, 80,000 years ago, by TOA JOVAN and his team, and returned after its successful use resulted in the death of one of the Toa. Numerous attempts were made to steal the mask, all of them stopped by Axonn and Brutaka.
The GREAT CATACLYSM caused Voya Nui to split off from its continent, rocket up through its dome, and end up on the surface of a strange ocean. A little more than 1,000 years later, the

PIRAKA came to the island seeking to steal the Ignika. They were followed by the TOA NUVA, and later the TOA INIKA. The Inika succeeded in defeating Umbra, VEZON and FENRAKK, and the Piraka, and getting the mask in hopes of using it to save the life of Mata Nui (1). But the mask was blown from their hands by KARDAS and flew away, falling beneath the sea off the coast of the island.

The Ignika drifted down to the sunken city of MAHRI NUI, where it was found by MATORAN. It was later taken by the BARRAKI, who entrusted it to one of their lieutenants, NOCTURN. When he wandered off with it, the Barraki were tricked into thinking one of them had taken it. War broke out beneath the waves as the TOA MAHRI attempted to use the confusion to search for the mask. When last seen, the mask was in the possession of HYDRAXON.

The full extent of the Ignika's powers are unknown. It has been shown to bring inanimate objects to life; take on different shapes; evolve/enlarge living things (see VENOM EEL, FENRAKK, GADUNKA, PROTODAX); levy curses (see VEZON, KYREHX, DEKAR); and totally change a being's form (see HYDRAXON). The Barraki believe it capable of reversing the mutations done to them by the waters of the Pit. What is known for certain is that it is the only object capable of restoring full life to Mata Nui, and that using it in that way requires that the wearer die.

IHU (EEE-hoo):

KO-MATORAN who acted as mentor to NUJU at the start of his career in the KNOWLEDGE TOWERS. Ihu taught Nuju that the most important thing in life was what you learned while living and how you used that knowledge. Ihu was killed when NUI-RAMA attacked the CHUTE in which he was riding. Later, TOA Nuju would name a mountain on MATA NUI (2) in his honor (see MOUNT IHU).

INFECTED MASKS:

Term used for KANOHI masks which have been tainted by the darkness of MAKUTA. Infected masks are created when a KRAATA makes physical contact with a mask. They can also be infected at long range by a SHADOW KRAATA. An infected mask takes on a rusted, pitted appearance. Anyone wearing such a mask becomes subservient to the will of Makuta. TOA LEWA was once forced to wear an infected mask and temporarily served Makuta.

INFERNAVIKA (in-FURN-nah-VEE-kah):

A small bird that made its home near the molten PROTODERMIS waste pipes on the coast of TA-METRU. Its love of ultra-hot places kept it safe, as few other creatures ventured near. These creatures would later migrate to MATA NUI (2) and make a home amid the lava near TA-KORO.

IRNAKK (er-NACK):

Legendary monstrous creature in the folktales of the SKAKDI. Irnakk never existed in reality, but was brought to life to fight the PIRAKA in the NIGHTMARE ZONE on VOYA NUI. Irnakk had the power to convert an opponent into pure thought and then draw him into its twisted brain. Its ZAMOR SPHERE LAUNCHER could cause the greatest fears of its target to become reality. Irnakk was defeated by ZAKTAN after the Piraka threatened to slay his comrades and thus deprive Irnakk of the fear it needed to survive.

IRUINI (EYE-roo-NEE):

Former TOA HAGAH of Air, later mutated by ROODAKA into a RAHAGA. Iruini had been part of an elite TOA team charged with being MAKUTA's personal guard. When they discovered Makuta was oppressing and enslaving MATORAN, they turned on him and attacked a fortress of the BROTHERHOOD OF MAKUTA. Iruini and NORIK got separated from the other Toa but managed to defeat the EXO-TOA and the DARK HUNTERS and drive Makuta off. They then went to rescue their friends, only to discover they had been turned into shrunken, twisted creatures with the faces of RAHKSHI by Roodaka. Although they saved their fellow Toa, they too were turned into Rahaga.

As a Toa, Iruini carried a CYCLONE SPEAR and a RHOTUKA SPINNER with the ability to heal. He wore the KANOHI KUALSI, the Great Mask of Quick Travel.

As a Rahaga, Iruini specialized in capturing Rahi climbers, such as BRAKAS and CABLE CRAWLERS. He carried a Rhotuka spinner with the *snag* power, which attached to its target and tangled up limbs like a net. He also carried a staff, the movements of which could hypnotize RAHI.

JALLER [JAH-luh]:
Former TA-MATORAN captain of the TA-KORO GUARD, later TOA INIKA and TOA MAHRI.

HISTORY

Jaller was employed as a tool maker in METRU NUI and was close friends with TAKUA, another worker. He was often kept busy covering for Takua's wanderings with the VAHKI to keep his friend out of trouble. During transport to MATA NUI (2), Jaller's KANOHI mask was badly damaged. Turaga VAKAMA replaced the mask with the late Turaga LHIKAN's Noble HAU. (Being a Matoran, Jaller could not access the powers of the mask.) Jaller rapidly became an important figure during the construction of TA-KORO, helping to defend the site from RAHI attacks. Vakama appointed him captain of the Ta-Koro Guard, a position he held for over 1,000 years. He showed great heroism during the BOHROK invasion, aiding the village of GA-KORO against a PAHRAK attack. He was rewarded with a name change during NAMING DAY ceremonies.

JALLER

Prior to an important kolhii match, Jaller went in search of the missing Takua only to find him in a forbidden lava cavern. He was there when Takua stumbled upon the legendary Mask of Light. Unwilling to accept responsibility for being HERALD of the Toa of Light, Takua tricked the Turaga into believing it was Jaller's destiny to fulfill that role. Jaller got even by insisting Takua accompany him on his search for the Seventh Toa. The two braved many dangers on their quest, including encounters with an ASH BEAR, RAHKSHI, and MAKUTA himself.

During the final battle between the Toa Nuva and the Rahkshi, Jaller sacrificed his life to save Takua. Later, TAKUTANUVA, a merged entity made up of TAKANUVA and Makuta, gave up part of its life force to restore life to Jaller. Since that time, the valiant Ta-Matoran has helped to oversee the construction of transport craft for the return to Metru Nui.

After arriving there and the subsequent disappearance of the Toa Nuva, Jaller grew angry at what he saw as the Turaga's reluctance to share information. He called a citywide strike. Finally, Turaga NOKAMA told him that the Nuva had been sent to find the KANOHI IGNIKA in order to save the life of Mata Nui (1). He assembled a team of five other Matoran and left the

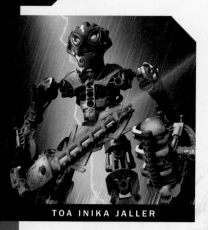

TOA INIKA JALLER

city in an attempt to find the missing heroes. During their adventures, they encountered KARZAHNI (1), who took their masks and replaced them with new ones. Jaller's original Hau has since been recovered by the Toa Nuva. The six Matoran eventually made it to the shores of VOYA NUI. Their transport canisters were struck by lightning from the RED STAR, which transformed all six into the Toa Inika. As Toa, they battled the PIRAKA, BRUTAKA, and others in an effort to claim the KANOHI IGNIKA.

Jaller led the team through the CORD, battling the ZYGLAK and Makuta, before arriving at Mahri Nui. A burst of energy from the Ignika transformed them into the aquatic Toa Mahri. They went on to battle the BARRAKI for possession of the Mask of Life. Jaller continued to function as nominal team leader, but was unable to keep Matoro from striking out on his own. He also felt hampered by being in an element so hostile to fire.

POWERS

Like TAHU NUVA, Jaller controls the power of fire.

PERSONALITY

Jaller wants to break the Tahu-Vakama mold and be a Toa of Fire who respects and listens to the opinions of his teammates. Although he has done a good job of this, he does have some resentment toward the more prominent role MATORO has taken on the team. He is also still haunted by the memory of dying as a Matoran.

EQUIPMENT

As a Toa Inika, Jaller wore the Kanohi CALIX, the Mask of Fate, and carried an ENERGIZED FLAME SWORD. As a Toa Mahri, he wears the Kanohi ARTHRON, the Mask of Sonar, and carries a CORDAK BLASTER and AQUATIC POWER BLADE.

JOVAN (JOE-vann):

Deceased former TOA of Magnetism and TURAGA of VOYA NUI. Jovan led the Toa team that recovered and used the KANOHI IGNIKA some 80,000 years ago. After returning the mask to its resting place on Voya Nui, Jovan transformed into a Turaga and became the leader of that region. When Voya Nui split off from its continent during the GREAT CATACLYSM and rose to the surface, Jovan was lost in the disaster. As a Toa, Jovan wore the Kanohi KADIN, and carried a ZAMOR SPHERE LAUNCHER and a magnetic bolt launcher.

KADIN (KAY-din):

KANOHI Mask of Flight worn by TOA INIKA NUPARU. He was given the MATORAN version of the mask during his time in the realm of KARZAHNI (1). The mask allows its user to fly under his own power, rather than relying on wind currents.

KAHGARAK [KAH-gah-rack]:

A powerful species related to the VISORAK used as guards by the hordes. Kahgarak ranged in height from 6 feet to 12 feet, and in width from 9 feet to 18 feet. Their coloring also varied. The Kahgarak's RHOTUKA SPINNERS had the power to envelop a foe in a zone of shadow. Their target would be unable to see or communicate with the world outside and would remain trapped unless another Kahgarak opened a gap in the zone. This power also meant that Kahgarak were the only creatures who could release the dreaded ZIVON from its domain of darkness, not to mention send it back there. A Kahgarak was responsible for the Zivon, TAHTORAK, and the KRAHKA all being transported to the realm of shadow. Kahgarak have, in the past, also been fitted with projectile launchers for use in sieges.

KAHGARAK

KAKAMA [kah-KAHM-mah]:

The Mask of Speed. This mask allowed the user to run great distances in an instant. POHATU wore the KANOHI Kakama when he first appeared on MATA NUI (2), and often put its power to good use. In one of his earliest adventures, he ran around the base of an erupting volcano at super speed, creating a trench into which molten lava could safely flow.

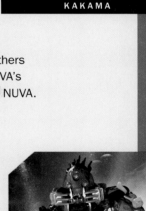

KAKAMA

KAKAMA NUVA [kah-KAHM-mah NOO-vah]:

The more powerful version of the KAKAMA worn by POHATU NUVA. This mask not only allowed super speed travel, but also gave the user complete control of the molecules of his body. This allowed someone wearing the Kakama to pass through solid objects without harm by simply vibrating at a different speed than the object. Like all Nuva masks, its power could be shared by the user with others in close proximity. The TOA used a combination of the Kakama Nuva and MIRU NUVA's powers to "fly" out of the BAHRAG chamber following their transformation into TOA NUVA.

KAKAMA NUVA

KALMAH [CAL-mahh]:

One of the six BARRAKI who menace MAHRI NUI.

As a member of the LEAGUE OF SIX KINGDOMS, Kalmah had a reputation as an ice-cold calculator without any feelings or emotions. When he had a goal, he would achieve it regardless of how many of his subjects got hurt or killed in the process. Originally, he had not wanted to join the League, unwilling to have others dictating any part of his actions. But when TAKADOX allied with PRIDAK, he was forced to join or risk having his empire cut off from the rest of the world.

Kalmah joined in the rebellion against MATA NUI (1) and was banished to the PIT with the other Barraki upon its failure. After their subsequent escape (and his mutation by seawater into his current squidlike appearance), Kalmah discovered a cavern filled with small, organic squid and an assortment of eggs. He rapidly learned that the squid were born hungry and were vampiric in nature, draining the life force from anything they attached themselves to. Seeing their possible use as a weapon, he prevented his allies from devouring them and began overseeing their breeding. By abusing and starving the creatures, he insured they would always be vicious and ready to attack. He designed launchers for use with the creatures and provided them to the other Barraki, in return for a larger realm undersea. (A clash over just how much bigger Kalmah's territory should be resulted in a battle between him and PRIDAK and the loss of sight in one of Kalmah's three eyes.)

KALMAH

After the KANOHI IGNIKA appeared in the region, Kalmah joined in the hunt for that artifact. When the TOA MAHRI arrived seeking it as well, Kalmah struck a deal with Jaller to let the Toa have the mask in return for using it to restore the Barraki to what they once were and for the death of Pridak. It is not yet known whether Jaller will hold up his end of this deal.

Kalmah possesses one powerful tentacle and carries a SQUID LAUNCHER. Tentacles on the back of his head allow him to sense movement behind him. He leads an army of giant squid, one of which was responsible for the disappearance of BRUTAKA.

KANAE BAY [kah-NIGH]:

A body of water on the southern shore of LE-WAHI. For a number of years, LE-MATORAN came here to attempt to overcome their dislike of water by swimming in the clear waters. The efforts proved to be a dismal failure and MATAU finally persuaded them that trees were far better than water, anyway.

KANE-RA [kah-NAY-rah]:

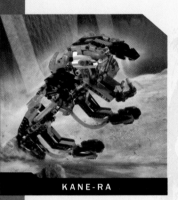

KANE-RA

One of the largest plant-eating land RAHI, the Kane-Ra bull would prove to be a menace on MATA NUI (2). Several specimens made it from METRU NUI to the island, only to be fitted with INFECTED MASKS and put under the influence of MAKUTA. Later, the TOA removed these masks and the Kane-Ra retreated to the valleys, no longer a threat.

KANOHI [kah-NO-hee]:

Matoran word meaning "mask." The Kanohi Masks of Power were vital to the survival of the MATORAN and the power of the TURAGA and TOA. Kanohi masks were created using KANOKA DISKS and were made in TA-METRU in METRU NUI.

There are three known types of Kanohi mask:

Matoran Masks: Worn by Matoran villagers, these masks do not have any extra powers. Wearing them is essential for Matoran, however, as having a mask off for too long can lead to a condition resembling a coma. Matoran masks are fashioned to look like Great Masks and Noble Masks. They are made from Kanoka disks with a power level of 6 and under.

Noble Masks: Less powerful than Great Masks, these are commonly worn by Turaga, but also used by Toa. Noble Masks are made from Kanoka disks with a power level of 7. Noble Masks were stored in the GREAT TEMPLE of Metru Nui. Noble Masks were brought from Metru Nui to MATA NUI (2) by the TOA METRU. They were later stolen from the Matoran villages by RAHI under MAKUTA's command, and remained missing until found by TAHU and the other Toa a thousand years later.

Great Masks: These masks can be used effectively only by Toa, and are made from Kanoka disks with a power level of 8. Great Masks were stored in the Great Temple in Metru Nui. An assortment of these masks was brought to Mata Nui by the TOA METRU and hidden in various spots on the island. They were later found by Tahu and his team of Toa.

Use of a mask power requires a high level of mental discipline and willpower. For this reason, Turaga are no longer able to use Great Masks despite having once been Toa, and Matoran cannot use mask powers at all.

Extremely powerful masks like the VAHI and IGNIKA are considered Legendary Masks.

Known Kanohi include the PEHKUI, KUALSI, HAU, HAU NUVA, KAKAMA, KAKAMA NUVA, AKAKU, AKAKU NUVA, HUNA, KOMAU, MAHIKI, MATATU, RAU, RURU, KAUKAU, KAUKAU NUVA, MIRU,

MIRU NUVA, PAKARI, PAKARI NUVA, OLMAK, RODE, CALIX, ELDA, SULETU, SANOK, KADIN, IDEN, GARAI, FAXON, ARTHRON, ZATTH, TRYNA, VOLITAK, AKAMAI, and RUA. See also KANOHI NUVA and INFECTED MASKS.

KANOHI DRAGON

KANOHI DRAGON [kah-no-hee]:

A mysterious beast said to have vanished from METRU NUI 3,000 years before the coming of the TOA METRU. The dragon was unleashed on the city at one point on the orders of the SHADOWED ONE, and defeated by Toa LHIKAN and ten of his comrades. The beast was then brought to the island of XIA, where it remains to this day. A creature of fire, the Kanohi dragon could fly and relied on its flame breath, smoldering tail blades, and claws in combat. Its name came from the Kanohi masks that seemed to line its body. Some MATORAN claimed they were real masks, while others said they were decoys designed to lure Toa in close.

KANOHI NUVA [kah-no-hee noo-vah]:

Masks exposed to ENERGIZED PROTODERMIS and transformed. Kanohi Nuva were more powerful than standard masks, and granted the user the ability to share the mask's power with anyone in close proximity. Kanohi Nuva included the AKAKU NUVA, HAU NUVA, KAKAMA NUVA, KAUKAU NUVA, MIRU NUVA, and PAKARI NUVA. They were worn by the TOA NUVA.

KANOKA DISK [kah-no-kah]:

Round disks of PROTODERMIS used for both sport and defense in the city of METRU NUI. Kanoka disks were made using liquid protodermis that had been purified in GA-METRU. Disks were made in every metru in the city and each had a special power. Each disk was stamped with a three-digit code, with the first digit representing the metru in which the disk was made, the second its power, and the third its level of power.

KANOKA DISK—MASK OF POWER CHART

Listed below are the various Masks of Power that have appeared in BIONICLE and, where known, the Kanoka disks used to create them.

Kanohi Hau, Mask of Shielding — Growth + Regeneration disks

Kanohi Miru, Mask of Levitation — Teleport + Weaken disks

Kanohi Kakama, Mask of Speed — Teleport + Reconstitutes at Random disks

Kanohi Pakari, Mask of Strength — Regeneration + Enlarge + Removes Poison disks

Kanohi Kaukau, Mask of Water Breathing — Regeneration + Shrink + Removes Poison disks

Kanohi Akaku, Mask of X-Ray Vision — Regeneration + Teleport disks

Kanohi Mahiki, Mask of Illusion — Reconstitutes at Random + Weaken disks

Kanohi Huna, Mask of Concealment — Enlarge + Shrink + Freeze disks

Kanohi Komau, Mask of Mind Control — Freeze + Weaken + Removes Poison disks

Kanohi Rau, Mask of Translation — Removes Poison + Enlarge disks

Kanohi Ruru, Mask of Night Vision — Enlarge + Teleport disks

Kanohi Matatu, Mask of Telekinesis — Teleport + Shrink disks

Kanohi Kiril, Mask of Regeneration — Regeneration disk

Kanohi Kualsi, Mask of Quick Travel — Teleport disk

Kanohi Pehkui, Mask of Diminishment — Shrink disk

Kanohi Kraahkan, Mask of Shadows — Unknown

Kanohi Avohkii, Mask of Light — Unknown

Kanohi Vahi, Mask of Time — Disk of Time, made by combining all six Great Disks

There were eight basic Kanoka powers: *enlarge, freeze, reconstitutes at random, regenerate, remove poison, shrink, teleport,* and *weaken.* These eight powers could also be combined in various ways to create new powers. A Kanoka's power and level of power were determined by the properties and purity of the protodermis used and the skill of the MATORAN making the disk. The metru in which it was made also determined the special flight properties of the disk.

Kanoka disks were used in various Matoran sports, including AKILINI, and for defense against RAHI. Disks were also made into KANOHI masks. Those disks with a power level of 6 or less became Matoran masks and had no power. Disks with a power level of 7 became Noble Masks, with a significant amount of power. Disks with a power level of 8 became Great Masks, with an enormous amount of power. Only six disks were ever known to have a power level of 9, the GREAT DISKS, which were used by VAKAMA to create the Kanohi VAHI. In addition to being launched and thrown, Kanoka disks were also used in other ways in Metru Nui. *Levitation* and *increase weight* disks were incorporated into the design of airships, and *regeneration* disks built into buildings.

KANOKA LAUNCHER
(kah-ПО-kah):
A tool carried by MATORAN and used for hurling KANOKA DISKS. Launchers had to be manually loaded and activated. These were used both for defense and in the sport of AKILINI.

KAPURA (KUH-purr-UH):
A TA-MATORAN. On METRU NUI, Kapura worked as a vat controller. During the time when the MORBUZAKH threatened the city, Kapura was dispatched to scout abandoned areas of the metru and retrieve any valuable items he might find.

On MATA NUI (2), Turaga VAKAMA worked with Kapura to teach him the secret art of traveling long distances very quickly by moving very slowly.

Although some considered Kapura to be not very bright, Vakama saw great potential in him and made him a trusted aide. Kapura served as part of the CHRONICLER's Company, a small group assembled by TAKUA to defend KINI-NUI against RAHI attack.

KANOKA RESEARCH AND INFORMATION

Keep track of your KANOKA disk collection! Each time you get a KANOKA disk, check out the first two digits of its code – the METRU of origin and the power. Then write the code in the appropriate box below. And don't forget to enter the codes on BIONICLE.com to earn valuable KANOKA points!

Disc Effects on Targets	TA-METRU Stronger, can knock obstacles out of the way.*	GA-METRU Can change direction in mid-air, guided by the thrower's thoughts.*	PO-METRU Deflects other discs from their course.*
	143	225	337

CODES • CODES • CODES • CODES • CODES • CODES • CODES • CODES

(1) reconstitutes at random			
(2) freezes			
(3) weakens			
(4) removes poison			
(5) enlarges			
(6) shrinks			
(7) regenerates			
(8) teleports			

Disc Effects on Targets	KO-METRU Dodges obstacles to get to target.*	LE-METRU Flies further.*	ONU-METRU Always returns to thrower if diverted from course.*
	473	574	685

CODES • CODES • CODES • CODES • CODES • CODES • CODES

(1) reconstitutes at random			
(2) freezes			
(3) weakens			
(4) removes poison			
(5) enlarges			
(6) shrinks			
(7) regenerates			
(8) teleports			

*Flight characteristics refer to story only, and do not reflect actual product performance.

KARDAS (CAR-dass):

Dragon who battled the TOA INIKA in the CHAMBER OF LIFE. Kardas was created when VEZON and FENRAKK were defeated by the Toa — under the terms of the curse upon the two of them, any defeat would result in Fenrakk mutating into a fiercer shape. The spider emerged from the lava as Kardas, a massive winged beast capable of discharging blasts of raw energy from its mouth. Temporarily defeated through the use of a ZAMOR SPHERE that created a stasis field, Kardas was abandoned by Vezon and surfaced on VOYA NUI, where it clashed with the TAHTORAK.

KARZAHNI (KARR-zah-NEE):

[1] Legendary ruler of a domain much feared by MATORAN in the dim past. According to ancient tales, in the time before the GREAT SPIRIT, Matoran labored in darkness. Those Matoran who excelled at their work were sent to ARTAKHA and allowed to work in the light. Those who worked poorly were sent to another place, one ruled by Karzahni, from which they never returned. The name "Karzahni" eventually became a term Matoran used to scare each other, with each new tale about him becoming more and more exaggerated and frightening. JALLER and his team of Matoran found themselves in the realm of Karzahni while journeying to VOYA NUI and clashed with the ruler. Karzahni carried a flaming chain and wore a mask that looked like four masks melded together. He had the power to make an enemy see a vision of an alternate future, normally a nightmarish one. The six Matoran escaped, but not before Karzahni stole their masks from them (these were later recovered by the TOA NUVA).
During this encounter, Karzahni learned of the existence of MATA NUI (1) and MAKUTA and decided to try to seize power for himself. He journeyed to MAHRI NUI, where he clashed with Makuta and Toa LESOVIKK and was defeated. His realm has since been destroyed and his Matoran prisoners freed.

[2] An intelligent plant creature created by MAKUTA with the help of the ENERGIZED PROTODERMIS ENTITY. Makuta named his creation Karzahni after the legendary ruler of a dread domain in ancient Matoran history. From the first, Karzahni proved to be too willful and ambitious to suit Makuta's needs, so eventually the master of shadows exiled his creation into the tunnels that linked METRU NUI to MATA NUI (2).
There Karzahni brooded and planned its revenge on its creator. When the TOA METRU defeated Makuta, Karzahni shifted its hatred to them. After NOKAMA was mortally wounded by the RAHI NUI, Karzahni struck a bargain with the Toa Metru: if they would retrieve for it a sample of energized protodermis from Makuta's lair, it would cure Nokama. Karzahni wanted the energized protodermis because it believed that the liquid would transform it into a far more powerful being.
The Toa Metru completed the quest and returned to Karzahni. Once there, NUJU revealed that he had deduced the plant creature was dying, the result of a fatal flaw Makuta bred into all of his creations. Forced to keep his bargain by Vakama, Karzahni cured Nokama and took the vial of energized protodermis from the Toa. But when it poured the contents onto itself, the liquid burned the plant from within. In a matter of moments, the Karzahni was dead.
When the Toa reached the shore of the silver sea around Metru Nui, they realized that they needed a ship to cross it. A Vahki transport was found, but there was nothing to keep it afloat. Toa ONEWA and Toa MATAU chopped up the dead plant's trunk and strapped the wood onto the bottom of the craft, making it seaworthy.
But Karzahni was not dead. It grew again and allied itself with Makuta as part of a plot to trick VAKAMA into giving up the VAHI. Karzahni betrayed Makuta and was killed by him as punishment. Karzahni also claimed to have slain a member of the ORDER OF MATA NUI.

[3] The realm ruled by Karzahni (1). Located in a canyon, it is a strange, frightening place filled with ice that burns, fire that freezes, dust that falls, and other bizarre features. It is inhabited by Matoran who were sent here for repairs and then kept as prisoners by the mad ruler. MANAS and DUST DARTERS can also be found here. Karzahni was the second location created by the GREAT BEINGS.

KAU KAU STAFF (KOW KOW):

TURAGA MATAU's tool and badge of office. Interestingly, its name is not related to the KANOHI KAUKAU mask. The name was a joke suggested by ONEWA based upon the noise made by BRAKAS in the trees. The nickname stuck and it has been called a kau kau staff ever since.

KAUKAU

KAUKAU (KOW-KOW):

The Mask of Water Breathing. Wearing this mask enabled the user to breathe underwater for an extended period of time. TOA GALI wore this mask when she first appeared on MATA NUI (2).

KAUKAU NUVA (KOW-KOW NOO-vah):

The more powerful version of the KAUKAU worn by GALI NUVA. In addition to allowing underwater respiration, this mask made it possible for the wearer to stay under longer and to breathe at greater depths. Like all Nuva masks, its power could be shared by the user with those in close proximity.

KAUKAU NUVA

KAVINIKA (KAH-vih-NEE-kah):

KAVINIKA

Wolflike creatures originally used as guards at some MATORAN facilities in METRU NUI. Their violent natures made them too dangerous and they were banned by TURAGA DUME, but efforts to drive them out of the city met with failure. Strangely, their population actually seemed to increase after the earthquake in Metru Nui. The RAHAGA believed that something in one of the GA-METRU labs caused the RAHI to duplicate. Kavinika did make their way to MATA NUI (2), surviving in the depths of the LE-WAHI jungle.

KAZI (kah-ZEE):

KO-MATORAN member of the RESISTANCE on VOYA NUI. He carries twin echo forks that, when slammed together, produce a devastating sound wave. Kazi was the first resident of Voya Nui to meet AXONN.

KEELERAK (KEY-le-rack):

One of the six breeds of VISORAK that invaded METRU NUI. The ends of a Keelerak's legs are razor sharp, and they have been known to leap high in the air and whirl at high speed, becoming Visorak "buzzsaws." Keelerak RHOTUKA SPINNERS have an acid venom that can melt any substance.

KEERAKH (key-RAHK):

The VAHKI model assigned to KO-METRU in METRU NUI. These mechanoids were known for their uncanny ability to predict where a target would run, allowing them to get there first. They were rarely seen by KO-MATORAN except for those who had broken the law and been apprehended. Keerakh carried STAFFS OF CONFUSION, which could scramble a target's sense of time and place and leave

KEERAKH

him disoriented. NUJU and WHENUA battled KEERAKH on top of a KNOWLEDGE TOWER during their search for the GREAT DISKS.

KEETONGU [KEE-tahn-GOO]:

A powerful RAHI previously unknown on METRU NUI and believed to be a myth by the populations of other lands. After the TOA METRU were mutated into HORDIKA, RAHAGA NORIK told them Keetongu was their only hope for a cure. Legend states that Keetongu's single "eye" can see the good or evil in any being, and that he will grant his cure only to those who are noble of spirit. His rotating shield array can absorb any power used against him and his blade claw can cleanse a being of VISORAK venom. Keetongu's true power is said to come from his armor and his spinners. The armor channels the power absorbed by the shield array, and the spinner can then send that energy back at his attacker. In this way, Keetongu can counteract any attack made upon him. The Toa Hordika and Rahaga launched a search for him in Metru Nui, in hopes that he would cure the Toa of their affliction. Keetongu was eventually discovered and he joined the Hordika in an attack on the COLISEUM. During that battle, Keetongu killed SIDORAK. He later used his powers to cure the Toa Hordika. Keetongu was badly wounded in a later clash with MAKUTA, but recovered. He now travels the universe, seeking to help other victims of the Visorak.

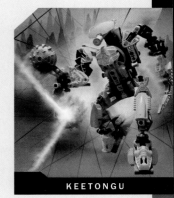
KEETONGU

KERAS [KEE-rahs]:

Large coral crabs found in the ocean off GA-METRU. At one time, MATORAN hoped that keras could be as useful to them as USSAL crabs were, but the hostile nature of the keras made that impossible.

KIKANALO [KEE-kah-nah-LOW]:

Herd beasts that roamed the canyons of PO-METRU before coming to MATA NUI (2). These creatures used their horns to dig up little bits of PROTODERMIS left behind by PO-MATORAN carvers. In addition to their great strength, Kikanalo are capable of letting loose a roar that can blow away enemies like dust in a windstorm. A Kikanalo herd aided the TOA METRU against the VAHKI in Po-Metru. During that adventure, Toa NOKAMA was able to use her Mask of Translation to communicate with the beasts, discovering that they were in fact quite intelligent.

KIKANALO

KINI-NUI [kih-NEE NOO-ee]:

The GREAT TEMPLE on the island of MATA NUI (2), constructed in part by the TURAGA and MATORAN shortly after their arrival on the island. TAKUA and the CHRONICLER's Company fought to defend this site from RAHI attack. Later, the Toa brought their KANOHI masks here and received GOLDEN MASKS that contained a full range of six powers. They entered Kini-Nui using the MAKOKI STONES and fought the MANAS, the SHADOW TOA, and MAKUTA. Later, Kini-Nui would be the site of the first appearance of the RAHKSHI on Mata Nui.

KINLOKA [kin-LOW-kah]:

A large, nasty species of rodent, Kinloka were the result of an experiment by the BROTHERHOOD OF MAKUTA to produce a RAHI with a more efficient digestive system. The result was a creature that was constantly hungry and

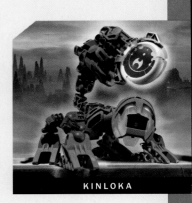
KINLOKA

ate anything. Although native to LE-METRU, they were seen all over METRU NUI. No reports of sightings were ever made on MATA NUI (2).

KIO [KY-oh]:
A unit of MATORAN measurement equal to 1,000 BIO. A kio measures 4,500 feet or 1,371 meters in Earth measurement. A kio is also equal to .85 miles or 1.37 kilometers. METRU NUI is 47.6 kio long and 24 kio wide. By contrast, MATA NUI (2) is 357 kio in length and 178 kio in width. There are 1,000 kio in a MIO.

KIRIKORI NUI [kih-rih-KOAR-EE NOO-ee]:
Locustlike insects known for their appearance in the skies over METRU NUI every ten years or so. They would alight in PO-METRU and GA-METRU, consume all the vegetation in sight, and then disappear. Their point of origin was unknown. Much to the dismay of the TURAGA, they later appeared on MATA NUI (2). MATORO was credited with discovering that they were afraid of NUI-KOPEN. Fake RAHI wasps were later constructed to try to scare the Kirikori Nui away.

KIRIL [kih-RILL]:
KANOHI Mask of Regeneration, worn by Turaga DUME. This mask allowed the wearer to restore inanimate objects or buildings to their previous, undamaged conditions. It could not be used to heal living things. Dume used a Kiril NOBLE MASK to begin repairs on the city of METRU NUI during the thousand years it was abandoned by the MATORAN.

KNOWLEDGE TOWERS:
Large crystalline structures in KO-METRU which were the workplaces of KO-MATORAN scholars. Knowledge Towers were not built but grown. Special knowledge crystals were thrown into cradles throughout the district, from which the towers grew at a rapid pace. Each Knowledge Tower boasted extensive library space, living quarters for scholars, observatories to monitor the stars, and special areas designed to hold ancient tablets and other valuable items. Many Ko-Matoran both lived and worked in the towers, never venturing out of doors. Before becoming a Toa, NUJU was employed in a Knowledge Tower. The Knowledge Towers were badly damaged in the earthquake that rocked METRU NUI.

KNOWLEDGE TOWERS

KO [KOE]:
A Matoran prefix meaning "ice."

KO-KINI [KOE-kih-NEE]:
A temple dedicated to KOPAKA located in KO-WAHI on MATA NUI (2).

KO-KORO [KOE-koar-OH]:
Village on MATA NUI (2) and home to the KO-MATORAN. Ko-Koro was hidden beneath a massive ice block that separates two glaciers, and surrounded by huge crevasses that could swallow the unwary. KO-KORO was led by TURAGA NUJU and protected by TOA KOPAKA. The village was severely damaged by the RAHKSHI.

KO-MATORAN [KOE-mat-OR-an]:
A resident of KO-KORO or KO-METRU. Ko-Matoran had white armor and commonly wore white or light-blue masks. Ko-Matoran in METRU NUI were primarily scholars. On the island of MATA

NUI (2), they were master trackers and trap builders. They tended to be quiet and not very social in both locations.

KO-METRU [KOH-MET-troo]:

Home of the thinkers in METRU NUI. Dubbed the "quiet metru" by MATORAN from other districts, Ko-Metru was the site of the KNOWLEDGE TOWERS and TOWERS OF THOUGHT. The entire area was dedicated to learning and the interpretation of prophecies. Just as living creatures and artifacts were stored in the ARCHIVES, so were all written records of Matoran past, present, and future stored here.
Ko-Metru was protected by TOA NUJU. One of the six GREAT DISKS was found here, hidden in ice at the top of a Knowledge Tower.

KO-METRU

KO-SUVA [KOH-soo-VAH]:

A shrine in the village of KO-KORO to honor KOPAKA NUVA. The NUVA SYMBOL was originally stolen from here by the BOHROK-KAL. Kopaka's Masks of Power were also kept on the suva.

KO-WAHI [KOH-wah-HEE]:

Icy region on MATA NUI (2) that encompassed MOUNT IHU and the DRIFTS. The village of KO-KORO was located here. Snowfall and avalanches are common here. TAKUA and JALLER traveled through Ko-Wahi on their quest to find TAKANUVA. A temporarily powerless KOPAKA NUVA and POHATU NUVA were menaced by a MUAKA in Ko-Wahi.

KODAN [KOH-dann]:

A PO-MATORAN in METRU NUI and the CHRONICLER for TOA LHIKAN's team. Kodan began his career as Chronicler when Lhikan arrived in the city with ten other Toa to fight the KANOHI DRAGON. Kodan continued to fill this role for centuries. He vanished along with two Toa on a mission for TURAGA DUME (actually MAKUTA in disguise).
Kodan was also credited with the invention of the sport of AKILINI. Numerous legends have arisen about how he first came up with the idea or how he first set up a crude akilini field in a PO-METRU canyon. However, over the years other metru have insisted that the idea for the sport actually came from one of their MATORAN. In the resulting confusion, no one is really certain anymore who deserves the honor. After Kodan disappeared and was presumed dead, a monument was erected to him in Po-Metru giving him credit for the discovery.

KODAN BALL [KOH-dann]:

A sphere formed by POHATU NUVA's CLIMBING CLAWS. In shape and size, it resembles the sphere used in METRU NUI for the very earliest versions of the sport of AKILINI. It was that resemblance which led TURAGA ONEWA to suggest the name "Kodan ball" to Pohatu Nuva. KODAN was the PO-MATORAN said to have invented the sport of Akilini. (See KODAN.)

KOFO-JAGA [KOH-foh JAH-gah]:

Small, fiery scorpions known for attacking in swarms, these were most often found near abandoned forges in TA-METRU and near the MANGAI volcano in TA-WAHI. They were attracted to the smell of molten PROTODERMIS and preferred dark places.
TA-METRU MATORAN investigating empty factories knew to carry bright LIGHTSTONES to protect themselves (temporarily) from these creatures. A swarm of Kofo-Jaga once drove off much larger and more powerful MANAS crabs.

KOHRAK [KOH-rahk]:

KOHRAK

One of the six breeds of BOHROK, insectlike mechanoids controlled by KRANA who menaced the island of MATA NUI (2). The Kohrak were tied to the element of ice, and their ICE SHIELDS could freeze anything, even open flames. The Kohrak's bodies gave off such intense cold that other Bohrok avoided their company. The Kohrak were part of the initial attack on TA-KORO which was repulsed by TAHU and his team of TOA. They spent much of their time on the lava plains and in the valleys of TA-WAHI. The Kohrak returned to their nests after the coming of the BOHROK-KAL.

KOHRAK-KAL [KOH-rahk KAHL]:

One of the six mutant BOHROK who made up the BOHROK-KAL. Kohrak-Kal's tool was a SONIC SHIELD capable of creating a sound barrier that could repel most forms of attack. It could also cause objects to vibrate until they shattered. After being fed TOA power via the TOA NUVA's symbols (see BOHROK-KAL), Kohrak-Kal was shaken apart by its own energies.

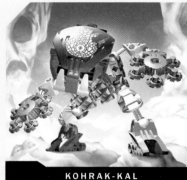

KOHRAK-KAL

KOHRAK VA [KOH-rahk VAH]:

One of the six BOHROK VA, Kohrak Va were connected to the element of ice. They relied on stealth and camouflage, hiding in snowdrifts to keep an eye on the movements of the TOA and MATORAN. When cornered, they used their claws to defend themselves.

KOHRAK VA

KOLHII [KOAL-lee]:

The most popular sport on MATA NUI (2). Kolhii was created by TURAGA ONEWA during a dispute between the carvers of PO-KORO and the miners of ONU-KORO. Seeking a way to settle the matter without violence, Onewa conceived of a competition between the two koro, and Turaga WHENUA readily agreed.

RULES OF KOLHII

1. Teams must number more than one but no more than six.
2. Teams may include any number of players greater than one, but no team may have more players than any other.
3. Prior to the game, all teams must agree to the number of goals required for victory.
4. The first team to reach the number of goals agreed to is the winner.
5. All goals are good goals (counting for a score) as long as they are not own goals (goals scored by a player in his own net). Own goals are not goals.
6. Each player is allowed one defender who carries a kolhii shield. No other player may use that shield, except when rule #11 is invoked.
7. All players may carry one kolhii staff, and one only.
8. Any number of kolhii balls may be played, but balls in play must number less than either the number of teams or the number of players per team, whichever number is the smallest.
9. Any player who strikes another player did not play well. Shield and staff strikes occurring during play and deemed innocent in intent are not considered a violation of this rule.
10. Any player who does not play well brings dishonor to his or her koro.
11. In the event of an invasion of the playing field by RAHI or other forces, play is postponed until the problem is dealt with.

In kolhii, two or more teams compete to get a KOLHII BALL into an opponent's goal. Variants of kolhii include a match where the ball can only be kicked, to the most popular version, in which KOLHII STAFFS are used to hurl the ball. Defending players carry KOLHII SHIELDS to deflect shots away from their goals.

PO-MATORAN have traditionally been the champions of the sport, to the point that POHATU is considered to be the patron TOA of kolhii. Prior to the coming of the Toa to Mata Nui, most matches were intramural within koro, due to the dangers of traveling to other villages. With the defeat of MAKUTA's RAHI, travel become much easier and inter-koro games were played once again. Kolhii became a centerpiece of Matoran life and matches an occasion of great celebration. Variants of the sport include an Onu-Koro version played on USSAL crabs and an aerial version played by LE-MATORAN flying on GUKKO birds.

Following the defeat of the BOHROK-KAL, the Toa and Matoran worked together to erect a great kolhii stadium. It was in the immediate aftermath of a match between TA-KORO, GA-KORO, and Po-Koro that it was discovered that TAKUA carried the Mask of Light.

KOLHII BALL [KOAL-lee]:

A sphere made of lightweight airstone bound in steel used in the sport of KOLHII. The most popular type of kolhii ball was the COMET, although it fell out of favor after AHKMOU sold several infected samples to MATORAN. These infected spheres brought the Matoran owners under the sway of MAKUTA.

KOLHII SHIELD [KOAL-lee]:

Tool carried by defenders in the sport of KOLHII, used to deflect shots.

KOLHII STAFF [KOAL-lee]:

A long staff with a macelike hammer on one end and a scooped hurler on the other, used in the sport of KOLHII. The hammer is used to deflect opponent's shots, while the hurler is used to toss the KOLHII BALL to a teammate or toward an opponent's goal.

KOMAU [koh-mow]:

KANOHI Mask of Mind Control. This mask allowed the wearer to make others do his bidding, although it could work only on targets that had a mind (and thus was ineffective against VAHKI and some forms of RAHI). ONEWA wore the Great Mask version of this as a TOA, and the Noble Mask version as a TURAGA.

KONGU [KAHN-goo]:

Former LE-MATORAN hero, later TOA INIKA and TOA MAHRI.

KONGU

HISTORY

On METRU NUI, Kongu was simply another worker, assigned to oversee the chute controls in the MOTO-HUB. The only excitement in his life came when he was captured by the DARK HUNTERS NIDHIKI and KREKKA and forced to reverse the flow in the chutes in an effort to trap the TOA METRU.

On MATA NUI (2), Kongu developed an incredible skill at dealing with RAHI. He became the best bird wrangler in all of LE-KORO and captain of the GUKKO BIRD FORCE. Kongu aided TAKUA on a rescue mission to save other Matoran from a NUI-RAMA nest. Later, he was part of a successful mission to save Toa LEWA, Turaga MATAU, and the other Le-Matoran from being controlled by the BOHROK swarm through the KRANA they had been forced to wear. Kongu worked with TAMARU, Takua, and NUPARU on this dangerous task, which was credited with saving the entire KORO. Following the return to Metru Nui, Kongu was one of five Matoran who accompanied JALLER

TOA INIKA KONGU

in search of the missing Toa Nuva. After a number of harrowing adventures, the canisters in which they traveled landed on the shores of VOYA NUI. The canisters were struck by lightning from the RED STAR, which transformed all six into the Toa Inika. As Toa, they battled the PIRAKA, BRUTAKA, and others in an effort to claim the KANOHI IGNIKA. Kongu was somewhat dismayed by the fact that NUPARU got to wear the Kanohi KADIN, the Mask of Flight, rather than himself, when he had so much more flight experience. Still, he took it upon himself to train Nuparu in basic flight skills and came to a newfound respect for his fellow Toa.

Kongu accompanied the Toa Inika through the CORD. Arriving at Mahri Nui, a burst of energy from the Ignika transformed them into the aquatic Toa Mahri. They went on to battle the BARRAKI for possession of the Mask of Life.

POWERS

Like LEWA NUVA, Kongu controls the element of air.

PERSONALITY

Kongu has had to make a lot of adjustments as a Toa. He spent a great deal of time as the commander of a defensive force on Mata Nui (2), yet the Toa already have a strong leader in Jaller. So Kongu has emulated his heroes, Lewa and MATAU, and taken on the role of cynic and humorist to help break the tension. It is a role he is still adjusting to, but one he has fulfilled well.

EQUIPMENT

As a Toa Inika, Kongu wore the Kanohi SULETU, the Mask of Telepathy, and carried a ZAMOR SPHERE LAUNCHER and an ENERGY CROSSBOW. As a Toa Mahri, he carries two CORDAK BLASTERs and wears the Kanohi ZATTH, the Mask of Summoning.

KOPAKA/KOPAKA NUVA [koh-PAH-kah/koh-PAH-kah NOO-vah]: TOA of Ice and protector of KO-KORO.

HISTORY

Little is known about Kopaka's history prior to his first appearance on the island of MATA NUI (2). He was one of six Toa who had been floating in the ocean around that land for 1,000 years. They were inside unique canisters and each was partially disassembled. A signal unwittingly sent by TAKUA called the canisters to shore. Kopaka emerged on the shores of KO-WAHI and almost immediately encountered MATORO. This MATORAN brought Kopaka to TURAGA NUJU, who explained that the island was besieged by the forces of MAKUTA.

KOPAKA

Kopaka's first act of heroism was saving Matoro from a NUI-RAMA. Shortly after, he encountered POHATU when the Toa of Stone accidentally buried him in a rockslide. The two proceeded to find a Kanohi HAU atop MOUNT IHU. Then Kopaka spotted a gathering of other beings, who turned out to be ONUA, TAHU, LEWA, and GALI.

Despite some misgivings, Kopaka agreed to team up with the other Toa. Together and separately, they searched for KANOHI masks and battled the RAHI servants of MAKUTA. Early on, Kopaka and Tahu began to get on each other's nerves, a condition that would only grow worse with time. He briefly merged with Gali and Lewa to form TOA KAITA WAIRUHA and fight the MANAS.

During the battle against the BOHROK, it was Kopaka who discovered that the enemy was not alien to the island of Mata Nui, but in fact came from underground. He also prevented Tahu from charging into a Bohrok nest and possibly getting killed.

Following the defeat of the twin Bohrok queens, the BAHRAG, the six Toa were transformed by ENERGIZED PROTODERMIS into TOA NUVA. Tahu and Kopaka fought shortly after, an argument which led to the break-up of the team. This damaged Kopaka's friendship with Gali for some time. Later, after the BOHROK-KAL had stolen the Toa Nuva's powers, Kopaka teamed with Pohatu to search for KANOHI NUVA masks.

Kopaka encountered TAKUA and JALLER during their search for TAKANUVA, saving them from a RAHKSHI attack. Discovering that Ko-Koro had been badly damaged by the invaders, Kopaka bid the Matoran farewell as he went to aid his village.

Later, Kopaka teamed with Tahu Nuva, Onua Nuva, and Pohatu Nuva to imprison KURAHK and VORAHK in frozen magma. He was there to witness Takanuva's victory over Makuta and the rediscovery of METRU NUI. Back on Mata Nui, Kopaka Nuva helped with the construction of boats for a journey back to the city of legends. He also joined with the others in listening to Turaga VAKAMA's tales of life in Metru Nui centuries before.

Kopaka Nuva returned to Metru Nui with the other Toa Nuva, Matoran and Turaga. Once there, he and his teammates were dispatched to VOYA NUI to retrieve the KANOHI IGNIKA. There they battled the PIRAKA and BRUTAKA, and were defeated in a treacherous attack from behind. They were imprisoned, but later freed by the MATORAN RESISTANCE. They have since returned to Metru Nui, beginning the preparations for the awakening of Mata Nui (1), including the freeing of the Bahrag, the unleashing of the Bohrok, and the destruction of the realm of KARZAHNI.

POWERS

Kopaka is the master of ice. He can stop or start blizzards; hurl ice darts; travel via ice slides; freeze an opponent solid in an instant; and, as a Toa Nuva, even freeze open flames. He also has a natural resistance to extreme cold.

PERSONALITY

Kopaka is the least social of all the Toa, preferring to spend time by himself. While he usually recognizes the importance of being in a team, he has never been comfortable with it. He has little patience for fools or reckless behavior. He and Tahu have clashed repeatedly, almost coming to blows once. Of all the Toa, it is only Gali and (though he would never admit it) Pohatu that he considers friends.

K

Kopaka carried an ICE SWORD and ICE SHIELD (2). As Kopaka Nuva, he carries an ICE BLADE that can be split in two and used as ice skates. Kopaka most often wears the Kanohi AKAKU or AKAKU NUVA, the Great Mask of X-Ray Vision.

KOPEKE [KOH-peek]:
A highly respected KO-MATORAN carver, known for his ice bridges and sculptures in honor of TOA KOPAKA. On METRU NUI, Kopeke worked at a variety of jobs, including messenger and chute station attendant. But it was on MATA NUI (2) that his true artistic gifts began to show themselves. In addition to being a fine sculptor, Kopeke was also an athlete. He excelled at both HUAI SNOWBALL SLING and KOLHII.
Kopeke served as part of the CHRONICLER's Company and helped to defend KINI-NUI against RAHI attack. Now serves as CHRONICLER.

KORO [KOAR-oh]:
Matoran word meaning "village." There were six villages on MATA NUI (2): GA-KORO, KO-KORO, LE-KORO, ONU-KORO, PO-KORO, and TA-KORO.

KOTU [KO-too]:
GA-MATORAN who worked as a Rahi handler on the island of MATA NUI (2). Kotu also served as an adviser to Turaga NOKAMA.

KRAAHKAN [krah-KAN]:
The Great Mask of Shadows worn by MAKUTA. The Kraahkan is capable of creating darkness, anger, and fear. Its origin is unknown, although legends hint that it may have been created on the island of ARTAKHA. The mask is capable of changing shape along with Makuta as needed. TAKANUVA defeated Makuta in part by removing this mask from his face. After Makuta's armor was shattered, the Kraahkan was lost beneath the waters surrounding METRU NUI when REIDAK attempted to steal it.

KRAAHU [KRAH-hoo]:
A specialized version of a VAHKI designed by NUPARU for use against RAHI stampedes and in other emergencies. Unlike the standard Vahki model, the Kraahu's knowledge centers are scattered throughout its structure. This allows the Kraahu to actually split apart and have its various pieces act independently. Kraahu parts give off an electrical charge that is triggered on contact. When intact, the Kraahu can emit clouds of stun gas.

KRAATA [KRAH-tah]:
Wormlike, sentient portions of MAKUTA's substance, created by him as the basis for RAHKSHI. Although Makuta could in theory create an infinite number of kraata, bringing them into being seems to diminish his energy temporarily. Kraata move like snakes and are capable of spreading infection to any inanimate object they touch, most often KANOHI masks. A kraata exposed to ENERGIZED PROTODERMIS will evolve over time into Rahkshi armor. Another kraata must then occupy the armor to activate and control it.
Kraata come in a variety of colors, with the colors indicating the power of the individual kraata. The Rahkshi created from those kraata will have identical powers.

Kraata go through six stages of development, with the evolution the result of time and experience. A select few kraata evolve to a seventh stage (see SHADOW KRAATA).
Although there were Rahkshi on METRU NUI, kraata were not a major factor there. The sole exception was TOA NOKAMA's realization that the Rahkshi he had encountered had to be KRAHKA in disguise because the armor lacked a controlling kraata.
These creatures were, however, a significant problem on MATA NUI (2), sent forth by Makuta to infect masks and bring RAHI and MATORAN under his sway. Many of these kraata were trapped by the TURAGA and placed into stasis tubes hidden in a PO-WAHI cave. The Turaga chose not to kill the kraata they encountered, believing that their energy would simply revert to Makuta.
Kraata were in control of the six Rahkshi who attacked Mata Nui. TAKANUVA's vehicle, the USSANUI, was constructed from the parts of these Rahkshi and powered by kraata. Their presence enabled the craft to detect Makuta's location and bring the Toa of Light right to it.

Kraata Colors and Powers
A kraata's power can be identified by its mix of colors. These powers can be used by the Rahkshi formed from the individual kraata. See the Rahkshi chart on pages 119-20 for the colors of different Rahkshi breeds.

Kraata Color	Power
Reddish Gold/Bright Red	Fear
Lemon Metallic/Bright Yellowish Green	Poison
Dark Gray/Metallic Gray	Hunger
Sand Yellow Metallic/Brick Yellow	Shattering
Sand Blue Metallic/Medium Blue	Disintegration
Light Gray Metallic/White	Anger
Lemon Metallic/Dark Gray Metallic	Weather Control
Bright Yellow Green/Bright Yellow	Elasticity
Black/Bright Orange	Heat Vision
Dark Green/Bright Yellow	Illusion
Lemon Metallic/Bright Red	Teleport
Lemon Metallic/Sand Blue Metallic	Quick Healing
Lemon Metallic/Dark Green	Laser Vision
Dark Gray Metallic/Lemon Metallic	Gravity
Bright Blue/Bright Red	Electricity
Black/Bright Yellow	Sonics
Bright Yellow/Bright Yellow Green	Vacuum
Dark Gray/Sand Blue Metallic	Plasma
Bright Orange/Black	Magnetism
Black/Bright Red	Fire Resistance
Bright Yellow/Dark Green	Ice Resistance
Bright Red/Lemon Metallic	Mind Reading
Dark Gray/Bright Yellow Green	Shape-shifting
Reddish Gold/Bright Yellow	Darkness
Reddish Gold/Black	Plant Control
Sand Yellow Metallic/Reddish Gold	Molecular Disruption (inorganic)
Sand Blue Metallic/Lemon Metallic	Chain Lightning
Sand Blue Metallic/Light Gray Metallic	Cyclone
Dark Green/Lemon Metallic	Density Control

Sand Yellow Metallic/Bright Yellow	Chameleon
Bright Red/Bright Blue	Accuracy
Sand Yellow Metallic/Black	Rahi Control
Bright Yellow/Black	Insect Control
Sand Blue Metallic/Dark Gray	Stasis Field
Black/Sand Yellow Metallic	Limited Invulnerability
Bright Red/Black	Power Scream
Bright Yellow/Sand Yellow Metallic	Dodge
Bright Yellow Green/Dark Gray	Silence
Bright Yellow/Reddish Gold	Adaptation
Light Gray Metallic/Sand Blue Metallic	Slow
Black/Reddish Gold	Confusion
Reddish Gold/Sand Yellow Metallic	Sleep

KRAATA-CU (KRAH-tah-KOO):
Controlling organism of the RAHKSHI KURAHK. Possessed the anger power. See KURAHK.

KRAATA-KAL:
DARK HUNTER who began life as a KRAATA before being mutated by MAKUTA into his current armored form. Kraata-Kal has power over water, fire, and shadow, and carries a double-bladed flame sword and a KANOKA DISK launcher.

KRAATA-UL (KRAH-tah-UHL):
Controlling organism of the RAHKSHI GUURAHK. Possessed the disintegration power. See GUURAHK.

KRAATA-VO (KRAH-tah-VOH):
Controlling organism of the RAHKSHI VORAHK. Possessed the hunger power. See VORAHK.

KRAATA-XI (KRAH-tah-ZEE):
Controlling organism of the RAHKSHI PANRAHK. Possessed the shattering or fragmenting power. See PANRAHK.

KRAATA-YE (KRAH-tah-YAY):
Controlling organism of the RAHKSHI LERAHK. Possessed the poison power. See LERAHK.

KRAATA-ZA (KRAH-tah-ZAH):
Controlling organism of a RAHKSHI TURAHK. Possessed the fear power. See TURAHK.

KRAAWA (KRAH-wah):
A RAHI with the special ability to absorb any force directed against it and use that energy to grow. The Kraawa was kept in the most secure portion of the METRU NUI ARCHIVES. How many specimens exist is unknown. An attempt by a kraawa to escape was blamed for the shattering of a container holding microscopic PROTODITES, and the subsequent spread of those creatures throughout the Archives.

KRAAWA

KRAHKA (KRAH-kah):

Intelligent, shape-shifting RAHI who lived in the area beneath the ARCHIVES maintenance tunnels in METRU NUI. Krahka was able to take on the form and powers of any living thing she had seen, as well as combine those forms and powers. She also gained knowledge with the transformation, enabling her to master the MATORAN (2) language among other things. Krahka first encountered the TOA METRU when they went into the maintenance tunnels to

KRAHKA

stop a leak that threatened the Archives. After capturing WHENUA, she impersonated him to lead the others into a trap. Believing the Toa and MATORAN (1) a threat to her domain, she intended to lure the Matoran into the tunnels and trap them, then claim the city for herself. She was defeated after using her power to take on aspects of all six TOA, when the mental strain proved too much for her. Turning herself into a lava eel, she escaped, with Toa VAKAMA making no effort to stop her.

She resurfaced after the VISORAK took over Metru Nui, challenging ROODAKA to single combat. Roodaka won and used Krahka as part of a plan to undermine the confidence of the TOA HORDIKA. Krahka later turned on Roodaka and sided with the Toa and RAHAGA against the Visorak horde. Summoning the TAHTORAK, Krahka rode it into battle against the horde and the ZIVON. During the struggle between the Tahtorak and the Zivon, Krahka spotted a KAHGARAK about to unleash a

spinner that would send the Tahtorak into the zone of darkness. Knowing she could not save him, Krahka slammed into the Zivon, forcing it into physical contact with its foe. When the spinner hit, all three — Tahtorak, Zivon, and Krahka — were transported into the zone. Krahka and Tahtorak later escaped through the use of BRUTAKA's mask, the OLMAK, and made it to VOYA NUI. Krahka transformed into a flying Rahi and left the island, heading for Metru Nui. Krahka believed that she was the only member of her species, but Rahaga POUKS revealed that many more had once existed in another land. They were overrun by the Visorak and are presumed lost.

KRAKUA (krah-KOO-ah):

TOA of Sonics who appeared to Toa VAKAMA in a vision. Krakua claimed to be from Vakama's future and warned him that a team of Toa would one day have to go on a journey to the "darkest place you can imagine" (now believed to be a reference to the TOA INIKA and TOA MAHRI). He also encouraged Vakama to persevere in his battle with MAKUTA for possession of the KANOHI VAHI, and be willing to destroy the Mask of Time, if need be, to keep it out of Makuta's hands. Krakua wore the Kanohi SULETU, the Mask of Telepathy.

KRALHI (KRAHL-hee):

The initial attempt to create an order-enforcing machine in METRU NUI was the Kralhi, designed by NUPARU under orders from TURAGA DUME. The Kralhi was able to launch an energy bubble from its tail at a target. The bubble would then envelop the target and drain a percentage of his energy. Unfortunately, this system proved inefficient as it left the MATORAN lawbreakers too weak to work. Dume decided to have the Kralhi retired, but the machines refused to be shut off. Some hid in KO-METRU, some in the ARCHIVES, and others ended up in the tunnels connecting Metru Nui to MATA NUI (2). The latter group allied with MAVRAH against the TOA METRU and were destroyed as a consequence. The Kralhi were replaced in Metru Nui by the VAHKI.

KRAΠA (KRAH-nah):

Living creatures that reside in and operate BOHROK mechanoids. There were eight types of krana: KRANA BO, KRANA CA, KRANA JA, KRANA SU, KRANA VU, KRANA XA, KRANA YO, and KRANA ZA (see individual entries). Each provided the Bohrok with a different power or ability. The first krana were created by the GREAT BEINGS by exposing the remains from the process used to create MATORAN into ENERGIZED PROTODERMIS. (What did not become krana became ZYGLAK.) Later, krana were created by the BAHRAG by introducing an unknown form of matter into energized protodermis.

Krana were unable to function independently, and relied on a telepathic link to the Bahrag. When that link was cut off by the Bahrag's defeat and imprisonment, the krana ceased to be a threat. If a krana was removed from a Bohrok, the mechanoid ceased to function properly. Bohrok were capable of ejecting their krana onto the face of an opponent. Once the krana was attached, the target's mind fell under the sway of the Bohrok swarm. TOA TAHU, Toa LEWA, TURAGA MATAU, and almost the entire population of LE-KORO experienced this harrowing ordeal.

During the battle with the Bohrok, the Toa collected the eight forms of krana from each species. Once they were fitted into niches in the floor of an underground chamber, six passages opened up revealing the way to the EXO-TOA armor. The Toa used that armor in their final battle with the Bahrag.

MATORAN also collected krana from Bohrok as a means to render the mechanoids helpless. Most of these krana wound up buried in a pit. Having survived thousands of years of dormancy, it is likely the krana simply willed themselves back into a suspended state to await rescue.

KRAΠA BO (KRAH-nah BOH):

One of the eight KRANA that served as controlling brains for the BOHROK. The krana bo gifted a Bohrok with the ability to see in the dark.

KRAΠA BO-KAL (KRAH-nah BOH-KAHL):

One of the eight KRANA-KAL that served as controlling brains for the BOHROK-KAL. The krana bo-kal granted the power of X-ray vision. A Bohrok-Kal with this creature could see in the dark and through most substances. Only the walls of caves and tunnels beneath MATA NUI (2) were impervious to this power.

KRAΠA CA (KRAH-nah KAH):

One of the eight KRANA that served as controlling brains for the BOHROK. The krana can give a Bohrok the power to shield itself and others from attack.

KRAΠA CA-KAL (KRAH-nah KAH-KAHL):

One of the eight KRANA-KAL that served as controlling brains for the BOHROK-KAL. A Bohrok-Kal with this creature could sense the minds of the BAHRAG and thus locate them no matter where they were.

KRANA CA-KAL

KRANA JA

KRAΠA JA (KRAH-nah JAH):

One of the eight KRANA that served as controlling brains for the BOHROK. The krana ja gave a Bohrok the power to detect distant obstacles in the swarm's path.

KRANA JA-KAL (KRAH-nah JAH-KAHL):

One of the eight KRANA-KAL that served as controlling brains for the BOHROK-KAL. This krana-kal granted its Bohrok-Kal a radar sense, enabling it to detect distant obstacles. It also magnified the senses of the Bohrok-Kal, particularly smell and hearing.

KRANA-KAL (KRAH-nah-KAHL):

Living creatures that reside in and operate BOHROK-KAL mechanoids. As with the KRANA, there were eight types of krana-kal: KRANA BO-KAL, KRANA CA-KAL, KRANA JA-CAL, KRANA SU-CAL, KRANA VU-KAL, KRANA XA-KAL, KRANA YO-KAL, and KRANA ZA-KAL. Each provided the Bohrok-Kal with a different power or ability. Unlike the krana, the krana-kal could function independently of the BAHRAG's influence and communicate with members of other species. If a krana-kal was removed from a Bohrok-Kal, the mechanoid ceased to function properly. At least some of the krana-kal escaped the destruction of the Bohrok-Kal.

KRANA-KAL

KRANA SU (KRAH-nah SOO):

One of the eight KRANA that served as controlling brains for the BOHROK. The krana su gave a Bohrok the power of enhanced strength.

KRANA SU-KAL (KRAH-nah SOO-KAHL):

One of the eight KRANA-KAL that served as controlling brains for the BOHROK-KAL. This krana-kal gave a Bohrok-Kal enhanced strength and resistance to heat and cold.

KRANA VU (KRAH-nah VOO):

One of the eight KRANA that served as controlling brains for the BOHROK. The krana vu gave a Bohrok the ability to fly short distances.

KRANA VU-KAL (KRAH-nah VOO-KAHL):

One of the eight KRANA-KAL that served as controlling brains for the BOHROK-KAL.
A Bohrok-Kal with this creature could move across the ground or through the air at high speed.

KRANA VU-KAL

KRANA XA (KRAH-nah ZAH):

One of the eight KRANA that served as controlling brains for the BOHROK. This krana was used only by swarm commanders and gave them the ability to form complex strategic plans.

KRANA XA-KAL (KRAH-nah ZAH-KAHL):

One of the eight KRANA-KAL that served as controlling brains for the BOHROK-KAL. This krana-kal was the most important of them all. It gave its Bohrok-Kal the power to free the BAHRAG from their prison, in conjunction with the activation of the NUVA CUBE.

KRANA YO (KRAH-nah YOH):

One of the eight KRANA that served as controlling brains for the BOHROK. The krana yo gave a Bohrok the power to tunnel through any substance on the island of MATA NUI (2).

KRANA YO-KAL [KRAH-nah YO-KAHL]:

One of the eight KRANA-KAL that served as controlling brains for the BOHROK-KAL. This krana-kal gave its Bohrok-Kal the ability to sense stress points in the earth, making for more efficient tunneling. It could also sense underground movement.

KRANA ZA [KRAH-nah ZAH]:

One of the eight KRANA that served as controlling brains for the BOHROK. The krana za made it possible for a Bohrok to communicate telepathically with others in the swarm.

KRANA ZA-KAL [KRAH-nah ZAH-KAHL]:

One of the eight KRANA-KAL that served as controlling brains for the BOHROK-KAL. This krana-kal was capable of communicating telepathically with other krana-kal, as well as reading minds and sensing strong emotion in the area.

KRANUA [KRAH-noo-ah]:

A specialized version of a VAHKI designed in secret by NUPARU and built by a select team of PO-MATORAN engineers. Its intended purpose was crowd control, particularly mass RAHI breakouts from the ARCHIVES. The powerful and bulky Kranua was capable of transforming its body into animated grains of PROTODERMIS, allowing it to flow through narrow openings before re-forming. The TOA METRU encountered a Kranua on their initial journey back to METRU NUI. After a brief but furious battle, VAKAMA used his fire power to fuse the sandy grains of the Kranua into glass. MATAU later tipped the crystalline Kranua over, shattering it.

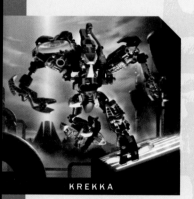

KREKKA

KREKKA [kreh-KAH]:

One of the three DARK HUNTERS sent to METRU NUI at the request of MAKUTA. Krekka's partner was NIDHIKI.

Krekka was originally part of a guardian/servant class on the same island from which SIDORAK came. Extremely strong and powerful but not very bright, Krekka earned a living by convincing intruders to go away, often in very painful ways. Unfortunately, he made the mistake of trying to do this to an emissary of the BROTHERHOOD OF MAKUTA. Exactly what happened next is not clear, but some believe the encounter was responsible both for Krekka deciding to leave home and for the loss of one of his eyes.

For a number of years, Krekka journeyed from island to island, usually getting into trouble and brawling his way out of it. This attracted the attention of the Dark Hunters, and Krekka was recruited into their organization. By order of the SHADOWED ONE, he was partnered with Nidhiki. It was an uneasy partnership at best, with Nidhiki being much smarter and more cunning than his bestial companion. But the Shadowed One had good reason for the decision he made. Nidhiki had betrayed the TOA in the past, and no one truly trusts a traitor. Krekka, on the other hand, would stick to a mission no matter what and make sure that Nidhiki did not stray too far from their objectives. For insurance, it was made extremely clear to Nidhiki that if anything happened to Krekka, the Dark Hunters would hold him responsible. Nidhiki and Krekka were sent to Metru Nui to aid Makuta in his plan to seize the GREAT DISKS and capture all the MATORAN in the city (see MAKUTA). Among their deeds were the capture of Toa LHIKAN and the recruitment of AHKMOU to help them get the Great Disks. They clashed repeatedly with the TOA METRU during and after this time (see NIDHIKI). Both Dark Hunters were drawn into Makuta's substance and became part of his new body. Krekka was killed by the process.

In addition to his enormous strength, Krekka carried a KANOKA DISK launcher and was capable of launching energy webs at his foes. He could also shift into an aerodynamic mode for flight. He was able to survive falls from great heights. Unlike Nidhiki, Krekka was not a Toa in the past.

KUALSI (KOO-ahl-see):
Mask of Quick Travel, worn by TOA IRUINI. This mask allows the wearer to travel by teleportation, although only to a spot that is in his or her sight line.

KUALUS (KOO-ahl-luss):
Former TOA HAGAH of Ice later mutated by ROODAKA into a RAHAGA. Kualus had been part of an elite Toa team charged with being MAKUTA's personal guard. When they discovered Makuta was oppressing and enslaving MATORAN, they turned on him and attacked a fortress of the BROTHERHOOD OF MAKUTA. Kualus was struck by one of Roodaka's RHOTUKA SPINNERS and mutated into a shrunken creature with the head of a RAHKSHI. He was later rescued by Toa IRUINI and Toa NORIK, who also ended up being mutated.
What masks and tools Kualus carried as a Toa has not yet been revealed.
As a Rahaga, Kualus specialized in capturing flying RAHI, such as ICE BATS and GUKKO. He carried a Rhotuka spinner with the *boomerang* power, which would adhere to a flying target and then bring it right to him. His staff could be used to send a high-pitched signal to Rahi, summoning them or warning them of danger.
Kualus was capable of speaking a strange language that was evidently understood by some Rahi, and of understanding some of their language. He later taught this skill to Toa NUJU, who eventually abandoned speaking Matoran altogether in favor of this Rahi dialect.

KUMA-NUI (KOO-mah-NOO-ee):
A giant rat creature found in the maintenance tunnels beneath the ARCHIVES, particularly in the TA-METRU and KO-METRU areas. A small number of these later migrated to MATA NUI (2). KORO defense forces were routinely dispatched to keep them away from the villages.

KUMU ISLETS (KOO-moo):
A group of small islands at the southern tip of MATA NUI (2). Efforts to colonize them met with failure owing to the large number of extremely dangerous RAHI who made their home there.

KURAHK (KER-rahk):
One of the six RAHKSHI sent by MAKUTA to stop the HERALD and recover the KANOHI AVOHKII. Kurahk's power, directed through its staff, caused his targets to grow enraged and often turn on each other. Along with TURAHK and VORAHK, Kurahk was responsible for the destruction of the village of ONU-KORO. Kurahk was trapped in an ice prison due to the efforts of ONUA NUVA, POHATU NUVA, TAHU NUVA, and KOPAKA NUVA.

KURAHK

KYREHX (KIGH-rex):
GA-MATORAN inhabitant of MAHRI NUI. Kyrehx was the first MATORAN there to come into contact with the KANOHI IGNIKA. As a result of her interaction with the Mask of Life, she found that plant life spontaneously grew anywhere she went and reacted violently to being uprooted. These experiences stopped when she passed the mask on to DEKAR.

LAKE OF FIRE:

A molten body of liquid PROTODERMIS on MATA NUI (2), site of the village of TA-KORO. The superheated lava was spanned by a bridge that could be lowered into the lake when danger threatened. Ta-Koro was later destroyed by the RAHKSHI and sank into the lake.

LAKE PALA (PAH-lah):

A small body of water in southeastern MATA NUI (2).

LARISKA (lah-RIS-kah):

Female DARK HUNTER. Little is known about Lariska's early life or where she originally came from, but it can safely be assumed it was from a land where every day was a battle for survival. Tough and cynical, Lariska is a skilled hand-to-hand fighter and an expert with many weapons, but prefers throwing daggers. Lariska joined the Dark Hunters some 10,000 years ago. After the capture of HAKANN and THOK, she defeated Hakann in a training match. During the TOA-DARK HUNTER war, she brokered the deal with NIDHIKI that led to his betrayal of the Toa. At some point in between those two events, Lariska angered the SHADOWED ONE and lost her arm as punishment. It was replaced by one that was completely mechanical. Lariska remains active, but her current whereabouts and mission are unknown.

LAVA:

Molten PROTODERMIS. Streams of this substance flowed from the MANGAI volcano on MATA NUI (2). It was farmed by TA-MATORAN, and IGNALU, or lava surfing, was a popular sport in the village.

LAVABOARD:

A flat, narrow piece of hardened PROTODERMIS used by TA-MATORAN in TA-WAHI to surf on lava. MATORAN use tree trunks from the CHARRED FOREST to make their boards, for they do not melt in molten magma.

LAVA CHAMBER GATE:

Entranceway to the CHAMBER OF LIFE. The lava chamber gate was located on a vast plain bisected by a river of lava, at the end of a bridge. The bridge was destroyed by TOA INIKA KONGU during a battle with the PIRAKA.

LAVA EEL:

A serpentlike creature of TA-METRU. When agitated, the surface temperature of a lava eel's skin increased to the point where it could melt through metal. Small lava eels were often kept as pets by TA-MATORAN, until they grew larger and more destructive, at which point they were normally abandoned.

LAVA FARM:

Areas worked by the TA-MATORAN in TA-WAHI. When the MATORAN lived on METRU NUI, objects could be crafted in TA-METRU from piped-in molten PROTODERMIS, then easily shipped to other districts for assembly and use. On the island of MATA NUI (2), things were not so simple owing to the number of RAHI serving MAKUTA who made the manufacture and transport of items more difficult. Ta-Matoran began harvesting lava from the MANGAI volcano and cooling it, then using tools to shape it into items that might be needed (these were rough carvings, nowhere near the level of what PO-MATORAN could do). These would then be shipped via underground tunnel to other villages. The BOHROK's initial attack on Ta-Wahi damaged some of the lava farms.

LAVA HAWK:
RAHI bird of VOYA NUI known for its immunity to molten lava. MATORAN collect the creature's scales to build crafts capable of surviving passage down lava rivers.

LAVA RAT:
A small rodent commonly found in TA-WAHI on MATA NUI (2). The lava rat was immune to fire and known for its tendency to burst into flames without warning. An old Matoran legend tells of an uneasy trip across water by a TAKEA shark carrying a lava rat upon his back.

LAVA SPEAR:
Tool carried by TOA NORIK. The lava spear could shoot a stream of molten lava at an enemy. In addition, the touch of the spear could either heat up an object and melt it instantly, or remove all heat from it in a split second. This was especially useful for turning a lava wave into an almost impenetrable wall of volcanic rock.

LE (LAY):
A Matoran prefix meaning "air."

LE-KINI (LAY-kih-NEE):
A temple dedicated to LEWA located in LE-WAHI on MATA NUI (2).

LE-KORO (LAY-KOAR-oh):
Village on MATA NUI (2) and home to the LE-MATORAN. Le-Koro was led by TURAGA MATAU and protected by TOA LEWA. The village was built in the treetops above the FAU SWAMP. Visitors to the area could often hear the Le-Matoran up in the trees, chattering to each other in TREESPEAK. The village was badly damaged by the LEHVAK and many of its residents captured and enslaved by the BOHROK swarm. Le-Koro was later rebuilt. It was protected by the GUKKO BIRD FORCE led by KONGU.

LE-MATORAN (LAY-mat-OAR-an):
A resident of LE-KORO or LE-METRU. Le-Matoran commonly had green armor and wore green masks. On METRU NUI, most Le-Matoran worked in the transport industry, either building or servicing vehicles and CHUTES, and used a slang known as CHUTESPEAK. This language was modified when they came to MATA NUI (2) to TREESPEAK.

LE-METRU (LAY-MET-troo):
Transport center of METRU NUI and site of the MOTO-HUB and TEST TRACK. Le-Metru was known for its feeling of barely controlled chaos as workers scrambled to and fro beneath a canopy of wires and cables. All chutes, ground, and air vehicles

LE-METRU

were manufactured here, and the entire chute system was supervised from here as well. Le-Metru was protected by TOA MATAU and the VAHKI VORZAKH. It suffered severe damage in the earthquake and became home to many of the species of RAHI who escaped the ARCHIVES.

LE-SUVA (LAY-SOO-vah):
A shrine to LEWA NUVA in LE-KORO. KANOHI masks and Lewa Nuva's symbol were kept here. BOHROK-KAL stole the NUVA SYMBOL from the Le-Suva, robbing Lewa Nuva of his elemental power of air.

LE-WAHI (LAY-WAH-hee):
A marshy, overgrown region located on the southern end of MATA NUI (2), known for its thick jungle. Le-Wahi was the site of the village of LE-KORO and home to numerous RAHI such as BRAKAS and GUKKO. LE-MATORAN live in the treetops above the FAU SWAMP. This area suffered badly at the claws of the LEHVAK during the BOHROK invasion.

LEAGUE OF SIX KINGDOMS:
Alliance of the BARRAKI, six conquerors and rulers — PRIDAK, EHLEK, MANTAX, KALMAH, CARAPAR, and TAKADOX — who dominated much of the Matoran universe in ancient times.

LEHVAK

Their attempt to lead their armies in rebellion against the GREAT SPIRIT MATA NUI (2) was crushed by an army of the BROTHERHOOD OF MAKUTA. Their legions were disbanded and the Barraki were condemned to the PIT by BOTAR. After the collapse of the League, the Brotherhood of Makuta assumed much of its former responsibility of guiding and managing the MATORAN.

LEHVAK (LAY-vahk):
One of the six breeds of BOHROK, insectlike mechanoids controlled by KRANA who menaced the island of MATA NUI (2). The Lehvak were tied to the swampy terrain of LE-KORO and their ACID SHIELDS were powerful enough to dissolve any substance. The Lehvak normally operated in small groups and rarely worked with other Bohrok. They were responsible for the destruction of LE-KORO and the capture of most of the LE-MATORAN. They were most often active in LE-WAHI. The Lehvak returned to their nests after the coming of the BOHROK-KAL.

LEHVAK-KAL (LAY-vahk-KAHL):
One of the six mutant BOHROK who made up the BOHROK-KAL. Lehvak-Kal's tool was a VACUUM SHIELD which could draw in all the air from a given area, causing a destructive implosion. It could then release that air in a single blast with the power to smash through solid rock. Lehvak-Kal lost control of its power after being fed Toa power through the TOA NUVA's symbols (see BOHROK-KAL) and blasted itself into orbit.

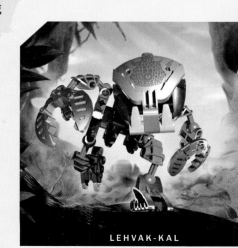
LEHVAK-KAL

LEHVAK VA (LAY-vahk VAH):
One of the six BOHROK VA, Lehvak Va were connected to swamp terrain. Unlike other Bohrok Va, who prided

LEHVAK VA

themselves on stealth, Lehvak Va were loud and aggressive creatures. They were more than willing to use their katana to defend themselves. Of all Bohrok Va, Lehvak Va stuck closest to their swarm.

LERAHK [LAY-rahk]:
One of the six RAHKSHI sent by MAKUTA to stop the HERALD and recover the KANOHI AVOHKII. Lerahk's staff was capable of poisoning anything it touched, from the ground to other beings. Along with GUURAHK and PANRAHK, Lerahk was responsible for the destruction of the village of TA-KORO. During an ensuing battle with TAHU NUVA, Lerahk scratched the TOA's mask, poisoning its foe. It took the combined power of the other five TOA NUVA to heal Tahu. Lerahk was trapped in a prison of glass due to the efforts of Tahu Nuva and LEWA NUVA.

LESOVIKK [LESS-oh-VICK]:
TOA of Air and a member of the first Toa team ever in existence. Originally stationed on one of the southernmost islands, the team clashed with a wandering tribe of ZYGLAK. During the battle, Lesovikk hesitated for a fatal split second. As a result, the zyglak gained the upper hand and killed all of the other members of the team. Only Lesovikk escaped. Returning to his home village to warn them of the impending danger, he found that the local TURAGA had gone mad and shipped the entire MATORAN population to the realm of KARZAHNI. These included Lesovikk's best friends, SARDA and IDRIS.
Guilt-ridden, Lesovikk became a wanderer, convinced he was not worthy to be a Toa. An attempt to rescue his friends from Karzahni met with failure (nor did he realize that those particular Matoran had already been transported to VOYA NUI by that time). Lesovikk continued to wander until he learned that Karzahni was planning an attack on an underwater Matoran city, backed by the zyglak. Seeing the chance to avenge himself on two of his oldest enemies, Lesovikk traveled to MAHRI NUI for a final confrontation.

LEWA/LEWA NUVA [LAY-wah/LAY-wah NOO-vah]:
TOA of Air and protector of LE-KORO.

HISTORY

As is the case with the rest of his Toa team, little is known about Lewa's history prior to his first appearance on the island of MATA NUI (2). He was one of six Toa who had been floating in the ocean around that land for 1,000 years. They were inside unique canisters and each was partially disassembled. A signal unwittingly sent by TAKUA called the canisters to shore. Lewa emerged on the shores of LE-WAHI and had to endure RAHI attacks before making it to the village of Le-Koro.
Lewa rapidly made contact with the other five Toa — ONUA, POHATU, GALI, LEWA, and KOPAKA. Together and separately, they searched for KANOHI masks and battled the Rahi servants of MAKUTA. He began a friendly rivalry with Gali, which grew out of Lewa's intense dislike of water. He briefly merged with Gali and Kopaka to form TOA KAITA WAIRUHA and fight the MANAS.
From the start, Lewa's impetuous nature got him into trouble. Onua had to save him twice, once when he was in thrall to an INFECTED MASK and once when his mind was stolen by

a KRANA. The latter experience made Lewa a bit more serious, as well as straining his relationship with Tahu, who feared Lewa might still be influenced by the Bohrok.

LEWA

Following the defeat of the twin Bohrok queens, the BAHRAG, the six Toa were transformed by ENERGIZED PROTODERMIS into TOA NUVA. When Kopaka and Tahu decided to break up the team, Lewa went along with them. Later, after the BOHROK-KAL had stolen the Toa Nuva's powers, Lewa teamed with Tahu to search for KANOHI NUVA masks.

Lewa encountered TAKUA and JALLER during their search for TAKANUVA, saving them both from an ASH BEAR. He led them both to KO-WAHI, where village drums informed him that TA-KORO had fallen to the RAHKSHI. He left the two MATORAN there while he went to join the other Toa Nuva.

Later, Lewa teamed with Tahu Nuva to imprison LERAHK, PANRAHK, and GUURAHK in a prison of glass. He was there to witness Takanuva's victory over Makuta and the rediscovery of METRU NUI. Back on Mata Nui, Lewa Nuva helped with the construction of boats for a journey back to the city of legends. He also joined with the others in listening to Turaga VAKAMA's tales of life in Metru Nui centuries before.

Lewa Nuva returned to Metru Nui with the other Toa Nuva, Matoran and Turaga. Once there, he and his teammates were dispatched to VOYA NUI to retrieve the KANOHI IGNIKA. There they battled the PIRAKA and BRUTAKA, and were defeated in a treacherous attack. They were imprisoned, but later freed by the MATORAN RESISTANCE. They have since returned to Metru Nui, beginning the preparations for the awakening of Mata Nui (1), including the freeing of the Bahrag and the unleashing of the Bohrok.

POWERS

Lewa is the master of air. He can create everything from a light breeze to a cyclone in a matter of seconds. He is extremely agile and nimble, moving through the treetops like a Rahi. He is also a highly skilled flyer.

PERSONALITY

LEWA NUVA

Lewa rarely takes life seriously. To him, being a Toa is an adventure. Although all six Toa were the same age, to an outsider Lewa might seem like the youngest of the group due to his boundless energy and sense of fun. Some of that enthusiasm was dampened after he was taken over by a krana, as if he suddenly realized that being a hero was not a game.

EQUIPMENT

Lewa carried an axe as a Toa, and twin AIR KATANA as a Toa Nuva. He is the only Toa to have worn both an infected mask and a krana at different points in the past. Lewa most often wore the Kanohi MIRU or MIRU NUVA, the Great Mask of Levitation. One of his air katana was shattered by REIDAK, but he later received a new one courtesy of VELIKA.

LHII [LEE-hee]:

A mythical MATORAN created by TURAGA VAKAMA to keep the memory of TOA LHIKAN alive without revealing the secrets of METRU NUI to the Matoran. Following the Matoran loss of memory on MATA NUI (2), the Turaga realized that they could not share the truth about the past without jeopardizing the safety of the villagers (see MATORAN). However, that also meant that all the old legends, particularly those of Toa Lhikan, would be lost forever. Turaga Vakama hit upon the plan of sharing some of Lhikan's exploits without revealing he was a Toa. He and Turaga NUJU crafted stories of Lhii, said to be the greatest Matoran lava surfer of all. His absence was blamed on his death in a surfing accident. Vakama even went so far as to tell JALLER he was part of the "clan of Lhii," a reference to the fact that Jaller unknowingly wore Turaga Lhikan's Noble Mask of Shielding. With the revelations about Metru Nui, the Matoran now know that Lhii never existed on Mata Nui.

LHIKAN [LEE-kan]:

TOA of Fire, protector of METRU NUI, and later a TURAGA.

HISTORY

LHIKAN

Little is known of Lhikan's past history. As a relatively new Toa, he helped man a Toa tower that contained the MAKOKI STONES. He was the lone defender to escape an attack of the FROSTELUS. He first came to Metru Nui 4,000 years ago along with 10 other Toa in response to a call for help from Turaga DUME. The Toa encountered and defeated a KANOHI DRAGON.

Lhikan personally saw the dragon delivered to the island of XIA. Afterwards, he, Toa NIDHIKI, and a handful of the other heroes elected to remain in the city as its protectors.

Lhikan led the Toa to victory in the conflict with the DARK HUNTERS over the latter group's plan to establish a base in the city. During this struggle, Lhikan discovered that Nidhiki planned to betray the city. Nidhiki left with the defeated Dark Hunters and did not return for hundreds of years.

Over time, some of the Toa left the city for other islands and more adventure. More recently, Turaga Dume ordered a number of the Toa to close off all the seaways that led from Metru Nui to other lands. No explanation was given for this strange order. Lhikan remained behind in the city while his companions left to carry out their missions. None of them ever returned. Lhikan began to grow suspicious but did not know that Dume was truly MAKUTA in disguise. Still, he felt it wise to make plans in case the worst should happen. He stole the TOA STONES from the GREAT TEMPLE and infused each of them with a portion of his power. Then he gave the stones, along with maps to the Great Temple, to six Matoran: MATAU, NOKAMA, NUJU, ONEWA, VAKAMA, and WHENUA. Lhikan could not know that Makuta had expected him to attempt to create other Toa. Believing it better for his plans if the new TOA METRU were a contentious and quarrelsome lot, Makuta planted the names of six Matoran into Lhikan's mind. He believed that Vakama and the others would never be able to get along well enough to work as a team, and therefore would be no threat to him.

When Lhikan brought the Toa stone to Vakama, he was followed by the Dark Hunters Nidhiki and KREKKA. They captured Lhikan, but not before he was able to help Vakama escape. Lhikan was carried way and placed in the PRISON OF THE DARK HUNTERS.

When the six Matoran used the Toa stones to turn themselves into Toa Metru, Lhikan had met the conditions to become a Turaga: he had fulfilled his destiny (creating new heroes) and he had willingly sacrificed his Toa power. He thus turned into Turaga Lhikan. (Note: a vision of Toa Lhikan appeared to the TOA INIKA on VOYA NUI, but this was merely a creation of the KANOHI IGNIKA and not Lhikan's genuine form.)

TURAGA LHIKAN

Lhikan remained in his cell as a Turaga and so was present when Whenua, Onewa, and Nuju were thrown inside. He used the time to teach the three of them new ways of thinking and approaching problems. This helped all three to discover how to use their KANOHI mask powers.

Later, when Vakama discovered a MATORAN SPHERE containing the sleeping form of the real Dume, Lhikan's suspicions were confirmed. The Dume who had ordered the Toa out of the city and branded the Toa Metru as criminals was an impostor. At the COLISEUM, the false Dume revealed himself to be Makuta. Lhikan was furious, reminding Makuta that he had sworn at one time to protect the Matoran.

During Vakama's confrontation with Makuta at the GREAT BARRIER, Lhikan saw that Vakama was unable to properly control the VAHI, the Mask of Time. He was in mortal danger. At the last possible moment, Lhikan leapt in the path of Makuta's attack, his body wracked by dark energies powerful enough to harm a Toa. They were too much for his weakened Turaga form, and Lhikan died. Vakama took his Mask of Power as a reminder of his heroic sacrifice, and later gave the mask to JALLER. Years later, realizing the Matoran had lost all memories of Metru Nui, Vakama began telling them stories of LHII, a mythical Matoran whose exploits were based on those of Lhikan. This was Vakama's way of ensuring that his hero would never be completely forgotten.

POWERS

As Toa of Fire, Lhikan controlled heat and flame. He could hurl fireballs, melt virtually any substance, create thermal updrafts to slow falling objects, and had all the abilities of later Toa of Fire such as Vakama and TAHU.

PERSONALITY

Lhikan saw himself as very much a "big brother" figure to the Matoran. Although he was not native to Metru Nui, he was deeply loyal to his adopted city and its population. When his services were not needed to deal with an emergency, he could often be found spending time with Matoran from various METRU, listening to their probems and offering advice. After Dume became a recluse (due to the fact that it was not truly Dume but Makuta in disguise), Lhikan began resolving disputes and helping to make day-to-day decisions in the city.

EQUIPMENT

Lhikan carried two FIRE GREATSWORDS, which could be fitted together to form a shield as well as a flying board. He wore the Kanohi HAU, the Great Mask of Shielding. As a Turaga, he wore the Noble Hau.

LHIKAN [LEE-kan]:

Name given to the VAHKI TRANSPORT used by the TOA METRU to sail from METRU NUI to MATA NUI (2). It consisted of a transport body with six MATORAN SPHERES strapped to the bottom to provide buoyancy.

LHIKAN II [LEE-kan]:

Name given to the VAHKI TRANSPORT used by the TOA METRU to sail back to METRU NUI on their mission to rescue the MATORAN. It consisted of a transport body with pieces of the KARZAHNI (2) used to provide buoyancy.

LIGHTFISH:

Small, glowing fish found in the deepest underwater caves around GA-METRU and GA-KORO. GA-MATORAN on MATA NUI (2) used lightfish to provide illumination in their dwellings.

LIGHTSTONE:

A glowing crystal mined by ONU-MATORAN both in METRU NUI and on MATA NUI (2). These crystals were used to provide illumination. In their raw, unrefined state, lightstones can be so bright as to be almost blinding to unshielded eyes. It was at one time believed that lightstones had a self-contained power source, but this was largely disproved by the fact that so many of them were doused when the Metru Nui power plant was wrecked. The fact that some of the stones continued to work, particularly on Mata Nui, would seem to indicate that there was a second source of energy for them other than the Metru Nui plant. What that source might be has not yet been discovered.

LOHRAK [LOH-rahk]:

A winged serpent found throughout METRU NUI and some portions of MATA NUI (2). The Lohrak was known for its sharp teeth and scaly hide covered in slime. Commonly found underground, Lohrak attacked in a swarm and were considered a dangerous menace, particularly by ONU-MATORAN miners. For a time, the creatures were even pronounced a protected species by TURAGA DUME, in hopes of stopping digging projects that might unearth more monsters. The TOA METRU fought and defeated a swarm of Lohrak after escaping the PRISON OF THE DARK HUNTERS, and later encountered a specimen mutated to monstrous size by the VISORAK.

LOHRAK

LONGFANGS:

Large, reptilian RAHI who elected to stay in METRU NUI when so many other creatures emigrated to MATA NUI (2). They traditionally lived in the tunnels beneath the ARCHIVES, but emerged following the GREAT CATACLYSM to feed on the surface. They average seven feet in length and their mouths are filled with multiple rows of sharp teeth. Their preferred prey is STONE RATS.

LURKER:

Banished from his home island for the crime of murder, Lurker accepted the offer to join the DARK HUNTERS. Modifications left him with claws, stingers, and built-in blades. He is a natural fighter and climber with a well-honed survival instinct.

LURKER

M&D:

Visorak shorthand for "mutation and disposal."

MACKU

MACKU (MAH-koo):

A GA-MATORAN known for her canoe racing and navigational skills. On METRU NUI, she received special permission to run her own business offering canoe tours of the coastline (see MACKU'S CANOES). On MATA NUI (2), she excelled in the NGALAWA canoe racing tournaments.

Macku helped to save her village from a RAHI attack by sending TAKUA to aid the other Ga-Matoran while she sought out TOA GALI. Later, she served as part of the CHRONICLER's Company and helped defend KINI-NUI against Rahi attack. Macku joined with HAHLI to form Ga-Koro's winning KOLHII team.

MACKU'S CANOES (MAH-koo):

Small business run by MACKU in GA-METRU. She offered guided tours of the METRU NUI coastline. Her most frequent customers were ONU-MATORAN searching for aquatic RAHI to add to the ARCHIVES.

MADU (MAH-doo):

A coconut-like fruit found on MATA NUI (2). The fruit's juices were extremely volatile and so the fruit was known to explode. Madu grew on trees.

MADU CABOLO (MAH-doo cah-BOH-loh):

An unripe MADU fruit. Also very volatile, Madu Cabolo would explode if exposed to elemental energy. When they did so, they emitted a foul-smelling gas that could be used to repel KANE-RA bulls.

MAGMA SWORDS:

Twin blades carried by TAHU NUVA. He could both channel his fire power through them and cross them in front of him to block attacks.

MAGNETIC SHIELD:

Tool carried by GAHLOK-KAL. This shield was capable of creating a magnetic force field, which proved itself capable of resisting TAHU NUVA's full power.

MAHIKI (mah-HEE-kee):

KANOHI Mask of Illusion. The Great Mask version of this, worn by TOA MATAU, actually allowed the user to shape-shift. The Noble Mask version, worn by Matau as a TURAGA, simply created illusions to confound enemies. Matau used the Great Mask to impersonate a VAHKI, NIDHIKI, and KREKKA.

MAHRI NUI (MAH-ree NOO-ee):

MATORAN city that broke off of the island of VOYA NUI and sank beneath the sea several centuries ago. In the years after Voya Nui rocketed to the surface of the ocean, molten PROTODERMIS cooled to form an additional segment of land. The Matoran residents of the island built Mahri Nui on this land, but it was unstable by nature. After a few centuries, it broke off and disappeared beneath the waves. It landed on top of a fortress built by EHLEK, crushing it, and also disrupted the FIELDS OF AIR, resulting in the release of air bubbles. The surviving Matoran of Mahri Nui were able to use that to sustain their own lives as well as resist the mutagenic properties of the seawater.

In the years that followed, the Matoran surrounded their homes and buildings with large air bubbles, domesticated HYDRUKA to harvest air, and did their best to survive. Their memories of Voya Nui were fragmentary at best and they did not realize there was another civilization above them. They were also unaware that their city was resting in the center of the outer regions of the PIT. Mahri Nui was often menaced by sea predators that served the BARRAKI. When the KANOHI IGNIKA floated down to Mahri Nui, the Matoran found themselves in the center of a war between the BARRAKI and the TOA MAHRI. The Matoran allied themselves with the Toa, despite knowing that if the Toa succeeded in their mission, Mahri Nui and all who lived on it would be destroyed.

Mahri Nui is connected to Voya Nui by a stone cord within which is a labyrinth of tunnels. The TOA INIKA traveled through these tunnels to reach the underwater city. The Matoran defended Mahri Nui by using launchers that fired SOLID AIR BUBBLES.

Known residents of Mahri Nui include DEFILAK, DEKAR, KYREHX, SARDA, IDRIS, and GAR.

MAKIKA (mah-KEE-kah):

A large and dangerous cave toad found in GA-METRU. It has few natural predators since it is poisonous to most other RAHI. MATORAN on MATA NUI (2) discovered that the Makika's acidic venom was useful for tunneling through earth and rock.

MAKOKI STONES (mah-KO-kee):

Six stone fragments used by the RAHAGA as a key to unlock the hiding place of the AVOHKII in the ARCHIVES. Later, they were collected by TAHU's TOA team shortly after their arrival on MATA NUI (2). Fitted together, the stones formed a key that opened a passage from KINI-NUI to MAKUTA's lair.

The history of the Makoki stones is a complicated one. Originally, they were all part of one tablet and contained secret inscriptions detailing information about the BROTHERHOOD OF MAKUTA. The tablet was guarded in a Toa tower, but stolen by VEZOK. Thousands of years later, HAKANN bought the freedom of the captured DARK HUNTERS from Toa LHIKAN by arranging the return of the tablet. Later, the Dark Hunters stole it back again and it was split into six pieces.

The stones later fell into the hands of the RAHAGA, who used them as the key to unlock the hiding place of the KANOHI AVOHKII in METRU NUI.

MAKUTA [mah-KOO-tah]:

Master of shadows, spirit of destruction, leader of the BROTHERHOOD OF MAKUTA, and sworn enemy of the TOA.

HISTORY

Information on Makuta's past is sketchy at best, much of it having come from either legend or his own statements (the truth of which is open to debate). According to Matoran lore, Makuta was MATA NUI (1)'s "brother" — however, since it was not a biological relationship, it is unclear just what their bond might have been. What has been verified is that at some point in the distant past, Makuta took an oath to protect the Matoran. He was so highly regarded that he had an elite team of Toa dedicated to serving and guarding him (see TOA HAGAH).

MAKUTA

After smashing a rebellion against Mata Nui (1) by the LEAGUE OF SIX KINGDOMS some 80,000 years ago, Makuta began to consider the possibility of seizing power for himself. Both he and the larger Brotherhood of Makuta began oppressing and enslaving the Matoran. Legend states that Makuta coveted the devotion the Matoran showed for Mata Nui and wanted it for himself. He set in motion events that would eventually lead to Mata Nui falling into an unending sleep, and worked with the ENERGIZED PROTODERMIS ENTITY to create dangerous RAHI mutations. In addition, he mounted an operation to raid ARTAKHA to steal the KANOHI AVOHKII, the Mask of Light. Discovering his treachery, the Toa Hagah turned on him. They succeeded in temporarily defeating Makuta and retrieving the Avohkii, but only at the cost of being turned into RAHAGA by Makuta's lieutenant, ROODAKA.

Centuries later, Makuta reappeared, this time posing as Turaga DUME and ruling METRU NUI. Reduced in stature due to his earlier defeat, he was forced to rely on DARK HUNTERS to achieve his ends. He ordered many of the city's Toa to go on dangerous missions, from which they did not return. He also sent NIDHIKI and KREKKA to capture Toa LHIKAN.

His plan was simple and frightening. He would have the city's Matoran placed into spheres which would render them comatose and erase their memories. Using the Kanohi VAHI, the Mask of Time, he would cause this to happen rapidly — years for the Matoran, but only days for Makuta. Then he would awaken them and be hailed as their rescuer.

At first, all went well. The Matoran were put to sleep. Makuta drained the energy of the city's power plant, and absorbed Nidhiki, Krekka, and NIVAWK, regaining his full power (and killing the three of them in the process). Mata Nui lapsed into unconsciousness. But the TOA METRU intervened, with VAKAMA keeping the Vahi from Makuta. In the ensuing fight, Lhikan, now a Turaga, was killed by Makuta. The six Toa then combined their powers and imprisoned Makuta behind solid protodermis branded with a TOA SEAL.

His body was trapped, but not his mind. He reached out and summoned Roodaka, SIDORAK, and the VISORAK hordes to Metru Nui. While the hordes attacked and captured the city's Rahi, Roodaka worked on a way to free Makuta. She eventually achieved this end by absorbing a portion of the elemental energy of the six Toa. Doing so brought her close to death, but she was rescued at the last moment by Makuta.

Free again, Makuta made an attempt to seize the Vahi, but was opposed by both the SHADOWED ONE and Vakama. This clash led to the outbreak of the DARK HUNTER-BROTHERHOOD OF MAKUTA WAR. Vakama was successful in keeping the Vahi away from Makuta.

After the Toa Metru transported the Matoran to the island of MATA NUI (2), Makuta became a constant menace to them. Operating out of one of his numerous lairs, this one called MANGAIA, he used infected KANOHI to take over Rahi and harass the Matoran. In fact, he was not trying to destroy them. He was simply trying to keep them from ever returning to Metru Nui, for he knew if they ever did Mata Nui might reawaken.

The tide began to turn with the arrival of six Toa: TAHU, POHATU, GALI, KOPAKA, ONUA, and LEWA. They opposed Makuta, defeated his Rahi, his MANAS guardians, and the SHADOW TOA he sent against them. Then they triumphed over the master of shadows himself, apparently saving the Matoran.

But Makuta was not defeated, merely weakened. He bought time by unleashing the BOHROK on Mata Nui while he regained his strength. But whatever plans he might have been making were changed by TAKUA's discovery of the Kanohi AVOHKII, the Mask of Light. Knowing the coming of a Toa of Light might mean his doom, Makuta sent his RAHKSHI to try and retrieve the mask. They were defeated by the TOA NUVA. Makuta challenged TAKANUVA, the Toa of Light, and in the resulting combat the two were merged into a combined entity called TAKUTANUVA. With Takanuva's mind dominating the entity, Takutanuva opened the gateway that led to Metru Nui.

In an act of great self-sacrifice, Takutanuva surrendered part of his life force to revive JALLER, who had been killed by a Rahkshi. Thus weakened, he could no longer support the gateway, which came crashing down even as the entity split back into its two halves. Takanuva was revived by the power of light, but of Makuta there was no sign. He was presumed dead by the Toa Nuva.

But Makuta had survived. His species had long ago evolved past the point of needing physical bodies, and instead consisted of energy inside armor. With his armor shattered, his energy was unleashed in the form of ANTIDERMIS. He used his powers to telepathically influence the PIRAKA to search for the KANOHI IGNIKA on VOYA NUI, and allowed his essence to be used in ZAMOR SPHERES to enslave the Matoran population of that island. During a battle between AXONN and BRUTAKA, the vat containing the antidermis was shattered, leaving Makuta without a body once more.

Undeterred, Makuta continued his pursuit of the Mask of Life, first possessing the body of MATORO and later the shell of MAXILOS. He has told Matoro that he does want the life of Mata Nui saved, but it is doubtful that is the full truth. He remains an enormous threat to the entire universe.

Note: "Makuta" is also the name of his species, as well as the title given by Matoran to its members. See BROTHERHOOD OF MAKUTA.

POWERS

One of the most powerful entities in the BIONICLE universe, Makuta wields the energies of darkness. He is an incredibly skilled shape-shifter and mimic, has strong telepathic powers, can summon a mighty vortex, and possesses all of the powers of the various Rahkshi. He also has the ability to create KRAATA from his own substance.

In his large, armored forms, he has physical strength exceeding that of a Toa. When weakened, he tends to rely more on surrogates to fight his battles. His knowledge of the universe exceeds both that of the Toa and Turaga, allowing him to use things like the Bohrok against them.

In the past, Makuta has been seen to use his mental powers to create Shadow Toa from the darkness inside the Toa; trigger sandstorms, tidal waves, and volcanic eruptions; transform his body into a vortex; and appear as everything from a Matoran to an armored, winged giant. He has been defeated at least three times, but never for long.

PERSONALITY

Makuta is ruthless, deceitful, and capable of almost any act in the furtherance of his cause. At the same time, if asked, he would insist that everything he is doing is for the good of Mata Nui and the Matoran. He sees Toa as annoyances who are committing a crime against the universe by defying his will. His strengths are his cunning, his imagination, his ability to rebound from defeat, his vast knowledge, and his sheer willpower. His weaknesses are overconfidence, pride, and a tendency to underestimate his opponents.

EQUIPMENT

Makuta wore the Kanohi KRAAHKAN, the Great Mask of Shadows, and carried the STAFF OF DARKNESS which channeled his power. The Kraahkan has since been lost beneath the sea around Metru Nui. The whereabouts of the staff are unknown.

MAKUTA FISH (mah-KOO-tah):
An incredibly ugly breed of fish capable of leaping from the water to attack larger creatures. It got its name during a battle with TOA METRU MATAU in an underground cavern. Matau noted that the faces of the grotesque fish reminded him of Makuta, and the name stuck. TOA NOKAMA would later fashion a trident out of Makuta fish bones which she would carry with her as a TURAGA.

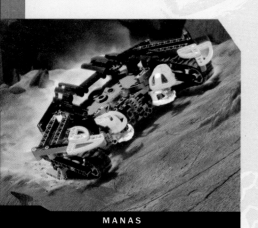

MANAS

MANAS (MAH-nuhz):
Huge, powerful crablike creatures who served as the guardians of MAKUTA's lair during the time the MATORAN were on MATA NUI (2). The word "manas" is Matoran for "monster," and it was said that no single TOA could ever hope to defeat one of these creatures. They were first spotted by the TOA METRU while sailing from METRU NUI to Mata Nui, but did not play a large role in the battle that followed. Later, the team of TAHU, KOPAKA, LEWA, GALI, ONUA, and POHATU would be forced to form two much more powerful entities — the TOA KAITA, AKAMAI, and WAIRUHA — to defeat the Manas. Onua and Turaga WHENUA later defeated the Manas again in a subterranean cavern by unleashing a swarm of KOFO-JAGA upon them.

Prior to the arrival of the Toa on Mata Nui, no Matoran of that land had ever seen the Manas and survived to tell the tale. They were so fierce that when not fighting opponents, they would turn on each other. Some have theorized that they were more than just RAHI, since they seemed to have some connection to energy towers constructed by Makuta. When those towers were destroyed, the Manas were apparently weakened, giving rise to the thought that they may have been drawing strength or sustenance from the towers. Manas were also found in large numbers in the realm of KARZAHNI.

MANA KO (MAH-nah KOH):

Fierce RAHI used by MAKUTA to guard his MANGAIA lair. Mana Ko are large, blocky-looking Rahi with the power to fire explosive blasts at opponents (or virtually anything else that attracts their attention). Although believed by the TOA and MATORAN to be evil creatures, the Mana Ko are in fact loyal to the ORDER OF MATA NUI and are expected to oppose the BROTHERHOOD OF MAKUTA in any final battle.

MANGAI (MAHN-gigh):

The great volcano of MATA NUI (2). Molten lava still streams from this site, feeding the lava farms of TA-WAHI. A potentially destructive eruption of the Mangai triggered by MAKUTA was countered by ONUA and LEWA, who used a combination of speed and strength to dig a trench for the lava to flow into.

MANGAIA (MAHN-gigh-uh):

One of a number of lairs of MAKUTA. Mangaia was located beneath KINI-NUI. It was here that the TOA fought the MANAS, the SHADOW TOA, and Makuta himself. Later, Makuta created the RAHKSHI here and sent them forth to battle the Toa Nuva. TAKANUVA used the USSANUI to travel to Mangaia and confront Makuta.

One of the major features of Mangaia was a huge stone gateway so heavy no Toa or group of Toa could lift it. Only TAKUTANUVA, the merged being formed from Makuta and Takanuva, could open this door. The gateway later crashed down upon Takutanuva, with only Takanuva known to have survived. The door led to the shores of a protodermis sea, beyond which was the city of METRU NUI.

Believing Makuta to be dead, the six PIRAKA traveled to Mangaia to loot his treasures. It was here that HAKANN found the SPEAR OF FUSION and used it to split VEZOK into two beings, the other being VEZON. It was also here that the essence of Makuta telepathically "suggested" the Piraka seek out the KANOHI IGNIKA on VOYA NUI.

A pool of ENERGIZED PROTODERMIS existed in Mangaia, used by Makuta to create Rahkshi from KRAATA. This same pool was responsible for the creation of TAKUTANUVA.

MANTAX (MAN-tacks):

One of the six BARRAKI who menace MAHRI NUI. Mantax was originally a member of the LEAGUE OF SIX KINGDOMS and ruled the central region of their empire. From the start, he was highly secretive in nature and rarely shared information on conditions in his realm. He even brokered separate trade deals with METRU NUI and XIA without informing the other League members.

Mantax joined the League in an attempt to rebel against MATA NUI (1), and he and his army were defeated by the BROTHERHOOD OF MAKUTA. He was condemned to the PIT by BOTAR and spent most of the next 80,000 years there. Then, some 1,000 years ago, a massive earthquake shattered the walls of his prison. He escaped with the others, but was mutated by the seawater into the form he has now. No longer able to breathe air, he was trapped beneath the waves.

This did nothing to change his loner attitude. He spent half his time buried in the sea floor, waiting for prey to swim by, and the other half no one knew where. In fact, Mantax was exploring his former prison, searching for proof that the Barraki had been betrayed from within.

When the KANOHI IGNIKA appeared underwater, Mantax joined with the other Barraki in an attempt to claim it. He later battled with TOA MAHRI HAHLI, who finally succeeded

MANTAX

in deceiving him into believing the other Barraki had betrayed him. Mantax invited Hahli to become his lieutenant and she accepted, leading an army of manta rays toward MAHRI NUI. When buried in sand, only Mantax's eyes and head spikes are visible. These spikes are coated with a paralyzing venom. His right hand is a massive pincer, and his left holds a SQUID LAUNCHER. The tail-like tentacle on his back is a lightning conductor and he has thick, armored shoulder plates to protect his body. Mantax rarely speaks, but is an excellent listener, which adds to his effectiveness as a hunter.

MATA NUI (MAH-tah NOO-ee):

[1] The GREAT SPIRIT revered by the MATORAN. Both the GREAT TEMPLE in METRU NUI and KINI-NUI on the island of MATA NUI (2)were dedicated to him, and of course the island of Mata Nui was named in his honor. According to Matoran legend, Mata Nui was sent from paradise by the GREAT BEINGS to care for all living things. After many thousands of years of his benevolent guidance, Mata Nui was struck down by his spirit brother MAKUTA. This resulted in Mata Nui sinking into an endless sleep and heralded a time of darkness for the Matoran.

MATA NUI

Upon Mata Nui's fall, a team of six TOA including TAHU, GALI, LEWA, ONUA, POHATU, and KOPAKA was dispatched to awaken him. While they have made progress, they have not yet been successful in reversing the effects of Makuta's actions.

Following the return of the Matoran to METRU NUI, it was discovered that Mata Nui was not just asleep, but dying. The TOA NUVA were dispatched to VOYA NUI to retrieve the KANOHI IGNIKA, the only artifact that could save his life. It is known that the Ignika was used at least one other time for a similar purpose by a team headed by Toa JOVAN. If Mata Nui were to die, the universe would die with him.

[2] Island in an unnamed sea, and home to the Matoran. The island was named after the Great Spirit Mata Nui (1) by Turaga VAKAMA. It consists of six regions: GA-WAHI, LE-WAHI, KO-WAHI, PO-WAHI, ONU-WAHI, and TA-WAHI. Each region has distinct geographic features and the climates are vastly different from one place to the other.

The TOA METRU brought the Matoran here when Metru Nui became unsafe for them. The Matoran constructed six KORO here, as well as Kini-Nui and other landmarks. RAHI also traveled from Metru Nui to this island. Initially, the Matoran were able to travel freely from place to place on the island. But Makuta used infected masks to take over Rahi and set them against the Matoran, making overland travel highly dangerous.

TAHU and his team of Toa washed up on the shores of Mata Nui after spending 1,000 years floating in the ocean in canisters. They defended the island from attacks by Rahi, BOHROK, BOHROK-KAL, and RAHKSHI. The Bohrok, in particular, did severe damage to the villages and the natural terrain of Mata Nui.

After the rediscovery of Metru Nui, the Matoran began building boats to transport them back to that city, which had been their original home. Whether the Matoran will ever have reason to return to Mata Nui again remains to be seen.

MATA NUI FISHING BIRD (MAH-tah NOO-ee):

Clever and noisy birds often spotted splashing along the LE-METRU coastline, and later in LE-WAHI. Too fast for most aquatic predators, these birds seem to delight in teasing their enemies by flying close, then soaring away at the last moment.

MATATU (MAH-tah-too):

KANOHI Mask of Telekinesis. TOA NUJU wore the Great Mask version of this, using its power to free himself, ONEWA, WHENUA, and LHIKAN from the PRISON OF THE DARK HUNTERS. As a TURAGA, he wore the Noble Matatu, once using it to save a powerless KOPAKA NUVA from plunging into a crevasse.

MATAU (mah-TOW):

TOA METRU of Air, guardian of LE-METRU, and later TURAGA of LE-KORO.

HISTORY

Matau was in the middle of doing one of his favorite things — testing a new vehicle on the Le-Metru TEST TRACK — when TOA LHIKAN gave him a TOA STONE and a map to the GREAT TEMPLE. Intrigued, Matau traveled there and encountered five other MATORAN — NUJU, ONEWA, WHENUA, NOKAMA, and VAKAMA. They placed their Toa stones into the TOA SUVA and were transformed into mighty Toa heroes. Matau was thrilled, believing that being a "Toa hero" was the key to lasting fame.

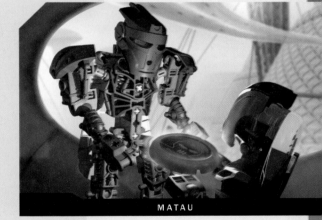

MATAU

He teamed with Nokama to find two GREAT DISKS in GA-METRU and Le-Metru, and was part of the successful effort to use the disks to destroy the MORBUZAKH plant. When the Toa went to the COLISEUM to present the disks to Turaga DUME, Matau was convinced they would be hailed as heroes. Instead, they were branded impostors by Dume, who ordered them arrested. (The Toa Metru did not realize at this point that Dume was MAKUTA in disguise.)

Whenua, Onewa, and Nuju were captured, with Vakama, Nokama, and Matau escaping. They survived a battle with Vahki and the DARK HUNTERS on an AIRSHIP, then stowed away on a VAHKI TRANSPORT into PO-METRU. There they fought the Dark Hunters again, formed an alliance with the KIKANALO, and helped to free their three friends and Lhikan, now a Turaga. During the battle, Matau discovered his mask power of shape-shifting and used it to confuse NIDHIKI and KREKKA.

Matau participated in the defeat of Makuta, the rescue of six Matoran spheres, and the trip to MATA NUI (2). He acted as pilot for both the *LHIKAN* and the *LHIKAN II*. His initial experience on LE-WAHI was not a positive one, as he promptly got lost in the FAU SWAMP.

On the return journey to Metru Nui, Matau grew increasingly annoyed with Vakama's harsh attitude. His mood was not improved any when the *Lhikan II* was shipwrecked and Nuju blamed "pilot error." Matau blamed Vakama for leading the Toa Metru into the trap that resulted in their being mutated into TOA HORDIKA. Of all the Toa, he had the hardest time adjusting to his new appearance and was torn between rescuing the Matoran and searching for KEETONGU, who might hold the key to a cure.

Matau later joined with the other Toa Hordika in a final battle with the Visorak horde, and convinced Vakama (who had defected to the enemy) to ally with the Toa once more. Victorious, the Hordika were transformed back into Toa Metru through the power of KEETONGU.

TURAGA MATAU

Matau traveled by airship with the other Toa and the sleeping Matoran to the island of Mata Nui (2). There, the Toa Metru willingly sacrificed their power to awaken the Matoran, transforming into Turaga in the process.

As a Turaga, Matau supervised the construction of LE-KORO, as well as its reconstruction after the BOHROK invasion. Along with the Toa LEWA and the LE-MATORAN, he was fitted with a KRANA and controlled by the Bohrok swarm for a short time.

He has since returned to Metru Nui with the other Turaga and the Matoran.

POWERS

TOA INIKA TURAGA MATAU

Matau was the master of air. He could summon a windstorm or cyclone, raise the air pressure in a chamber until the walls burst, or absorb all the air in a room into his body before releasing it in a massive blast. He was also a skilled flyer with the aid of his Toa tools.

PERSONALITY

Matau loved being a Toa Metru. To him, it was all excitement and fun and the chance to be remembered forever for heroic deeds. Even in the darkest moments, he never fully lost his sense of humor or his taste for adventure. Only when he was transformed into a Toa Hordika did Matau succumb to bitterness. But even then, he remained fiercely loyal to Nokama and the other Toa. Only his relationship with Vakama suffered during this period.

As a Turaga, Matau could be calm and wise one moment, and pull a practical joke the next. His motto was "talk ever-quick, and move ever-quicker." Although he could be a prankster, he was also seen as a brave leader who would never ask a Matoran to do something he would not do himself. As a result, the Le-Matoran were fiercely loyal to him.

EQUIPMENT

As a Toa Metru, Matau carried twin aero slicers that doubled as wings. He wore the Kanohi MAHIKI, the Great Mask of Illusion. As a Toa Hordika, he carried twin FANG BLADES. As a Turaga, he carried a Kau Kau staff and wore the Noble Mahiki.

MATORAN (mat-OAR-an):

Villagers on METRU NUI, MATA NUI, VOYA NUI, MAHRI NUI, and elsewhere. There are seven known types of Matoran: KO-MATORAN, PO-MATORAN, GA-MATORAN, ONU-MATORAN, TA-MATORAN, LE-MATORAN, and AV-MATORAN, normally identified by the color of their armor and KANOHI. Matoran are the only beings so far shown to be able to evolve into TOA. Groups of six Matoran, one from each village, are capable of merging into the MATORAN NUI. Matoran were the first creation of the GREAT BEINGS in this universe. The leavings from the process that brought them into being were used to create KRANA and ZYGLAK. Matoran built ARTAKHA, KARZAHNI, Metru Nui, and many other cities.

The Matoran lived on Metru Nui until they were captured by MAKUTA and forced into MATORAN SPHERES. There they were thrown into a form of suspended animation. This lasted until they were brought to MATA NUI (2) and awakened by the TOA METRU. Over time, the Matoran's bodies shrank in stature and they lost all memory of their lives on Metru Nui, after-effects of their time in the spheres.

They built six villages, or KORO, on Mata Nui and lived there for 1,000 years, much of it spent fighting off RAHI sent by Makuta. The Matoran universally welcomed the coming of TAHU and his team of Toa, believing they would reawaken MATA NUI (1) and defeat Makuta.

Following the defeat of the BOHROK-KAL, the TURAGA taught the Matoran how to rebuild themselves so that they could be stronger and more agile. It is believed the Turaga may have learned this secret from the RAHAGA at some point in the past.

These Matoran have since returned to Metru Nui to bring that city back to life.

The Matoran of Voya Nui and Mahri Nui originally came from a number of different places. They were sent to the realm of KARZAHNI for repair, where they were changed for the worse. Karzahni then shipped them out to one of the mainland continents, where they took up residence. During the GREAT CATACLYSM, a portion of the continent called Voya Nui was torn free and ended up on the surface of the ocean. Its Turaga was killed and the Matoran had to survive on their own. Much later, a portion of Voya Nui called Mahri Nui broke off and sank into the PIT, taking its Matoran with it. Voya Nui was later attacked by the PIRAKA, with most of the Matoran being enslaved and those who remained forming the MATORAN RESISTANCE. Beneath the waves, the Matoran of Mahri Nui fought a no less spirited war against the BARRAKI.

Known Matoran have included AHKMOU, NUHRII, VHISOLA, ORKAHM, EHRYE, TEHUTTI, HAHLI, HEWKII, HAFU, JALLER, TAKUA, KOPEKE, KONGU, MACKU, KAPURA, ONEPU, NUPARU, MAVRAH, MATORO, KODAN, KOTU, SARDA, IDRIS, DEFILAK, DEKAR, KYREHX, GARAN, BALTA, DEZALK, VELIKA, DALU, PIRUK, and KAZI. See individual entries.

THE MATORAN ALPHABET

◐ = A	⊘ = N
◓ = B	◒ = O
◑ = C	◍ = P
◪ = D	◖ = Q
⊖ = E	◉ = R
⊟ = F	◎ = S
⊕ = G	⊝ = T
⊞ = H	○ = U
◫ = I	⊗ = V
◩ = J	⊗ = W
⊘ = K	⊗ = X
◧ = L	⊗ = Y
◫ = M	⊘ = Z

MATORAN NUI [mat-OAR-an NOO-ee]:
A being formed by the merging of six MATORAN. The Matoran Nui has been created at least twice, once on METRU NUI by AHKMOU, EHRYE, NUHRII, ORKAHM, TEHUTTI, and VHISOLA, and once on MATA NUI by HEWKII, JALLER, KONGU, MACKU, MATORO, and ONEPU.

MATORAN RESISTANCE:
Name given to a small band of VOYA NUI villagers who fought a valiant battle against the invading PIRAKA. The Matoran resistance briefly clashed with the TOA NUVA, allied with the TOA INIKA, and eventually rescued the Nuva from the Piraka's trap. The six members were GARAN, BALTA, DALU, VELIKA, PIRUK, and KAZI.

MATORAN SPHERE [mat-OAR-an]:
Rounded silver containers in which MAKUTA imprisoned the MATORAN of METRU NUI. These spheres caused the Matoran to go into suspended animation. They were later rescued and reawakened by the TOA METRU.

MATORO

MATORO [mat-OR-oh]:

Former KO-MATORAN translator for Turaga NUJU, later TOA INIKA and TOA MAHRI, and destined bearer of the KANOHI IGNIKA.

HISTORY

During his time on METRU NUI, he spent many days and nights in the ARCHIVES studying the language and behavior of RAHI. He later opened a small trading post offering small Rahi to other MATORAN for use as pets.

TOA INIKA MATORO

Once on MATA NUI (2), Matoro swiftly built a reputation as an efficient tracker and hunter of Rahi. He gave that up when he was tapped to lead KO-KORO's KOLHII team. But easily his most important role on the island has been aide to Turaga Nuju. Only Matoro fully understands Nuju's strange language of clicks and whistles. It is his job to translate for the Turaga, even at the councils of the village leaders. This has put him in the uncomfortable position of having knowledge he cannot share with the other Matoran, or having to translate some of Nuju's ruder comments to Turaga and Toa alike.

Matoro was the first to encounter Toa KOPAKA after that hero arrived on Mata Nui. Kopaka later saved Matoro from a NUI-RAMA attack. Later, Matoro rescued TAKUA when the Chronicler was lost in the snow drifts of KO-WAHI.

After the Matoran returned to the city of Metru Nui, Matoro was one of five Matoran who joined JALLER on a mission to find the missing Toa Nuva. Along the way, they encountered KARZAHNI, who stole their original masks from them and replaced them with others. Matoro also had the bizarre experience of feeling himself holding someone's hand in a dark tunnel, only to find there was no one there. What he did not know was that the power of the Kanohi Ignika was reaching out to him from a great distance, testing his courage and resolve.

Lightning from the RED STAR struck the TOA CANISTERS the Matoran used to reach the island of VOYA NUI. This energy transformed Matoro and the others into Toa Inika. Matoro was never entirely comfortable as a Toa, feeling that his background as a scholar did not leave him well-suited for the role. When the Inika encountered a situation where one of them had to willingly sacrifice himself or herself for the mission to continue, Matoro volunteered to die. He ceased to exist but then was immediately reborn, and now truly destined to be the bearer of the Mask of Life.

After the defeat of VEZON, Matoro wrested the mask from him, but then lost it when KARDAS hurled a blast of energy at him. The mask flew to the surface of the island and then plunged beneath the sea. The Inika had to travel through the CORD to try and retrieve it. Along the way, Matoro used his mask power to unleash his spirit and scout ahead. During that time, when his body was vacant, MAKUTA possessed it and attempted to manipulate the Inika into serving his ends. Makuta was eventually driven out and Matoro restored to his true body.

When the Toa Inika reached the end of the Cord, a wave of energy from the Kanohi Ignika transformed them into TOA MAHRI. While scouting on his own, Matoro was captured by HYDRAXON, who had mistaken him for an escapee from the PIT. He was freed by the robotic guard MAXILOS, whose body was now inhabited by Makuta. Maxilos/Makuta warned him that if he revealed the truth to the other Toa, Makuta would destroy them. Matoro has been forced to accept Makuta's help in the quest to find the Mask of Life once more.

POWERS

Like KOPAKA NUVA, Matoro controlled the element of ice.

PERSONALITY

Matoro has grown used to the burden of keeping secrets. During his time on the island of Mata Nui, he learned many things from sitting in on Turaga meetings, none of which he could share with his fellow Matoran. Now he is the only one who knows Makuta is in the midst of the Toa Mahri. Although he first doubted his fitness to be a Toa, his experiences on Voya Nui have increased Matoro's confidence. His relationship with Jaller has become strained as a result of the importance of his role with regard to the Ignika.

EQUIPMENT

As a Toa Inika, Matoro wore the Kanohi IDEN, the Mask of Spirit, and carried an energized ice sword. As a Toa Mahri, he wears the Kanohi TRYNA, the Mask of Reanimation, and carries a CORDAK BLASTER and twin CUTTERS.

MATORO'S RAHI (mat-OR-oh rah-HEE):
Small business run by MATORO in METRU NUI, selling little RAHI for use as pets.

MAVRAH (MAHV-rah):
An ONU-MATORAN archivist in METRU NUI. Along with WHENUA, Mavrah was part of a secret project to study ancient aquatic RAHI who had appeared in the ocean around the city. When it became obvious that keeping the beasts confined was a threat to the ARCHIVES and the rest of Metru Nui, TURAGA DUME ordered that the project be shut down and the Rahi driven back out to sea by the VAHKI. Unwilling to give up his work, Mavrah led the creatures out of the Archives himself and through a tunnel in the GREAT BARRIER. There he took up residence in a cavern while his Rahi lived in an underground river. He also allied with a small number of KRALHI, mechanical order enforcers who had been driven from the city long ago.
Many years later, the TOA METRU traveled that same river as they attempted to find a new land in which the MATORAN could live. Believing them to be agents of Dume sent to take him back, Mavrah unleashed his Rahi on them and attempted to kill the TOA. In the middle of a three-way battle between Toa, Rahi, and Vahki, Toa ONEWA forced Mavrah to see the destruction his methods were causing. Guilt-ridden and dismayed, Mavrah rushed to the water's edge, calling for the fighting to cease. But the battle had turned the river waters violent, and Mavrah was washed away by a sudden wave. He is presumed to be dead.

MAXILOS (MACKS-ih-LOHS):
Robot guardian of the PIT. After that prison area was shattered by the GREAT CATACLYSM and the jailer, HYDRAXON, killed, Maxilos and his RAHI "bloodhound" SPINAX wandered the waters without purpose. When the KANOHI IGNIKA appeared in the region, HYDRAXON mysteriously returned and recruited Maxilos to serve as a guard once more. Shortly after that, Maxilos's robot body was possessed by the energy of MAKUTA. While inhabiting that shell, Makuta struck up an uneasy alliance with TOA MAHRI MATORO to get the Ignika away from the BARRAKI. Other than Matoro, no one knows that Maxilos is truly Makuta. Maxilos carries

a CORDAK BLASTER and a power sword. He now also has access to all 40-plus of Makuta's powers.

MEMORY CRYSTAL:

Objects used in KNOWLEDGE TOWERS to store information.
Data can be recorded in the crystal by means of physical contact with a scholar, but the operation must be triggered by the will of that scholar. FROST BEETLES are believed to have attained greater-than-average intelligence by consuming memory crystals.

METRU (MET-troo):

Districts in the city of METRU NUI. There are six metru: GA-METRU, KO-METRU, LE-METRU, ONU-METRU, PO-METRU, and TA-METRU. See individual entries.

METRU MANTIS (MET-troo):

Nocturnal, meat-eating insectlike creatures found on both METRU NUI and MATA NUI (2). Their favorite prey was NUI-RAMA, NUI-JAGA, and other insectoids. They averaged six to eight feet in height and tended to be tame unless provoked. After the arrival of the VISORAK, Metru Mantis began feasting on them as well, and the RAHAGA considered them a potent strike force against the invaders. Metru Mantis hunted by grabbing their prey with their forelegs and then injecting a sedating venom through their bite.

METRU NUI (MET-troo NOO-ee):

Island city that floats on a PROTODERMIS sea far beneath the surface of MATA NUI (2). Metru Nui is the original home of the MATORAN who later settled on Mata Nui (2). It is divided into six districts, or metru: KO-METRU, TA-METRU, GA-METRU, ONU-METRU, PO-METRU, and LE-METRU. It is also known as the "CITY OF LEGENDS."

During much of its existence, Metru Nui was ruled by Turaga DUME, protected by Toa LHIKAN and other Toa, and guarded by the VAHKI. Metru Nui was once the site of a major conflict between the Toa and the DARK HUNTERS.

When MAKUTA impersonated Dume, he sent all the Toa but Lhikan out of the city and invited the DARK HUNTERS in to capture the remaining hero. He also unleashed the MORBUZAKH plant, which wrecked many outlying areas. Before he was through, the city power plant had been destroyed, most of the Vahki blown to pieces by a power surge, Lhikan had been killed, and the Matoran had been placed in MATORAN SPHERES which kept them comatose. The city was wracked by a major earthquake that damaged buildings throughout the metru. Only the actions of the six TOA METRU stopped Makuta before things got worse.

After the TOA METRU departed the city to search for a new home for the Matoran, the VISORAK horde moved in and shrouded the city in webs. The Toa Metru, transformed into TOA HORDIKA, had to challenge the Visorak for control of the city.

METRU NUI

After the Matoran reached Mata Nui (2), they eventually lost all memory of Metru Nui due to the aftereffects of being in the spheres. The city was not rediscovered until TAKANUVA, the Toa of Light, defeated Makuta. The Matoran and Turaga have since repopulated the city and are at work rebuilding it. Takanuva remains there on guard by order of Turaga Dume.

After a mission to VOYA NUI, the Toa Nuva returned to Metru Nui and broke into the GREAT TEMPLE to retrieve a mysterious scroll. Its contents list all that the Toa must do to prepare the universe for the reawakening of the Great Spirit Mata Nui (1).

MIMIC:
DARK HUNTER capable of duplicating any physical feat he sees perfectly and without practice.

MINION:
Mute former enforcer for the BROTHERHOOD OF MAKUTA who now works for the DARK HUNTERS. His claws are long and razor-sharp and his armor is impenetrable.

MIO (MY-oh):
A unit of MATORAN measurement. A mio is equal to 1,000 kio, or 850 miles/1,370 kilometers.

MIRU (MEAR-roo):
The Mask of Levitation. Although often mistaken for a mask of flight, what this KANOHI actually did was to prevent a flying wearer from falling to earth. While wearing a Miru, a user could ride on air currents and rely on the mask's power to repel the ground and keep him aloft. By controlling the mask, the being could then descend slowly. The Miru did not allow flight from a standing start. This mask was worn by TOA LEWA when he first appeared on MATA NUI (2).

MORAK

MIRU NUVA (MEAR-roo NOO-vah):
The more powerful version of the Mask of Levitation, this mask actually did allow a semblance of flight. With a proper head start, a user could rise into the air and remain aloft without having to rely on updrafts.

MORAK (more-ACK):
One of the HYDRUKA used by the MATORAN of MAHRI NUI to harvest air from AIRWEED.

MORBUZAKH (MORE-boo-ZACK):
An intelligent plant creature created by MAKUTA as part of his plan to capture the MATORAN of METRU NUI. The Morbuzakh was actually Makuta's second attempt at such a creation, the first being the KARZAHNI (2). When the Karzahni proved to be too ambitious and willful, Makuta banished it and made the Morbuzakh.

MORBUZAKH

The purpose of this creature was to drive the Matoran away from the outskirts of the city and toward the COLISEUM, making it easier for them to be rounded up by the VAHKI. The Morbuzakh also captured a number of Matoran for Makuta. Its primary tools were its vines, which were so long they could reach anywhere in the city. The massive king root of the Morbuzakh was hidden inside the GREAT FURNACE in TA-METRU.

The Morbuzakh thrived on heat and flame. It was able to spread via seeds, which clung to the ceilings of furnaces and foundries throughout the METRU. When these seeds struck a solid object, they sprouted and the vines immediately wrapped themselves around whatever was nearest. The TOA METRU were almost smothered by these baby vines.

Using the power of the GREAT DISKS, the Toa Metru were able to defeat the Morbuzakh even as it brought the Great Furnace down around itself. The king root and all its vines crumbled to dust. No further sign of it has ever been seen.

While it lived, the Morbuzakh was able to communicate by telepathy with other species and to gather information about the world outside through its vines. Shortly before its death, it claimed that its ultimate purpose was to conquer the city and enslave the Matoran. It is doubtful Makuta would have reacted well to this change of plan.

MOTO-HUB

MOTO-HUB:

Site of the vehicle manufacturing factories and CHUTE system controls in METRU NUI. The Moto-Hub was the center of LE-METRU and the place of employment for roughly half of the LE-MATORAN. Chutes, air vehicles, and ground vehicles were all produced there, with the latter often being tried out on the TEST TRACK. KONGU worked here as a chute controller and MATAU spent much of his spare time here when he was a MATORAN.

The Moto-Hub was badly damaged in an earthquake prior to the VISORAK invasion. The TOA METRU hid here to avoid a VAHKI squad and later defeated a mutant LOHRAK who was on the loose in the structure.

MOUNT IHU (EEE-hoo):

A high, snow- and ice-capped mountain in the center of MATA NUI (2). It was named by NUJU for IHU, his late Matoran mentor. KOPAKA found his first KANOHI mask, the HAU, on Mount Ihu, and later spied the other TOA gathering from there using his AKAKU. It would eventually become a place where Kopaka would go to be alone and think.

MOUNTAIN:

A sentient rock formation in the center of the island of XIA. Members of the VORTIXX species climb the Mountain in pairs as a rite of passage, a task made extremely dangerous by the fact that the Mountain can sense their presence and will try to consume them.

MOUNT VALMAI:

Volcanic mountain on the island of VOYA NUI. The PIRAKA initially believed the KANOHI IGNIKA was located somewhere inside the mountain and had the enslaved MATORAN working to drain the lava from inside of it. At least one Matoran died during this period from falling into the mouth of the volcano. AVAK and HAKANN combined their elemental powers to create a stone-lava monster who seemed to emerge from inside of Valmai.

MUAKA

MUAKA (moo-AH-kah):

A powerful tigerlike beast that plagued both METRU NUI and MATA NUI (2). Solitary hunters, Muaka were extremely quick for their size and more than strong enough to bring down most other RAHI. Muaka were particularly fond of RAHKSHI and were the only natural enemy of those creatures on Metru Nui. Perhaps because of that, MAKUTA made extensive use of Muaka when he set out to use Rahi against the MATORAN on Mata Nui. TOA KOPAKA and Toa LEWA challenged a number of Muaka shortly after arriving on the island, eventually defeating them and removing the INFECTED MASKS Makuta used to control them. KOPAKA NUVA and POHATU NUVA were menaced by a Muaka on MOUNT IHU after losing their elemental powers. TOA METRU WHENUA set a Muaka against a Rahkshi in an effort to save TEHUTTI. The Muaka relied primarily on its claws in a hunt. Sinking them into its prey, it forced the unfortunate victim to the ground and then finished the job with its teeth.

NAHO BAY:
A large body of water in GA-WAHI on MATA NUI (2), and site of the village of GA-KORO. Unknown to the MATORAN, Naho Bay covers one of the two openings in the surface of the island that once served as "suns" for METRU NUI. Also known as Lake Naho and Gali's Bay.

NAMING DAY:
Matoran holiday in which those villagers who have performed some great service for their KORO are rewarded with name changes. Past recipients of this honor include JALLER, HEWKII, and MACKU, among others. The exchange of gifts was also a part of Naming Day ceremonies, although that practice was more prevalent on METRU NUI than MATA NUI (2).

NEKTANN (NECK-tan):
Robotic weapons built by the PIRAKA to defend key points on VOYA NUI. Nektann fire concussive blasts and are heavily armored, except on the bottom. There are two types of nektann, fixed and mobile. TOA INIKA NUPARU defeated nektann outside of the PIRAKA STRONGHOLD.

NGALAWA (NIH-gah-LAH-wah):
A boat-racing competition popular in GA-KORO. Winners of Ngalawa tournaments received a COPPER MASK OF VICTORY.

NIDHIKI (nih-DEE-kee):
Former TOA of Air, betrayer of METRU NUI, and vicious DARK HUNTER. Nidhiki was one of 10 Toa summoned by LHIKAN to help defend Metru Nui against the KANOHI DRAGON. He remained in the city for many years afterward, helping to defend it against RAHI and occasionally venturing to other islands. But over time, he began to feel dissatisfied with his role. Turaga DUME and the Matoran were not, after all, as powerful as he and the other Toa — so why should the Toa serve their interests? Powerful beings should serve only themselves, and lesser beings should obey them, he decided. When the DARK HUNTERS attempted to create a base in the city, Dume opposed them and the Toa mobilized to defend Metru Nui. Nidhiki secretly made contact with the enemy and offered to betray the city into their hands. Before he could so, Lhikan discovered his treachery. The Dark Hunters were defeated and Nidhiki went with them when they departed. On the island of ODINA, Nidhiki attempted to become accustomed to life as a Dark Hunter, but found he missed the glory that came with being a Toa. He schemed with ROODAKA to escape the island, but she betrayed him and used her RHOTUKA SPINNER

NIDHIKI

to mutate him into an insectoid form. In this shape, he knew he would never be accepted on any Matoran-held island.

Nidhiki found that he was not fully trusted by the Dark Hunters (since no one trusts a traitor). As a result, he was teamed with KREKKA, a strong, dumb brute who was nevertheless scrupulously honest and devoted to carrying out orders. Krekka would make sure Nidhiki did not turn their missions into occasions for personal profit. Nidhiki was also told that he would be held responsible if any harm came to Krekka. He went along with this because he felt certain he could get around Krekka at some point if he had to, and because he hoped to use his place in the Dark Hunters to someday take over the entire organization.

After many adventures together, Nidhiki and Krekka were sent to Metru Nui to aid MAKUTA in his plans to capture the Matoran. They began by capturing Toa LHIKAN, an act Nidhiki found particularly satisfying. Then they intimidated AHKMOU into helping them get the six GREAT DISKS. When that plan was frustrated by the TOA METRU, they attempted to hunt down the new heroes. They battled the Toa in an airship, in PO-METRU, and outside of the COLISEUM, without success.

Finally, Makuta used his powers to absorb Nidhiki, Krekka, and NIVAWK into his own body, enhancing his power. Nidhiki was killed by the process.

In addition to his natural cunning, Nidhiki was capable of spitting force bolts at opponents and of flight. As a Toa, he wore the Kanohi VOLITAK, the Mask of Stealth.

NIGHT CREEPER:

A nocturnal creature found in ONU-METRU. Roughly seven feet long, squat, with powerful legs, night creepers forage for small insects and rodents. RAHAGA BOMONGA once saved a night creeper from a VISORAK in Onu-Metru.

NIGHTMARE CHAMBER:

Section of the 777-step staircase that led to the CHAMBER OF LIFE. In this area, the greatest fears of those passing through could come to life. The PIRAKA encountered and defeated IRNAKK here, and the TOA INIKA encountered illusions of LHIKAN and their greatest foes and were tricked into believing they had accidentally slain the Toa NUVA.

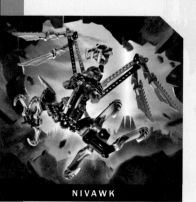

NIVAWK

NIVAWK [NEE-vawk]:

Given name of a RAHI hawk that served as a pet and spy for MAKUTA during the time he was posing as TURAGA DUME in METRU NUI. Though strong enough to transport its owner, it was used primarily to keep watch on the activities of TOA LHIKAN and later the TOA METRU. It would then report back to Makuta/Dume, who was capable of understanding its language. Makuta used a shadow claw to absorb Nivawk into his substance, later reappearing with Nivawk's wings as part of his new body. Nivawk is presumed dead.

NOBLE MASKS:
See KANOHI.

NOCTURN [KNOCK-turn]:

Hulking, tentacled prisoner of the PIT whose disappearance while in possession of the KANOHI IGNIKA set off a conflict among the BARRAKI. Nocturn was originally exiled to the Pit for destroying his home island. After the GREAT CATACLYSM shattered the cells, he fled into the black water with the other inmates. Being already amphibious, he had no problem surviving in the depths, and in fact proved to be immune to the mutagenic effects of the seawater. He became a sometime lieutenant to EHLEK and lost an arm in a clash with PRIDAK (the arm eventually grew back minus its tentacle). His dim intellect made him a bit unreliable in combat, but he did have a fierce loyalty to Ehlek (when he remembered who Ehlek was). After the Barraki got possession of the Ignika, it was decided it should be kept in a neutral spot so that no one warlord controlled it. They left it with Nocturn, along with a SQUID LAUNCHER and instructions to guard the mask and not leave its resting place. Nocturn promptly discovered that touching the mask had cursed him so that his slightest touch killed. Puzzled by this, he took the mask and wandered off to try and find Ehlek. When the Barraki checked back and found him gone, suspicions were born that one of them had taken the mask. Meanwhile, Nocturn battled HYDRAXON, who defeated him and took the Ignika with the intent of destroying it.

Nocturn has four arms, one of which is a tentacle, bulbous red eyes, and a spiked head. Lean, muscular, and extremely powerful, Nocturn is able to single-handedly defeat giant squid and RAZOR WHALES. In addition to his squid launcher, he carries sharp-bladed weapons.

NOKAMA (noh-KAH-mah):

TOA METRU of Water, guardian of GA-METRU, and later TURAGA of GA-KORO.

HISTORY

Nokama was in the middle of a lecture on the translation of ancient texts when TOA LHIKAN gave her a TOA STONE and a map leading to the GREAT TEMPLE. She traveled there and encountered five other MATORAN — MATAU, NUJU, ONEWA, VAKAMA, and WHENUA. They placed their Toa stones into the TOA SUVA and were transformed into mighty Toa heroes. Vakama had a vision that the city was in peril and that only finding the six GREAT DISKS would save it, but not all of the Toa Metru took him seriously. It was Nokama who insisted that as long as the chance existed that his visions might be a message from the GREAT SPIRIT, the Toa were obligated to act upon them.

Nokama teamed with Matau to retrieve the Ga-Metru and LE-METRU Great Disks. The Toa Metru used these disks to destroy the MORBUZAKH plant that threatened the city. But when they went to present the disks to Turaga Dume, he denounced them as impostors and ordered their arrest. Whenua, Onewa, and Nuju were captured, with Vakama, Nokama, and Matau escaping. They survived a battle with VAHKI and the DARK HUNTERS on an AIRSHIP, then stowed away on a VAHKI TRANSPORT into PO-METRU. There they fought the Dark Hunters again. Shortly after this battle, Nokama discovered how to trigger her mask power of translation and was able to communicate with the KIKANALO. With her help, the Toa were able to form an alliance with those RAHI and rescue the other three Toa and Lhikan (who was now a Turaga).

Nokama helped to rescue six of the Matoran, still trapped in their MATORAN SPHERES, and aided in the defeat of Makuta. During the initial voyage to MATA NUI (2), she carved a trident from the bones of a MAKUTA FISH (which would later be her symbol of office as a Turaga). She also carved an image of the six Toa Metru into the side of a tunnel.

On the journey back to Metru Nui, Nokama was seriously wounded in a fight with the RAHI NUI. The Toa were forced to make a deal with KARZAHNI (2) in order to get the herbs necessary to save her life.

NOKAMA

Along with the other Toa Metru, Nokama was transformed into a TOA HORDIKA by the VISORAK upon returning to Metru Nui. But unlike her friends, Nokama seemed to revel in the new connection she felt with nature and sea creatures as a Hordika. This, combined with her frequent rages, worried RAHAGA GAAKI, who feared that Nokama might come to like being a Hordika too much and never want to turn back. Nokama joined with the other Toa Hordika in a final battle with the Visorak horde, which the Toa won. The Rahi KEETONGU later used his powers to transform the Hordika back into Toa Metru.

TURAGA NOKAMA

Nokama traveled by airship with the other Toa Metru and the sleeping Matoran to Mata Nui (2). The Toa Metru willingly sacrificed their power to awaken the Matoran, transforming into Turaga in the process.
As a Turaga, Nokama supervised the construction of GA-KORO. When GALI arrived, Nokama stuck to the agreement made by the Turaga not to share any information about Metru Nui and the events there. But of all the Turaga, she was the least comfortable with the arrangement. She went so far as to lead Gali to the tunnel where her carving of the Toa Metru could be seen, though she denied having any connection with the figures in the picture.

TURAGA NOKAMA

Nokama returned to Metru Nui with the other Turaga, the Toa Nuva, and the Matoran. After discovering that the life of Mata Nui (1), and thus the entire universe was in danger, she broke ranks with the other Turaga and informed JALLER of the situation. This prompted him to gather a team of villagers and go in search of the missing Toa Nuva. See TOA INIKA.

POWERS

Nokama controlled the power of water. She could hurl jets of water at a foe, summon everything from a trickle of moisture to a tidal wave, calm raging waters, and survive for prolonged periods at great depths. Combined with a knack for strategy, this made her a formidable opponent. Perhaps her greatest victory was when she singlehandedly defeated three RAHKSHI.

PERSONALITY

Although she represented an element usually associated with peace and tranquility, Nokama was capable of flashes of temper and could be too sure of her own wisdom at times. Of all the Toa, she had the hardest time adjusting to the fact that her old Matoran friends did not know how to treat her after she transformed. After taking some time to get comfortable with her new self, she was able to forge friendships with the other Toa Metru that continued when they became Turaga. She was a strong supporter of Vakama, even after his actions led to the Toa Metru being transformed into Toa Hordika.
As a Turaga, Nokama was known for her logical approach to things. She had seen how often deciding things based purely on emotion had led to trouble. The GA-MATORAN respected her for the fact that she would always listen to every side carefully before making a decision on what action to take. She was strongly in favor of telling the Toa Nuva the truth about Metru Nui.

As a Toa Metru, Nokama carried twin HYDROBLADES that could pull her through the water at high speed. She wore the Kanohi RAU, the Great Mask of Translation. As a Toa Hordika, she carried twin FIN BARBS, which could dig through most substances and aid in climbing, as well as charge up her RHOTUKA SPINNER. As a Turaga, she carried a trident carved from Makuta fish bones and wore the Noble Rau.

NORIK (NOAR-ick):

Former TOA HAGAH of Fire, later mutated by ROODAKA into a RAHAGA. Norik had been the leader of an elite Toa team assigned to MAKUTA's personal guard. When they discovered Makuta was oppressing and enslaving MATORAN, they turned on him and attacked a fortress of the BROTHERHOOD OF MAKUTA. Norik and IRUINI were separated from the other Toa but managed to defeat the EXO-TOA and the DARK HUNTERS and drive Makuta off. They then went to rescue their friends, only to discover they had been turned by Roodaka into shrunken, twisted creatures with the faces of RAHKSHI. Although they saved their fellow heroes, they, too, were turned into Rahaga.

Norik later suggested that the Rahaga begin a search for KEETONGU, a legendary RAHI said to be able to reverse any affliction. Although Norik firmly believed that this beast existed, many of the other Rahaga did not share his faith. Still, they agreed to join him and eventually made their way to METRU NUI. There Norik saved Toa VAKAMA after he had been turned into a TOA HORDIKA, but he was unable to keep Vakama from turning away from his friends and succumbing to his bestial side.

As a Toa, Norik carried a LAVA SPEAR and a RHOTUKA SPINNER with the ability to slow an opponent. He wore the KANOHI PEHKUI, the Great Mask of Diminishment.

As a Rahaga, Iruini specialized in capturing RAHI reptiles and other crawling creatures, such as FURNACE SALAMANDERS. He carried a Rhotuka spinner with the *snare* power, which tangled the limbs of a target. His staff could be used to distract his intended target until he was ready to strike.

NORTH MARCH:

An icy pass near where KO-WAHI meets TA-WAHI. Shortly after the construction of KO-KORO, a guard post was established here by KO-MATORAN.

NOTCH:

An old portion of the CHUTE system in METRU NUI. A number of chutes met and wound around each other here. TOA MATAU retrieved a GREAT DISK from inside a FORCE SPHERE here.

NUHRII (NOO-ree):

A TA-MATORAN mask maker in TA-METRU. Resentful of VAKAMA's success, Nuhrii decided to use the Ta-Metru GREAT DISK to create a mask that would make him famous. Unfortunately, the DARK HUNTERS also wanted the disk and arranged for Nuhrii to be trapped in a house under attack by the MORBUZAKH. Vakama rescued Nuhrii and learned the location of the disk. The TOA and MATORAN worked together to retrieve the Great Disk from the FIRE PITS. Later, Nuhrii joined with AHKMOU, EHRYE, ORKAHM, TEHUTTI, and VHISOLA to form a MATORAN NUI to aid the TOA METRU against the Morbuzakh. Shortly after this, Nuhrii was captured by VAHKI and

NUHRII

placed into a sphere that rendered him comatose. Evidence was later discovered that Nurhii may have been destined to become a Toa of Fire. This evidence later proved to be false. On MATA NUI (2), Nuhrii served in the TA-KORO GUARD with honor.

NUHVOK (noo-vahk):

One of the six breeds of BOHROK, insectlike mechanoids controlled by KRANA who menaced the island of MATA NUI (2). The Nuhvok were tied to the element of earth, and their EARTH SHIELDS could weaken structures from below, causing them to collapse. Nuhvok were accomplished tunnelers and could see in the dark but had weak eyesight in daylight. The Nuhvok returned to their nests after the coming of the BOHROK-KAL.

NUHVOK

NUHVOK-KAL

NUHVOK-KAL (noo-vahk-KAHL):

One of the six mutant BOHROK who made up the BOHROK-KAL. Its tool was a gravity shield, capable of negating or increasing gravity around a target. After being fed Toa power via the TOA NUVA symbols (see BOHROK-KAL), Nuhvok-Kal's power turned back upon itself and transformed the Bohrok-Kal into a black hole.

NUHVOK VA (noo-vahk VAH):

One of the six BOHROK VA, Nuhvok Va were connected to the element of earth. They were gifted with the ability to see in the dark and were adequate tunnelers. When threatened, they used their claws to defend themselves.

NUHVOK VA

NUI-JAGA (noo-ee-JAH-guh):

Slow-moving, scorpionlike creatures found in both PO-METRU and PO-WAHI. Pack hunters, they relied on numbers and their powerful stingers to bring down prey. MAKUTA used INFECTED MASKS to control Nui-Jaga on MATA NUI (2) and send them against the MATORAN. One Nui-Jaga was defeated by a merged entity called a MATORAN NUI, made up of HEWKII, JALLER, KONGU, MACKU, MATORO, and ONEPU. On METRU NUI, Nui-Jaga stingers were prized by collectors and were often the subject of highly dangerous hunts.

NUI-JAGA

NUI-KOPEN (noo-ee-KOH-pen):

A giant, wasplike insect and a bitter enemy of the NUI-RAMA and the KIRIKORI NUI. ROODAKA rode a Nui-Kopen to visit MAKUTA's PROTODERMIS prison on the GREAT BARRIER.

NUI-RAMA (noo-ee-RAH-mah):

Winged, insectlike creatures who menaced both LE-METRU and LE-WAHI. Their primary tool was their stinger, which could be used both for offense and for feeding (Nui-Rama fed on liquid PROTODERMIS in METRU NUI and on plant sap and other natural fluids on MATA NUI (2)). Its wings were strong enough to allow it to carry a TOA into the air, and gave it sufficient speed to outdistance its natural enemy, the GUKKO bird. Nui-Rama were among the earliest recorded RAHI menaces in Metru Nui and followed the MATORAN when they migrated to Mata Nui (2). Large numbers of them were fitted with INFECTED MASKS by MAKUTA and used against the KORO. The first Rahi encountered on

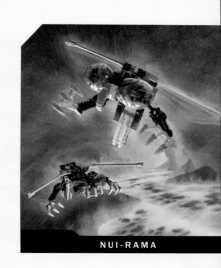

NUI-RAMA

Mata Nui by Toa KOPAKA was a Nui-Rama who attempted to knock him and MATORO off a cliff. Nui-Rama were also responsible for the death of IHU on Metru Nui.

∩UJU (∩OO-joo):
TOA METRU of Ice, guardian of KO-METRU, and later TURAGA of KO-KORO.

Nuju was a scholar and seer working in a KNOWLEDGE TOWER when TOA LHIKAN gave him a TOA STONE and a map to the GREAT TEMPLE. His reaction was annoyance that his work had been interrupted for such a strange gift. Still, he traveled to the temple and there encountered five other MATORAN — MATAU, NOKAMA, ONEWA, VAKAMA, and WHENUA. They placed their Toa stones into the TOA Suva and were transformed into mighty Toa heroes.

From the start, Nuju regarded being a Toa and saving the city as something of an inconvenience. He once mused that the reason Toa had to be chosen by destiny for the job was that no one would ever volunteer for it. Despite this, he teamed with Whenua to find the ONU-METRU and Ko-Metru GREAT DISKS and used them to help destroy the MORBUZAKH plant that threatened the city. Nuju's stated reason for doing this was that the sooner the city was out of danger, the sooner he could go back to worrying only about Ko-Metru.

When the Toa Metru presented the Great Disks to Turaga DUME, he denounced them as impostors and ordered their arrest. (The Toa did not discover until later that this Dume was MAKUTA in disguise.) Whenua, Onewa, and Nuju were captured and locked up in the PRISON OF THE DARK HUNTERS. There they encountered a mysterious Turaga who counseled them on what it meant to be a Toa and helped Onewa and Nuju discover their KANOHI mask powers. (Later, they discovered this Turaga was in fact Lhikan.) Nuju used his mask's telekinesis power to tear stones out of the prison wall, allowing the Toa and Lhikan to escape. Shortly after, they were reunited with Vakama, Matau, and Nokama.

Nuju aided in the subsequent battle with Makuta by using his mask powers to lift Vakama up to a plateau on the GREAT BARRIER for a showdown with their enemy. He later joined with the other Toa in using their powers to trap Makuta behind a wall of PROTODERMIS.

After the Toa's initial journey to MATA NUI (2), Nuju proved himself a hero on the return trip to Metru Nui. He teamed with Vakama to defeat the RAHI NUI that had severely wounded Nokama. It was also Nuju who deduced that KARZAHNI (2) was dying and therefore could not afford to back out of the deal it had made to save Nokama in exchange for a sample of ENERGIZED PROTODERMIS. Over time, Nuju became the most skilled of all the Toa at solving mysteries, applying careful logic and keen powers of observation.

Nuju found his intellect under siege when he was transformed along with the other Toa Metru into TOA HORDIKA. His rational side warred with the beast inside of himself, and he found his already short temper becoming even hotter and nastier. Worse, he was teamed with RAHAGA KUALUS, who persisted in wasting time talking to RAHI in their own language. Ironically, Kualus would later teach that language to Nuju and it would become the only one he ever spoke.

Nuju later joined with the other Toa Hordika in an assault on the COLISEUM, which led to the defeat of ROODAKA and the temporary disbanding of the VISORAK horde. Nuju was turned back into a Toa Metru through the power of KEETONGU.

NUJU

TURAGA NUJU

After reaching MATA NUI (2), the Toa Metru willingly sacrificed their power to awaken the Matoran, transforming into Turaga in the process.

TURAGA NUJU

As a Turaga, Nuju supervised the construction of KO-KORO. When KOPAKA arrived on Mata Nui, Nuju warned him about the threat of Makuta and his Rahi, but said nothing about Metru Nui or past events there.

The biggest change in Nuju was his language. After becoming a Turaga, he stopped speaking Matoran and spoke only the Rahi language taught to him by Kualus. MATORO served as his translator. His stated reason for the change was that if someone was not willing to make the effort to understand him, that being was not worth Nuju's time to talk to. He has only been heard to speak the Matoran language twice in the last 1,000 years.

During the BOHROK-KAL invasion, Nuju used his mask power to save Kopaka Nuva, who had fallen into a crevasse after beng stripped of his elemental ice power.

Nuju is one of the Turaga who strenuously objects to Vakama telling the tale of the Toa Hordika. He tried his best to talk his old friend out of it, and when that failed, he signaled his displeasure by sitting apart from the other Turaga as Vakama began the story.

Nuju is now back on METRU NUI with TAKANUVA, the MATORAN, and the other Turaga.

POWERS

Nuju was the master of ice. He could cause ice storms and blizzards, travel via ice slide, and create virtually anything out of ice. Perhaps his most impressive feat was freezing attacking VAHKI in mid-leap to create an ice bridge between two Knowledge Towers for himself and Whenua.

PERSONALITY

Nuju's personality changed little between his time as a Matoran, Toa Metru, and Turaga. He was impatient with fools, had no use for those who did not plan for the future, and was more than willing to use his cutting wit to voice his dislike of anyone or anything. Despite all this, his razor-sharp mind and incredible analytical skills made him a valuable ally. Like all residents of Ko-Metru, his orientation was toward the future, so he was always thinking ahead. More than once, this helped the Toa Metru escape extremely dangerous situations.

EQUIPMENT

As a Toa Metru, Nuju carried twin CRYSTAL SPIKES. He wore the Kanohi MATATU, the Great Mask of Telekinesis. As a Toa Hordika, he carried HORDIKA TEETH. As a Turaga, he carried an ICE PICK and wore the Noble Matatu.

NUPARU (noo-PAH-roo):
Former ONU-MATORAN inventor, later TOA INIKA and TOA MAHRI.

HISTORY

Nuparu was employed as a RAHI Receiving Official in the ONU-METRU ARCHIVES in METRU NUI, but he could not suppress a natural talent for invention and engineering. He designed

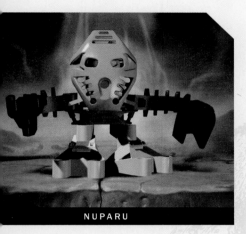

NUPARU

the KRALHI, the VAHKI, the KRAAHU, and the KRANUA, all of which were constructed in PO-METRU.

Nuparu's curiosity sometimes led him into dangerous situations. While searching the Archives sublevels for RAHKSHI pieces, he stumbled upon a large crack in one of the sea walls through which liquid PROTODERMIS was leaking. Returning to the surface, he warned TOA WHENUA. The TOA METRU went belowground in response to his report and encountered KRAHKA for the first time. On MATA NUI (2), Nuparu was best known for inventing the BOXOR. This one-Matoran vehicle was used by villagers to combat the BOHROK and BOHROK VA. Nuparu's greatest regret is that he never got to see an EXO-TOA in person, as he would have loved to have studied its design and possibly reproduced it in some form.

Unknown to the Turaga, Nuparu salvaged some of the wreckage of those armored suits and brought it with him on the return journey to Metru Nui.

After arriving there and the subsequent disappearance of the Toa Nuva, Nuparu joined with JALLER and four other Matoran on a mission to find the missing heroes. During their adventures, they encountered KARZAHNI (1), who took their masks and replaced them with new ones.

The six Matoran eventually made it to the shores of VOYA NUI. Their transport canisters were struck by lightning from the RED STAR, which transformed all six into the Toa Inika. As Toa, they battled the PIRAKA, BRUTAKA, and others in an effort to claim the KANOHI IGNIKA. Nuparu distinguished himself in battle with NEKTANN and by single-handedly defeating ZAKTAN.

Nuparu led the team through the CORD, battling the ZYGLAK and Makuta, before arriving at Mahri Nui. A burst of energy from the Ignika transformed them into the aquatic Toa Mahri. They went on to battle the BARRAKI for possession of the Mask of Life.

TOA INIKA NUPARU

POWERS

Like ONUA NUVA, Nuparu controls the power of earth.

PERSONALITY

Nuparu loves to learn, and being a Toa allows him to see places and encounter things he never would have been able to as a Matoran. He has shown himself to be both quick-witted and extremely brave, to the point where even KONGU shows respect for him. He does occasionally become too much the scientist and get distracted by the wonders around him, but being in the hostile underwater environment has tempered that somewhat.

EQUIPMENT

As a Toa Inika, Nuparu wore the KANOHI KADIN, the Mask of Flight, and carried a shoulder-mounted ZAMOR SPHERE LAUNCHER and a LASER DRILL. As a Toa Mahri, he wears the Kanohi VOLITAK, the Mask of Stealth, and carries a CORDAK BLASTER, AQUA BLASTER BLADE, and a shield.

NUURAKH (NER-rahk):

VAHKI model assigned to TA-METRU on METRU NUI. These mechanoids were extremely swift and enormously patient, preferring to lurk in ambush than initiate direct confrontation. Their STAFFS OF COMMAND allowed them to fill a MATORAN's mind with a single overriding directive. The TOA METRU battled Nuurakh on their initial journey from Metru Nui to MATA NUI (2).

NUVA CUBE:

Floating square object that serves as the "lock" on the cage of the BAHRAG. It can be opened using the six NUVA SYMBOLS, or destroyed through the power of six Toa of the proper elements striking at once.

NUVA SYMBOLS:

Six objects mysteriously connected to the elemental powers of the TOA NUVA, which served as the "keys" to the NUVA CUBE "lock" on the BAHRAG cage. The symbols were stolen by the BOHROK-KAL, which resulted in the Toa Nuva losing their elemental powers. The Toa theorized that the symbols must remain in the care of the MATORAN for their powers to remain intact. The Toa defeated the Kal by channeling their powers through the symbols to such a great extent that the Kal could not handle the surplus of energy. The symbols were regained following their defeat.

ODINA (oh-DEE-nah):

Primary island base of the DARK HUNTERS. Odina is located well away from any trade routes and its steep cliffs make it highly defensible. Its northern reaches are wild and barren, while the main feature of its southern side is the fortress of the SHADOWED ONE. It is here that Dark Hunters are trained, housed, and given their missions. Another feature of note is NIDHIKI Beach, named after the deceased ex-TOA who was transformed into a monstrous, insectlike being here by ROODAKA. Odina is heavily defended and home to vicious RAHI, like the CLIFF SCREECHER.

OLMAK (ohl-MACK):

KANOHI Mask of Dimensional Gates, which allows the user to open portals to other dimensions and either pass through them himself or force others into them. BRUTAKA used the mask to send a TAHTORAK to METRU NUI at some point in the past. He attempted to use it to thrust AXONN out of this dimension, but instead the Tahtorak and KRAHKA emerged from the portal. The ORDER OF MATA NUI suspects that the BROTHERHOOD OF MAKUTA has access to a more powerful version of the mask, or something similar, and is using it to transport the island of DESTRAL from place to place.

ONEPU

ONEPU (oh-NEE-poo):

An ONU-MATORAN. Onepu served as an archivist in METRU NUI, but did not have the patience for the work. He preferred to be out capturing RAHI rather than just waiting for them to be brought in by VAHKI. He was best known for leading an expedition that discovered an intact BOHROK nest beneath LE-METRU.

On MATA NUI (2), Onepu was appointed captain of the USSALRY, the Onu-Matoran defense force. He established himself as a great rider of USSAL crabs and was a five-time winner of the GREAT USSAL RACE.

ONEWA [AH-new-wah]:
TOA METRU of Stone, guardian of PO-METRU, and later TURAGA of PO-KORO.

Onewa was employed as a carver in Po-Metru when TOA LHIKAN gave him a TOA STONE and a map to the GREAT TEMPLE. He traveled there and encountered five other MATORAN — MATAU, NOKAMA, NUJU, VAKAMA, and WHENUA. They placed their Toa stones into the TOA Suva and were transformed into mighty Toa heroes.

After Vakama had a vision warning of the destruction of the city, Onewa reluctantly agreed to join the others to find the six GREAT DISKS. From the start, he clashed with Toa Vakama, whom he derisively referred to as "fire-spitter." Still, he teamed with the new Toa of Fire to recover both the TA-METRU and Po-Metru disks. Vakama even saved Onewa's life twice, once from a MORBUZAKH vine and once when the two of them were about to be incinerated in the PROTODERMIS RECLAMATION FURNACE. Later, Onewa identified AHKMOU as the Matoran who had betrayed the city to the DARK HUNTERS. The Toa used the Great Disks to defeat the Morbuzakh plant that threatened the city.

TOA ONEWA

When the Toa Metru presented the Great Disks to Turaga DUME, he denounced them as impostors and ordered their arrest. (The Toa did not discover until later that this Dume was MAKUTA in disguise.) Whenua, Onewa, and Nuju were captured and locked up in the PRISON OF THE DARK HUNTERS. There they encountered a mysterious Turaga who counseled them on what it meant to be a Toa and helped Onewa and Nuju discover their KANOHI mask powers. (Later, they discovered this Turaga was in fact Lhikan.) Onewa used his mind control mask power to make Whenua sit down on the cell floor. Shortly after, they escaped the cell and were reunited with Vakama, Matau, and Nokama. Onewa aided in the ensuing battle with the Dark Hunters by making KREKKA attack NIDHIKI. Later, he joined his power with that of the other Toa Metru to trap Makuta behind a wall of solid PROTODERMIS.

The Toa Metru then departed Metru Nui with the six Matoran spheres. Along the way, they encountered monstrous sea RAHI and powerful KRALHI under the command of an ONU-MATORAN named MAVRAH. During a huge battle between the Toa, the Kralhi, the VAHKI, and the RAHI, Mavrah was swept into the underground river by a great wave. Onewa prevented Whenua from sacrificing his life to save Mavrah.

After reaching MATA NUI (2) and then returning to Metru Nui, Onewa and the other Toa Metru encountered VISORAK. All six Toa were captured and mutated by Visorak venom into TOA HORDIKA. As half Toa, half beast, Onewa found it difficult to control his rage. Later, he stumbled upon a secret lair of Makuta's that contained evidence that Ahkmou may have been destined to become Toa of Stone. This evidence later proved to be false.

Onewa joined with the other Toa Hordika in an assault on the COLISEUM, headquarters of Sidorak, ROODAKA, and the Visorak. The horde was defeated and the Rahi KEETONGU used his power to transform the Hordika back to Toa Metru.

TURAGA ONEWA

The Toa Metru escaped Metru Nui via airship with the sleeping Matoran and willingly sacrificed their power to awaken them, transforming into Turaga in the process.

As a Turaga, Onewa supervised the construction of PO-KORO. Of all the villages, it looked the most like its Metru Nui counterpart. Onewa became known for his firm and fair resolutions of disputes, earning the nickname "Referee." He also invented the sport KOLHII. When POHATU arrived, Onewa informed him of the threat Makuta posed to the island but did not share any information regarding Metru Nui or his life as a Toa.

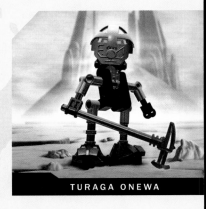

TURAGA ONEWA

During the BOHROK invasion, Onewa led the Po-Matoran across the coast to GA-KORO to avoid the TAHNOK. Still, it was only the Toa's defeat of the BAHRAG that saved the Po-Matoran from the PAHRAK.

Onewa has since returned with the TOA NUVA, the other Turaga, and the Matoran to Metru Nui.

POWERS

Onewa was the master of stone. He could cause jagged pillars of stone to erupt from the ground, stone hands to grab enemies, or stone walls to form around a target. He also had the ability to shatter stone at will, a power he used effectively during the battle with the ENERGIZED PROTODERMIS ENTITY.

PERSONALITY

Onewa was courageous and daring as a Toa, but not always the easiest to get along with. He was always quick with a wisecrack, and frequently made Vakama and Whenua the butt of his jokes. Like Matau, he could see the thrilling side of being a Toa, but he also knew that it was serious business.

Perhaps because he had provoked so many arguments as a Toa, he became skilled at resolving them as a Turaga. Where once he had lived only for the present, he came to see the virtues of an awareness of both past and future.

EQUIPMENT

As a Toa Metru, Onewa carried twin PROTO PITONS. He wore the Kanohi KOMAU, the Great Mask of Mind Control. As a Toa Hordika, he carried twin CLAW CLUBS, which could hurl stones or energize his RHOTUKA SPINNER. As a Turaga, he carried a STONE HAMMER and wore the Noble Komau.

ONU (oh-noo):
A Matoran prefix meaning "earth."

ONU-KINI (oh-noo-KIH-nee):
A temple dedicated to ONUA located in ONU-WAHI on MATA NUI (2).

ONU-KORO (oh-noo-KOAR-oh):

A village of tunnels, caves, and mines located beneath the surface of ONU-WAHI. It was home to TURAGA WHENUA and the ONU-MATORAN and was protected by TOA ONUA. Onu-Koro was the site of PROTODERMIS mines as well as USSAL crab races. The village was flooded by the GAHLOK during the BOHROK invasion, and later destroyed by the RAHKSHI. The ONU-SUVA was located here.

ONU-MATORAN (oh-noo mat-OAR-an):

A resident of ONU-KORO or ONU-METRU. Onu-Matoran commonly had black armor and wore purple or orange masks. On both METRU NUI and MATA NUI (2), Onu-Matoran were skilled miners. They also served as archivists in the Onu-Metru ARCHIVES. Onu-Matoran generally have good night vision but weak eyes in the daylight. Their favorite sport is USSAL crab racing, and they make up the membership of the USSALRY.

ONU-METRU (oh-noo-MET-troo):

Home of the archivists and miners in METRU NUI. Onu-Metru was best known for the presence of the ARCHIVES, place of employment for most Onu-Matoran in the city. It was also the site of solid PROTODERMIS mines, with blocks of the substance shipped by boat and airship to PO-METRU for carving. Onu-Metru was also the site of the PRISON OF THE DARK HUNTERS.

ONU-SUVA (oh-noo-SOO-vah):

A shrine to ONUA NUVA in ONU-KORO. KANOHI masks and Onua Nuva's symbol were kept here. BOHROK-KAL stole the NUVA SYMBOL from the Onu-Suva, robbing Onua Nuva of his elemental power of earth.

ONU-WAHI (oh-noo-WAH-hee):

A largely barren region located in northwestern MATA NUI (2). On the surface, it appeared nothing lived there but the occasional RAHI. In fact, there was a thriving village in the tunnels beneath the surface. ONU-KORO was home to the ONU-MATORAN. TOA ONUA's canister washed up on the shore of ONU-WAHI. Onu-Wahi suffered serious damage during the BOHROK invasion, and the village was destroyed when the RAHKSHI attacked. Subterranean tunnels linked Onu-Wahi to other regions.

ONUA/ONUA NUVA (oh-noo-ah/oh-noo-ah noo-vah):

TOA of Earth and protector of ONU-KORO.

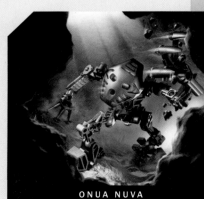

ONUA NUVA

HISTORY

Onua's early history is a mystery. He was one of six Toa who had been floating in the ocean around MATA NUI (2) for 1,000 years. They were inside unique canisters and each was partially disassembled. A signal unwittingly sent by TAKUA called the canisters to shore. Onua emerged from his canister on the coast of ONU-WAHI and instinctively headed underground. There he met ONEPU and TURAGA WHENUA.

Later, he made contact with the other five Toa — GALI, KOPAKA, LEWA, POHATU, and TAHU. Together and separately, they searched for KANOHI masks and battled the RAHI servants of MAKUTA. It was during this period that Onua saved Lewa, who'd had an INFECTED MASK affixed to his face and been transported to a NUI-RAMA nest.

He briefly merged with Pohatu and Tahu to form the TOA KAITA called AKAMAI and battle the MANAS. During the invasion of the BOHROK, he risked his life to help Lewa when the latter's mind was taken over by a KRANA.

Following the defeat of the twin Bohrok queens, the BAHRAG, the six Toa were transformed by ENERGIZED PROTODERMIS into TOA NUVA. Onua said nothing as his teammates grew arrogant and quarrelsome, nor did he step in to prevent Tahu and Kopaka from splitting up the team. This made Gali angry with Onua for his failure to act.

During the BOHROK-KAL invasion, Onua teamed with Whenua to find KANOHI NUVA, encountering and driving off Manas in the process. When the RAHKSHI attacked Onu-Koro, he battled them alongside Pohatu. He was later part of the Rahkshi's final defeat, and a witness to TAKANUVA's defeat of Makuta.

Onua joined with the others in listening to Turaga VAKAMA's tales of life in METRU NUI centuries before. Onua Nuva traveled with the other Toa Nuva, Turaga and Matoran, back to Metru Nui. Shortly after their arrival, he and his teammates were sent to VOYA NUI to retrieve the KANOHI IGNIKA. They encountered the PIRAKA and BRUTAKA on that island and were defeated and imprisoned. They were later saved by the MATORAN RESISTANCE. They have since journeyed back to Metru Nui as the first part of their quest to prepare for the reawakening of Mata Nui (1).

POWERS

Onua is the master of earth. He can erect walls of earth in an instant, cause the soil to strike a foe like a battering ram, or make the dirt shift under an enemy's feet so that he sinks into the ground. He is a skilled tunneler, often helping ONU-MATORAN to dig new mine shafts. He has excellent night vision, but his eyesight is weak in daylight.

PERSONALITY

Onua was arguably one of the wisest of the Toa as well as being the least talkative. This caused problems, for he was too quick to let the others go their own way without speaking up, even when he knew they were making a mistake. He has tried to be the conscience of the Toa, helping them to keep a sense of perspective about their place in the universe.

EQUIPMENT

OOHNORAK

Onua relied on his claws as a Toa and on a pair of QUAKE BREAKERS as a Toa Nuva. He most often wore a Kanohi PAKARI or PAKARI NUVA, the Great Mask of Strength.

OOHNORAK (ooh-NOAR-ack):
One of the six breeds of VISORAK that invaded METRU NUI. Oohnorak have limited telepathic abilities and are skilled mimics, allowing them to trap a foe by speaking in the voice of a trusted friend. The Oohnorak

used this trick to get TOA MATAU to open a hangar door and let them in. Oohnorak RHOTUKA SPINNERS are capable of numbing a target, making an escape extremely difficult.

ORDER OF MATA NUI:

Secret organization devoted to carrying out the will of MATA NUI (1). The Order was formed very early in the history of the universe, with its original members formerly part of the HAND OF ARTAKHA. It was decided from the outset that while TOA would be the public face of order and justice, the Order would remain hidden so that they could do things Toa could not. Among the actions known to have been taken by the Order are: the placing of AXONN and BRUTAKA on VOYA NUI as guards for the KANOHI IGNIKA; working with Mata Nui (1) to engineer a six-month TIME SLIP during which AV-MATORAN were planted on various islands in disguise; tampering with EHLEK's native species in an effort to create a race that could battle the Brotherhood of Makuta; planting agents in places of importance to monitor events; eliminating all those who knew the location of ARTAKHA; planting evidence to make it look as if six MATORAN other than those who became the TOA METRU were intended to be Toa; and more, still unrevealed.
Known members of the Order include AXONN, BRUTAKA, and BOTAR. Order agents sent to METRU NUI and MATA NUI (2) were killed by KARZAHNI (2) and MAKUTA respectively.

The Order's primary base of operations is on the island of DAXIA and the group boasts hundreds of agents. Over time, the Order has checked the plans of the DARK HUNTERS, the Brotherhood of Makuta, and the LEAGUE OF SIX KINGDOMS, all without its existence being revealed. Currently, the existence of the Order is known to the TOA MAHRI, the TOA NUVA, and the members of the MATORAN RESISTANCE on VOYA NUI.

ORKAHM

ORKAHM (OR-kam):

An USSAL crab rider in LE-METRU. Orkahm was one of six MATORAN to discover the locations of the legendary GREAT DISKS. Orkahm was slow and meticulous and known for having little imagination. His favorite Ussal crab was PEWKU. He originally intended to find some way to profit from his knowledge of the Le-Metru Great Disk's location, but shortly after finding it, he began being followed by NIDHIKI and KREKKA. Lured to an out-of-the-way spot, he was trapped in a snare set by AHKMOU. The TOA METRU of Air, MATAU, came to his rescue. Orkahm led Matau to the Great Disk, which was stuck inside a FORCE SPHERE in one of the CHUTES.
Later, Orkahm joined with Ahkmou, VHISOLA, TEHUTTI, EHRYE, and NUHRII to form a MATORAN NUI to aid the Toa in their battle against the MORBUZAKH. Shortly afterward, he was captured by VAHKI and put into a SPHERE. He remained there, comatose, until awakened on MATA NUI (2) by the Toa Metru. Evidence was later discovered that Orkahm may have been destined to become a Toa of Air. This evidence later proved to be false.
Orkahm later became a GUKKO rider in LE-KORO.

PAHRAK (PAH-rahk):

One of the six breeds of BOHROK, insectlike mechanoids controlled by KRANA who menaced the island of MATA NUI (2). The Pahrak were tied to the element of ice and their STONE SHIELDS could cause violent seismic disruptions. The Pahrak came dangerously close

PAHRAK

to destroying GA-KORO, stopped once by HAHLI and MACKU's efforts and once by the TOA's defeat of the BAHRAG. The Pahrak returned to their nests after the coming of the BOHROK-KAL.

PAHRAK-KAL [PAH-rahk KAHL]:
One of the six mutant BOHROK who made up the BOHROK-KAL. Its tool was a PLASMA SHIELD, capable of superheating any substance until it becomes plasmoid. It could also be used defensively to melt incoming projectiles. After being fed Toa power via the TOA NUVA symbols (see BOHROK-KAL), Pahrak-Kal superheated, melted through the floor, and vanished, possibly falling all the way through to the core of the planet.

PAHRAK-KAL

PAHRAK VA [PAH-rahk VAH]:
One of the six BOHROK VA, Pahrak Va was connected to the element of stone. Slow-moving, this Bohrok Va proved the easiest for the MATORAN to capture. It used stone hammers to defend itself.

PAHRAK VA

PAKARI [PAH-kar-EE]:
The KANOHI Mask of Strength, capable of increasing the physical power of the wearer. ONUA wore the Great Mask of Strength when he first washed ashore on MATA NUI (2).

PAKARI NUVA [PAH-kar-EE NOO-vah]:
The powerful Great Mask of Strength worn by ONUA NUVA. It was capable of increasing his strength and that of those around him to their ultimate. See KANOHI NUVA.

PANRAHK [PAHN-rahk]:
One of the six RAHKSHI sent by MAKUTA to stop the HERALD and recover the KANOHI AVOHKII. Panrahk was able to use its staff to make any object fly into tiny fragments. This Rahkshi's energies were so potent that small explosions would go off wherever it walked. Along with GUURAHK and LERAHK, Panrahk was responsible for the destruction of the village of TA-KORO. Panrahk was trapped in a prison of glass through the efforts of TAHU NUVA and LEWA NUVA.

PANRAHK

PAPA NIHU REEF [PAH-pah nee-HOO]:
Name given to the ONU-WAHI coastline on MATA NUI (2).

PARAKREKKS [PAH-rah-KRECKS]:
These vicious amphibians follow in the wake of the PROTOCAIRNS, feeding off of the rubble the larger creatures leave behind. Long after the protocairns have died, these nasty beings linger, tearing down structures with their claws and feasting on the fragments. Extremely good at finding concealment, they can be very difficult to root out once they have gotten a foothold in a place. Left unchecked, they can eventually destroy an entire city due to their rapacious appetite.

PEHKUI [peh-KOO-ee]:
Mask of Diminishment, worn by TOA NORIK. This mask allows a user to shrink to a minimum height of six inches while still retaining normal strength and power.

PEWKU (POO-koo):

A retired Ussal racing crab who was friends with TAKUA. Pewku originally served in METRU NUI pulling an USSAL CART, driven by ORKHAM. After migrating to MATA NUI, Pewku was a racing crab and later a means of transport for Matoran traveling between ONU-KORO and PO-KORO. She was TAKUA's companion during the search for TAKANUVA. She was then adopted by JALLER. Although she has not been adopted by a new owner since Jaller's departure from the city of Metru Nui, she has befriended KAPURA.

PHANTOM:

A member of the DARK HUNTERS with one of the more bizarre origin stories. He was originally a humble crafter from an island far from METRU NUI where there were no Toa. His people felt the need for a hero, and so he was chosen for a "rebuilding project." After numerous experiments, including exposure to an ENERGIZED PROTODERMIS variant, Phantom emerged with increased strength, the power of limited flight, dramatically improved eyesight, and the ability to turn invisible. His career as a hero was short-lived. Frightened and ashamed of what they had done, the locals shunned him. Disheartened and without purpose, he was easily recruited into the Dark Hunters. However, his conscience has so far made him of limited use on missions.

PHASE DRAGON:

Flying reptilian RAHI of METRU NUI, known for its great speed and ability to alter its density so as to pass unharmed through solid objects. Although frightening in appearance, phase dragons were largely harmless as long as there were vehicles for it to chase. Once Metru Nui became a dead city, phase dragons became a menace to anything that moved. None of these creatures were ever seen on MATA NUI (2).

PHASE DRAGON

PIRAKA (PIE-rock-ah):

Name adopted by six ex–DARK HUNTERS who broke away from that organization and attempted to steal the KANOHI IGNIKA. It is a MATORAN term meaning "thief and murderer." The Piraka were THOK, HAKANN, ZAKTAN, AVAK, REIDAK, and VEZOK, with VEZON unofficially considered a seventh Piraka. See individual entries.

PIRAKA STRONGHOLD:

Fortress built on VOYA NUI by MATORAN under orders from the six PIRAKA. The stronghold contained, among other things, the vat containing ANTIDERMIS and the imprisoned TOA NUVA. The stronghold was badly damaged by battles between the Piraka and the Toa (both Nuva and INIKA) and by a fight between AXONN and BRUTAKA. KRAHKA and the TAHTORAK emerged from the zone of darkness into the Piraka Stronghold.

PIRUK (PIE-rook):

LE-MATORAN member of the RESISTANCE on the island of VOYA NUI. Good at sneaking around but not the most courageous member of the group, he was primarily used as a scout and spy. Piruk carries two shredder claws as weapons.

PIT:

Name given by the ORDER OF MATA NUI to its place of imprisonment for those deemed beyond redemption. The Pit was a series of cells within a dome, overseen by HYDRAXON and guarded by

MAXILOS and SPINAX. Inmates were brought there by BOTAR and included the worst criminals in the universe. During the GREAT CATACLYSM, the walls of the Pit were shattered, allowing the inmates to escape (Hydraxon was badly injured in the quake, and later killed by TAKADOX). Their path to "freedom" led them to the black water of the sea bottom outside the dome. The mutagenic properties of the seawater transformed all the inmates (with the exception of NOCTURN), altering their bodies so that they could breathe water, and in other ways as well. Now no longer able to survive on land, they felt themselves to be imprisoned again, and so named this area of the ocean "the Pit" as well. Known inhabitants of this area include PRIDAK, Takadox, KALMAH, CARAPAR, MANTAX, EHLEK, Nocturn, and BRUTAKA.

A few centuries after the cataclysm, the landmass upon which the village of MAHRI NUI rested broke off its island and sank into the Pit. Later, the TOA INIKA journeyed here in search of the KANOHI IGNIKA and were transformed by that mask into the aquatic TOA MAHRI.

PLACE OF SHADOW:

Name given by the MATORAN to a pass along the border of KO-WAHI and TA-WAHI on MATA NUI (2). This area was avoided at all costs, even by the BOHROK. TAHU NUVA, KOPAKA NUVA, and GALI NUVA came here in search of KANOHI NUVA masks.

PLASMA SHIELD:

Tool carried by PAHRAK-KAL. The plasma shield was able to emit a stream of superheated plasma at a temperature of roughly 2,000 degrees.

PO (POH):

A Matoran prefix meaning "stone."

POISON:

DARK HUNTER capable of spitting a paralyzing venom at his enemies. He bears a special hatred for MATORAN, as they hunted his species to near extinction. Interestingly, Poison's only vulnerability is to his own venom.

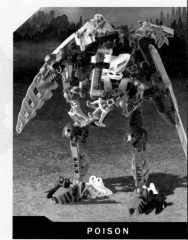

POISON

PO-KINI (POH-kih-NEE):

A temple dedicated to POHATU located in PO-WAHI on MATA NUI (2).

PO-KORO (POH-koar-OH):

Village on MATA NUI (2) and home to the PO-MATORAN. Po-Koro was located in the desert to the far north of the island. Structures here were carved from rock and intended to blend in with the surrounding area. The climate was harsh, with unrelenting heat and sandstorms. During the BOHROK invasion, the Po-Matoran temporarily fled their village and took up residence in caves.

PO-MATORAN (POH-mat-OAR-an):

A resident of PO-KORO or PO-METRU. Po-Matoran commonly had tan armor and wore black or dark orange masks. On both METRU NUI and MATA NUI (2), Po-Matoran were known as extremely skilled carvers. Po-Matoran, as a rule, hate water and cannot swim. The sport of KOLHII originated among the Po-Matoran and they were some of its best players.

PO-METRU (POH-MET-troo):

Home of the carvers in METRU NUI. Unlike the other districts of the city, Po-Metru is largely a wild and barren place, dotted with mountains and canyons. Po-Matoran labor out of doors, assembling goods and carving great statues. Po-Metru is protected by TOA ONEWA and is home to the SCULPTURE FIELDS, the FIELDS OF CONSTRUCTION, the ASSEMBLER'S VILLAGE, the PRISON OF THE DARK HUNTERS, and the PROTODERMIS WAREHOUSE. One of the six GREAT DISKS was found here. Three of the TOA METRU were held captive here, and the other three came to Po-Metru to save them and LHIKAN. A major skirmish between VAKAMA, NOKAMA, and MATAU and the DARK HUNTERS took place in Po-Metru.

PO-SUVA [POH-soo-VAH]:
A shrine to POHATU NUVA in PO-KORO. KANOHI masks and Pohatu Nuva's symbol were kept here. BOHROK-KAL stole the NUVA SYMBOL from the Po-Suva, robbing Pohatu Nuva of his elemental power of stone.

PO-WAHI [POH-wah-HEE]:
A barren, rocky wasteland located in the far northern region of MATA NUI (2). It was home to PO-KORO and the PO-MATORAN. TOA POHATU's canister washed up on the shore of Po-Wahi. Numerous RAHI live here, including NUI-JAGA, SAND TARAKAVA, TUNNELERS, HUSI, and many more. Po-Wahi suffered some damage during the BOHROK invasion, but was largely spared by the BOHROK-KAL and RAHKSHI.

POHATU/POHATU NUVA [poe-HAH-too/poe-HAH-too NOO-vah]:
TOA of Stone and protector of PO-KORO.

HISTORY

Nothing has been revealed about Pohatu's history prior to his first appearance on the island of MATA NUI (2). He was one of six Toa who had been floating in the ocean around that land for 1,000 years. They were inside unique canisters and each was partially disassembled. A signal unwittingly sent by TAKUA called the canisters to shore. Pohatu's canister washed up on the shores of PO-WAHI. He first encountered another Toa in spectacular fashion, when he accidentally buried KOPAKA in a rockslide.

Later, the two of them made contact with the other heroes of Mata Nui — GALI, LEWA, ONUA, and TAHU. Together and separately, they searched for KANOHI masks and battled the RAHI servants of MAKUTA.

Pohatu briefly merged with Tahu and Onua to form the TOA KAITA called AKAMAI and fight the MANAS. Following the defeat of Makuta, he joined the other Toa in battling the BOHROK invasion. Pohatu teamed with Gali, Kopaka, and Onua to trap a swarm of TAHNOK in TIRO CANYON in PO-WAHI.

Following the defeat of the twin Bohrok queens, the BAHRAG, the six Toa were transformed by ENERGIZED PROTODERMIS into TOA NUVA. Despite the increase in power, Pohatu remained modest and friendly. After the BOHROK-KAL stole the Toa's elemental powers, Pohatu teamed with Kopaka to track down KANOHI NUVA.

Pohatu was in attendance at the KOLHII match when it was revealed that TAKUA had discovered the Kanohi AVOHKII, the Mask of Light. Pohatu later joined with Onua in a futile effort to defend ONU-KORO against the RAHKSHI. During this period, he was infuriated to discover that the Turaga had been keeping captured KRAATA in a Po-Wahi cave without informing him.

The two Toa Nuva were part of the final defeat of the Rahkshi, aided by TAKANUVA, the Toa of Light. Pohatu Nuva and other Toa Nuva are now preparing to meet their destiny.

POHATU

POWERS

Pohatu is the master of stone. He can create rockslides, make stone spring from the ground, bring rock walls into being by his will, and more. His strength is prodigious, particularly in his legs. He is capable of kicking a massive boulder a distance of several miles.

PERSONALITY

Pohatu has always been the most easygoing of the Toa. His philosophy from the start was that everyone would be better served by getting along, and he maintained that attitude even in the face of such extreme personalities as Tahu and Kopaka. He is widely regarded as a loyal and reliable comrade and a good being to have beside you in a fight. He rarely took himself or others too seriously. Like most residents of Po-Wahi, he disliked water and could not swim.

EQUIPMENT

Pohatu initially carried no special Toa tool, relying on his own strength, As Pohatu Nuva, he wielded CLIMBING CLAWS, which could be thrown or put together to form a KODAN BALL. He most often wore a Kanohi KAKAMA or KAKAMA NUVA, the Great Mask of Speed.

POKAWI (POH-kah-WEE):
Flightless fowl that live high among the peaks of PO-METRU, feeding on whatever vegetation that might be there. Their high vantage point is all that saves them, since they can usually spot predators long before they get too close. On MATA NUI (2), they were known for scattering in all directions when enemies approached, confusing them with their sudden movement.

POUKS (POOKS):
Former TOA HAGAH of Stone later mutated by ROODAKA into a RAHAGA. Pouks had been part of an elite Toa team charged with being MAKUTA's personal guard. When they discovered Makuta was oppressing and enslaving MATORAN, they turned on him and attacked a fortress of the BROTHERHOOD OF MAKUTA. Pouks was struck by one of Roodaka's RHOTUKA SPINNERS and mutated into a shrunken creature with the head of a RAHKSHI. He was later rescued by TOA IRUINI and Toa NORIK, who also ended up being mutated.
What masks and tools Pouks carried as a Toa has not yet been revealed.
As a Rahaga, Pouks specialized in capturing large land RAHI, such as KIKANALO and MUAKA. He carried a Rhotuka spinner with the *lasso* power, which skimmed just above the ground and then wrapped around the legs of a target, bringing it down and immobilizing it. He also carried a staff that could be used to make an invisible mark on Rahi so that they could be tracked. Pouks was familiar enough with the natural movements of Rahi that he could spot impersonations by KRAHKA. He persuaded Krahka to side with the TOA METRU against the VISORAK, and later rode with her and Toa ONEWA on the back of a TAHTORAK.

PRIDAK (PRY-dack):
Leader of the six BARRAKI who menace MAHRI NUI. It was Pridak who first devised the idea of an alliance between the leaders of the six most powerful empires in the universe. This became the infamous LEAGUE OF SIX KINGDOMS, with Pridak dominating the northeastern region, including the island of XIA. Later, Pridak led the League's efforts to overthrow MATA

NUI (2). Pridak was defiant even in the face of defeat by the BROTHERHOOD OF MAKUTA and would have welcomed execution as the only honorable outcome of failure. Instead, he and his allies were transported to the PIT by BOTAR.

Freed by a massive earthquake (see GREAT CATACLYSM), Pridak and the others escaped into a vast ocean. But the mutagenic properties of the seawater transformed them, making them water-breathers, but also changing them into monstrous forms. Unable to reclaim his kingdom, Pridak contented himself with creating a new one under the sea and assembling an army of TAKEA SHARKS. When MAHRI NUI sank, crushing the Barraki fortress, it was Pridak who prevented EHLEK from attacking and destroying the MATORAN (believing they might be of some use at some point). This was not the first time he settled disputes with the other Barraki or their allies. In the ensuing years, he ruined one of KALMAH's eyes in battle and bit off NOCTURN's arm. When the KANOHI IGNIKA appeared underwater, Pridak captured DEFILAK, SARDA, and IDRIS in an effort to discover its location. He believed he had killed Sarda, unaware the Matoran had been saved by TOA LESOVIKK. He later got his claws on the Ignika, ignoring its legendary curse. Pridak believed no curse could be worse than what the Barraki were already enduring. When the Toa MAHRI arrived in the Pit, Pridak at first mistook them for other villains. But that did not stop him from leading an army against MATORO and MAXILOS. When Ehlek's legions launched a surprise attack against him, he turned his sharks against his former ally, launching an all-out undersea war.

EQUIPMENT

Pridak's teeth are powerful enough to bite through PROTOSTEEL. He carries a SHARK TOOTH BLADE and a SQUID LAUNCHER.

PRIMAL:
DARK HUNTER who relies on strength and speed to complete his missions, using his paralysis device only in emergencies. Primal belongs to a species largely wiped out by the VISORAK. He has proven to be a difficult operative due to his refusal to accept missions that don't involve the possibility of getting a trophy from the hunt.

PRIMAL

PRISON OF THE DARK HUNTERS:
A series of cells inside a cave network in ONU-METRU, used by the DARK HUNTERS to keep important prisoners. LHIKAN, WHENUA, NUJU, and ONEWA were held here after their capture. Lhikan, then a TURAGA, taught the three TOA METRU skills that would help them focus and learn to use their KANOHI mask powers. Both Onewa and Nuju discovered their powers while in captivity, and Nuju's Kanohi MATATU, the Mask of Telekinesis, made it possible for him to tear stones from the wall and free them. The prison of the Dark Hunters was guarded by squads of VAHKI.

PROTO PITONS:
Tools carried by TOA METRU ONEWA. These allowed him to scale buildings and swing from one to the other.

P

PROTOCAIRNS (PROE-toe-CARE-nz):

Surely one of the most bizarre creatures ever seen on METRU NUI, perhaps only their rumored origin is stranger than their behavior. According to legend, the Protocairns were once a small group of villagers from another land who willingly exposed themselves to ENERGIZED PROTODERMIS. They were transformed into monstrous amphibious beasts. Every hundred years or so since then, Protocairns appear on the shore of various islands and wreak enormous destruction, actually disintegrating large portions of the coastline. After a short time of this, the Protocairns die and their bodies fuse together, forming new land in place of the old they destroyed. While they live, they are extremely difficult to stop, although VAHKI squads have had success driving them away over the past few centuries.

PROTODAX (PROE-toe-DACKS):

A Toa-sized version of a PROTODITE, enlarged by the power of the KANOHI IGNIKA to serve as another guardian of the mask. Protodax are wild and savage by nature, with the unique ability to split into two beings of equal size and strength anytime they are physically struck (resulting in rapid multiplication in battle). The TOA INIKA battled protodax, with the creatures being driven off by laser bursts from UMBRA.

PROTODERMIS:

The most important substance in the BIONICLE universe. Protodermis can exist in solid, liquid, and gaseous form, and virtually everything known to the MATORAN is made of it. This includes Toa armor and organic tissue, buildings, tools, KANOKA DISKS, KANOHI masks, and even the silver sea that surrounds METRU NUI.
Solid protodermis was mined in both ONU-METRU on Metru Nui and ONU-KORO on MATA NUI (2). All buildings, statues, and other structures on both islands were made from solid protodermis. Liquid protodermis, such as makes up the Metru Nui ocean, must be purified before being used to create items. (See PROTODERMIS PURIFICATION.) No significant sources of liquid protodermis existed on Mata Nui. Due to the fact that liquid protodermis took the place of water for the Metru Nui Matoran, it was dubbed the "stuff of life."
The third, and rarest, form of protodermis is ENERGIZED PROTODERMIS.

POTODERMIS PURIFICATION:

A process performed in GA-METRU on METRU NUI to remove impurities from liquid protodermis so that it could be used in the making of KANOKA DISKS. Liquid protodermis was drawn from the sea into the GREAT TEMPLE. Here a special group of GA-MATORAN waited to begin purification work. While some read ancient passages calling on the GREAT SPIRIT MATA NUI for aid and protection, others supervised the rapid heating and cooling needed to cleanse the liquid. Once this was done, the liquid protodermis lost its silver coloring and become a clear fluid with a bluish tinge.

PROTODERMIS RECLAMATION FURNACE:

An enclosure containing an extremely hot flame, used to melt down flawed creations in TA-METRU. Items stored in the PROTODERMIS RECLAMATION YARD were sent here to be reduced to liquid protodermis. NIDHIKI attempted to kill VAKAMA and ONEWA here.

PROTODERMIS RECLAMATION YARD:

Area of TA-METRU in which damaged masks and tools were kept prior to their being melted down. TOA VAKAMA journeyed here while searching for the missing NUHRII. The Matoran caretaker of the facility is reported to talk to the KANOHI masks in his care as if they were living beings.

PROTODERMIS WAREHOUSE:
Structures in PO-METRU that held an assortment of parts awaiting assembly. Components of VAHKI, furniture, and other items were shipped to Po-Metru from TA-METRU and put together in ASSEMBLER'S VILLAGES. TOA ONEWA came to a protodermis warehouse during his search for AHKMOU.

PROTODITES (PROE-toe-DIGHTS):
Microscopic creatures accidentally freed in the ARCHIVES and still infesting some sections. These creatures were being studied by archivists when efforts to escape by a KRAAWA rocked their container and shattered it. The protodites spread rapidly, kept in check only by their one predator, the ARCHIVES MOLES. Whether any protodites made it to MATA NUI (2) is unknown. A unique feature of the protodite is that a physical impact causes one to split into two of equal size and strength.
ZAKTAN was transformed into a mass of protodites by the eyebeams of the SHADOWED ONE. The KANOHI IGNIKA used its power to enlarge protodites into the monstrous PROTODAX.

PROTO DRAKE:
Amphibious creatures found in the waters off GA-METRU. These creatures got their name from their habit of bathing in molten PROTODERMIS, which was believed to be their way of burning off parasites that clung to their skin. They were regarded with respect by the GA-MATORAN, particularly because they helped to keep coastal areas safe by feeding on sharks. Proto drake were later spotted off the coast of TA-WAHI on MATA NUI (2).

PROTO DRAKE

PROTOSTEEL:
Hardest substance known to exist, protosteel was created by the artisans of ARTAKHA and used to craft the armor of the BROTHERHOOD OF MAKUTA. While protosteel is not unbreakable or invulnerable, it does require tremendous force to pierce or crack. MAKUTA's protosteel armor was shattered by the collapse of the gateway leading from MANGAIA to METRU NUI.

PROTOSTEEL TALONS:
Weapons carried by TOA MAHRI HAHLI and made of the hardest substance known in the universe.

PROTOTYPE

PROTOTYPE:
DARK HUNTER created when a TOA of Fire and a Toa of Earth were merged by the power of the SPEAR OF FUSION. Driven mad by the experience, Prototype was recruited into the Dark Hunter organization. He is extremely strong and virtually invulnerable.

QUAKE BREAKERS:

ONUA NUVA's twin Toa tools which could dig through earth and rock, as well as serve as all-terrain treads when attached to his feet.

RAHAGA (rah-HAH-gah):

Name given to six former TOA HAGAH who were transformed by ROODAKA into shrunken, bent creatures with the heads of RAHKSHI. The name was coined by Roodaka as a play on the words "Hagah" and "Rahkshi." Rahaga were partially RAHI and had enhanced sense and agility as a result. Each carried a staff and had a RHOTUKA LAUNCHER as part of their anatomy. The Rahaga continued to oppose Roodaka and the VISORAK, making every effort to rescue Rahi before the Visorak could capture them. The Rahaga acted to save the TOA HORDIKA from certain death and to educate them about their new forms, new powers, and hopes for a cure for their condition. The six Rahaga were BOMONGA, GAAKI, IRUINI, KUALUS, NORIK, and POUKS (see individual entries).

RAHI (rah-HEE):

Overall name applied to all animals, fish, birds, insects, and reptiles by the MATORAN. A rough translation of the term is "not us," since it is used by Matoran to describe living things other than themselves. The majority of Rahi are sentient, multi-celled biomechanical beings, ranging from dangerous and hostile beasts to easily domesticated creatures. The precise origin of the different species is unknown to the Matoran, since the Rahi they have encountered have all migrated from other lands.

RAHI NUI (rah-HEE NOO-ee):

A bizarre creature that appeared to be a combination a MUAKA, a TARAKAVA, a NUI-JAGA, a NUI-RAMA, and a KANE-RA bull. It was created by MAKUTA to serve as a tracking beast for the DARK HUNTERS NIDHIKI and KREKKA. In addition to its natural tools — horns, wings, teeth, power forelegs, and hindlegs — the Rahi Nui originally possessed all the base KANOKA DISK powers, including *teleportation*. Using that particular ability, it could home in on TOA wherever they might be. The Rahi Nui actually fed on Toa power, making it immune to elemental blasts. The first recorded encounter was with the TOA METRU, during which the Rahi Nui severely wounded NOKAMA. It was defeated by NUJU and VAKAMA and its atoms dispersed. Over 1,000 years later, the Rahi Nui reappeared on MATA NUI (2), minus its special powers. It was defeated by the TOA NUVA with the aid of TURAGA Vakama. Its current whereabouts are unknown.

RAHKSHI (RAHK-shee):

Powerful and destructive armored beings created by MAKUTA to do his bidding. A Rahkshi consists of a suit of armor that houses a KRAATA, a wormlike creature that controls the being's movements and actions. Without a kraata, Rahkshi armor is unable to move or act.

Rahkshi are created by exposing kraata to ENERGIZED PROTODERMIS. Over time, the protodermis evolves the kraata into a suit of Rahkshi armor. A second kraata then crawls into the head of the armor and activates it. Since kraata are created by Makuta, Rahkshi have been nicknamed the "sons of Makuta." There are 42 known types of Rahkshi, differentiated by their powers and the color of their armor.

Most Rahkshi on METRU NUI were "wild Rahkshi," beings operating without orders from Makuta and acting like pure beasts. They lived in tunnels underneath the city, occasionally venturing out and battling VAHKI. Some of these Rahkshi ended up on display in the ARCHIVES.

When the search began for the TOA of Light on MATA NUI (2), Makuta unleashed six Rahkshi against the TOA NUVA and Matoran: GUURAHK, KURAHK, LERAHK, PANRAHK, TURAHK, and VORAHK (see individual entries). So powerful were they that even Makuta expressed reluctance about setting them free. All six were defeated by the Toa Nuva and TAKANUVA, and their parts were used to build the USSANUI.

Rahkshi Power Chart

A Rahkshi's power can be identified by the color of its armor. This chart contains all known Rahkshi, although it is possible that others may exist which have not yet been encountered.

Rahkshi Armor Color	Power
Gold	Weather Control
Tan	Elasticity
Yellow	Heat Vision
Tan-Blue	Illusion
Blue-Green	Teleport
Black-Brown	Quick Healing
Red-Orange	Laser Vision
Blue-Silver	Gravity
Blue-White	Electricity
Yellow-Green	Sonics
Orange-Black	Vacuum
Tan-Red	Plasma
Black-Gold	Magnetism
Aquamarine	Fire Resistance
Red-Yellow	Ice Resistance
Light Purple	Mind Reading
Blue-Gold	Shape-shifting
Black-Red	Darkness
Green-Brown	Plant Control
Light Blue	Molecular Disruption (inorganic)
Silver	Chain Lightning
Black-White	Cyclone
Black-Green	Density Control
Red-Gold	Chameleon
Blue-Purple	Accuracy
Magenta	Rahi Control
Orange	Insect Control

Blue-Black	Stasis Field
Gray	Limited Invulnerability
Purple	Power Scream
Red-Silver	Dodge
Gray-Black	Silence
Black-Purple	Adaptation
Blue-Yellow	Slow
Gray-Green	Confusion
Maroon	Sleep
Red	Fear
Black	Weakness
White	Anger
Blue	Disintegration
Green	Poison
Brown	Shattering

RAHKSHI KAITA VO (RAHK-shee KIGH-ee-TAH VOE):

Being created from the merging of three RAHKSHI — VORAHK, PANRAHK, and GUURAHK. It had the power to absorb energy from its foes.

RAHKSHI KAITA ZA (RAHK-shee KIGH-ee-TAH ZAH):

Being created from the merging of three RAHKSHI — TURAHK, LERAHK, and KURAHK. It had the power to transform itself into a cyclone.

RANAMA (rah-NAH-mah):

Long considered a pest by MATORAN in TA-METRU, the Ranama are giant fire frogs who thrive in molten PROTODERMIS. Their presence in that fluid forced TA-MATORAN to filter it carefully before using it to mold tools and masks. Ranama fed on small insects, leaping out of molten protodermis vats to snare them with its tongue. They later made their way to MATA NUI (2), where they lived in molten lava in TA-WAHI.

RAU

RAU (ROW):

KANOHI Mask of Translation. The Great Mask version of this allowed TOA NOKAMA to understand both written and spoken languages. She used its power to communicate with the KIKANALO as well as to translate ancient writings related to the GREAT DISKS. The Noble Rau, worn by Nokama as a TURAGA, enabled translation of written languages only.

RAVAGER:

Amnesiac DARK HUNTER known for his destructive nature and stinger tail. His sword and shield are said to automatically increase in strength to match any foe he encounters. Efforts to determine who he really is or where he comes from have so far proved unsuccessful.

RAVAGER

RAZORFISH:

Although called a fish, this creature is actually an aquatic mammal. Its primary defense was the razor-sharp scales that lined its body. Brushing against a razorfish could result in a serious wound. They were found both in the ocean around METRU NUI and the waters surrounding MATA NUI (2).

RAZOR WHALE:

RAZOR WHALE

Massive aquatic mammals who rely on the sharp spines on their backs to protect them from predators. At a certain point in their lives, the spines naturally fall off, making it possible for MATORAN to ride the great beasts. TOA HORDIKA NOKAMA made a point of defending the razor whales against the VISORAK BOGGARAK. Since few specimens were ever sighted off MATA NUI (2), it is unclear how many of the species still survive.

RED STAR:

A blazing star in the heavens above MATA NUI (2). Of all the celestial bodies, it is this one that most governs the interpretation of prophecies about the island and its inhabitants. Lightning from the red star caused the transformation of six MATORAN into the TOA INIKA.

REIDAK (ray-DACK):

One of the six PIRAKA who attempted to steal the KANOHI IGNIKA. Reidak joined the Dark Hunters after a dispute on the island of ZAKAZ resulted in the destruction of one of the few settlements still standing there. He possesses the elemental power of earth, thermal and infrared vision, and the ability to adapt to defeats so that the same method cannot be used to beat him twice. He carries a ZAMOR SPHERE LAUNCHER and a combination buzzsaw and drill, which can turn the ground into quicksand on contact. Known more for his brawn than his brains, Reidak was part of the failed effort to overthrow the SHADOWED ONE, the expedition to free the KANOHI DRAGON, and the TOA-Dark Hunter War. He later joined with five other ex–Dark Hunters to form a loose alliance under the name PIRAKA. During a raid on an abandoned lair of MAKUTA, Reidak attempted to seize the KANOHI KRAAHKAN, only to be lashed with dark energy. Reidak journeyed with the other Piraka to the island of Voya Nui to steal the Ignika, only to encounter the TOA NUVA. Reidak fought LEWA NUVA and broke one of his AIR KATANA. He was later defeated (temporarily) by Lewa, ONUA NUVA, and POHATU NUVA. Reidak also did battle with the TOA INIKA, VEZON and FENRAKK, IRNAKK, and ultra-powered versions of HAKANN and THOK. Vezon used the SPEAR OF FUSION to merge Reidak and VEZOK into one monstrous being to fight the other Piraka. When last seen, Reidak was with the other Piraka, still scheming how to get the Kanohi Ignika, and unaware that his body was being affected by an earlier exposure to mutagenic seawater.

REIDAK

RHOTUKA LAUNCHER (roe-TOO-kah):

A tool, either natural or artificially created, capable of hurling an energy spinner a long distance at a target. These were used for both offense and defense. The RAHAGA, TOA HORDIKA, KEETONGU, VISORAK, and some RAHI had natural launchers as parts of their bodies. TOA IRUINI, TOA NORIK, ROODAKA, and SIDORAK carried mechanical launchers.

RHOTUKA SPINNER (roe-TOO-kah):

A wheel of energy generated by the willpower of the user and able to be hurled great distances using a RHOTUKA LAUNCHER. These spinners were the primary offensive and defensive tools of the TOA HORDIKA, RAHAGA, KEETONGU, and VISORAK, and were also used by ROODAKA, SIDORAK, TOA IRUINI, TOA NORIK, and some RAHI. The power of the spinner was determined by the individual being who launched it — for example, due to his identification with his element, Toa Hordika VAKAMA launched fire spinners, something no one else could do. Sidorak, who favored blind obedience from his horde above all else, could generate a spinner that produced such obedience in anyone it struck. Generating a Rhotuka spinner cost the user energy, so only a certain number could be created in a given time.

ROCK LION:

Little is known about this creature, which was said to occupy the lowest levels of the ARCHIVES. Those few MATORAN who claimed to have seen one said that it had sharp teeth and claws and a mane which became white-hot when the beast was angered. No rock lion was ever seen on MATA NUI (2).

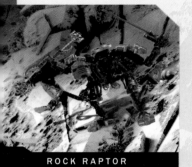

ROCK RAPTOR

ROCK RAPTOR:

A successful predator in PO-METRU, rock raptors suffered badly at the claws of VISORAK ROPORAK until only a few specimens remained. Prior to the arrival of the VISORAK, rock raptors were known for capturing much larger prey by using their natural tools to trigger rockslides. Their aggressive, independent nature made it impossible for the RAHAGA to help them against the hordes and most raptors were captured or killed.

RODE (ROAD):

KANOHI Mask of Truth worn by AXONN. This mask allows the user to see through any deception or disguise. It also enabled Axonn to see and communicate with TOA INIKA MATORO when the latter was in spirit form.

ROODAKA (roo-DAHK-ah):

Former viceroy of the VISORAK and lieutenant to MAKUTA, current freelance operative.

HISTORY

Little is known of Roodaka's past. She is a native of the island of XIA, a land where ruthlessness and the ability to deceive were required to survive, two traits she had in abundance. She committed her first betrayal while participating in a rite of passage with a companion, which involved successfully scaling a living mountain. When her partner's foot became caught, Roodaka abandoned him to die while she completed the climb.

How she met MAKUTA and SIDORAK are stories that have yet to be told. But later years found her partnered with Sidorak as lieutenants to Makuta, a job she enjoyed. Both of these powerful beings attempted to gain favor in the eyes of their employer, with neither succeeding at truly outdoing the other. After the TOA HAGA attacked the BROTHERHOOD

ROODAKA

OF MAKUTA, Roodaka ambushed them and used her KANOKA DISK to transform them into bestial RAHAGA.

Sidorak claimed credit for this idea and was rewarded with command of the Visorak horde, with Roodaka as his viceroy. Together, they led the horde to many victories in many lands. Sidorak hoped to cement an alliance with Roodaka and so gain influence in her native land. Roodaka, on the other hand, schemed to eliminate Sidorak and rule by the side of Makuta. Both got their opportunity when Makuta was defeated and imprisoned by the TOA METRU. Responding to his mental summons, they led the horde to METRU NUI. Once there, Roodaka began scheming how to win favor with Makuta by freeing him from the protodermis prison into which the TOA METRU had placed him. As part of her plan, she had the Toa transformed into TOA HORDIKA and lured VAKAMA into taking over as commander of the Visorak horde. During an attack by the Hordika, Roodaka struck out at the powerful RAHI KEETONGU, angering him. She then left Sidorak to deal with the maddened creature, who slew the horde king in battle. Disgusted by her role in Sidorak's death, the Visorak lost faith in her and so were quick to desert when Vakama gave them permission to leave the city.

Roodaka challenged the Hordika as a means of gathering the elemental energy needed to free Makuta. It appeared as if she had been fatally struck, but in truth Makuta saved her at the last moment. She returned to Xia, from which she began working for both sides in the DARK HUNTER-BROTHERHOOD OF MAKUTA WAR. It was during this period that she encountered ZAKTAN at a former Brotherhood fortress and directed him to a secret chamber that contained inscriptions related to Makuta's overall plan. It is believed that Roodaka herself has never seen this information.

POWERS

Roodaka is immensely strong and capable of harnessing her body's natural shadow energy and unleashing it in a devastating blast. Her catcher claw can snatch Kanoka disks out of the air so she can fling them back at her foe.

PERSONALITY

Roodaka is cunning, cruel, and thoroughly evil. A grand strategic thinker, she sees all other beings as pawns in her game. The only entity she admires is Makuta, and her time on Metru Nui was spent devising a means of rescuing him from his prison. Roodaka can be subtle, scheming, and capable of brilliantly complex plans one moment, and irrational and violent the next. Her favored approach to problems is to work on the weak spot of an opponent and twist them until they are willing to do her dirty work for her. Roodaka enjoyed the loyalty of the BOGGARAK who made up her personal guard, but many of the other Visorak feared and hated her.

EQUIPMENT

Roodaka carries a Kanoka disk launcher. Her disk is capable of causing instantaneous, permanent mutation in whoever it strikes. She also at one time carried a shard of the solid protodermis that had imprisoned Makuta.

ROPORAK

ROPORAK (ROE-poe-RACK):
One of the six breeds of VISORAK who invaded METRU NUI. Roporak have the power to blend in with their surroundings, becoming virtually invisible. This makes them excellent spies for the horde. Their RHOTUKA SPINNERS can disrupt the function of living creatures, causing an abrupt "power outage" effect. Of all Visorak, Roporak are capable of launching their spinners the farthest distance.

RORZAKH (ROAR-zahk):
VAHKI model assigned to ONU-METRU on METRU NUI. These mechanoids were relentless, willing to continue a pursuit even to their own destruction. Their Staffs of Presence allowed them to see and hear whatever their target saw or heard. The Rorzakh used this power on TOA WHENUA to lead him, NUJU, and ONEWA into a trap in the PRISON OF THE DARK HUNTERS. The TOA METRU also battled Rorzakh in the COLISEUM after being branded traitors by MAKUTA in his disguise as DUME.

RORZAKH

RUA (ROO-ah):
The Silver Mask of Wisdom, possessed of the powers of Water Breathing, X-Ray Vision, and Levitation.

RURU

RUKI (ROO-kee):
Small fish found in the waters around both METRU NUI and MATA NUI (2). Although no threat individually, schools of Ruki had been seen to drive off TARAKAVA and other much larger creatures. Their powerful jaws made them a consistent problem for GA-MATORAN, since they would chew through nets, dams, and any other object they might find in the water.

RURU (ROO-ROO):
KANOHI Mask of Night Vision. The Great Mask version, worn by TOA WHENUA, allowed him not only to see in the dark but to have X-ray vision as well. The Noble Ruru, worn by Whenua as a TURAGA, allowed night vision only.

SAFE HOUR:
Period of time during which MATORAN of the undersea city of MAHRI NUI felt they could wander beyond their borders without risk of harm. Careful observation had revealed that there was one hour of the day during which no predators were active in the waters. The primary activity during this time was the harvesting of AIRWEED by Matoran with the aid of HYDRUKA.

SAND SCREAMER:
Mysterious RAHI found on the island of VOYA NUI. The agonized shrieks of sand screamers are often heard, but the creature itself has never been seen. Tracks sighted by MATORAN

vanish in seconds. Evidence indicates that whatever the sand screamer is, it is capable of bringing down larger beasts.

SAND SNIPE:
A small, biting insect found in PO-METRU. Sand snipes could be annoying creatures, often burrowing beneath MATORAN armor and biting the organic PROTODERMIS underneath. Fortunately, they were easy to trap. Living in a barren METRU, they were enthralled by the sight of liquid protodermis and would march headlong into any puddle and promptly drown. This odd quirk led to the Matoran saying "foolish as a sand snipe."

SAND TARAKAVA (TAH-rah-KAH-vah):
This smaller cousin of the aquatic TARAKAVA made its home in the sandy wastes of PO-METRU and PO-WAHI. Its usual hunting method was to lurk beneath the sand and then strike when prey passed near. It was a natural enemy of the KIKANALO, usually preying on the weak or injured in a herd.

SANOK (sah-NOCK):
KANOHI Mask of Accuracy worn by TOA INIKA HEWKII. He was given the Matoran version of this mask while in the realm of KARZAHNI (1). The Sanok allows its wearer to use virtually any object as a missile weapon and to hit whatever it is aimed at.

SARDA (SAR-dah):
TA-MATORAN resident of MAHRI NUI who accompanied DEFILAK on his exploratory mission into the PIT. Captured by PRIDAK, Sarda was believed to have been killed by TAKEA sharks. In fact, he was rescued by TOA LESOVIKK and later participated in the battle against KARZAHNI (1).

SAVAGE:
Insane TOA HORDIKA who has been recruited into the DARK HUNTER organization. He possesses a highly developed tracking sense and a RHOTUKA SPINNER that can paralyze his enemies. His tri-claw has the power to liquefy solid matter.

SAVAGE

SCHOOLS:
GA-METRU was the educational center of METRU NUI and boasted many schools. Among the subjects taught here were PROTODERMIS PURIFICATION, translation, and MATORAN history. Ga-Metru employed Matoran from other districts to do menial tasks so that GA-MATORAN could focus on their studies. Prior to becoming a TOA, NOKAMA was a teacher in a Ga-Metru school and VHISOLA was one of her students.

SCULPTURE FIELDS:
Great, barren plains in PO-METRU used for the creation and display of massive statues. Anything too big to be carved in an enclosed space is worked on here. Portions of the Sculpture Fields became unstable due to RAHI activity, and MATORAN were barred from entire sections. TOA ONEWA pursued AHKMOU through the Sculpture Fields. The Po-Metru GREAT DISK was found embedded in a rock pillar here.

SCULPTURE FIELDS

SEA SPIDER:

An amphibious RAHI that first appeared off GA-METRU after the VISORAK invasion. The RAHAGA rapidly discovered that the sea spiders were a natural predator of the Visorak, one of the only ones known. Sea spider venom shrinks its prey to a more manageable size. The creature then throws its target into stasis using its spinner. Sea spiders have never been spotted anywhere on or around MATA NUI (2).

SEA SPIDER

SEA SQUID:

Organic life-forms found in the PIT and used as weapons by the BARRAKI. Sea squid hatch from eggs and come into the world hungry, and their preferred diet is the life energy of other beings. They attack by latching on to their prey with an almost unbreakable grip and then draining the energy directly. KALMAH discovered the cave that acted as their hatchery and began keeping them from food and abusing them to insure they would be constantly hungry and aggressive. He then created mechanical launchers that could be used to hurl the squid swiftly at a target. All six Barraki carried these launchers.

SECTOR THREE:

An area of LE-METRU just across the PROTODERMIS canals from TA-METRU. It had long been the site of numerous CHUTE breakdowns, which were eventually tied to the MORBUZAKH. LE-MATORAN repair squads who traveled there vanished, never to return, even when protected by VAHKI. Despite its reputation, ORKAHM allowed himself to be lured there by AHKMOU, part of the latter's efforts to get his hands on the six GREAT DISKS. Orkahm walked into a trap there and had to be rescued by TOA MATAU.

SEEKER:

Former servant of the BROTHERHOOD OF MAKUTA who was cast out for failing to securely guard the AVOHKII, the Mask of Light. Currently employed by the DARK HUNTERS, he is dedicated to finding the RAHAGA and getting the mask back. His primary weapon is his staff, which weakens an opponent physically and delivers seismic shocks.

SEEKING:

The name given to the study of prophecies in KO-KORO.

SEEKER

SENTRAKH [sen-TROCK]:

DARK HUNTER who inhabits a shadow state between living and death. His strange condition is the result of experiments performed on him by the SHADOWED ONE, and he remains that being's most loyal servant. Sentrakh possesses the natural powers of illusion casting, darkness, molecular transmutation, and mind wipe. His RHOTUKA SPINNER can cause a target to temporarily dematerialize. Sentrakh battled TOA VAKAMA in METRU NUI and saved the Shadowed One's life after his losing battle with MAKUTA.

SENTRAKH

SHADOW KRAATA:

Rare seventh stage of the KRAATA, shadow kraata are identified by their purple coloring as opposed to their shape (as they can appear in the shape of any of the previous six stages). Shadow kraata are capable of infecting KANOHI masks from a distance.

SHADOW PLAGUE:

Mysterious illness that struck the inhabitants of the island of MATA NUI (2) prior to the coming of the TOA MATA. It was created by MAKUTA by reducing SHADOW KRAATA to pure essence, and transforming that essence into an airborne virus. Those afflicted became influenced by the will of Makuta. He eventually abandoned this project upon realizing that the effects did not have the same permanence that came from infected masks and that the supply of shadow kraata was so limited as to make the effort impractical. The effects of the virus eventually faded from those afflicted, but not before large portions of the various KORO had been damaged, requiring years of repair.

SHADOW STEALER:

A former member of the HAND OF ARTAKHA, the band of heroes who predated the first TOA. After that group's time passed and they were replaced by the Toa, he turned to the DARK HUNTERS seeking adventure. The relationship was a stormy one, because the Dark Hunters' goals and his own were so vastly different. After his first mission, he decided to strike out on his own. He is currently making his way back to the Dark Hunter base on ODINA, defeating Toa and Dark Hunters as he goes. Shadow Stealer is able to absorb shadows and convert them into energy. He can also disappear into shadow and reappear somewhere else.

SHADOW STEALER

SHADOW TOA (TOE-ah):

Dark essences of GALI, KOPAKA, LEWA, ONUA, POHATU, and TAHU, given independent life by MAKUTA. The Shadow Toa were unleashed against their counterparts shortly after the TOA arrived on MATA NUI (2) as a test of their power. Faced with essentially fighting themselves, the Toa still managed to triumph by acknowledging that the darkness was a part of them, just as it was a part of all beings. This realization enabled the Toa to reabsorb the Shadow Toa back into their bodies, ending their threat.

SHADOWED ONE

SHADOWED ONE:

Legendary leader of the DARK HUNTERS, the Shadowed One lives on the island of Odina, from which he directs the actions of his mercenaries. His power is rumored to be second only to that of the BROTHERHOOD OF MAKUTA. It was he who dispatched NIDHIKI and KREKKA to METRU NUI in answer to MAKUTA's summons. After learning that Makuta was responsible for the deaths of his two agents, the Shadowed One declared war on the Brotherhood of Makuta. The conflict between the Dark Hunters and the Brotherhood has now raged for over 1,000 years. The Shadowed One's staff can create solid, crystalline PROTODERMIS, and his RHOTUKA SPINNER induces temporary madness. The Shadowed One also possesses highly destructive eyebeams. When ZAKTAN led a rebellion against his rule, the Shadowed One used his eyebeams in an effort to destroy him. For reasons that remain mysterious,

Zaktan survived the attack but his body was changed from solid matter to a collection of billions of microscopic PROTODITES.

SHALLOWS CAT:
Dangerous RAHI native to the island of DAXIA. The shallows cat resembles a MUAKA and lives along the coastline. It will stretch itself out near the surf, appearing harmless, and wait for the unwary to approach. Once someone gets too close, it will grab them, drag them into the water, and devour them.

SHARK TOOTH BLADE:
Weapon carried by PRIDAK, and made from the fused teeth of 10,000 TAKEA SHARKS.

SIDORAK (sih-DOAR-ack):
King of the VISORAK horde.

SIDORAK

HISTORY

In his early life, Sidorak was a minor power in a land filled with conflict. He rapidly discovered that by claiming credit for victories won by those beneath him, he could advance in the eyes of his leaders. If a commander objected to the credit being stolen, Sidorak would simply dispatch him on a dangerous mission from which he would not return.
This talent for treachery attracted the attention of MAKUTA. Sidorak was made one of that powerful being's lieutenants, along with ROODAKA. He immediately saw the advantage that might be gained if he and Roodaka formed an alliance, but she refused to agree. Instead, the two ended up competing for Makuta's favor, with Roodaka doing her best to hamper Sidorak.
When the TOA HAGAH turned on Makuta, and Roodaka transformed them into RAHAGA, Sidorak claimed credit for the idea. Makuta rewarded his cleverness by making him king of the Visorak, while Roodaka became viceroy. Sidorak grew into the job, becoming a respected leader of the horde and carrying them to many victories. He continued to hope that he and Roodaka could join forces at a some point, a wish that may have blinded him to her true intentions.
Sidorak led a successful invasion of METRU NUI during which the TOA METRU were captured and turned into TOA HORDIKA. Roodaka talked him out of having them immediately executed because she wished to use their powers to free Makuta. Sidorak later approved of Roodaka's decision to name VAKAMA field commander of the horde. Following an ill-advised attack on KEETONGU, Sidorak was killed by the Rahi while Roodaka looked on, refusing to help.

POWERS

Sidorak's primary power was his strength. Although not at the level of KEETONGU, he was far stronger than a TOA. He was also an excellent strategist and tactician, having masterminded a number of Visorak campaigns. He was skilled at manipulation, so much so, in fact, that it never occurred to him that he might be manipulated in turn.

PERSONALITY

Sidorak was not a king who hid in a fortress — he preferred to be out leading his Visorak into battle. Deep down, though, he knew that he had not really earned the position he held, and it made him try that much harder to be a successful and ruthless conqueror. He came across most of the time as confident, strong, and in control. He had done a good job at hiding from the Visorak any doubts he may have had about his leadership. Unfortunately, he had not managed to hide them from Roodaka.

EQUIPMENT

Sidorak carried a herding blade which could be used to communicate orders to the Visorak in the field. He also carried a RHOTUKA LAUNCHER with an *obedience* spinner which would force whoever it struck to obey his commands.

SILENCE:

DARK HUNTER who is believed to have been mutated by ROODAKA into his current form. Silence's specialty is the abduction of TOA, TURAGA, and BROTHERHOOD OF MAKUTA members. He is capable of creating a field around himself that deadens all sound. He carries a double-edged blade mounted on his forearm and a KANOKA disk launcher equipped with freeze disks.

SILVER CHUTE SPIDER:

A voracious predatory arachnid whose favorite hunting ground was near METRU NUI CHUTES. Its favorite prey was the GUKKO bird, which it would trap using fast-acting paralyzing venom in its webs. GA-MATORAN made a study of this creature's incredibly light and strong webbing, with the hope of duplicating it, but their efforts were unsuccessful. Interestingly, silver chute spiders were the only RAHI not hunted by the VISORAK hordes. As a result, many survived to make their way to LE-WAHI on MATA NUI (2).

SILVER CHUTE SPIDER

SKAKDI (SKOCK-dee):

Native species of the island of ZAKAZ. Up until about 70,000 years ago, the Skakdi were regarded as an unfriendly but generally peaceful people. Then a "renegade" BROTHERHOOD OF MAKUTA member arrived on the island and began tampering with the natives, resulting in their gaining vision-based powers and elemental powers. This led to the Skakdi becoming more warlike and destructive. Civil wars broke out all over the island. Today it is home to scattered hordes of natives fighting over ruins. The island has been quarantined by the Brotherhood and only the DARK HUNTERS ever venture there. A number of Skakdi have been recruited into that organization, including the six PIRAKA. Skakdi are known for their substantial physical strength, foul tempers, and the perpetual evil smiles they seem to be wearing. See also TAHTORAK and SPINE SLUGS.

SONIC SHIELD:

Tool carried by KOHRAK-KAL. This shield could create a sonic barrier that responded to blows with a sound so loud it could stun a TOA NUVA.

SPEAR OF FUSION:

Ancient weapon used most recently by VEZON. The designers of this powerful artifact remain unknown, but its uses are obvious. The spear is capable of either fusing two or more objects or beings together or splitting an object or being apart into two separate entities. The spear was originally stolen from its makers by the DARK HUNTERS, who sold it to the BROTHERHOOD OF MAKUTA. It was found by the PIRAKA in MANGAIA, and its accidental use resulted in the splitting of VEZOK into two beings, himself and Vezon. The latter wielded it in his capacity as guardian of the KANOHI IGNIKA. It was shattered by REIDAK but repaired again using its own power. The spear was later burnt to ashes by JALLER.

SPINAX (SPY-nacks):

RAHI companion of MAXILOS. Spinax is the equivalent of a bloodhound, capable of tracking a target anywhere and maintaining pursuit over the course of centuries. His primary weapons are claws and teeth.

SPINE SLUGS:

Parasites who attach themselves to the organic tissue of SKAKDI spines and apparently feed somehow on the energy produced by the host's battle rage. There are theories that the spine slugs somehow encourage that rage, though nothing has ever been proven.

SPINNER

SPINNER:

Former TOA of Air who defected to the DARK HUNTERS. Spinner's eyes cause vertigo in a target and his RHOTUKA SPINNERS can also affect an enemy's sense of balance. The combined power of his spinners can throw a target into a coma, but doing that weakens Spinner as well. The atmosphere around Spinner tends to be heavy and poisonous, making it difficult for him to sneak up on anyone.

SPINY STONE APE:

A tremendously strong RAHI that lived in caves in PO-METRU and PO-WAHI. Aggressive only when threatened, the stone ape relied on its claws, blade-tipped tail, and spiny armor when fighting. Its normal reaction to an intruder was to roll up into a defensive ball and growl, warning away anyone foolish enough to enter its lair. Stone apes favored the caves carved out of the canyon walls by ROCK RAPTORS.

SPIRIT STARS:

Points of light said to appear in the sky to represent TOA. Following the path of a spirit star in the night sky above METRU NUI enabled Toa VAKAMA, Toa NOKAMA, and Toa MATAU to find the prison in which LHIKAN was being held. After the TOA METRU defeated MAKUTA, Lhikan's spirit star split into six new ones, representing the new Toa.

Six stars above MATA NUI (2) were believed to represent TAHU and his team of Toa. The appearance of a seventh star above the island heralded the coming of TAKANUVA, the Toa of Light. Spirit stars also appeared above VOYA NUI upon the creation of the TOA INIKA.

STAFF OF DARKNESS:
Tool carried by MAKUTA through which he could channel his dark energies. Makuta used this as a sort of KOLHII STAFF in his battle with TAKANUVA.

STAFF OF LIGHT:
Tool carried by TAKANUVA. In the final combat with MAKUTA, Takanuva used this as a KOLHII STAFF, catching and hurling balls of energy with it.

STARS, METRU NUI (MET-troo NOO-ee):
A sky full of stars seemed to light the METRU NUI night, despite the fact that the city was inside a hollow cavern. It is clear that these stars were not the same as those in the skies above MATA NUI (2), but exactly what their true nature might have been has never been discovered. Still, beings as diverse as KO-MATORAN scholars and MAKUTA himself studied the stars to divine prophecies of the future and the will of the GREAT SPIRIT MATA NUI (1).

STONE HAMMER:
TURAGA ONEWA's tool and badge of office.

STONE RAT:
Voracious rodents who lived beneath the ground in METRU NUI. A stone rat plague once struck TA-METRU when the creatures were driven from their nests by NUI-RAMA. Later, the TOA METRU encountered stone rats while searching for KRAHKA.

SUBTERRANEAN:
Mutated ONU-MATORAN from METRU NUI who joined the DARK HUNTERS following the conclusion of the TOA-DARK HUNTER WAR. Subterranean is capable of disassembling objects with a touch and immobilizing enemies with his glance. He wears armor designed to deaden sound, as his hearing is painfully acute.

SUBTERRANEAN

SUBTERRANEAN WORM:
Great, blind, pale, white-tentacled creatures that lived in the deepest tunnels beneath ONU-WAHI on MATA NUI (2). They were believed to eat raw PROTODERMIS and the appearance of one was enough to shut down an Onu-Matoran mine for good. ONUA NUVA and WHENUA encountered one of these creatures while searching for KANOHI NUVA masks. Onua defeated it by slamming two rocks together and deafening the beast.

SULETU (SOO-lay-TOO):
KANOHI Mask of Telepathy worn by TOA INIKA KONGU. The mask was found during the journey Kongu and his friends made to VOYA NUI when they were still MATORAN. Kongu was able to get it back after it was taken from him during their time in the realm of KARZAHNI (1). The Suletu gives its user the ability to read thoughts as well as project them. Kongu used the Suletu to make VEZON hear the Kanohi IGNIKA's thoughts and realize the mask was prepared to reject him as its guardian. Toa KRAKUA also wore a Suletu.

SUUKORAK

SUUKORAK (SUE-coe-rack):

One of the six breeds of VISORAK that invaded METRU NUI. Suukorak have a natural resistance to cold and the ability to slow their life processes down to almost zero, making it extremely difficult for others to detect their presence. Suukorak RHOTUKA SPINNERS create an electrical field around a target. The field surrounds and moves with the target, gradually shrinking as time goes on. It is impossible to escape the field without sustaining a shock, so a prisoner's only hope is that the field dissipates before it contracts completely.

SUVA (SOO-vah):

Shrines found in the villages of MATA NUI (2), the GREAT TEMPLE of METRU NUI, and in various other places. These are commonly dedicated to individual TOA or groups of Toa, and are used as a storage space for KANOHI masks. Toa are able to teleport their masks directly from the suva to their faces. The six MATORAN who become TOA METRU did so by placing TOA STONES into the suva located in the Great Temple, unleashing energy that transformed them.

TA (TAH):

A Matoran prefix which means "fire."

TA-KINI (TAH-kih-NEE):

A temple dedicated to TAHU located in TA-WAHI on MATA NUI (2).

TA-KORO (TAH-koar-OH):

Village on MATA NUI (2) and home to the TA-MATORAN. Ta-Koro was located in the Lake of Fire and its citizens lived in homes made of cooled lava. A small lava stream flowed through the village, providing it with heat. Ta-Koro was governed by TURAGA VAKAMA and protected by TOA TAHU and the TA-KORO GUARD. The village was destroyed by the RAHKSHI, vanishing beneath the lava without a trace. It has not been rebuilt.

TA-KORO GUARD (tah-KOAR-oh):

Defense force that protected the village of TA-KORO against all threats. The Guard was led by JALLER.

TA-MATORAN (TAH-mat-OAR-an):

A resident of TA-KORO or TA-METRU. Ta-Matoran commonly had red armor and wore red or yellow masks. On METRU NUI, most Ta-Matoran worked in foundries and forges, creating KANOHI masks and other items for use throughout the city. On MATA NUI (2), many Ta-Matoran were lava farmers or members of the TA-KORO GUARD.

TA-METRU (TAH-MET-troo):

Home of the "makers" on METRU NUI, where molten PROTODERMIS was fashioned by skilled workers into tools, KANOHI masks, and other items used throughout the city. Ta-Metru was filled with factories and foundries, and the temperature in the METRU was too hot for most other MATORAN to handle. The skies above Ta-Metru were traditionally filled with steam and smoke, making it a place residents of other metru preferred to avoid. Ta-Metru was the site of the GREAT FURNACE, where the final battle with the MORBUZAKH plant took place. The FIRE PITS, PROTODERMIS RECLAMATION YARD, PROTODERMIS RECLAMATION FURNACE, and VAKAMA'S FOUNDRY could all be found here. One of the six GREAT DISKS was hidden in a fire pit in this metru.

TA-SUVA [TAH-soo-VAH]:
A shrine to TAHU NUVA in TA-KORO. KANOHI masks and Tahu Nuva's symbol were kept here. BOHROK-KAL stole the NUVA SYMBOL from the Ta-Suva, robbing Tahu Nuva of his elemental power of fire. The suva was destroyed, along with the village itself, by the RAHKSHI.

TA-WAHI [TAH-wah-HEE]:

The hot, volcanic region surrounding TA-KORO on MATA NUI (2). Lava falls, rivers of molten magma, and other fiery features can be found here, flowing from the mouth of the MANGAI volcano. It is home to TA-MATORAN and scores of RAHI that thrive on heat and flame. TOA TAHU's canister washed up on the shore of Ta-Wahi. This region was the site of one of the first BOHROK attacks, as well as a devastating onslaught by the RAHKSHI that resulted in the destruction of Ta-Koro. The largest Matoran KOLHII stadium is also located here.

TAHNOK

TAHNOK [TAH-nahk]:
One of the six breeds of BOHROK, insectlike mechanoids controlled by KRANA that menaced the island of MATA NUI (2). The Tahnok were tied to the element of fire and their FIRE SHIELDS could melt any substance. Dangerous and unpredictable, the Tahnok were the most aggressive of all the Bohrok swarms. They were part of the initial attack on TA-KORO and a subsequent one on PO-KORO. Later, a swarm of Tahnok (minus their krana) was led by TAHU NUVA against the BOHROK-KAL. They were sent into space due to NUHVOK-KAL's negation of gravity and remain in orbit. The rest of the Tahnok returned to their nests after the coming of the Bohrok-Kal.

TAHNOK-KAL [TAH-nahk-KAHL]:
One of the six mutant BOHROK who made up the BOHROK-KAL. Its tool was an electricity shield, able to be used both for defense and to hurl lightning bolts. After being fed Toa power via the TOA NUVA symbols (see BOHROK-KAL), Tahnok-Kal was overloaded with electricity and its moving parts fused together.

TAHNOK KAL

TAHNOK VA [TAH-nahk VAH]:

One of the six BOHROK VA, Tahnok Va were connected to the fire element. They used their FIRESTAFFS to defend themselves in combat and to light their way through the dark BOHROK tunnels. Upon realizing the Tahnok Va were not living creatures, the TA-MATORAN diverted a lava stream into the path of some of the couriers and melted them.

TAHNOK VA

TAHTORAK [tah-TOAR-ack]:

The largest land RAHI ever seen in METRU NUI, the intelligent, reptilian Tahtorak stood over 40 feet tall. It was more than powerful enough to destroy a city, with a single sweep of its tail able to bring down entire buildings. Tahtorak was once a herd animal in another land who was transported to Metru Nui through a dimensional gate by BRUTAKA, using the KANOHI OLMAK. It made a home far beneath the ARCHIVES maintenance tunnels, where it slumbered. It was awakened by the TOA METRU's battle with the KRAHKA and later tore its way through the surface, demanding to know "the answer." (Rahaga POUKS later theorized that the answer it seeks is just how it ended up in Metru Nui, so far from its home.) The Toa defeated it by weakening the ground beneath its feet, sending it plunging back down below.

TAHTORAK

The Tahtorak reappeared after the VISORAK invaded the city. Summoned by Krahka, the great beast allied itself with her, the Toa and the RAHAGA. The Tahtorak fought a great battle against the monstrous ZIVON, which ended when both creatures and Krahka were transported into the zone of darkness by a KAHGARAK spinner.

The Tahtorak has since escaped with Krahka onto the island of VOYA NUI, where it has done battle with the KARDAS dragon.

TAHU/TAHU NUVA [TAH-hoo/TAH-hoo NOO-vah]:

TOA of Fire on MATA NUI (2), leader of the TOA NUVA, and protector of TA-KORO.

HISTORY

TAHU

Nothing is known about Tahu's history prior to his first appearance on the island of Mata Nui. He was one of six Toa who had been floating in the ocean around that land for 1,000 years. They were inside unique canisters and each was partially disassembled. A signal unwittingly sent by TAKUA called the canisters to shore. Tahu emerged on the coast of TA-WAHI, assembled himself, and headed into the CHARRED FOREST. There he walked into a Rahi trap set by JALLER. The Matoran set him free upon realizing that this was indeed the Toa whose arrival they had awaited for so long.

Tahu rapidly made contact with the other five Toa — ONUA, POHATU, GALI, LEWA, and KOPAKA. Together and separately, they searched for KANOHI masks and battled the RAHI servants of MAKUTA. Over time, Tahu came to be acknowledged as the group's leader, though that role did not always sit well with the others.

The Toa of Fire led his friends into battle against the SHADOW TOA and later against Makuta himself. He also briefly merged with Pohatu and Onua to form the Toa Kaita called AKAMAI. During the invasion of the BOHROK, Tahu began to display a recklessness and lack of patience that grated on the nerves of Kopaka. At one point, Tahu's impetuous nature led to him being trapped in a TAHNOK nest. Only by using his powers to superheat the air in the nest and cause an explosion was he able to escape. (It was during this period that Tahu was briefly stripped of his mask and forced to wear a parasitic KRANA, but this is an encounter he has refused to speak about.)

Following the defeat of the twin Bohrok queens, the BAHRAG, the six Toa were transformed by energized protodermis into TOA NUVA. Tahu Nuva grew, if anything, more overconfident and arrogant. This led to arguments with Kopaka and eventually a decision to split up the team. None of the Toa Nuva could know that this would leave them vulnerable to a later attack by the BOHROK-KAL. It was Tahu's potentially dangerous use of the Kanohi VAHI, the Great Mask of Time, that helped to end that threat.

Despite how close the Toa came to being defeated in that instance, Tahu Nuva had not yet learned a badly needed lesson about unity. His stubbornness alienated him from Gali. When the Rahkshi attacked Ta-Koro, Tahu Nuva attempted to challenge them on his own. The result was defeat, the destruction of the village, and a scratch from the poisonous LEHRAK. The poison ravaged Tahu Nuva's system, causing him to easily become enraged and turn on his friends. It took Kopaka's ice power to stop his rampage, and the power of all five Toa Nuva to remove the poison.

Their unity now restored, the Toa Nuva challenged the Rahkshi and won with the aid of TAKANUVA, the Toa of Light. They later witnessed Takanuva's victory over Makuta and the rediscovery of METRU NUI. Back on Mata Nui, Tahu Nuva helped oversee the construction of boats for a journey back to the city of legends. He also joined with the others in listening to Turaga VAKAMA's tales of life in Metru Nui centuries before.

Tahu Nuva led the Toa Nuva, Turaga and Matoran, back to Metru Nui. Shortly after their arrival, he and his teammates were sent to VOYA NUI to retrieve the KANOHI IGNIKA. They encountered the PIRAKA and BRUTAKA on that island and were defeated and imprisoned. They were later saved by the MATORAN RESISTANCE.

Tahu and the team have since returned to Metru Nui and begun preparations to awaken MATA NUI (1). Along the way, Tahu retrieved JALLER's old mask from the realm of KARZAHNI (1).

POWERS

Tahu was the master of heat and flame. In his time on Mata Nui (2), he created everything from small brush fires to raging infernos; used his flame to fuse a wall of sand into glass; superheated the air in an enclosed space until it caused an explosion; and created cages and other structures made of flame. Tahu also had in theory the ability to absorb all heat and flame in an area into himself, but never demonstrated this skill. He was an accomplished lava surfer and has a natural resistance to extreme heat.

PERSONALITY

Tahu took being a leader extremely seriously. This often caused him to be impatient with the other Toa, too quick to take on dangerous tasks, and not inclined to include his comrades in strategy sessions. While very protective of the other Toa, especially Gali, he had a habit of plunging into risky situations without waiting for a plan. He could be fierce, short-tempered, and stubborn, but was also an extremely brave and loyal Toa.

EQUIPMENT

Tahu carried a fire sword and (as Tahu Nuva) twin magma swords. He most often wore a HAU or HAU NUVA, the Great Mask of Shielding. He was also the only one of the six Toa to ever wear the Kanohi Vahi, the Great Mask of Time.

TAIPU [TAY-poo]:

Taipu was a junior ONU-MATORAN archivist of no particular renown on METRU NUI. On MATA NUI (2), he served as a miner in ONU-KORO. He first met TAKUA while participating in a digging project to construct a tunnel to LE-WAHI. He informed the newcomer about Onu-Matoran mining and what was known about TOA ONUA. Later, Taipu was captured by a swarm of NUI-RAMA and an infected Toa LEWA. Only Onua's intervention saved him. Taipu would later join with Takua, KAPURA, KOPEKE, TAMARU, MACKU, and HAFU in the CHRONICLER's Company and defend KINI-NUI against RAHI attack. He participated in a great battle with various forms of Rahi which ended successfully, thanks to the intervention of the TA-KORO GUARD, the ONU-KORO USSALRY, and the LE-KORO GUKKO BIRD FORCE.

TAKADOX [TACK-ah-DOCKS]:

One of the six BARRAKI who menace the residents of MAHRI NUI.

TAKADOX

Takadox was the first to join with PRIDAK in the formation of the LEAGUE OF SIX KINGDOMS, immediately seeing an advantage in having strong allies. He joined his eastern kingdom to Pridak's northwestern one, essentially forcing Kalmah (based in the northeast) to join or have his kingdom cut off.

Takadox was the least visible of all the Barraki, generally staying in his fortress and using his hypnotic power to make his lieutenants carry out his will. The commands he made them deliver were so harsh that they became targets of hatred throughout the empire, resulting in many of them being slain by Takadox's subjects.

Takadox had serious doubts about the League's ability to overthrow MATA NUI (1), but joined in the rebellion anyway (for fear of being excluded from power if it succeeded). When it failed, he was banished along with the other Barraki to the PIT. After the GREAT CATACLYSM shattered the prison, Takadox killed HYDRAXON, the jailer. He escaped into the sea and was mutated by the water into an insectoid form.

Disturbed by his new appearance and reluctant to be part of any more Barraki schemes, Takadox retreated to a cavern where he spent most of the next 1,000 years. Anything he needed was provided either by his underwater insect army or by Carapar, who he frequently entranced. When the KANOHI IGNIKA drifted into the region, Takadox decided to end his seclusion and join in the hunt for it. (He was briefly sidetracked by an attempt to hypnotize a 300-foot-long VENOM EEL.)

He allied with Pridak against MATORO and MAXILOS, and later against EHLEK when he believed that Barraki had betrayed the group. With open warfare now raging between the various BARRAKI, the TOA MAHRI, and the MATORAN of Mahri Nui, Takadox is busy working out a way he can profit from the carnage.

Takadox possesses a hypnotic power and carries long daggers and a SQUID LAUNCHER.

TAKANUVA [TAH-kah-NOO-vah]:

The TOA of Light, also known as the "Seventh Toa."

HISTORY

Matoran legend stated that in a time of great darkness, a defender would emerge who would wield the power of Light. His coming would be heralded by the discovery of the KANOHI

TAKANUVA

AVOHKII, the Mask of Light. The mask was discovered by a MATORAN named TAKUA. He and his best friend, JALLER, were sent by the TURAGA on a mission to bring the mask to the waiting Toa. The mission proved to be extremely dangerous, as MAKUTA sent his RAHKSHI to find the HERALD of the Seventh Toa and the mask. Takua eventually realized that he was the one destined to become the Toa of Light, and putting on the mask, he was transformed.

As Takanuva, he helped to defeat the Rahkshi. With the assistance of the Toa, he built a vehicle called the USSANUI from Rahkshi parts and used it to travel to Makuta's lair. There light and darkness clashed, until the two powerful beings fell into a pool of ENERGIZED PROTODERMIS and were merged into one entity, TAKUTANUVA.

After being returned to his individual form, Takanuva used his light powers to help illuminate the newly rediscovered METRU NUI. He returned to Mata Nui with the TOA NUVA to oversee the building of transport craft and is currently preparing for the return to Metru Nui. He believes that he has fulfilled his destiny — defeating Makuta — but only time will tell if Takanuva has achieved all that he was meant to achieve.

Takanuva returned with the Toa Nuva and Matoran to Metru Nui. He was ordered by TURAGA DUME to stay behind when the Nuva went to VOYA NUI. Later, he joined Jaller and a team of Matoran in a search party for the missing heroes, but was forced to turn back when he encountered an archway through which no one with the power of light could pass. As of this writing, he remains in Metru Nui, guarding the city.

POWERS

Just as Tahu controls fire and Gali water, Takanuva controls light. He can illuminate the darkness, create blinding flares, focus his power into a laser beam, and create holographic images of himself. He has also been experimenting with other potential powers, such as increased speed and the creation of solid light projections.

PERSONALITY

Although now a Toa, Takanuva has not changed a great deal from when he was Takua. He still has an insatiable curiosity about new things and new places and prefers exploring to doing more mundane work. He is awed by the power and responsibility he has as a Toa and by being in the company of Tahu and his other heroes. He has proven to be a good student of their training, driving himself hard to master his powers. What he has not shared with them is that he secretly worries Makuta will return someday and seek vengeance for the defeat at Takanuva's hands. The Toa of Light is determined to be ready should that happen. Although he has been welcomed into the company of the other Toa, Takanuva still feels most comfortable with his Matoran friends, especially Jaller and HAHLI.

EQUIPMENT

Takanuva carries the STAFF OF LIGHT, which he can use to channel and direct his powers. He wears the Kanohi Avohkii, the Mask of Light.

TAKEA (TAH-kay-AH):

An ocean predator, the Takea's name means "king of sharks" in MATORAN (2). Takea consider virtually everything in the water an enemy, from TARAKAVA to Matoran fishing boats. The TOA METRU witnessed Takea sharks attacking prehistoric beasts along the underground river that linked METRU NUI to MATA NUI (2).
Takea made up PRIDAK's army in the PIT.

TAKU (TAH-koo):

A small, ducklike bird distantly related to the GUKKO. It is best known for its ability to dive deep beneath the water in search of fish.

TAKUA (tah-KOO-ah):

An AV-MATORAN, former CHRONICLER, and currently TAKANUVA, the Toa of Light.
Little is known about Takua's life prior to his arrival on METRU NUI. During the TIME SLIP, he

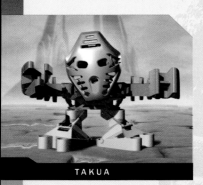

TAKUA

was transported to Metru Nui in the guise of a TA-MATORAN and given false memories of a life in the city. He worked in TA-METRU as a toolmaker and operated a small business offering souvenirs from other metru he had picked up in his wanderings. Unfortunately, since he often made these trips during his working hours, he attracted a lot of attention from VAHKI patrols. A running joke in Ta-Metru was that an entire squad was assigned just to keep watch on Takua. On MATA NUI (2), Takua continued to be more interested in exploring than working. But his life changed when the TURAGA asked him to travel the island and collect the TOA STONES. These had been hidden long before by the TOA METRU, but the Turaga believed that MAKUTA might attempt to steal them. Takua carried out his task and brought all six stones to the KINI-NUI. When he placed them there, beams of light shot up into the sky. Takua was carried high in the air by one of the beams, then slammed onto the ground, the blow resulting in amnesia.

Without realizing it, Takua had succeeded in summoning TAHU and the rest of the Toa from the sea, where they had been floating in canisters for 1,000 years.
Stripped of his memory again, Takua stumbled into more adventures as he wandered the island. He helped to save GA-MATORAN trapped underwater, aided ONU-MATORAN miners, aided PO-MATORAN dealing with infected COMET balls, and helped save the LE-MATORAN and Toa LEWA from NUI-RAMA. As a reward for his service, he was named CHRONICLER of the Toa.
One of his first acts was to form the CHRONICLER's Company to aid in the defense of the island. When the Toa went to battle Makuta underground, the Chronicler's Company was assigned to defend Kini-Nui from RAHI attack. Before going below, Toa GALI established a mind link with Takua so he would be aware of all that went on and could keep an accurate record.
After the defeat of the Rahi, Takua journeyed down to MANGAIA to witness the Toa's fight with Makuta. He saw both this and the awakening of the BOHROK, and barely escaped with his life. During the Bohrok invasion, Takua aided the Le-Matoran and the Ga-Matoran. He and his best friend, JALLER, journeyed with Tahu for a brief time after the appearance of the BOHROK-KAL.
Takua's greatest adventure began when he wandered off before a KOLHII match and found a lava cave. Fascinated by a strange stone marker, he was investigating it when Jaller found him. Stumbling, he dropped the marker, which dissolved in the lava to reveal the KANOHI AVOHKII, the legendary Mask of Light.
Although the mask's illumination clearly fell on Takua, marking him as the HERALD of the Seventh Toa, he did not want the responsibility. He convinced the Turaga that it was Jaller who

was meant to be the herald. Together, the two were sent by Turaga VAKAMA to find the Toa of Light and bring him his mask. Accompanied by PEWKU, Takua's pet USSAL crab, they set out. Their journey took them through LE-WAHI and KO-WAHI and ONU-WAHI, dodging RAHKSHI attacks along the way. It became clear that the Rahkshi were seeking the herald and the mask. Takua continued to refuse to accept responsibility for the quest, even going so far as to quit the journey entirely at one point after Makuta warned him that continuing would cost Jaller his life. It was, in fact, Jaller's sacrifice that saved Takua from the TURAHK and made the MATORAN realize what he must do. As Jaller lay dying, Takua donned the Mask of Light and transformed into Toa TAKANUVA (something that could only happen to a destined Av-Matoran). (See TAKANUVA.) Vakama later told him that after being a Chronicler for so long, "you have finally found your own story."

TAKUTANUVA (tah-KOO-tah-NOO-vah):

A merged entity formed when TAKANUVA and MAKUTA fell into a pool of ENERGIZED PROTODERMIS together during their battle. The creature that emerged had a mask formed of half the KANOHI AVOHKII and half the Kanohi KRAAHKAN. Due to the fact that Makuta's mask had been torn off him just prior to immersion, Takutanuva was apparently dominated by Takanuva's more benevolent personality. Takutanuva used his great strength to open the gateway leading from Makuta's lair to METRU NUI. He then used a portion of Makuta's life force to revive the dead JALLER. The gateway immediately collapsed on the weakened Takutanuva. The Toa of Light survived, his body reconstituted by the power of light, but of Makuta there was no sign.

TAMARU (tah-MAH-roo):

A friendly, fast-talking LE-MATORAN, Tamaru once dreamed of being an AIRSHIP pilot in METRU NUI. Unfortunately, he washed out of training due to a fear of heights. He later opened his own shop, Tamaru's Transports, renting and selling used vehicles and failed test-track prototypes.
On MATA NUI (2), Tamaru similarly failed to become a GUKKO rider and ended up working as the keeper of the LE-KORO throwing disk range. He served as part of the Chronicler's Company, a small force assembled by TAKUA to protect KINI-NUI from RAHI attacks. Later, he was one of only two Le-Matoran who were not captured by the BOHROK and fitted with a mind-controlling KRANA. He joined with the other Le-Matoran, KONGU, along with Takua and NUPARU to lure TOA LEWA, TURAGA MATAU, and the rest of the Le-Matoran into a trap and remove their krana.

TARAKAVA (tah-RAH-kah-VAH):

Lizardlike amphibians who live in shallow waters, around both GA-METRU and GA-KORO. Their common hunting method is to lurk beneath the water until a target comes by and then strike with their powerful forearms. Tarakava tend to avoid deep water, as it is home to TAKEA sharks and other natural enemies of this RAHI. These beasts were among the creatures used by MAKUTA against the TOA and MATORAN on MATA NUI (2). Although the Rahi caused a great deal of destruction, GA-MATORAN on Mata Nui showed a willingness to care for those Tarakava who had been freed from Makuta's dark influence.

TARAKAVA

TARAKAVA NUI (tah-RAH-kah-VAH noo-ee):

A mutant version of the TARAKAVA and one of the last creatures created by MAKUTA and the ENERGIZED PROTODERMIS ENTITY. The Tarakava Nui was responsible for wrecking early efforts to build the village of GA-KORO on MATA NUI (2), before it was temporarily driven off by TURAGA NOKAMA and the GA-MATORAN.

TEHUTTI (tuh-HOO-tee):

ONU-MATORAN archivist who discovered the location of the ONU-METRU GREAT DISK. Initially, Tehutti planned to give the disk as a gift to the ARCHIVES, thus securing his reputation as a master archivist. But when NIDHIKI threatened him, the MATORAN thought better of his plan. Rescued from a wild RAHKSHI by TOA WHENUA, Tehutti led him and Toa NUJU to the proper section of the Archives where the disk could be found.

TEHUTTI

Later, Tehutti joined with AHKMOU, EHRYE, NUHRII, ORKAHM, and VHISOLA to form the MATORAN NUI and assist the TOA METRU against the MORBUZAKH. After they had split back into their separate forms, Tehutti departed for Onu-Metru. He was captured on the way by VAHKI and placed in a MATORAN SPHERE. Evidence was later discovered that Tehutti may have been destined to become a Toa of Earth. This evidence later proved to be false.

He would later be rescued by the Toa Metru and transported to MATA NUI (2), where he worked as a miner.

TEST TRACK

TEST TRACK:

A portion of the MOTO-HUB in LE-METRU devoted to testing new land vehicles. MATAU was a frequent visitor here when he was a MATORAN, often volunteering to test the latest creations. Like the Moto-Hub in general, the test track was badly damaged by the earthquake that struck METRU NUI. Matau was using the test track when LHIKAN gave him a TOA STONE.

THOK (THOCK):

One of the six PIRAKA who invaded the island of VOYA NUI. Thok was originally recruited into the DARK HUNTERS after attempting to steal the weapons of three of its members. He later joined in ZAKTAN's unsuccessful rebellion against the SHADOWED ONE and broke ranks with the Dark Hunters to become a Piraka. He traveled with the others to Voya Nui in search of the KANOHI IGNIKA, planning all the time to betray them and seize it for himself. He is an expert at manipulating others and then abandoning them when things go wrong. Along with HAKANN, Thok stole the power of BRUTAKA and fought the TOA INIKA and the other Piraka, only to be defeated. When last seen, he and the other Piraka were still on Voya Nui, and unaware their bodies were changing as a result of exposure to mutagenic seawater.

THOK

Thok carries an ice peg gun, possesses spellbinder vision that can disorient opponents, and has the power to bring inanimate objects to life under his control. He also has elemental ice power, but it can only be used in conjunction with the powers of another Piraka.

THULOX (THOO-locks):
Name of one of the HYDRUKA who was used to harvest air for the residents of MAHRI NUI. See HYDRUKA.

THUMPERS:
Tools carried by TOA HORDIKA WHENUA. These could be used to summon subterranean RAHI or charge up his RHOTUKA SPINNER.

TIME SLIP:
Six-month period tens of thousands of years ago engineered by MATA NUI (1), the events of which are not remembered by anyone in the universe except members of the ORDER OF MATA NUI. It was during this period that the Order "seeded" AV-MATORAN on various islands in disguise, including TAKUA.

THULOX

TIRO CANYON (tee-ROE):
A gorge in the desert of PO-WAHI on MATA NUI (2). POHATU, GALI, ONUA, and KOPAKA combined forces to trap a swarm of TAHNOK here and rob them of their KRANA.

TOA (TOE-ah):
Heroes who serve the GREAT SPIRIT MATA NUI, defend the MATORAN and other innocent beings, and honor the three virtues, Unity, Duty, and Destiny. All Toa seem to have certain things in common, including the ability to use Great KANOHI Masks of Power, control of a single elemental power, and possession of a tool to focus that power. Toa commonly operate in groups of six, although smaller and larger groups have been known to exist when circumstances dictate. Certain Toa are known to have begun their lives as MATORAN, while others may have been Toa for the entirety of their existence. Known means of transforming from Matoran to Toa include via the power of TOA STONES (the TOA METRU), donning the Mask of Light (TAKANUVA), and being struck by lightning from the RED STAR. Whether these are the only ways a Matoran can become a Toa is unknown.

Toa are said to have a destiny to fulfill. Once they have done so, they will at some point be presented with a great choice. If they choose to sacrifice their Toa power for the greater good, then they will be transformed into TURAGA, respected leaders of the Matoran. If they choose to retain their power, they can remain as Toa indefinitely. Toa have been active on METRU NUI, Mata Nui (2), and in numerous other lands. Toa have faced numerous foes including MAKUTA, the RAHKSHI, the BOHROK, the BOHROK-KAL, the MORBUZAKH, KARZAHNI (2), the RAHI, the DARK HUNTERS, ROODAKA, SIDORAK, the PIRAKA, BRUTAKA, the BARRAKI, and KRAHKA, among others. Their greatest and most persistent enemies to date have been the BROTHERHOOD OF MAKUTA and the DARK HUNTERS.

Known Toa include TAHU, GALI, LEWA, ONUA, POHATU, KOPAKA, VAKAMA, NOKAMA, ONEWA, WHENUA, NUJU, MATAU, LHIKAN, DUME, NORIK, IRUINI, BOMONGA, GAAKI, POUKS, KUALUS, DUME, NIDHIKI, JALLER, HAHLI, HEWKII, MATORO, KONGU, NUPARU, KRAKUA, JOVAN, and LESOVIKK. See individual entries.

TOA CANISTER:
Transport vehicle built by MATORAN in a place referred to as "the world that feeds the world" and placed in various spots throughout the universe. The canisters were said to be safe for use only by Toa, although others have used them and survived. The TOA MATA took canisters to the island of MATA NUI (2), although the craft malfunctioned and floated in the ocean for 1,000 years.

Canisters were also used by the PIRAKA, VEZON, the TOA NUVA, and JALLER's team of Matoran (later the TOA INIKA). Canisters are capable of moving at high speed, can pass through solid rock, and appear to be able to hone in on a location based on a traveler's thoughts.

TOA-DARK HUNTER WAR:

Conflict that spanned six months in the city of METRU NUI. Sparked by a conflict between TURAGA DUME and the SHADOWED ONE over the latter's desire to build a base in the city, the war raged throughout the various METRU. It came to an end when LARISKA convinced Toa NIDHIKI to betray his comrades and lead them into a trap. What neither of them knew was that Toa LHIKAN had overheard their plot. Lhikan led the Toa into the trap, but then sprang one of his own, capturing the Dark Hunter army. In return for the MAKOKI STONE, Lhikan agreed to let the Dark Hunters leave the island in peace, provided they took Nidhiki with them.

TOA HAGAH [TOE-ah HAH-gah]:

Name given to the six elite Toa whose job was to safeguard MAKUTA. Each Toa Hagah wore unique armor that identified him or her as a member of this special group. The Toa Hagah later discovered that Makuta was oppressing and enslaving Matoran and turned against both him and the BROTHERHOOD OF MAKUTA. They broke into the fortress at DESTRAL and stole the KANOHI AVOHKII, the Mask of Light. They were later turned into RAHAGA by ROODAKA, but still managed to escape to METRU NUI with the mask. The six Toa Hagah were NORIK, IRUINI, GAAKI, KUALUS, POUKS, and BOMONGA (see individual entries).

TOA HORDIKA [TOE-ah hoar-DEE-kah]:

Name given to the six TOA METRU who were transformed into half hero, half beast forms by the venom of the VISORAK. The Toa Hordika were equipped with new tools and KANOKA LAUNCHERS, but had to constantly fight their own bestial sides. They challenged the Visorak and aided the RAHAGA in their search for KEETONGU.

TOA INIKA [TOE-ah i-NEE-kah]:

Team of heroes who came into being when lightning from the RED STAR struck six TOA CANISTERS on the shores of VOYA NUI, transforming the MATORAN inside into Toa. The Toa Inika all had organic KANOHI and elemental powers that were mixed with lightning. When their masks were removed, their faces gave off a blinding glow. The Toa Inika were JALLER, HAHLI, KONGU, NUPARU, MATORO, and HEWKII. They fought the PIRAKA, BRUTAKA, UMBRA, the PROTODAX, VEZON, and FENRAKK in their quest to obtain the KANOHI IGNIKA. After finding and losing the mask, they traveled through the CORD to reach the sunken village of MAHRI NUI. Upon entering the water, a wave of energy from the Ignika transformed them into the TOA MAHRI.

TOA KAITA [TOE-ah KIGH-ee-TAH]:

Two distinct beings formed by the merging of the six TOA. WAIRUHA was created when GALI, KOPAKA, and LEWA combined, and AKAMAI by the joining of TAHU, ONUA, and POHATU. The Toa Kaita were first seen by Gali in a vision. Later, the Toa chose to bring them into being to defeat the MANAS guardians of MAKUTA. They have not been seen to form Kaita since that time.

Although the TOA METRU also had the potential to form Toa Kaita, they never did so simply because they did not know how to accomplish the feat.

TOA KAITA NUVA (TOE-ah KIGH-ee-TAH NOO-vah):

Two distinct beings who could have been formed by the merging of the six TOA NUVA. Although the potential for such unions existed, only Wairuha Nuva has ever been formed.

TOA MAHRI (TOE-ah MAH-ree):

Name given to the TOA INIKA after their transformation by the KANOHI IGNIKA into beings capable of surviving underwater. The title was awarded to the Toa by DEFILAK, in honor of their efforts to save the city of MAHRI NUI from the BARRAKI. Each Toa Mahri is fitted with special breathing tubes that act as gills and make it possible for them to breathe water, but not air. The six Toa Mahri are JALLER, HAHLI, HEWKII, NUPARU, MATORO, and KONGU.

TOA MATA (TOE-ah MAH-tah):

TOA METRU

Name given to the six TOA who appeared on the island of MATA NUI slightly over 1,000 years ago and battled to save it from MAKUTA. The six Toa Mata were TAHU, GALI, LEWA, POHATU, ONUA, and KOPAKA. They fought RAHI, BOHROK, and BOHROK-KAL before immersion in ENERGIZED PROTODERMIS transformed them into TOA NUVA.

TOA METRU (TOE-ah MET-troo):

Name given to the six TOA heroes who defended METRU NUI against MAKUTA, the MORBUZAKH, and the DARK HUNTERS. The six Toa Metru were MATAU, NOKAMA, NUJU, ONEWA, VAKAMA, and WHENUA. It is believed that these six were the first Toa to have this designation, as the previous Toa serving in Metru Nui were not native to that city (see LHIKAN and NIDHIKI).

TOA NUVA (TOE-ah NOO-vah):

Heroes gifted with greater strength, stronger armor, and greater control of their elemental powers than ordinary Toa possess. Toa Nuva also have the ability to use KANOHI NUVA, masks that allow the wearer to share their power with those in close proximity. The only known means of transforming a Toa into a Toa Nuva is via exposure to ENERGIZED PROTODERMIS. Only six Toa Nuva have ever been known to exist: GALI NUVA, TAHU NUVA, KOPAKA NUVA, POHATU NUVA, ONUA NUVA, and LEWA NUVA (see individual entries). Originally TOA MATA on MATA NUI (2), these six heroes were immersed in energized protodermis shortly after their defeat of the BAHRAG. The experience transformed them and made them more powerful than before. Although that enhanced power for a time threatened to shatter their unity, they were able to combine forces to defeat the BOHROK-KAL and the RAHKSHI. They later led the TURAGA and MATORAN back to their homeland of METRU NUI. Once there, the Toa Nuva were told by Turaga DUME that MATA NUI (1) was dying and they had to travel to the island of VOYA NUI to retrieve the KANOHI IGNIKA in order to save him. On Voya Nui, they battled the PIRAKA and BRUTAKA and were defeated and imprisoned. They were later freed by a group of Matoran led by GARAN.

Following a conversation with AXONN and BOTAR, the Toa Nuva left Voya Nui and returned to Metru Nui. There, they broke into the GREAT TEMPLE and uncovered a list of tasks that had to be done to awaken Mata Nui (1), including freeing the Bahrag and unleashing the Bohrok once again. That has been done, and they are currently pursuing the other tasks they must do in order to prepare the universe for the Great Spirit's return.

TOA STONES (TOE-ah):

Powerful relics that have loomed large in the history of the Matoran civilization. From all evidence, it appears that Toa stones are ordinary rocks until they are invested with some portion of a TOA's power. Once so invested, they seem always to be linked to the creation of or the coming of Toa heroes. Two sets of Toa stones are currently on record as existing. Toa LHIKAN shared his power with six stones in METRU NUI, which were later used to transform six MATORAN into the TOA METRU. Those same Toa Metru later put a portion of their power into six more stones and hid them on the island of MATA NUI (2), in places they believed only a true Toa could reach. One thousand years later, a Matoran named TAKUA found the stones and placed them on the KINI-NUI, unwittingly triggering a signal that brought TAHU and five other Toa to shore. Whether more Toa stones exist elsewhere is unknown.

TOA SUVA (TOE-ah SOO-vah):

Shrine located in the GREAT TEMPLE in METRU NUI. Six MATORAN placed TOA STONES into special slots here and unleashed energy that transformed them into TOA METRU.

TOWERS OF THOUGHT:

Special structures in the METRU NUI district of KO-METRU intended for scholarly projects requiring absolute silence. A squad of VAHKI KEERAKH was always in the area to insure that the work of the MATORAN in the Towers of Thought was not disturbed.

TRACKER

TRACKER:

DARK HUNTER who, along with his pet bull, is extremely skilled at hunting down quarry. His most notable accomplishment was finding ROODAKA after her apparent "death" at the hands of the TOA HORDIKA.

TRANSPORT CARTS:

Wheeled vehicles used for transporting exhibits through the subterranean tunnels of the ARCHIVES.

TREESPEAK:

Slang spoken by LE-MATORAN of various islands.

TREN KROM BREAK:

An area marked by lava streams outside of TA-KORO, site of a number of lava farms and IGNALU lava surfing competitions.

TRIDENT OF NOKAMA (noh-KAH-mah):

TURAGA NOKAMA's tool and badge of office. It was crafted to resemble the tridents that GA-MATORAN used to catch fish in GA-METRU. Nokama carved it while still a TOA from the bones of a MAKUTA FISH.

TRYNA (TRI-nah):

KANOHI Mask of Reanimation worn by TOA MAHRI MATORO. This mask allows the wearer to fill the shells of deceased beings with artificial life energy. The subjects remain reanimated for only as long as the mask wearer focuses on them, but it is possible to revivify more than one subject at a time. Removal of the mask or a loss of concentration or consciousness on the part of the wearer negates the power of the Tryna.

TUNNEL STALKER:

A gigantic desert RAHI from PO-METRU known for its unusual hunting technique. The stalker lurks in tunnels just below the sand, with its bladed tail poised to strike. When it picks up movement from above, it lunges up through the ground and traps whatever luckless creature was going by. Only two specimens of tunnel stalker were ever seen in METRU NUI, one of which was captured by the VAHKI and put in the ARCHIVES. Tunnel stalkers did make scattered appearances in PO-WAHI on MATA NUI (2). In addition to its tail, the tunnel stalker could rely on sharp pincers and mandibles to defend itself.

TUNNELER:

A reptilian creature of PO-METRU capable of taking on the properties of any physical object used against it (a fireball, for example, turns it into a creature of fire). TOA VAKAMA and Toa ONEWA defeated one by tricking it into turning itself to glass. They have appeared periodically in PO-WAHI on MATA NUI (2).

TURAGA [too-RAH-gah]:

Leaders of the MATORAN and protectors of the legends of the TOA. Turaga come into being when Toa have fulfilled their destiny and have chosen to sacrifice their Toa power for the greater good. That act leads to the transformation of Toa to Turaga. The city of METRU NUI was led by Turaga DUME, a benevolent leader who was captured and impersonated by MAKUTA for many months. He remains somewhere in the city, comatose inside a silver sphere. The six TOA METRU fulfilled their destiny by saving the Matoran from Makuta and sacrificed their power to awaken those same Matoran from their comas. In that instant, they transformed into Turaga MATAU, Turaga NOKAMA, Turaga NUJU, Turaga ONEWA, Turaga VAKAMA, and Turaga WHENUA. In these forms, they oversaw the construction of the six villages of MATA NUI (2) and helped to defend the Matoran from the attacks of RAHI.

When TAHU and his team of Toa arrived on the island, the Turaga chose to tell them only part of the truth about the past. It was not until the defeat of Makuta and the rediscovery of Metru Nui that the Turaga shared with Tahu and the others the fact that they had once been Toa and that the Matoran had once lived on Metru Nui.

Once a Toa becomes a Turaga, he loses the ability ever to wield Toa power or use Great Masks of Power again. Turaga are able to master Noble Masks of Power and have limited elemental abilities. Physically, they are slightly stronger than Matoran but nowhere near as powerful as Toa. Although generally wise and able leaders, Turaga have shown themselves capable of resentment, deception, and lack of trust. How much recent revelations about their past will damage the relationship between the Turaga and the TOA NUVA remains to be seen.

Known Turaga have included Dume, LHIKAN, JOVAN, Matau, Nokama, Nuju, Onewa, Vakama, and Whenua.

TURAGA NUI [too-RAH-gah NOO-ee]:

Legend states that if six TURAGA merge their minds and bodies, they will form a great and wise leader called a Turaga Nui. To this point, the idea remains merely legend, as no Turaga have ever been known to attempt this.

TURAHK [TER-rahk]:

One of the six RAHKSHI dispatched by MAKUTA to capture the HERALD of the Seventh TOA. Turahk's job was to fill the TOA NUVA with fear so that they would forget their duty to MATA

NUI (1). Using its staff, it could cause a foe to break into a terror-filled run or freeze in fear. Turahk killed JALLER by overwhelming him with fear, but the MATORAN was later brought back to life by TAKUTANUVA. Turahk was defeated by TAKANUVA, the Toa of Light.

TWO-HEADED TARAKAVA (tah-RAH-kah-VAH):

A mutant aquatic beast (see TARAKAVA) created by the ENERGIZED PROTODERMIS ENTITY. TOA NUJU encountered this creature in the ARCHIVES.

TYRANT:

DARK HUNTER who made a failed attempt to overthrow the SHADOWED ONE. He was later set up for a defeat by TOA and vanished beneath the waves, but rumors persist that he is still alive. Tyrant is capable of absorbing heat and releasing it in a massive blast. He is immune to the effects of extreme heat or cold.

TYRANT

UMBRA:

One of the guardians of the KANOHI IGNIKA. Umbra was the first sentinel put in place by the GREAT BEINGS to guard the mask 100,000 years ago and continues to serve to the present day. Umbra's powers include the ability to transform into a beam of light. He also possesses skates that let him move at superspeed, a staff that fires lasers, and a RHOTUKA SPINNER that can create hard light projections. Umbra encountered the TOA INIKA and was defeated by them.

USSAL (uss-SUL):

Crablike creatures long domesticated by MATORAN and used for both racing and transport. Docile and friendly, Ussal seem to genuinely enjoy Matoran company. In METRU NUI, they were used to pull carts and carry heavy loads. On MATA NUI (2), they served much the same purposes, along with being used for sport in Ussal crab races and for defense.

USSALRY (uss-SUL-ree):

The ONU-MATORAN defense force on MATA NUI (2) consisting of MATORAN riding on USSAL crabs. The Ussalry was under the command of an Onu-Matoran named ONEPU. The Ussalry was instrumental in helping to defend KINI-NUI against attacking RAHI and ONU-KORO against invading BOHROK.

USSAL

USSANUI (uss-ah-NOO-ee):

Vehicle constructed by TAKANUVA and the TOA NUVA for transport to MAKUTA's lair. The Ussanui was built using RAHKSHI parts and was powered by KRAATA. The vehicle was wrecked when Takanuva used it to break into the lair. Whether or not it will be repaired remains to be seen.

VACUUM SHIELD:

Tool carried by LEHVAK-KAL. The vacuum shield could absorb and hold a large amount of air for a long period of time before releasing it in a powerful blast.

VAHI (VAH-hee):

The Great Mask of Time. This mask was able to either slow down or speed up time around a target. Originally created by TOA VAKAMA using all six of the GREAT DISKS, it was lost in the ocean surrounding METRU NUI during battle with MAKUTA. Vakama later recovered the mask and brought it to MATA NUI (2).

VAHI

One thousand years later, Vakama, now a TURAGA, gave the mask to TAHU NUVA. The Toa of Fire used the mask to slow down time around the BOHROK-KAL and prevent them from freeing the BAHRAG. Tahu later returned the mask to Vakama's care, where it remains.

VAHKI (VAH-kee):

Mechanical order enforcement units who patrolled METRU NUI. There were six models of Vahki: BORDAKH, KEERAKH, NUURAKH, RORZAKH, VORZAKH, and ZADAKH. They were put into operation after the failure of the KRALHI experiment. Vahki received recharges of power in their HIVES, located throughout Metru Nui.

The primary purpose of a Vahki was to maintain order. This involved anything from containing a RAHI rampage, to pursuing a lawbreaker, to making sure MATORAN worked when they were scheduled to do so. Vahki communicated by speaking the Matoran language at an extremely high speed. Turaga DUME's chambers contained technology that could slow the speech down enough to be understood.

Vahki were capable of three modes of transport: flight, walking on two legs, and walking on four legs using their tools as forelegs. They were equipped with stun staffs, nonlethal devices that acted on the mind rather than the body of the target. The point was to correct behavior without damaging valuable workers.

When the Metru Nui power plant was destroyed by MAKUTA, a power surge struck the hives and destroyed most of the Vahki. Those that survived were altered for the worse. Their speech centers had slowed so that other beings could understand them. Their stun staffs had become incredibly destructive. In addition, their fundamental mission had been warped. They now believed that living things created disorder, and that therefore the way to maintain order was to eliminate anything that lived.

The Vahki were used by Makuta (posing as Dume) to capture Matoran, guard the PRISON OF THE DARK HUNTERS, and battle the TOA METRU. After their transformation, small squads of Vahki continued to patrol the city, often clashing with VISORAK. Eventually they were all destroyed by the horde.

VAHKI HUNTER (VAH-kee):

Massive RAHI who seem to have a particular hatred for machinery. They have been known to use their claws and teeth to demolish VAHKI, FIRE DRONES, and other mechanical creations. Once confined to PO-METRU and TA-METRU, they later spread out all over METRU NUI. Vahki

Hunters spent most of their time underground, emerging only to strike before returning to the safety of their tunnels.

VAHKI TRANSPORT [VAH-kee]:

A vehicle propelled by mechanical insectoid legs and used to transport VAHKI squads, KRAAHU, and KRANUA to trouble spots. NOKAMA, VAKAMA, and MATAU snuck onboard a transport while fleeing from the DARK HUNTERS. The transports were being used to carry the MATORAN SPHERES to the COLISEUM. Later, the TOA METRU used a Vahki transport with spheres affixed to the bottom as a boat to escape METRU NUI, and a second transport to sail back again.

VAKAMA [vah-KAH-mah]:

TOA METRU of Fire, guardian of TA-METRU, and later TURAGA of TA-KORO.

VAKAMA

HISTORY

Vakama began his life as a TA-MATORAN working in a foundry. Shortly after being promoted to mask maker, he was asked by Turaga DUME (secretly MAKUTA in disguise) to make the KANOHI VAHI, the Mask of Time. Later, he was visited by Toa LHIKAN, who gave him a TOA STONE. Lhikan warned him that dark times were coming to METRU NUI. Before he could explain, NIDHIKI and KREKKA attacked. Lhikan was captured, but not before helping Vakama escape.

Vakama traveled to the GREAT TEMPLE and encountered five other MATORAN — MATAU, NOKAMA, NUJU, ONEWA, and WHENUA. They placed their Toa stones into the Toa suva and were transformed into mighty Toa heroes. Vakama had a vision that the city was in peril and that only finding the six GREAT DISKS would save it.

Despite many dangers, the TOA METRU succeeded in finding the disks, eluding the VAHKI, and destroying the MORBUZAKH plant that threatened the city. But when they went to present the disks to Turaga Dume, he denounced them as impostors and ordered their arrest. Whenua, Onewa, and Nuju were captured, with Vakama, Nokama, and Matau escaping. They survived a battle with Vahki and the DARK HUNTERS on an AIRSHIP, then stowed away on a VAHKI TRANSPORT into PO-METRU. There they fought the Dark Hunters again, formed an alliance with the KIKANALO, and helped to free their three friends and Lhikan, now a Turaga. Vakama believed they had achieved what they set out to do, and was crushed to find out that Lhikan had wanted them to save the Matoran, not him. Already plagued with self-doubt, discovering he had made such a serious error was a blow to his confidence. Despite this, he led the Toa against Makuta and the Dark Hunters. They succeeded in rescuing six Matoran, still in the MATORAN SPHERES in which the Vahki had placed them. Vakama confronted Makuta, using the Vahi he had made by combining the six Great Disks. During the battle, Vakama's inability to control the Vahi placed him in mortal danger. Lhikan intervened at the last moment, taking a blow meant for Vakama and dying as a result. Vakama and Makuta battled to a stalemate until the other Toa Metru arrived and their combined might trapped Makuta behind a wall of solid PROTODERMIS.

The Toa Metru then departed Metru Nui with the six Matoran spheres. After a dangerous journey, they reached the island of MATA NUI (2). There Vakama suggested they create Toa stones and hide them in places on the island only one with the heart of a true Toa could reach. This, he believed, would ensure that a new generation of Toa would follow the Toa Metru someday.

On the return journey to Metru Nui to rescue the rest of the Matoran, Vakama grew short-tempered and frustrated. He blamed himself for Lhikan's death and the fate of the Matoran. Eager to prove he deserved to be a Toa, he recklessly led the Toa Metru into the heart of the city where they were captured by the VISORAK. The venom of these creatures mutated the Toa into TOA HORDIKA, half hero, half beast and monstrous mockeries of their former selves. Vakama saw this as another example of his poor leadership and the other Toa, particularly Matau, blamed him as well.

Vakama's mood was not improved by the discovery of evidence that apparently indicated that NUHRII, a Ta-Matoran, had been destined to become the Toa of Fire. Convinced now that his becoming a Toa Metru was a mistake from the start, Vakama grew increasingly bitter and distant from his friends. He eventually allied with ROODAKA and assumed command of the Visorak horde. During this period, he was responsible for an attack on NORIK and significant damage to the GREAT TEMPLE.

During a battle with the Toa Hordika, MATAU was able to convince Vakama that his place was with his friends. He turned on Roodaka and ordered the horde to leave the city. Following the battle, KEETONGU used his power to restore the Toa Hordika to their former selves, the Toa Metru.

During the evacuation of the Matoran from Metru Nui, Vakama returned to the city on his own to search for the missing Vahi. He was tricked by Makuta into believing the events leading up to his becoming a Toa had never happened and that Metru Nui was still intact. Vakama eventually threw off the illusion, but was forced to ally with Makuta to stop the DARK HUNTERS from stealing the mask. Vakama prevented Makuta from taking the Vahi himself by threatening to destroy the mask and unleash the power of time if he made the attempt. The two reached an agreement — Vakama would leave the city with the Vahi and Makuta would not attack the Matoran for one full year, in exchange for Vakama not destroying the mask. Both sides honored the bargain.

TURAGA VAKAMA

After reaching MATA NUI (2), the Toa Metru willingly sacrificed their power to awaken the Matoran, transforming into Turaga in the process.

As a Turaga, Vakama supervised the construction of TA-KORO. When TAHU arrived, Vakama welcomed him but did not share any information regarding Metru Nui or his life as a Toa. He revealed details about the BOHROK and RAHKSHI only after those enemies had appeared on Mata Nui.

Finally, after consulting with the other Turaga, Vakama chose to share the tales of Metru Nui with the TOA NUVA. Over the objections of Onewa and Nuju, he has begun relating the history of the Toa Hordika.

Vakama lived in PO-KORO after the destruction of Ta-Koro. He is now on Metru Nui, assisting in the management and rebuilding of that city.

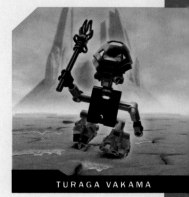

TURAGA VAKAMA

POWERS

Vakama was the master of fire. Among the powers he demonstrated on Metru Nui were the ability to create and absorb heat and flame, to survive for a brief period in molten protodermis, and to turn stone red-hot with just a touch of his hand. He was also capable of creating a nova blast, a massive explosion of flame, but wisely refrained from ever doing so. He was skilled with a KANOKA LAUNCHER and had a natural resistance to extreme heat.

PERSONALITY

Vakama was always a reluctant hero. Most of the time, he did not feel he deserved to be a Toa or that he was equal to what was being asked of him. At first, he reacted by hanging back and letting others take the lead. Later, he tried so hard to be a leader that he irritated his fellow Toa. He was the most affected emotionally by the transformation into a Toa Hordika, because he blamed himself for leading the Toa into a trap.

As a Turaga, Vakama was wise and patient, but highly secretive. After realizing that the Matoran had lost their memories of Metru Nui, it had been his suggestion that the Turaga never tell them of the city until some chance existed that they could go back there. It was also his idea to create the fiction of LHII to preserve some fragment of the memory of Lhikan. His experiences with the false Dume made it difficult for him to fully trust powerful beings, including Toa Tahu, so a great deal of time passed before he told the Toa Nuva the truth about the past.

EQUIPMENT

As a Toa Metru, Vakama carried a Kanoka disk launcher that could also be used as a rocket pack for flight. He wore the Kanohi HUNA, the Great Mask of Concealment. As a Toa Hordika, he was armed with BLAZER CLAWS. As a Turaga, he carried a fire staff and wore the Noble Huna.

VANISHER

VAKAMA'S FOUNDRY (vah-KAH-mah):
One of a number of forges in TA-METRU in the city of METRU NUI. Vakama used this work area to create KANOHI masks. It was here that he first began work on the VAHI, and this was also the site of TOA LHIKAN's battle with NIDHIKI and KREKKA.

VANISHER:
DARK HUNTER suspected of being a double agent for the BROTHERHOOD OF MAKUTA. Vanisher was capable of appearing and disappearing at will via dimensional transport, as well as diverting energies hurled against him into other dimensions.

VATUKA (VAH-too-kah):
A legendary creature of stone. TURAGA WHENUA was once captured by the Vatuka in the tunnels of ONU-WAHI and later rescued by TAKUA. It is now believed the Vatuka may have been a creation of the ENERGIZED PROTODERMIS ENTITY, who once sent a similar stone creature against the TOA METRU.

VELIKA (vuh-LEEK-ah):
PO-MATORAN member of the RESISTANCE on the island of VOYA NUI. Velika is a skilled inventor known for speaking in complex riddles. He carries twin power carvers. Velika copied the design of the ZAMOR SPHERE LAUNCHER to provide the TOA INIKA with weapons. He also created the ENERGIZED PROTODERMIS-filled ZAMOR SPHERES that were used to cure the enslaved Matoran of the island.

VENOM EEL:

Vicious, poisonous creature found in the black waters of the PIT around the city of MAHRI NUI. Venom eels made up the bulk of the undersea army of EHLEK. The creatures average about a foot in length, but one specimen was evolved by the KANOHI IGNIKA to a length of 300 feet. It attacked the BARRAKI, Mahri Nui, and the TOA MAHRI, and was last seen locked in battle with another gigantic sea creature.

VENOM FLYERS:

Flying RAHI can be extremely difficult for the largely land-bound VISORAK to capture. That is why each horde travels with a small group of venom flyers. Naturally skilled at aerial maneuvers and captures, the venom flyers make extremely effective hunters. While they lack the extra powers normal Visorak have, their spinners can negate the ability of a target to fly, regardless of whether their ability is based on natural or mechanical means.

VEZOK

VEZOK (vay-ZOCK):

One of the six PIRAKA who traveled to VOYA NUI in an attempt to steal the KANOHI IGNIKA, the Mask of Life. Vezok was originally recruited into the DARK HUNTERS by ANCIENT after he stole the MAKOKI STONE from a TOA fortress. Later, he was part of an ill-fated attempt to overthrow the SHADOWED ONE and helped release the KANOHI DRAGON on the city of METRU NUI. He joined with ZAKTAN, AVAK, HAKANN, THOK, and REIDAK to loot the lair of MAKUTA, and it was there that the power of Makuta implanted the idea in all six of seeking out the Mask of Life. It was during this adventure that an accidental use of the SPEAR OF FUSION resulted in Vezok splitting into two beings, himself and VEZON. As a result of the division, Vezok lost his ability to think strategically and came to rely on brute force in combat.

On Voya Nui, Vezok struck the final blow in the initial battle against the TOA NUVA, felling ONUA NUVA. Later, he was the first Piraka to meet and fight the TOA INIKA. When last seen, he was with the other Piraka on Voya Nui, still scheming to get the Kanohi Ignika, unaware that his body was being affected by an earlier exposure to mutagenic seawater. He is also determined to somehow reabsorb Vezon into his body.

Vezok possesses the elemental power of water as well as impact vision. His body is resistant to the corrosive effects of some types of water. He also has the power to temporarily duplicate the natural abilities of others, allowing him to combine and use those powers himself. He carries a ZAMOR SPHERE LAUNCHER and a combination harpoon and buzzsaw, which can hurl water daggers at an enemy.

VEZON (vey-zonn):

The unwilling PIRAKA guardian of the KANOHI IGNIKA, Vezon was created when HAKANN accidentally fired the SPEAR OF FUSION at VEZOK while the weapon was set in reverse, splitting the target into two beings — Vezok and Vezon (whose name is the MATORAN word for "double"). Vezon promptly betrayed the other Piraka, stole the spear, and made his way to VOYA NUI in search of the Ignika. He was able to make it to the CHAMBER OF LIFE and actually touch the Kanohi mask, but at that moment he was cursed by its power. The Mask of Life fused to his head, evolved a spider into the monstrous FENRAKK, and then fused Vezon to Fenrakk. He was then condemned to remain there and guard the mask, with the knowledge that as long as he possessed it, he could not die.

Vezon defeated the Piraka and was himself defeated by the TOA INIKA. He later attempted to pursue the Toa to MAHRI NUI and was defeated a second time. Vezon was last seen being carried off by the murderous ZYGLAK.

Vezon was gifted by the Ignika with two powers: a limited ability to see into the future, and the ability to absorb kinetic energy so that any blow struck against him would make him stronger. He was also granted immortality as long as he possessed the mask. Vezon lost all of these powers when the mask was taken from him.

VHISOLA (vih-SO-lah):

VHISOLA

A GA-MATORAN. Vhisola was a student of NOKAMA's on METRU NUI and considered the future TOA METRU to be her best friend. But from the beginning, Vhisola was possessive of Nokama and got angry if she spent time with her other friends. When Nokama became a Toa Metru, Vhisola decided to use her knowledge of a GREAT DISK's location to make herself more famous than her friend.

But the plan backfired. Vhisola's knowledge attracted the attention of NIDHIKI, who pursued her in hopes of getting the disk. TOA Nokama ended up saving the MATORAN. Vhisola shared the location of the disk and her theory that the Great Disks could be used to defeat the MORBUZAKH. Later, Vhisola joined with AHKMOU, NUHRII, TEHUTTI, EHRYE, and ORKHAM to form a MATORAN NUI and help in the fight against the Morbuzakh. Shortly after that, she was captured by VAHKI and placed in a sphere that rendered her comatose. Evidence was later discovered that Vhisola may have been destined to become a Toa of Water.

Vhisola would later be revived on MATA NUI (2) by the Toa Metru.

VISORAK (vih-SOAR-ack):

Spiderlike creatures who operate as a horde under the command of SIDORAK and ROODAKA. The Visorak invaded METRU NUI following the initial departure of the TOA METRU for MATA NUI (2). Their primary focus seemed to be the capture and either containment or mutation of RAHI.

VISORAK

Little is known about the Visorak's point of origin, but an ancient tablet in the ARCHIVES states that their name meant "poisonous scourge" in their own language. They were also known as the "stealers of life." The Visorak were well organized, cunning, efficient, and highly skilled at the job of hunting. They had been active in a number of different places before coming to Metru Nui, and had driven herds of Rahi before them. Almost all of the Rahi who were in Metru Nui had arrived there as a result of fleeing the hordes.

The Visorak had four natural tools:

1. **Webbing:** Visorak produced webbing from internal glands and spun it using their mouths. It was strong enough to support a large number of the creatures as they moved from place to place. It could also be used to form a thick cocoon strong enough to hold the most powerful Rahi.

2. **Pincers:** All Visorak had strong, sharp pincers that could inflict a painful bite.

3. **Venom:** Visorak venom was mutagenic, capable of transforming Rahi or other targets into horrifying versions of their former selves. The most common venom delivery system was barbs in the cocoons. Visorak venom turned the Toa Metru into TOA HORDIKA, as well as causing many other mutations among the Rahi. The only known cure for the effects of Visorak venom was the counteragent abilities of KEETONGU.

4. Rhotuka spinners: Visorak have natural RHOTUKA LAUNCHERS and can generate wheels of energy by willpower. All Visorak have a default spinner power that can stun and paralyze an opponent, in addition to their other powers.

Although intelligent creatures, Visorak were unable to understand or speak the Matoran language, with one exception (see OOHNORAK). Their relationship with Sidorak was a simple and straightforward one: they gave him their loyalty in return for his providing them with constant opportunities to hunt. The horde was led temporarily by TOA HORDIKA VAKAMA, as part of a plot by ROODAKA to overthrow Sidorak. Following Sidorak's death, the Visorak horde was ordered out of Metru Nui by Vakama and scattered. The horde was later reassembled by the BROTHERHOOD OF MAKUTA and continues to serve the Brotherhood to this day.
There were six known Visorak breeds: VOHTARAK, OOHNORAK, SUUKORAK, BOGGARAK, ROPORAK, and KEELERAK. See individual entries.

VISORAK BATTLE RAM [vih-SOAR-ack]:
A massive siege vehicle capable of shattering the thickest wall in METRU NUI. The battle ram was so large and heavy it required five VISORAK to pull it. The Visorak Battle Ram was among many war engines built on the island of XIA.

VOHTARAK [VOT-ah-rack]:
One of the six breeds of VISORAK who invaded METRU NUI. Vohtarak had a natural resistance to fire and heat. Their preferred method of attack was to charge wildly while launching multiple spinners. They were also capable of making "berserker charges," during which their outer shells became virtually invulnerable. Vohtarak RHOTUKA SPINNERS caused a burning sensation in a target, so intense that it would distract him from any other action.

VOHTARAK

VOLITAK [VOHL-ih-TACK]:
The KANOHI Mask of Stealth. This mask has the combined effect of camouflaging the wearer and deadening sound around him so he cannot be heard. The Volitak has been worn by TOA MAHRI NUPARU and TOA NIDHIKI.

VOLO LUTU [VOE-loe LOO-too]:
A launcher that could be used to grab on to objects over great distance. TAKUA used a Volo Lutu launcher in ONU-WAHI during his search for the VUATA MACA CRYSTALS.

VOPORAK [VOE-poe-RACK]:
A huge and powerful servant of the DARK HUNTERS with an intriguing history. He came from an island populated by a highly competitive and prideful species. Anytime any of them succeeded in building something, their neighbors would grow jealous and destroy it. This resulted in a land made barren and a culture that bordered on anarchy.
Voporak might have remained there forever had an emissary of the BROTHERHOOD OF MAKUTA not arrived, seeking a being of power. Seeing that Voporak dominated his region, the Brotherhood selected him for an experiment in mutation. Combining ENERGIZED PROTODERMIS, the RHOTUKA SPINNER of ROODAKA, and possibly other more dangerous ingredients, they succeeded in transforming Voporak into a being sensitive to shifts in time. Believing it inevitable that one day the KANOHI VAHI, the Mask of Time, would be created, the Brotherhood now had a servant capable of tracking it and capturing it.

In the interim, Voporak was loaned out to the Dark Hunters to learn discipline. He discovered that he now gave off a temporal force field that aged any power used against him. For example, a rock thrown at him would age rapidly and crumble to dust before ever striking him. He also found that his touch could age anyone and anything if he willed it to do so.

After VAKAMA used the Vahi against MAKUTA, Voporak sensed its power and began heading for METRU NUI. While the legend of what happened when he arrived there has not yet been told, it is known that Voporak survived the encounter and may well be seeking out the TOA NUVA following TAHU's use of the Vahi.

VORAHK [VOH-rock]:

One of the six RAHKSHI sent by MAKUTA to stop the HERALD and recover the KANOHI AVOHKII. Vorahk's staff could be used to absorb the power of an enemy and transfer it temporarily to Vorahk. The staff had to be in physical contact with the target to do this. Vorahk was partially responsible for the destruction of ONU-KORO.

VORTIXX [VOAR-ticks]:

Native species of the island of XIA. Vortixx society is dominated by females, and the population as a whole is made up of tall, lean, powerful beings in black armor. Males labor in the dirtiest and most dangerous jobs on the island. The Vortixx are an industrious and greedy people, best known for producing weaponry for whoever pays them. They were initially employed by the LEAGUE OF SIX KINGDOMS, and have since done work for the DARK HUNTERS and the BROTHERHOOD OF MAKUTA. The Vortixx are officially neutral in the war between those two factions. Easily the most famous Vortixx is ROODAKA, who served as viceroy of the VISORAK horde during the invasion of METRU NUI. She still resides on Xia, although much of her time is spent off-island.

VORZAKH

VORZAKH [VOAR-zahk]:

VAHKI model assigned to LE-METRU on METRU NUI. These mechanoids were known for being destructive, preferring to smash through an obstacle rather than going around or over it. Their STAFFS OF ERASING allowed them to temporarily eliminate higher mental functions in their targets. A group of VORZAKH destroyed a chute in an effort to capture TOA MATAU. Along with the other Vahki, most Vorzakh were destroyed in the GREAT CATACLYSM. Those who survived fell in combat with the VISORAK.

VOYA NUI [VOE-yah NOO-ee]:

Island that contains the hiding place of the KANOHI IGNIKA. Voya Nui was once part of a larger, underground continent, but it broke off during the GREAT CATACLYSM and ended up on the surface of the ocean (the same ocean in which MATA NUI (2) rests). Voya Nui floated a far distance before finally coming to rest in its present location. Over time, the MATORAN residents noticed that the island was expanding as molten PROTODERMIS cooled in the water, forming new land. They built a second village called MAHRI NUI on the coast, only to see it break off and sink beneath the waves centuries later. (The Voya Nui Matoran do not know that the residents of Mahri Nui still survive in the PIT.)

Due to its connection to the Kanohi Ignika, the island has been guarded for tens of thousands of years by ORDER OF MATA NUI members, AXONN and BRUTAKA. The island was invaded by

PIRAKA, seeking to steal the mask, and was the scene of battles between those criminals and the TOA NUVA and TOA INIKA. Axonn currently resides on the island with the Matoran, but it is believed he is aware that if the mask is used to save the life of MATA NUI (1), all life on Voya Nui may be destroyed.

Among the many features of Voya Nui are the PIRAKA STRONGHOLD; MOUNT VALMAI; the mysterious "green belt," an unexplained area of vegetation along the coast; and the Matoran fortress.

VUATA MACA (voo-AH-tah MAH-cah):

A tree that provided fruit which the ONU-MATORAN used for energy. The tree, in turn, was energized by VUATA MACA CRYSTALS. Prior to the coming of the TOA to MATA NUI (2), the Vuata Maca tree was poisoned. TAKUA was asked to locate two Vuata Maca Crystals to cleanse the tree and make the fruit safe again.

VUATA MACA CRYSTAL (voo-AH-tah MAH-cah):

Two objects that provided energy to the VUATA MACA tree. TAKUA retrieved these in ONU-WAHI in order to cleanse poison from the tree.

WAHI (wah-HEE):

Regions on the island of MATA NUI (2). There are six wahi: GA-WAHI, KO-WAHI, LE-WAHI, ONU-WAHI, PO-WAHI, and TA-WAHI.

WAIKIRU (WHY-kee-ROO):

A walruslike creature that dwelled on the shores of GA-METRU. Swift and agile in the water, they were clumsy on land. They relied on their tusks to drive away predators, primarily TAKEA sharks. On MATA NUI (2), TOA GALI placed the species under her protection after a storm she summoned accidentally injured a number of the beasts.

WAIRUHA (ware-ROO-hah):

One of the two TOA KAITA who defeated MAKUTA's MANAS guardians. Wairuha was formed by the merging of TOA GALI, TOA KOPAKA, and TOA LEWA. He wore the KANOHI RUA, the Silver Mask of Wisdom. Following the defeat of the Manas, the Toa split back into their individual forms again and have not formed Wairuha since.

WAIRUHA NUVA (ware-ROO-hah NOO-vah):

A TOA KAITA NUVA formed by the merging of KOPAKA NUVA, GALI NUVA, and LEWA NUVA. Wairuha Nuva came into being only once, when the TOA NUVA joined together in an ultimately futile effort to defeat the BOHROK-KAL.

WALL OF HISTORY:

A large stone structure in TA-KORO upon which TAKUA the CHRONICLER recorded the history of MATA NUI (2). The wall was destroyed along with the rest of Ta-Koro during the RAHKSHI attack. HAHLI, Takua's successor as Chronicler, has begun a new wall in GA-KORO.

WALL OF PROPHECY:

A large structure of ice in KO-KORO upon which was recorded the prophecies and legends regarding the GREAT SPIRIT MATA NUI. Unknown to the MATORAN, the Wall of Prophecy largely duplicated the function of METRU NUI's KNOWLEDGE TOWERS.

WATER SHIELD:

Tool carried by the GAHLOK. It was capable of drawing water from any source and then redirecting it at a target. Gahlok used their water shields to flood ONU-KORO.

WHENUA (wen-noo-ah):

TOA METRU of Earth, guardian of ONU-METRU, and later TURAGA of ONU-KORO.

HISTORY

Whenua was working in the ONU-METRU ARCHIVES when TOA LHIKAN gave him a TOA STONE and a map to the GREAT TEMPLE. He traveled there and encountered five other MATORAN — MATAU, NOKAMA, NUJU, ONEWA, and VAKAMA. They placed their Toa stones into the Toa suva and were transformed into mighty Toa heroes.

After Vakama had a vision warning of the destruction of the city, Whenua joined with the others to find the six GREAT DISKS. He teamed with Nuju to recover both the KO-METRU disk and the ONU-METRU disk. The Toa Metru used the disks to destroy the MORBUZAKH plant that threatened the city.

WHENUA

Afterward, Whenua led the Toa into the maintenance tunnels beneath the Archives to stop a possible flood. Whenua was captured by KRAHKA, who impersonated him to try to capture the other Toa Metru. He was the subject of a failed rescue attempt by Nuju, but both were later saved by the other Toa.

When they emerged from the tunnels and went to present the Great Disks to Turaga DUME, he denounced them as impostors and ordered their arrest. (The Toa did not discover until later that this Dume was MAKUTA in disguise.) Whenua, Onewa, and Nuju were captured and locked up in the PRISON OF THE DARK HUNTERS. There they encountered a mysterious Turaga who counseled them on what it meant to be a Toa and helped Onewa and Nuju discover their KANOHI mask powers. (Later, they discovered this Turaga was in fact LHIKAN.) After Nuju's telekinesis power helped them escape, Whenua discovered that his mask lit up the darkness and so led the way. Shortly after, they were reunited with Vakama, Matau, and Nokama.

Whenua aided in the ensuing battle with the DARK HUNTERS and the rescue of six Matoran, still trapped in MATORAN SPHERES. He joined his power with that of the other Toa Metru to trap Makuta behind a wall of solid PROTODERMIS.

The Toa Metru then departed Metru Nui with the six Matoran spheres. Along the way, they encountered monstrous sea RAHI and powerful KRALHI under the command of an ONU-MATORAN named MAVRAH. Whenua had once been a friend and colleague of Mavrah and was deeply disturbed by the fact that his old companion was now either badly misguided or insane. During a huge battle between the Toa, the Kralhi, the VAHKI, and the RAHI, Mavrah was swept into the underground river by a great wave. Onewa prevented Whenua from sacrificing his life in a vain attempt to save the Matoran.

After reaching MATA NUI (2) and then returning to Metru Nui, Whenua and the other Toa Metru encountered VISORAK. Although he had once read something in the Archives about these creatures, Whenua did not immediately identify them and was harshly criticized by Vakama because of it. Shortly after, the Toa were captured and mutated by Visorak venom into TOA HORDIKA. As half Toa, half beast, Whenua found the lure of being a full Rahi was strong. It was only the presence of RAHAGA BOMONGA that kept him from running off and joining the wild packs of beasts that roamed the city.

TURAGA WHENUA

How the Toa Hordika transformed back into Toa Metru and escaped to Mata Nui with the rest of the Matoran has not yet been revealed. But they did make it to that island with close to 1,000 sleeping villagers. The Toa Metru willingly sacrificed their power to awaken the Matoran, transforming into Turaga in the process.
As a Turaga, Whenua supervised the construction of ONU-KORO. When ONUA arrived, Whenua informed him of the threat Makuta posed to the island but did not share any information regarding Metru Nui or his life as a Toa. He led the rebuilding of the Onu-Koro mines after they were flooded by a BOHROK attack and aided Onua in his search for Kanohi NUVA masks.
Whenua has since returned with the TOA NUVA, the other Turaga, and the Matoran back to Metru Nui.

TURAGA WHENUA

POWERS

Whenua was the master of earth. He could cause earthquakes, raise earthen walls, and even make hands of earth reach out and grab an enemy. His time as an archivist left him with an encyclopedic knowledge of Rahi and Metru Nui history. He had strong night vision but his eyes were weaker in daylight.

PERSONALITY

Whenua was not the boldest of Toa, preferring to hang back and analyze a situation before plunging in. The only exception to this is when the Archives were threatened, at which point Whenua behaved like a mother ASH BEAR defending her territory. He quarreled often with Nuju and Onewa, though he and the Toa Metru of Stone later became good friends. He firmly believed history repeated itself and that a knowledge of the past was essential to success. As a Turaga, Whenua had a reputation for fairness and honesty. Although he had a more balanced view of life, he still believed the answer to many problems lay in memories of what had gone before.

EQUIPMENT

As a Toa Metru, Whenua carried twin earthshock drills. He wore the Kanohi RURU, the Great Mask of Night Vision. As a Turaga, he carried the drill of ONUA and wore the Noble Ruru.

WIDGETS:
Currency used on MATA NUI (2), which took the place of barter and trading systems on the island. It was based on the protodermic currency used on METRU NUI.

157

ZIVON [ZEE-vahn]:

A massive RAHI, well over 30 feet tall, who has been known to assist the VISORAK hordes in battle. Its head resembles that of a Visorak, but its claws are crablike and its stinger that of a NUI-JAGA. When fighting something of its own size, it will seize the enemy in its claws and then sting repeatedly. Its hard shell protects it from most damage. The Zivon is also capable of shooting webbing from its legs to entangle a foe.

ZIVON

The Zivon has four natural RHOTUKA LAUNCHERS as part of its anatomy. Its spinners target the senses of a foe, rendering him temporarily blind, deaf, or mute, or robbing him of his sense of touch. Although they are quite effective, the Zivon was rarely seen to use them, preferring physical combat.

The Zivon lived in a dimension of darkness which could be accessed only by the RHOTUKA SPINNERS of a KAHGARAK. Though technically an ally of the Visorak, its appearance was not welcomed by the hordes. The Zivon considered the spider creatures to be a delicacy and had been known to consume a large portion of the horde in celebration following a victory.

This creature made one appearance in METRU NUI, summoned by order of SIDORAK. It fought TAHTORAK and the KRAHKA before being sent into the darkness again by a Kahgarak spinner, along with both of its opponents. Whether it still survives inside that realm of shadows is unknown.

ZYGLAK [ZIGH-glack]:

Bipedal reptilian race who were encountered by the TOA INIKA in the CORD connecting VOYA NUI and MAHRI NUI. The zyglak was one of the first species created by the GREAT BEINGS, a result of remnants left over from the creation of the MATORAN being exposed to ENERGIZED PROTODERMIS. Those remnants that did not become KRANA became zyglak, but the Great Beings had no use for this new species, particularly after it was discovered that they were plague carriers. They were shunned and hated wherever they went and nursed a deep resentment toward Matoran, who they saw as occupying the favored position in the universe that should have been theirs. Zyglak extended their desire for revenge to any krana or BOHROK they encountered and anyone who spoke the language of the MATORAN. They were responsible for the massacre of almost all of Toa LESOVIKK's team as well as an unknown number of other Toa and Matoran over the millennia.

Zyglak relied on crude tools and weapons but made up for it with their natural advantages, including almost complete invulnerability to elemental attack and their ability to spread an organic protodermis-destroying disease through contact.

Although the Toa Inika escaped from them, they may pose a renewed threat to the Matoran at some future time.